THE EYE OF TIME

A PREHISTORIC SAGA

T. S. ROBEY

A Character list can be found at the back of ebook edition and before the Prologue in the print edition.

ACKNOWLEDGMENTS

I could not have finished this book without the help, encouragement, and ideas of a number of people. When I started working at Stonehenge, I thought I knew a lot about it. I soon found out I had barely begun to learn. So I'd like to thank my teachers, especially Tim Daw and Simon Banton, who gave me the whole idea of Stonehenge as the Heart of the World, a microcosm of the universe, in a discussion about the level horizon and palaeo-astronomy. I would also like to thank all the archaeologists and palaeo-environmentalists whose work I pillaged to create the detail behind the story.

I am truly grateful to Katherine White for two edits of the text, for her knowledge of writing and publishing which saved me days of frustration, and for her support and patience throughout the long gestation of this novel: I love you and remember you end up getting half the proceeds!

I would also like to express my gratitude to Mary Armour, Janet Reedman, and Nick Jones for their comments on the draft manuscript. I hope the final version meets your approval.

My gratitude also goes to Eve Pendle for undertaking the vital task of formatting the text.

Finally thanks to Iain Cox for his brilliant artwork on the cover - Thank you, it is just the ticket!

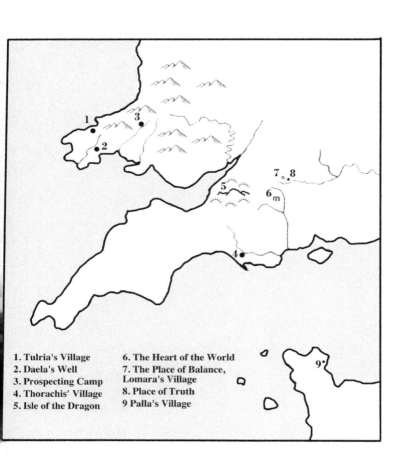

1. Tulria's Village
2. Daela's Well
3. Prospecting Camp
4. Thorachis' Village
5. Isle of the Dragon

6. The Heart of the World
7. The Place of Balance,
Lomara's Village
8. Place of Truth
9 Palla's Village

CHARACTERS

Children of Gehana (White Mountains) *{Alps}*

Gehana: Founding mother of Weyllan's lineage.

Kefhan: Father to Orelac and Weyllan's grandfather.

Orelac: Weyllan's uncle & adopted father.

Hegea: Weyllan's lost love.

Torlyr: Hegea's new love interest.

Llanys: Dutehar's weaver wife.

Weyllan: Shaman/Seer and bronze-smith, the Amesbury Archer.

Kefhan: Weyllan's brother.

Kirah: Wife to Kefahn, mother to Ulrac.

Ulrac: Son of Kefhan & Kirah, adopted by Weyllan.

Aslena: Daughter to Weyllan and Kirah.

Children of Ashila (Mainland Coast)
    {Brittany}
Cuhal: Shaman/Seer.
Palla - The Matriarch, leader of the
    Children of Ashila.
Ashila: The founding mother of Cuhal's
    lineage.

**Thorachis' People (Britain South
    Coast)** *{Dorset}*
Thorachis: Chief of the tribe bearing his
    name.
Granadh: Son of Thorachis, warrior.
Mikhan: Weasel-face, arrow poisoner, &
    assassin.
Tennec: One of Thorachis' seer-
    advisors.

Hatha's Children (The Plain)
    {Stonehenge}
Atharon: Leader of Hatha's Children,
    grandson of Merthyn.
Sylwa: Atharon's wife, mother to Athlan
    and Syllan.
Athlan: Elder son of Atharon.
Syllan: Second son and ultimate heir to
    Atharon.
Tokhan: A warrior, bodyguard to Syllan.
Dutehar: Syllan's second bodyguard,
    linguist and philanderer.
Turac: A senior shaman on the Plain,
    mentor to Weyllan.
Ursehan: Leader of a kin group allied to
    Urda.

Useris: Father of Ursehan.

Reirda: Shaman/Seer of Ursehan's kin group

Kerta: Wife to Syllan, mother to Kyrthan and Hathis.

Kyrthan: Son of Syllan.

Hathis: Daughter of Syllan.

Aslena: Old healer, a friend to Weyllan.

Aslena II: Daughter to Weyllan & Kirah.

Witlan: Elder from the northern Plain.

Withan: son of Witlan.

Tarohan: Youth killed in 2nd raid.

Tufakin: Half-blind shaman overseeing Weyllan's initiation.

Dobris: Shaman at Weyllan's initiation.

Pithan & Suaric: Flintworkers and miners.

Hatha: The founding mother of the Plains tribe.

Tyris: Ancestor of Myrthis, shaman, began the spirit circle.

Myrthis: Builder of the new Temple, The Eye of Time.

Dersa: neice of Myrthis and his successor.

Yrthyn: Grandson of Myrthis and father of Atharon.

Urda: Shaman from the plain, she created the Spirit Path.

Leca: wife of Myradoc and shaman descended from Urda.

Jysthan: Kinsman to Useris, Reirda's uncle.

Kharis: founder of a lineage who joined Hatha's Children.

Children of Ayena (The Place of Balance) *{Avebury}*

Lomara: Matriarch of the Children of Ayena, mother of Afron and Lomhan.

Afron: son of Lomara, husband to SeKerta

SeKerta: Wife to Afron and mother of Kerta.

Lomhan: Shaman, son of Lomara.

Miranis: Sister to Lomara and keeper of the flame.

Enthis: Slave to Weyllan and Kefhan.

The Sunset Mountains *{Wales}*

Teyrin: Hermit seer, keeper of Daela's Well.

Tulria: Matriarch and shaman/healer of the tribe.

Idranan: Husband to Tulria.

Rathon: Old man, Weyllan's uncle.

Rathonan: Son to Rathon

Fenratha: Daughter of Rathon, wife to Weyllan.

Meyrana: Daughter to Fenratha and Weyllan.

Myradoc /Mynradys: Shaman. Brought the old stones to the Plain.

Moranan: Ancestral leader of herding tribe.

The Northerners *{Cumbria}*

Jahrain: seer and leader of the Northerners.

Maklyr: brother to Jahrain.

Tamkris: seer from Cumbria, of the People of Tamwyr.

Sterhun: Companion to **Tamkris,** another seer.

Verhain: Young Northerner, Bellik's final victim.

Tamakis: Ancestral seer, who led the Northerners.

Tamhain: Nephew to **Tamakis**, and his successor.

The Mainlanders *{Europe}*

Nyren: A metallurgist & prospector.

Wheris: wife to Nyhren, a potter, mother to Nykhin.

Nykhin: Son of Nyren and Wheris.

Yarta: a potter, wife to Nykhin.

Emaris: Witness to Bellik's killing.

The Nature Spirits

Koh, Kas: the life force that runs through us all

Lukan: The sun spirit.

Lena: The moon spirit.

Turash/yi: (sing/pl)The sky spirits.

Aynturash: the milky way (river of sky souls).

Kylri: Spirit of the North Star.

Domash/yi: (sing/pl) The earth spirits.

Verash/yi: (sing/pl) The forest or woodland spirits.

Aynash/yi: (sing/pl) The river spirits (Aynash also the name of the Kennet R).

Gerash: Spirit of summer.

Leus: [Loek]: Spirit of the wild wind, personification of chaos.

Reya: Weyllan's spirit guide, appears as a vixen or a kite.

Brwslyi: Dragon spirit under the sacred hill.

Bellik: A demonic bear spirit from the bog beside the Avon.

Daela: A water spirit at the spring in Wales.

Wobai: Ancient hill spirit of the Preseli Mountains.

PROLOGUE

Arriving in the depths of winter, we had a cold, wet welcome to the shores of the Great Ocean. It had been such a long journey, for we had set out from the White Mountains a moon after midsummer, and we should have reached the coast by the onset of autumn. First, my brother Kefhan fell ill, so that we wasted almost a whole moon beside a broad river. Then I had a fall and was out of my wits for ten nights or more. A hard time we had of it, and often I feared this whole adventure was just folly. Now the winter weather set in; in village after dirty village, we could find no boatmen to carry us over the water to Syllan's island home, just beyond the horizon.

The first snow fell a few days before midwinter, then the skies cleared for several days. We could perhaps have crossed the straits then, but no one in their right mind would go to sea during the Soul Days, when the sun paused in its endless journey across the sky, when the spirits roamed freely through the long nights as the world waited for the cycle of life to turn once again and a new year to begin.

We celebrated the year's end with the Children of Ashila,

a people scattered across a peninsular that jabbed like a pointing finger out into the Great Ocean. They spent most of the year feuding with each other over petty grievances that went back sometimes three or four generations but as the midwinter approached each year, the families made truces and came together at a place called Wyreshi, the Spirit Road. There, they maintained a short avenue of standing stones leading to a massive wooden enclosure in which the chosen among the dead were laid to rest and celebrations were held to honour their passing.

Our host was Cuhal, a healer of some renown in the region, and the seer officiating at the ceremonies. I remember him as a gaunt man, with a wispy beard and a belt of plaited fox-hide, the paws hanging down at intervals around his waist. He looked every inch a man of power and influence, and we automatically paid great heed to his words.

"The Children of Ashila greet you, Seer, and bid you welcome. I have seen your coming in the wind, have waited for you as the seasons changed, but you join us at last at the time of our gathering, and that must be a good sign."

"I am honoured and not a little surprised that you should see any significance in our coming." I replied, "I am Weyllan of the Children of Gehana, far towards the Great River of the Dawn. My companions and I will gladly join your gathering, for we have no wish to travel further in these dying days."

I introduced my brother Kefhan, Kirah, his wife, our guide Syllan, and the young warrior Tokhan, who served him as his companion and bodyguard. I explained that it was at Syllan's behest that we were on this journey, travelling to their country to practice my art and to teach his people the skill of making the moon-gold. The speeches over, he led us into a cluster of huts where two women stood by an open fire in the clay-floored yard, stirring what smelled deliciously like a hare stew whilst several small children played around them.

As we entered the hut beyond, Kirah held back, thinking I suppose to stay with the women, but Cuhal motioned her forward to go in with us. When my eyes adjusted to the gloom, I saw before me an elderly woman with a mass of curly grey hair, a prominent beak of a nose, and an air of relaxed authority. I realised with a start I was facing the Matriarch of the group, who raked us with sharp, intelligent eyes before breaking into a broad grin that revealed a mouth still filled with good teeth. Beside her stood her consort, a man not much older than myself, muscular and stocky, who remained silent but alert throughout our interview. I bowed my head cautiously to each in turn.

Even as Cuhal introduced her as Palla, the Matriarch stepped forward to examine me, then nodded to herself as if confirming an opinion.

"You and your companion wield true power in your work." She produced from beneath her cloak a small, shiny moon-gold knife. " Are you not the makers of such wonderful things as this? He who gave it to me said a mage from a distant land transformed a rare blue rock with fire to make it. And in my vision, I saw you working at such a fire, saw you pour the liquid rock– I knew that you had made this blade."

I could see at a glance it was not in truth one of my blades, nor yet one of my family's, but I was impressed at the clarity of her vision and the sharpness of her inference. I suspected that she would know it was unlikely the one blade she had seen was by the only stone-changer she had encountered. She was making a point, so I just bowed my head, acknowledging the compliment.

The meeting over, we were escorted to an empty hut adjacent to the Matriarch's little compound. Cuhal called it 'the guest hut' although from its small size and recently added hearth, it was more likely a store-room converted for us when our coming was foreseen. Still, it was comfortable, a space to rest up away from the comings and goings in both Cuhal's and Palla's households as the final arrangements were made for the midwinter celebrations.

The following day I went with Cuhal to Wyreshi where he told me what was planned for the celebrations. A freshly scoured ditch enclosed an area perhaps fifty paces across and seventy long, within which the earth had been thrown up into a waist-high bank surmounted by a palisade of close-set posts. Each of these stood taller than a man's reach, and they were set so that the activity and lights inside would be visible between them whilst remaining inaccessible to the onlookers. At intervals around the perimeter, a few of the posts were shorter, providing, as Cuhal explained, clear views of the horizon at key points. Through these slots seers could witness the sunrise and sunset at the limits of their traverse, as well as the moonrise at the turning of the Great Cycle.

Inside, nine chest-high stones were arranged in a rough circle half the diameter of the palisaded bank. Whereas ditches and palisades were not uncommon in our homeland, this was the first stone circle I had encountered since our journey began, and the power of the place made the hairs rise on my neck and brought on a familiar tingle between my shoulders.

"You will join us in the spirit-dance tomorrow?" He seemed taken aback when I shook my head.

"I have little skill in the dance," I explained. "I have made the journey to the far side twice, but I cannot say I came back with any great truths or answers – I think the ancestors do not speak through me by choice. I can draw down the power to change stone, and I can channel the heat of the wild fire-spirits to lock it into an axe or a blade, but almost never do I feel the ancestors – mine or anyone else's – acting through me when I work or when I dance."

"And yet our Mother told me to ask you. She sees some purpose in it, and if she sees, there is always something there. Will you join us to find what Palla has foreseen?"

"Then, how can I not? Your Mother must rule me while I am a guest in your homes, and I hope that my participation will add something of use."

Cuhal smiled broadly at this response and slapped me on my back, chuckling. "You will see. Indeed, you will!".

And so it was I came to be a player in the dance that year. I found myself the next day fully occupied in a cleansing rite in a choking, steaming sweat-lodge filled with vapours that by the end had me almost staggering into the ghost-world before the drumming had even begun. Kirah crushed the red and yellow earth, and the white with some eye-watering herbs, wetted the mix and marked me with the white of the ancestors and the colours of my own wild fire-demons. Then she gave me a small beaker of something foul and fiery to drink before releasing me into the enclosure with the drummers, the dancers, and the helpers who would try to keep their bodies safe when their spirits travelled in the other reality.

I recall it all so clearly. Yet, as ever, I wonder how much is memory and how much is rationalisation of an experience beyond reason, of sensations beyond words; all of it so much beyond what I had expected to occur. I remember the rhythm of the dance and the first wave of dizziness that swept over me so that I tottered drunkenly forward. Then the heat, spreading from between my shoulders as the power entered me, and I slipped across the boundary into the other world. The colours faded, and the edges of my vision snapped into sharp focus.

I was walking – well, wading would be a more accurate description – across a plain of fine grey sand that stretched away in front of me and to each side. I knew better than to glance behind me; there would be nothing to see but darkness. Darkness up, darkness down, and darkness flowing away in every other direction. To look back was to risk losing the reality ahead and to fall forever into the nothing behind. I had been here before and knew to heed the warnings: move forward; it is the way in, the way out, and every direction you need in between.

At each step, I sank to my ankles in the sand, then lifted a cupful of it on my shoe, tossing it about as my foot swung forward. The sand sparkled, each step releasing a thousand tiny white lights blinking in and out of existence. I was grinning like a child with a new toy. Then I saw other lights in the dark sky, hundreds of stars that as I looked towards them, flickered in all the colours I could imagine. Spreading from a source above me, coloured filaments began to appear between them, linking each to the other and turning the sky into a vast spider's web with strands that sparked momentarily between the lowest stars and the grains of sand kicked up by my feet. It was a wonderful sight; the joy radiated from me as the power welled up inside me, hot and sparking in my gut, warming my soul, making me more alive, more focused than I had felt in an age.

Between the lines of the web, weaving among the stars, a multitude of shadows drifted alongside, keeping pace with me, merging with and splitting from one another like tendrils of kelp in an ocean swell. And we all moved with the current, flowing across the sandy plain. In the strands of shadow, I could now see faces, some deep in conversation with their companions, while others moved alone, quite unaware of those around them. As I gazed, the faces grew clearer. I was aware that some swirling around me were familiar and reminded me of individuals I had recently met among the Children of Ashila. I guessed they were the ancestors of my hosts, so I drifted with them a while until, at last, an old woman spoke to me. She had a strong face, with a sharp nose and close-set eyes, her mouth twisted out of shape by a thin scar running down her chin. Her long hair was tied in a single plait that streamed off into the shadow behind her.

" Why do you travel with us? You are not one of us, Seer. You cannot stay here. Your fate lies elsewhere."

"These folk, your kin, have given me shelter, so I do this for them. Can you give me something to take back to them? Give me healing, or give me news."

"News? There is no news here. We are here now, here always, and always it is now. You know this, Seer."

"And yet you know what has been and what will be. And some of what *will* be might aid those on the other side if you were to share it with me."

Another face appeared out of the shadows, a hollow-cheeked old man leering at me with a toothless grin. "You could say that my child Menya will bear a daughter in the spring. The girl will grow wise and strong and one day lead the people into a time of great prosperity."

"Ay-y-y," said another, "You know well that is not fixed. It is not for us to pass on yet."

"It will come to pass. I know it and fixed it will be. The daughter of Menya will be long remembered!"

Then the old woman moved behind me, placing her hands between my shoulder blades, and I felt healing power flow into my body. When she spoke, it was in a quieter voice, yet one that brooked no argument.

"There, you have what you need. Now go. Go back to my

children and give them this to close the rifts between them, that all my people can start this year in harmony, with all slights and sins forgotten. I have fixed it, and it will be so."

The shadows swirled away; there was only the glittering sand and the stars as the threads of the web faded, and the night slipped back in. I felt suddenly exhausted. I stumbled, then quickly sat myself down on the sand as the dizziness returned, as I heard again the rhythm of the drums and the clapping. Then Kefhan was at my side, the first time I had been aware of his presence as my guardian that night; he wrapped me in my leather cloak, speaking low in my ear words to bind me into our normality and to hold me from sliding back into the shadow realm. I shivered uncontrollably, then slowly calmed, focussing on the *now* as I tried to recall my journey clearly before it slipped from my head to disappear in the night.

Cuhal and the Matriarch came across, and I related my experience to them.

"Hardly an epic journey, I know, but more than I expected. Thank you for persuading me to join in." Palla looked thoughtful and asked me to describe the older woman from my vision. Cuhal and one or two others nearby looked stunned by my description. I turned to them questioningly.

"You describe our great mother, Ashila, in fine detail," the Matriarch explained. "Your message and the healing are for us all. You have been given a great gift for a stranger – we must call the people in to share it tonight."

As the other dancers one by one returned to us, Cuhal and others brought in the leaders of each family of Ashila's offspring until there were almost fifty people in the enclosure. Then the Matriarch spoke to them and bade them stand in a ring that included the nine stones of the circle, with their hands linked to each other over the stones. She gestured me to join the circle next to her, where she stood with her back to the entrance, then called for quiet.

"Now, Weyllan, friend of our Mother Ashila, release your gift to us all," she said gently to me. "Draw it up as you would the power of your fire-spirit, and pass it through me to the circle."

And as she spoke, I reached into my heart, deep into my very soul, to where the power dwelt, and felt a bright light burst up and flow through my body, surging out through my hands and bursting into the circle in both directions. For a moment eternal, I heard such a sweet singing in my ears that the very cosmos turned, the heat and the light seemed to flare in the night as my skin flickered and sparked – and tingled and crawled with it – until a strong sense of peace flowed through me. I felt completely drained, so that I fell to the floor, remembering nothing more.

Although I had been into the spirit realm when I began my training, I had never had much to show for it and had not even tried for several summers. So, this occasion, as you may imagine, shocked me as much as it deeply pleased me. It was the first time I had travelled with the departed from another people, the first time I brought back any healing worth talking about. The strength and goodwill that had been channelled through me would soften hearts to bring an end to many of the feuds and minor squabbles that seemed rife amongst these folk. I was happy for myself, in that I began to see I had opened a new doorway in my soul, and I was glad also to be able to repay the hospitality of Ashila's people so well.

I had plenty of time to reflect on my fortune and to recover my strength, for by dawn, the weather had turned. The cold frostiness gave way to a gale and squalls that knocked grown men over, soaking everyone in the blink of an eye. Any thought of crossing the sea had to wait till the spirits had settled down again.

Looking back, I think how young I was, how full of expectation, when first I set out for the island at the edge of the world. Had I known then what trials would await me, would I have refused to go?

PART I
FROST AND FIRE

CHAPTER ONE

After following the steep path up the ridge from the River, Syllan led his two young companions at last into the village. He looked across the slope at a settlement scattered along a broad meadow, consisting of twenty or thirty huts around two much larger longhouses. It had been a long, hard journey across the mainland from their island home, but it looked now as if the end of his quest was finally in view.

He sat himself down on a stone at the edge of the settlement, sending Tokhan and Dutehar in to make enquiries. They looked a tough pair, in their dusty deerskin leggings and waistcoats, laden with their bags and weapons, but Dutehar's curly red hair and sunny countenance made their appearance much less threatening as they greeted the locals. Tokhan was every inch a warrior, but when his chiselled face broke into a welcoming smile, no-one could ever doubt his sincerity or intentions.

Even at this height, it was a warm summer's day with very little breeze, and Syllan found himself dozing lightly as he reflected that they were at last near their goal. With a nod of acknowledgement to the spirits, he hoped they would be successful after all this time.

Two grubby children came over to where he sat and stood staring at him with intense interest from a safe distance. He watched them from beneath his half-closed lids as they whispered to each other, each daring the other to approach him. At last, the young boy lost the argument and tentatively crept towards Syllan. When he was a step away, he stopped and bent forward, reaching out a hand to tag the stranger. Syllan opened his eyes and cocked his head to one side, making the boy leap back as if he'd been bitten. Smiling at his little trick, he greeted the children in their own language and took from his pouch a strip of dried venison which he broke in two and offered to them. They took the food readily, and after chewing thoughtfully for a moment, the girl found her tongue.

"You're not a demon! But you dress so strangely – do you come from the other side of the lake?"

"I've seen the lake people," her companion scoffed. "They dress just like us! These men come from far away, from the wilds beyond the sunset. Am I right?" he demanded of Syllan, who laughed, nodding slightly.

"I suppose that's true, in a way. But we don't think of it as the wilds. We think of it as home. We come from an island far towards the setting sun, but be certain the sun sets still further away for us, too. It has taken us four whole moons to travel here, seeking a seer who is a master at working with the spirits of rocks and stones."

"You mean Orelac! He's the best stone-changer in our land! He is a ..."

At that moment they were interrupted by a female voice loudly calling them home.

"Oh, we have to go!" The girl seized the boy's arm as they

turned and ran towards the woman, who at that moment appeared around the side of one of the huts. Syllan leaned back, but before he could return to his daydreaming, Tokhan reappeared to tell him that a message had been sent to the seer Orelac.

"We must walk to the far side of the village to meet the messenger on his return. He will tell us there whether Orelac will see us or not."

Tokhan admitted he had not seen Dutehar for some time. He grinned ruefully; the young warrior had once again managed to disappear completely in a community of fewer than thirty households. No doubt he would be back by night-fall with some laughing woman on his arm and an invitation for the three of them to eat with a family in the next village. Syllan sighed, replaced his straw sun-hat, and hefted his bag onto his back to follow the more responsible of his companions.

As his eyes adjusted to the gloom inside the hut, Syllan was able properly to take in the man who stood before him. Lit by the flickering flames of the small fire in the centre of the floor, he stood facing Syllan with his arm raised in formal greeting. The seer was a hand-span shorter than Syllan himself, with a weatherworn face that had seen at least forty summers, framed by a thinning crop of curly grey hair and a dense white beard. He wore a plain, woven tunic and leggings in the local style, without any of the fancy decorations and animal bones so often favoured by other seers to advertise their status. Apart from a brindled hound curled up by the fire, he was alone. His smile of welcome was qualified by the curiosity evident in his gaze.

"Welcome to my house, young man. You have travelled a

great distance to come asking for me by name. From beyond the Great River and over the water I see you have journeyed, yet I had no forewarning of your coming or your purpose, which surprises me. So, I must await your explanation like any other person. Sit you down and tell me your tale."

Syllan dutifully lowered himself onto the log to the right of the entrance, the area traditionally reserved for guests.

"My name is Syllan, son of Atharon, son of Yrthyn, son of Merthyn Stone-raiser. I come from an island over the water, where we consult our ancestors in stone-built spirit houses. My great-grandfather put up the greatest of these, on the Plain at the Heart of the World. Our tribe has become widely known and respected by this act, and now is perhaps the most powerful in the land."

He paused to let the inference sink in, then continued, "Many years ago, before I was born, the first stone-changers came to the Plain and my father saw for himself the shining soul of the stone. It has been his desire ever since that we should have living with us such a man to teach our people the way to unlock the stone spirit and help us make our spirit house the most wonderful in existence. We heard from our visitors that the greatest of the stone-changers came from this region, in the shadow of the White Mountains, and so in time I was sent to find you and to ask you to return with me to fulfil my father's vision."

Orelac seemed lost in thought, or perhaps he had lost interest. Thinking he needed a new angle to impress the seer, Syllan opened his mouth to continue, but Orelac raised his hand to silence him.

"Many things in your story interest me. My father Kefhan – Wanderer they named him – travelled many years ago to the islands beyond the sea. I wonder if he was one of the visitors you have had, and whether it was he who sang my praises so loudly. For I know my skills are widely appreciated, but I doubt I am the only man in the land with such skill, or that I should be singled out for such fame."

"I know not what their names were, I am sorry," Syllan replied. "Nor can I say why they came or where they went. I only remember one, when I had perhaps eight summers, but I think he came from the land near the Great River, and I was not party to any discussions he had with my father and grandfather."

They talked a little longer, without – in Syllan's view – making any progress, until Orelac brought the interview to a close.

"I will think on what you have told me, young Syllan, and I will tell you my decisions in three days' time, when my nephew returns from a trip. I would discuss this all with him before we talk again. I will ask my friends in the village to find you and your companions a house, and you may rest or explore our beautiful land until then."

The old seer's tone indicated that the interview was over. Syllan stood and, bowing his head slightly, touched a hand to his breast and raised his open palm in a gesture of farewell. He backed out of the hut and stood blinking in the sunlight a moment, before turning with Tokhan to walk back through the forest to the village. He was disappointed at the delay but determined, when next they met, to persuade Orelac to go with him to his home.

The time passed quickly for Syllan and his companions. They were by now seasoned travellers and soon adjusted to the broadly familiar routine of village life. A guest hut had been quickly cleaned up for them with a kinsman of Orelac's; food was brought to them each morning and they ate their evening meal with the family. Syllan went hunting or exploring with Tokhan, but they saw very little of their other companion. Dutehar had, as expected, found a young woman whose company he enjoyed and he disappeared for days at a time, returning with an increasingly dreamy smile and evasive answers to their enquiries. When they walked about with him, he seemed to know everybody and their dogs by name: they all greeted him like old friends. He had a gift for languages that allowed him to converse with total strangers within a day or so after arriving in a new place. That had been the main reason for Syllan including him in the party.

"I think the poor lad must be in love!" laughed Tokhan.

Syllan sighed. "Just as long as we can finish our business here before he falls foul of the family and we have to run for our lives, like we did in the hill country last spring!"

One afternoon, a young boy came to Syllan with a summons to visit the seer. He set off up the path through the forest to the little clutch of huts Orelac occupied, turning over in his mind the possible arguments he could use if the stone-changer had decided not to return across the water with him.

Orelac was waiting for him outside the hut this time, and he was not alone. Beside him stood two clean-shaven young men, a few summers older than Syllan himself, who returned his formal greetings with warm smiles on their faces. Not bodyguards, then. Like Orelac, they wore plain deerskin leggings and woven shirts, though theirs were grubby and travel-stained. The old seer introduced them as his son and nephew.

"They have only today returned. I have told them of your quest, but not yet of my answer to you. So, let me say it now to all at one time. I will not go with you, Syllan. I am now too old and would like to end my years in a familiar place where family and friends will care for me, as I have tried to care for them. In my stead, however, I offer my nephew Weyllan, a fine stone-changer, well taught by me, and long overdue to leave his teacher and find his own way."

Syllan watched Weyllan's backward step and his look of shock at these words with some unease. Orelac's nephew was the shorter of the two cousins, a well-built young man with pleasant features who only looked a little plain when outshone by his handsome kinsman. But where the son was confident and composed, Weyllan seemed apprehensive or even fearful. He did not seem at all the sort of inspirational visionary his father had sent him to fetch. Syllan watched as the young smith turned to his tutor in amazement, finding his voice only after several moments.

"Uncle, I cannot go! I have still so much to learn and … and you will need my help in the coming years. And what of Hegela? I must wait until she is ready to marry me, I …"

Orelac raised his hand to silence the youth. Syllan was at once impressed by the seer's easy authority and at the same time amused to see that Weyllan was as instantly quieted by the gesture as *he* had been a few days earlier.

"Weyllan, you know everything I do about rocks; which ones can give of their spirit and which will not, and the properties and uses of those that will. Your skill is already acknowledged far beyond this village and whilst I believe you have more to learn, you will be able to teach yourself any new skills you require. I am just as sure that you have the Sight, perhaps more even than do I, if you ever choose to use the skill."

Orelac paused and rested his scarred old hand on his nephew's shoulder as he spoke. "I have two young pupils who will in a year or two be able to assist me and look after the village when I am gone, so that is no reason for you to stay. As for Hegela, I understood she had rejected you absolutely. You know I have spoken with her, and there seems no chance of a reconciliation. Has anything happened this last moon that makes you think this is no longer her feeling?"

Weyllan shuffled. "No, not as such," he mumbled, then gathered himself to say, "But I am sure she is just going through a phase. She will come around again and will want me for her partner before the summer is out ... she has to!"

"I wish to the stars that she would, and bring an end to your moping!" Orelac scowled at his nephew. "But from what she told me, I doubt it. She is not for you at all. Ever. And the sooner you accept that and take a new path, the happier we will all be."

The second young man chuckled at this, but nonetheless, put a comforting arm around Weyllan's shoulders.

"He is right, brother. She is already making full-moon eyes at that Torlyr from down the valley. It is time we found you another woman."

Weyllan sat down heavily on a log bench just behind him, putting his head in his hands and shaking it slowly as if to rid himself of this unwanted truth.

"I cannot ..."

"You can and you will, nephew," said Orelac. "There will never be a better time to leave, nor a better opportunity for adventure and status as this!"

"My father may not be happy with this outcome." Syllan bit back on the sudden tide of anger that swept through him. "He wanted a man of stature and skill who could influence his seers and work his art upon our stones. I mean no disrespect, but Weyllan here seems not to fit that description in any way."

"If you mean no disrespect, young man, then try to trust my judgement," was Orelac's instant retort. "Weyllan will be as great a seer as I before long – I have already foreseen it and I know he is capable. He will get over this loss and will be able to do whatever can be done. Now, I have decided. I will not go. I offer you my nephew, my equal, in my stead. It is for you to persuade him to accompany you and you will not do that by insulting him."

Deep inside, a voice was telling Syllan that the old seer was right. He looked over at Weyllan, catching the young man's eye briefly and nodding slightly in his direction.

"My apology, Weyllan. I do not know you well enough to have made such a judgement of you and should have kept my tongue still."

"My nephew, I instruct you to spend time with this Syllan and his fellows, to take them out hunting or climbing, and to consider your options. I will respect your choice in the end, but here and now I feel you should grasp this chance with both hands."

The seer turned and strode into his house, leaving the younger men to continue the conversation. The second interview was over. Syllan had had his answer and would have to make the most of it, at least for a while.

For the next few days, the village huddled under grey clouds and persistent rain, sometimes heavy but mostly just an irritating, soaking, drizzle. Syllan had watched Weyllan slouch off after the meeting, leaving his cousin and adopted brother, Kefhan, to entertain the visitor. Syllan had been invited, along with Tokhan, to eat with Kefhan and his young wife Kirah, and they had been introduced to other families and young people in the village and nearby. Weyllan, still slightly truculent, at last overcame his despondency enough to join them on an excursion.

The young men were passing a small farmstead when they spotted Dutehar helping a pretty young weaver set up her loom. Syllan realised they had, at last, discovered his companion's latest love-interest, and he turned to Tokhan, shaking his head in mock resignation. Both Islanders laughed, and even Weyllan was seen to break into a watery smile. They sat down to talk as Dutehar's new friend began weaving while he meekly passed her the yarn when she asked for it. As evening came, the skies cleared and they made up their minds to go hunting early the next day.

On the day of the hunt, Weyllan for the first time took the lead, working his way up through the hills into a long valley dotted with small clumps of woodland, where he was certain they would find game. As they followed an old deer track through the tall grass, Syllan fell in beside Kefhan.

"He seems confident," he said, waving towards the young seer. "Do you often hunt here?"

"I bow to my cousin when it comes to hunting," was the reply. "He has a feeling for where the animals are. It goes beyond simple knowledge of the game. It is as if he can listen in to their thoughts when he wants to, and track them with his mind. Not that he isn't also good at reading sign the usual way – he excels at that too. If Weyllan says the deer are grazing this valley today, then we will find them. And he will shoot one, mark my word!"

And so, it proved to be. Within a short time, they had located a herd and taken positions, spread out along the downwind flank of the animals. Weyllan brought down a young buck with a sure arrow to the heart that dropped it with barely a sound, and Syllan got a clear shot at a large doe that fell kicking in the grass until Tokhan dispatched her with his flint knife. Kefhan's shot came a little late and only grazed his target, since she sprang away when Syllan's doe went down. They removed the buck's antlers to prevent damage and snagging, then tied the animals to long poles cut from the trees nearby. Feeling more cheerful than they had for several days, they set off down to the village, hefting each of their substantial burdens between two men.

As they cut up the meat outside Kefhan's house, Weyllan for the first time struck up a conversation with Syllan.

"That was a good shot you made back there," he began. "Just a handspan lower and the doe would have dropped quietly through to the Other Side. I think perhaps she was tensing to leap as you released, so that she crouched a fraction as the shaft flew to her."

It was a subtle way out of having to admit he had missed the heart, and Syllan warmed to the other young man. "Perhaps, but in truth I think I was not concentrating enough." He wiped his knife absently. "I am a fair shot, but I think I will never be a gifted archer, like you."

"When I work the fires and when I hunt, are the times when I feel the power course through me," acknowledged Weyllan. "As I take aim, I see a shimmering line that joins me to the beast, and so long as I shoot along that line, the arrow flies true. I am not convinced that I will ever be able to see what really is and what will be, the way my uncle can, but I can see the death of a stag or sense the moment a rock will release its spirit, even though the lid is hard on the melting pot."

" I fear I have not even that degree of vision." Syllan smiled but shook his head ruefully. "My father Atharon has some. He even went on a vision quest as a young man and is accepted as a seer, but I have never been called. In the end, it matters not at all, since my elder brother, not I, will take the chieftain's cloak when my father dies. He looks to be a more powerful seer than our father. I wish him well in that, and hope he lives long enough to bear sons so that I need never have the burden of ruling our people placed on my shoulders!"

"I have heard of people whose leaders are chosen by birthright rather than acknowledged merit, but you are the first one from such a tribe I have met." Kefhan joined in the conversation, his curiosity aroused by the change of topic. "If we are to come – to send Weyllan away with you to your land, tell us more about it."

Syllan noted the hesitation with interest. Was Kefhan considering coming with them? What would his wife think about that? He said nothing; instead, he obligingly began to explain his tribe and their system to his hosts. It was not easy; his grandfather Yrthyn had been chosen by the Moot, although he was the third of his family to lead the tribe. He had himself picked his eldest son Atharon to lead after his death, and in turn, Syllan's father would make the same choice. In Syllan's mind, there was no doubt who it would be. He felt only relief that his brother would be the next chief and not himself.

Kirah brought out a large pot of barley beer with several small beakers to dip in and drink from. Syllan had seen this custom several times in the course of his travels, and knew it was for him to take the first drink and approve the brew. He did so, after which all four men sat back and rested while Kirah gathered the butchered joints of meat and went off, Syllan supposed, to distribute them to friends and relatives.

He was impressed by the lightness of the tall, carinated cups and the finely wrought decoration on them, and he said so to his hosts. Kefhan straightened his back and proudly stated that the vessels were all his wife's work.

"Young she may be, but she is already widely acknowledged as a skilled potter, well-versed in the craft and adept at the magic that is required to control both fire and earth."

Syllan raised his eyebrows and pictured this paragon in his mind, appreciating the strong, intelligent face and the way her light-brown hair was tied firmly back out of the way. She was slight of build, but with well-muscled limbs; he decided she was a woman who would walk beside her man and never behind him. He gave a respectful hum in response and concluded, "You are fortunate indeed to have such a gifted wife, Kefhan."

"No luckier than is she to have Kehan." Weyllan smiled at his cousin. "His gifts may not be so apparent as hers, but Kefhan is the truest and most steadfast companion anyone could ever hope for. He holds me to reality when I let my emotions take over, and has my back when trouble comes seeking me ... he is as much my big brother as if we had shared the same breast as babes!"

There was an awkward silence after this outburst, until Weyllan laughed out loud, rocking back on his haunches at his cousin's obvious discomfort. They all joined in, and the moment passed. They talked again of hunting and Tokhan, eyes sparkling, regaled them with tales of the wild boar they had encountered on their way from the coast. In the forested hills on the far side of the Great River, a local chieftain had taken them on a boar hunt. Tokhan had been in his element – boar were hunted with spears rather than bows, making the kill a true demonstration of a warrior's courage.

Syllan confirmed that Tokhan had himself skewered a charging boar during the hunt, and he was quietly pleased at the open admiration shown by their hosts. Weyllan, in a warmer mood now, laughed at the story and praised Tokhan for his prowess. At last the young man was climbing out of the pit he had dug for himself over his lost love. The seer might, after all, be worth getting to know better.

Two days later, they were able to go hunting again, this time following Weyllan towards the rising sun along the ridge and into the next valley. The wind gusted unseasonably cold along the ridge, so that Syllan was glad he had taken the advice to bring his bark-fibre cloak to keep it out. Even Tokhan had wrapped his cloak tightly about him as they strode along the path. The valley was sheltered from the wind but despite a thorough search, the deer eluded them. So, towards midday, they climbed out of the foothills to the slopes of a mountain, on the rocky sides of which Weyllan assured them they would find ibex. Sure enough, they rounded a corner of the path to see a pair of the animals balanced on the rocks forty paces from them. Weyllan moved aside to give Syllan the lead.

"This one is for you," he whispered.

Syllan paused, suddenly uncertain at this unexpected move. "But if we try to close in, they will be gone in a breath, and I don't think I can get a sure shot from this range."

"We will try something I have never done before. Trust me, and we will have one of those fellows for supper. Take your aim."

So Syllan nocked an arrow and slowly drew the bow, lifting it as he did so. As he reached full draw, he took in a steady breath. At that moment, Weyllan touched his fingers to the base of Syllan's neck, pressing lightly into his spine. His other hand he spread over Syllan's right ear, the finger-tips pressed against his temple. Syllan felt the tingling of power flow through his head, and his eyesight sharpened tenfold in an instant. He could almost see the beating heart of the ibex as it gazed out across the valley, and for a moment he saw an arc of reddish light that shimmered between his eyes and the beast's heart. Placing the arrowhead into the arc, he lined up the shaft and with all the focus he could muster, released the bowstring.

He was aware of the shaft tearing along the already fading arc of light, aware of the shock in his own breast as the arrow struck home, and conscious as never before of a sense of loss as the ibex reared briefly, collapsed on its haunches and rolled from its perch onto the rocks beneath it. He sat unsteadily down on a rock beside the path, sucking fresh air into his lungs to clear his head.

"I ... I ... I ... Thank you! Do you ... do you ... experience that every time you make a kill?" he stammered. "If so, I think I'd rather miss sometimes."

Weyllan collapsed on the ground beside Syllan, drained by the transfer of power. He grinned ruefully.

"You get used to it. But it helps to remember the way our forefathers felt when killing an animal, so that there is not too much joy in the extinction of a life. You were joined with the spirit of that ibex for a moment. You felt its end."

"Each gift comes with its burden," Kefhan nodded towards his kinsman. "Now you see why my brother is so aware of the game and where they are. His is a spirit connection which few of us feel to the same degree, although he is usually unwilling to acknowledge his gift."

"I am honoured to have shared it." Syllan, greatly impressed, gazed at the fallen ibex. This man Weyllan might after all be a prize worth bringing home, and an interesting friend and ally for a young prince.

They scrambled over and down to the kill to join Tokhan. Weyllan placed a hand on the animal's throat, perhaps to check it was truly dead, but Syllan saw his lips move and realised he was saying a prayer for the beast's soul. He followed suit and placed his hand on the wound left by the now-broken arrow and offered his own thoughts to the departing spirit, feeling a small sorrow lift from him as he did so.

The Islanders stayed in the village until the moon was swollen almost to full once more. Syllan watched as Weyllan came gradually out of his depression, and began to enjoy himself as the pair grew closer together. He continued to warm to the young seer and conversed with him more and more, trying to understand as he did so the complexity of his new friend.

But the summer was drawing on and Syllan was aware that they should be on their way before the leaves turned in order to get home before the winter set in too hard. He arranged another meeting with Orelac to agree to the old man's offer, and thank him for suggesting Weyllan travel in his stead.

Weyllan attended, and for his part declared his readiness to go with Syllan. "Once again, Uncle, I bow to your insight. You knew that, given time, Syllan and I would become friends. Thank you for giving us that time. We will go, and one day I will send word back as to how we fare and what adventures we have had."

"I am glad you've seen the sense of it after all. You will be a credit to our people, I am certain. I need no mystical fore-sight to know that. Now here is another task for you. You know your grandfather wandered off to see the world all those years ago, and that he intended to travel to the very island to which you are bound. Yet I have seen nothing of him in my visions in all the years since, and I fear he came to a bad end. Make enquiries when you are there and see if you can find out what became of him."

When the two returned to the village, Syllan sent Tokhan off to find Dutehar, while he and Weyllan sat down with Kirah and Kefhan. When they told the couple of their deci-sion to leave, Kefhan looked across at his partner, receiving an emphatic nod in response to his unspoken query.

"We are coming with you," he announced. "No, there's no point arguing. We have talked it through several times and we are decided. I can be your assistant when we smelt our ores, and who better than Kirah to make your fire-pots for you, or the beakers for our mead? We may never get another

THE EYE OF TIME | 29

chance for such an adventure and we have no intention of missing it!"

Syllan watched Weyllan turn, nonplussed, from one to the other, bemused at their beaming grins. But when the young seer looked to him in appeal, he merely shrugged, spreading his hands wide in acceptance of the inevitable.

"Six can travel just as easily as four," he pointed out. "There is no reason for them not to come. And besides, they will be friends and allies when you arrive in my country; believe me, I was glad to have Tokhan – and Dutehar when we could find him – with me on my travels. I think it an excellent idea."

Weyllan sighed loudly and embraced both of his kinsfolk. "You have always been a brother to me, Kefhan, and now it seems I have adopted a sister too! We will take this road together and follow it to our destiny, be it glorious or not."

The group broke up to begin packing their belongings. Relieved as he was to be turning for home again, Syllan spared a thought for his newly acquired companions. Choosing what to take was a difficult task for them; it was possible they would never come back again, so what they took now might have to serve a lifetime as reminders of home. In addition, they had to be able to carry what they chose.

Weyllan came back in time to share the evening meal with them all. Syllan watched as he placed a heavy bag in front of his cousin.

"I will need to take some materials with me, for who knows how long it will be before we find suitable rocks on the islands. Will you carry a bag for me?"

Kefhan nodded and smiled, taking the bag and putting it with his gear. Then in came Tokhan, followed after a moment by Dutehar, who turned back to invite in the young weaver he had been seeing during their stay.

"Dutehar," said Syllan. "Welcome back! Tokhan will have told you we are leaving tomorrow. Get your things together, say your goodbyes, and be ready to go at first light, please."

There was a short silence, then Dutehar cleared his throat loudly. "The thing is … the thing is, I won't be coming back with you. I decided some time ago to stay here with Llanys … my new wife! I just didn't find the right time to tell you, and now it's … well, I am sorry Syllan, but I will be staying."

As he spoke, he squared up his shoulders, and eyed his leader warily, expecting some resistance. But Syllan and the others had instantly seen the aptness of the exchange of one couple for the other, and as they looked at each other, they began to laugh. Syllan thought this woman who had tamed Dutehar must be someone special. He held out a hand to his bodyguard.

"My friend, if you truly wish to stay, you have my blessing and my thanks for your companionship on our journey here. But it seems we are already going home with one married couple. Are you sure you and your wife would not prefer to join us on our homeward journey?"

"No, Syllan, I am honoured by your words, but I think I would rather stay here. There is nothing for me to return to, and I have grown to love the view of the mountains in the morning and the taste of food cooked in water that has not spent a lifetime flowing through chalk!"

And so it was that at dawn the next day, the small party of five hoisted their bags onto their shoulders and Syllan led them off down the track with their backs to the rising sun. The chief's son was excited to be heading at last for home, and nothing could puncture his optimism. He saw that several people came to say farewell. Dutehar was there with Llanys, and even Orelac came down from his house in the woods to see them on their way. Syllan noticed the tear in Kirah's eye, and both the cousins were subdued as they left

their childhoods behind, but he and Tokhan just waved dutifully at the well-wishers, then turned their smiling faces and
their hearts to the long journey home.

And Syllan, not normally blessed with visions, had the
clear impression that this was the beginning of something
momentous. Whatever it might turn out to be, his destiny lay
before him in his homeland, not here at the foot of the
mountains.

CHAPTER TWO

I soon recovered from my little excursion into the spirit realm, although the experience affected me deeply. I felt as if a door had opened within me, and what I had seen through it would always draw me back for another look. I was, as Kefhan said to me, a real seer now!

We had to wait six days at the coast with the Children of Ashila for the wind to die down and cease its dance from one direction to another. I was happy to rest, but Syllan was edgy and eager to be back on his home soil after so long away. Once we tried to set out but were beaten back before we left the bay. Eventually, a weatherworn old fisherman told me the portents were good enough and agreed to take us in his boat across the sea to the Sunset Isles.

We put out on the morning tide, and with a following wind made good progress, keeping the coast in sight as a dark line on the horizon. For most of the day, the weak winter sun showed only as a slightly brighter patch in the plains of grey cloud that stretched from horizon to horizon, but sometimes it appeared briefly in small lakes of clear sky. We were reassured by the friendly warmth of the sun-spirit

Lukan and the signs that the storm spirits were asleep or occupied elsewhere. By mid-afternoon we had passed the cape and the master turned the boat to put the sun-glow over on our left side. Progress was slower with the wind now on our quarter, but we were not reduced to rowing, for which I was thankful.

The master informed us we might expect to make landfall in the dawn. "Try to get some sleep if you can. If the wind holds, we will have no need of help or magic to reach the Islands tomorrow."

This was easier said than done. There were altogether ten of us in an open vessel just three times the length of a man; we had to leave room for the crew to work the sail and move the steering oar, which left only one or two cramped spaces to settle in. But these were fishermen and traders, used to working around a bulky cargo, and I thought they would manage to cope with us and our few possessions.

We five hunched down in the lee of the steersman's raised bench in the stern, but none of us could find sleep with all the pitching and rocking as our boat danced upon the swell. Kirah and Kefhan put their heads close and held a whispered conversation that excluded the rest of the world, so I turned to young Syllan to pass the time.

"Tell me more about this island of yours, my friend. It will take our minds off this sickening motion and give me some inkling of what I have let myself in for."

"My people live on the rolling upland we call the Plain, a land that with all my travels I still find the most beautiful I have ever seen. There is a sense of a very ancient power there, not at all the same as the raw grandeur of your home. My land has just a thin layer of soil covering soft white chalk that goes down forever, if the legends are true. There are few trees on the hills, and the sky seems vast because of it. It is so old, but still it lives and breathes in its own way, the great, slow-beating heart of the world. We live on it and with it, our Spirit House standing at its very centre. Ah, but I have missed it so much!"

He paused to wipe some spray from his face before continuing. "Where the soil is shallowest, the open grassland is superb for grazing stock or hunting, but of only limited use for crops. The heavier soils cover a deep band of clay which holds rain close to the surface and rots the roots of the grain in wet years. But between these are good, deep soils over well-drained rocks where the spirits of the barley thrive. There, our people have built solid homes, running their stock on the clay and the chalk while growing a little grain on the brash and the stone." He sat back, smiling wistfully, and it made my heart glad that he was coming home at last after his travels.

We talked for half the night, until Syllan's speech slurred and his eyes grew heavy. In the darkness, I let him slide into a fitful sleep. The sea had become wilder again and, though the wind blew steady, the pitching of the boat seemed each time to approach the very brink of disaster. The crew were alert and stern-faced, speaking only when necessary. Like me, they appeared to be waiting for the storm spirits to find us again and tear us asunder, casting our broken bodies into the waves as food for the fishes and the monsters of the deep.

I wished I had some skill in calming the waters, as I had heard some seers along the coast possessed, but there was little call for that in my home, where the lakes took no time at all to traverse, and the waves were only a handspan high. In the end, though, I too began to nod. I fell fearfully into dreams of shipwreck and disaster in which I clung to a single plank as the wind tore at my hands and the waves threw me towards the rocks and my bloody destruction.

. . .

I awoke in the grey half-light, the first moments of the dawn, stiff and cold and damp in my corner. Syllan was already awake, holding the side as he stood with his feet braced on the curved hull against the movement of the boat. My kinsfolk still slept beside me. I stretched and joined the Islander as he turned towards me.

"The wind has dropped. They tell me it often does at dawn. A good time to seek harbour, though we may yet have to row to make it." He paused, nodding towards the master standing in the bows. "He says we are too far beyond our harbour and we will have to follow the coast back a while yet. Once we make landfall anywhere, that is!"

Yet even as he spoke, one of the crew called out to the master, pointing towards a smudge of land appearing out of the murk to our right. The master called to the steersman to turn towards it and, with the crew, trimmed the sail as close as he could. It flapped sullenly, almost losing the wind, then caught the breeze again as the steering oar turned the bows. We continued our slow progress through the low swell towards land. He had seen we were awake and stepped aft to where we stood. Three men standing together in such a small vessel made me feel too unsteady – I crouched down and the others did likewise.

"With the wind as it blows now, we can't bring the ship round any further. I reckon that is the island we call Toroth and that mist to the left rises above the great bar of cobbles that guards the coast and connects Toroth to the mainland. If I'm right, then we will try to put in behind the island and wait for the wind to veer later in the morning. That should allow us to slip back down the coast to the mouth of the River we seek. There is no sign of the storm spirits, so if all stays well, we will beach there before nightfall and put you all safely ashore."

And so it proved. In no time at all, we were watching the

breakers on the long stone bar, until with a slight lift of the morning breeze, we were able to squeeze the boat close in past Toroth and drop anchor in the calm harbour beyond. As a landsman, I was impressed by the anchor, a hefty boulder in a rope net that took three men to lift and drop overboard. It gave me a feeling of confidence and safety to think we were held in our anchorage by such a stout boulder. If I had known then how easily the wind can drag a ship and anchor across the water to the rocks, I might have felt less secure, but sometimes a little ignorance is a great boon.

We sat by the mast to eat some of our supplies – a little bread and some dried venison, with a tiny wild apple each, bitter and hard, but refreshing after the saltiness of the venison. Then we swam off the boat, revelling in the feeling of being clean even as we gasped at the chill of the midwinter sea. It was a brief dip, as you can imagine; we rubbed ourselves vigorously and put on all our layers to warm up again afterwards. Then there was nothing to do but wait. After a little conversation I fell asleep, as I suppose did the others.

I woke to something of a commotion on board. It was immediately apparent that the wind had risen, and not in the direction our master had expected. Even with the sail stowed, we were being blown broadside-on across the anchorage, dragging our anchor as we went. Then with a soundless jerk, the cable broke and the boat turned into the wind. We were now moving backwards towards the shore, albeit at a reduced pace now the ship had turned freely to face its opponent. Frantically the crew put out the oars and we were called to help work them, but before we could make more than a token stroke, a shudder ran the length of the boat as we ran hard aground.

The stunned silence that followed was punctuated by the creaking of the ship for a short while, but then, as it settled into its new role as an offshore breakwater, the creaking decreased and we began to breathe again more freely. The sea spirits had played a last trick, taking us completely unawares. The master came over to us, the apology clear in his face before a word was spoken.

"This will take us a long while to mend. The tide is still half out and we cannot hope to re-float her till late in the afternoon. We may miss the breeze as a result – it may be tomorrow before we can make the river mouth."

So it was that we found ourselves being ferried ashore in the ship's little coracle two at a time, with a fourth trip for the last of our baggage. Syllan was the most worried amongst us. Between us and our destination now lay the lands of the people of Thorachis, one of the emerging chieftains of the Islands, and a man ill-disposed towards Syllan's people, whom we were bound to join.

"They are warlike folk in these parts, all of them. Every man a warrior and spoiling for a fight, I'm told. I have also heard rumours of strange customs – more than a few travellers have disappeared in this land, sacrificed to their river spirits, or so we believe," Syllan told us as we gathered our possessions. "We should avoid contact with them – even being seen – as we move inland. We can head more toward the rising sun as well, to be out of their lands the sooner."

Kefhan and I exchanged glances, wondering how much of this was truth and how much embellishment. But we had to trust to our local guide and anyway, the proposed route would take us more quickly to the river we sought. I watched Tokhan smile to himself, looking carefully about and shifting the balance of the spear in his hand. It occurred to me that Thorachis' people might not be the only ones spoiling for a little action! I was glad to be warned of this tendency and the potential it held for trouble.

We set out from the beach and headed into the open

woods that covered the coastal hills in this part of the island. We walked alongside a small stream for a while, then crossed it, climbing up a side valley until the woods thinned out and we walked through a heath thick with ferns and bracken, dotted with patches of sedge-grass that hid from view the waterlogged ground beneath. The sun was well past the zenith when we came at last out of the valley head up on to the ridge-top, dotted with solitary oaks and occasional clumps of hawthorn and broom, where the tall grass swayed and bowed in the steady breeze that blew up from the valley beyond.

We stood a while enjoying the cool wind after the warmth generated by our exertions – despite the cold of the winter day. The view was breath-taking. Behind us, the bay formed a sweeping curve that ended in the rocky island at the end of the gravel bar. Beyond that the sea occupied the view from horizon to horizon.

"It looks almost flat calm from this height. You'd think there was no swell out there at all!" Kirah pointed down, to where we could see the ship still fast aground in the bay, the shallows on which it had grounded clearly visible from our vantage point. "At least the tide will soon have risen enough for them to raise sail and free her."

"And do you see those two canoes setting out from the shore? There on the far side of the bay; now they are paddling fast towards our ship."

I wondered if the occupants were fearsome warriors or simply local farmers or fishermen, come to offer their help to other mariners in need of it. It was unlikely we would ever find out, and I smiled as I thought that any troublesome warriors would find their hands full if they started anything with the master and his crew today. But Syllan frowned and turned away.

"I don't like the look of it. We should put as much distance between us and the bay as we can. If Thorachis hears we are ashore in his lands, he will come looking for us."

I turned and followed Syllan as he headed off along the ridge, away from the afternoon sun. It was really more a line of hills than a true ridge, dissected as it was by the heads of winter-borne valleys, sometimes linked to form boggy saddles between the hilltops. We kept to the high ground for a full march, angling inland onto a second ridge line before we stopped again before a deeper combe that cut through to the broad river valley inland.

We sat ourselves down with our backs to a small clump of trees just off the ridge and ate a little food. I was pleased when Tokhan suggested we take time to hunt something for the pot, but Syllan shook his head and looked worried, refusing to allow us to hunt before we were over the rivers and out of Thorachis' territory. He pointed to the landscape below us, at the occasional cleared patches that in summer would be gardens, and the several smudges of smoke that were now appearing at intervals across the valley.

"Each smoke is a homestead or a camp populated by folk loyal to Thorachis and the river spirits. Those people will be about the lands and will report our presence back to any warriors out seeking us."

I turned to look at my companions, seeing the concern on their faces. Syllan's fears were contagious.

We were aware as we watched that the sun had gone behind the clouds, and our gaze turned back the way we had come to see the rapidly building cloud-bank spreading along the coast towards us. It darkened the horizon in its shadow until it blurred into a gloomy smudge beneath a curtain of rain. No one needed to tell us we were in for a drenching. We packed up our gear, donned cloaks and hats, and considered our next move.

"We need to head down the inland slope." Kefhan pointed

down to our left. "We will be out of the wind there, and perhaps we can find shelter in a byre or against a fence when the storm hits."

Syllan was unhappy with the idea of approaching the settlements, but his companion decided for him as, hefting one of my bags of stones as if it were empty, Tokhan set off down the hill with Kefhan and his wife close behind.

"Where we lead, so we also follow, it seems," I joked, while Syllan and I hastened after our companions as the first peal of thunder rolled across the hillside.

The rain hit us a little before we reached the upper terrace of the broad riverine plain, turning in an instant to stinging hail that rattled on our leather cloaks and stabbed at our exposed arms and faces. Our conical bark-bast hats kept the worst of it out of our eyes but in moments the water was cascading off the rims in waterfalls that obscured our vision of the path and each other. I glanced back towards the ridge just as a great thunderbolt split the sky, bursting on the ground not far from where we had just rested. For a moment I was blinded as the thunder crashed around us; I saw in the dazzling whiteness a vision of several men – other men, not our party – running before the rain along the top of a ridge, each with one hand holding their cloaks tight, the other carrying a spear or two at the trail. Then my sight returned, apart from a fuzzy red blotch in the middle of my view, and the image disappeared. We broke into a stumbling run, ducking for a little shelter into a patch of woods as we reached the valley floor.

As the hail turned back to rain, we left the copse and trotted across a damp meadow to the edge of the forest, slowing to a walk as we followed a faint path between the trees. It led us to a boggy clearing through which flowed a small stream, where we were obliged to turn further aside to follow the bourne until we could find a safe crossing. Sure enough, after a hundred paces or so, we found a place where willow hurdles had been laid across the bog, making a dryish path through to a split-log bridge over the stream. We came off the hurdles on the far side, through a thin strip of woodland and into a broad clearing covered in the remnants of barley stubble. On the far side stood a small clutch of huts, their thatched roofs reaching right to the ground. There was no way through the bracken and brambles of the wood, so we picked our way around the edge of the field, keeping the farmstead on the opposite side as we searched for a path away from the clearing. The continuing rain and fading light helped us; nobody came out from the houses to see our passing before we found the way we sought and headed back to relative safety in the shelter of the forest once more.

By this time, we were soaked through, exhausted from the descent and flight from the storm. So, when a short while later we came to another clearing and homestead, we paused at its edge to consider our options. No smoke could be seen, and after some argument we decided to chance approaching the houses to seek shelter if possible in a storehouse or byre. Perhaps twenty paces from the buildings we first smelled and then saw the smoke of a new-lit fire curling through the thatch of the nearest house. We looked at one another in shock for a moment, but before we could react, a dog barked, the door-curtain was pulled aside, and a man looked out into the evening, seeing us almost immediately.

We stood frozen, each as surprised as the others by this sudden meeting, until the man broke into a smile of welcome and waved us to come in out of the rain. He hushed the still-growling hound beside him as he stood back from the doorway to let us pass. Syllan was clearly unhappy, but the rest of us required no second invitation and gratefully stepped into the smoky interior of the house.

By the light of the fire we could see the rest of the family;

a woman, an older boy and two girls, who moved to make room for us with nervous smiles of welcome. We hung our cloaks over the low wicker and hide wall that ran around the room before squatting by the fire to warm as Syllan and Tokhan introduced us in the local dialect. Over the last few months, we had come to understand our guides quite well through a combination of common words and the learning of as much of the island tongue as we could, but it was hard to follow the conversation taking place around the fire. I suspected that our hosts were only being given a part of the truth, leaving out our connections to the Plains folk and our ultimate destination.

As we began to steam, the girls moved around and helped us out of our sodden smocks, giving us each a fur blanket or deerskin cloak to wrap around us. Some salted meat was produced, with two flat discs of bread to share amongst us, until by and by we began to relax a little as the fire settled and the smoke cleared towards the roof.

After the food I became drowsy, watching the flames dance and the smoke twist up into the thatch. Then, with the walls fading into darkness, I became aware that the faces around the fire were no longer familiar. For what seemed some time I sat among the huddled group of warriors from my earlier vision as they cursed at the rain and argued about I know not what in their melodious tongue. Then one addressed me directly but as I tried to form words to reply, the image shimmered and the inside of the house returned.

Several of the group were looking at me and Kefhan asked if I was well. I just smiled to reassure them, but said I felt sleepy. Our host immediately stood, indicating an area to the right of the doorway where he and his son cleared space for us while the women shared out their straw to give us something to lie on. I thanked them and curled up at one side of the bedding. Kefhan soon joined me, followed by Syllan.

Tokhan stayed talking a while longer to the farmer and Kirah spoke a little with the wife as they damped down the fire. It seemed I was asleep in less time than an arrow takes in flight.

We were awakened by a thunderous banging on the doorpost and a furious barking from the dog in reply. The farmer's daughter rolled from her bed on the far side of the doorway and stood to open the wicker hurdle a little and peek through the curtain. Rough male voices on the outside spoke to her in dialect, their words bringing the farmer himself to the door and eliciting gasps from Syllan and Tokhan.

"They've come for us!" gasped Syllan as the first warrior pushed his way across the threshold. I knew him straight away as one of the men from my daydreams, and I knew instinctively that the others would be gathered outside in the grey half-light. A rapid exchange now passed between Syllan, the farmer, and the lead warrior. Syllan turned to me with a worried look on his face.

"They say we must go with them to Thorachis' camp. I am sorry, Weyllan. Truly, I fear now for our lives!"

More discussion followed, an argument that I couldn't follow. I found out later the warrior leader threatened the farmer with dire but unspecified punishments for harbouring us, but our guides argued that they had acted out of kindness to strangers without any more idea than we had ourselves that we were fugitives. Eventually he agreed to defer the decision to his chieftain. Meanwhile, we gathered our belongings and filed out into the yard, where dawn was slowly taking hold of a cold grey sky. There would be no sunrise this morning, although thankfully there was also little chance of more rain.

Before we left, I turned to thank the farmer, unaware he was under threat, and took his hand briefly in both of mine. I had a flashing impression of him as an old man, standing in thought before this same house, and I felt instinctively he would be well. He smiled, gripped my hand and bade us go safely. Then we turned to walk off with our escort of armed warriors.

There were seven of them, armed with spears and bows or slingshots, and a tough bunch of brawlers they looked. It was not that we were unarmed or unable to defend ourselves; I was a good shot with a bow and Kefhan was a handy friend in any fight, but Tokhan was the only real warrior among us, with Syllan as an unknown quantity. Kirah was quite capable of defending herself against someone like me, but she would have little chance against these warriors. The odds were against us, and even Tokhan could see that, so we followed without complaint. That we still had our weapons was in itself encouraging, making it seem as if we were being escorted rather than taken prisoner. Even so, we were aware that that impression might change in an instant if we tried to run, or yet when we came at last to see Thorachis.

We walked along the valley bottom away from the growing day, with the ridge we had traversed the previous day on our left. Below it, the land sloped gently down towards the river in a cutting somewhere to our right. A short march beyond that another low ridge, a patchwork of cleared fields and oak woodland, rose up to divide the valley in two. I guessed there was a second river beyond the ridge which joined the nearer one close to where we had spent the night.

Rather less than half the land in the valley appeared to have been cleared for fields, while most of the pastures dotted here and there had the look of natural clearings. Some fields were bare, the crop ploughed back in ready for sowing in another moon or so; others looked as if they had lain fallow for two or three years, gradually recovering their fertility beneath a covering of weeds, brambles and bushes. We passed a couple of farmsteads, then a small hamlet of perhaps fifteen houses and storerooms, home to four or five families, with their livestock already bawling to be taken to their pasture for the day.

After a good walk we began to angle towards the river, heading directly for a point where the low ridge ended in a steeper hill rising several times higher than the rest of the slope. We now crossed two or three marshy streams flowing across our way to the river, each one swollen from the last night's rain. A hundred or so paces to the right lines of alder and hazel appeared, marking the banks of the river, here running in several intertwining channels. Beyond the river, the ridge was covered in gorse and bracken, a broad clear swathe of heathland on the sandy saddle between the ridge and the hill. We crossed the river above the braids, wading through up to our knees in the icy water, then headed diagonally across the heath towards the base of the hill.

Tokhan turned and pointed, as Kefhan said quietly to me, "Smoke. Several columns! It looks as if we are nearly there, wherever that may be."

"The village of this Thorachis, I'd imagine. Yes, look! You can see the houses now. Quite a large place, by the look of it."

Around the shoulder of the hill we could see it spread before us, over seventy houses and shelters huddled together inside a fence of woven hurdles. The place was already bustling with activity as herdsmen gathered their cows and their goats up, heading for the pastures on the ridge or in the open valley that now appeared before us.

As we walked into the village past the middens, a few dogs yapped half-heartedly or trotted out to sniff at our legs as we went by, and people turned to watch our small parade pass. A few called greetings to our escort and one clearly asked a question of them, answered with a single word I recognised as "foreigners" or "outlanders". Further comment was silenced by a glare from the leader and we were led directly to a newly emptied cattle enclosure near the top of the settlement. He spoke briefly to Syllan, who relayed his message to the rest of us.

"We are to wait here while they speak to their chief. He says we are not to leave, nor even look around, or his warriors may use us for spear practice. Tokhan, take that look off your face! We will do as they say for now."

To reinforce the order, the leader left three of his fellows standing at the gate into the byre, and we again had to wonder at our status here, still uncomfortably somewhere between guests and prisoners.

And there we remained for the rest of the morning. A few folk came to look us over, and a child threw a few sticks at us until one of our guards sent him packing. A woman came by with a large pot of water, but no food, so that we were forced to dig into our own supplies for our breakfast and midday meal. Syllan was despondent, but Tokhan tried to talk to the guards, although without much success. It was Kirah who made some progress, communicating in a mix of learnt words and signs to the woman who brought our water. She found out that Thorachis had gone off shortly before our arrival and was not expected back until well after noon. We passed the time talking amongst ourselves, waiting for the inevitable confrontation when he returned.

CHAPTER THREE

When the time finally came, we were surprised to find Thorachis was a slightly built man with an open countenance, in a plain deerskin smock and a short leather cloak. A tall staff and a fine polished axe were all that marked him from the men around him, or perhaps it was the very simplicity that made him different. The two seers at his side could hardly have been more obvious, with their esoteric headdresses cascading over long bone-bedangled tunics with medicine pouches and animal parts hanging from their girdles. The warriors around the chief favoured bear- and wolf-skin cloaks worn fur outwards, with their spears, clubs, and axes clearly on display.

He indicated the bearded leader of our escort party. "My nephew Granadh has told me you landed from a boat aground in the bay and that, instead of coming here to me for assistance, you skulked along the hills doing all you could to avoid this place. That is the manner of an enemy, not a friend. He also tells me you speak the dialect of our enemies on the Plain, the children of Hatha. Explain yourselves to me now or face the consequences!"

A hot flush of anger spread through me as I listened to these words. Threats and insults so early in the interview were uncalled for; I was in no mood now to dissemble to a bully. Syllan opened his mouth to speak, but before he could say anything, I held a hand up towards him and spoke up myself. Thorachis had used the general Island tongue rather than his own dialect and I hoped to be able to make him understand me with my limited knowledge of the language.

"I am Weyllan, of the people of Gehana, far away across the water by the White Mountains. I am a seer and a craftsman, and I am bound for the Plain to see the great stone house built there. In my country we had heard of that wonder and when I discovered that Syllan here was from the region, I asked him if he would be my guide on the journey. We had meant to land at a river mouth much further towards the sunrise from here, but the wind spirits drove us into your bay. We sought to travel back towards the river and did not seek help because none was needed."

I paused to let my narrowed eyes sweep the room.

"You speak to us of consequences, yet we came here willingly and in peace when invited. We hardly expected to be treated as spies or thieves. You speak of consequences, but I tell you I am called to this island and have yet to play the role the spirits have decreed for me. If harm comes to my companions or me, my curse will be on you and your people, and the spirits may show you your consequences in ways you willnot enjoy!"

It was a fable, and I was certain my deception was painted all across my face, but I had learnt over the last year or so that foreign magic is often feared much more than the home-born varieties. I wanted to regain some control over our fates. To my surprise, it seemed to work, so that when Thorachis spoke again, it was with a more conciliatory tone.

"If it is wonders you seek, Seer, then you need travel no further, for we have a spirit house here as great as the stone ring on the Plain, where we call on the river Lord Magh. And I wager he hears us more than those adopted ancestors they sing to inland. Seers, leatherworkers and stone-smiths we have in full measure, and potters too." He paused, then said, "Granadh says you are carrying two skins filled with stones. Tell me, is this just a burden you bear to atone for something, or do they perhaps polish up as well as my axe here?"

"My craft is one I doubt you possess," I replied. "And my stone is not for flaking or polishing as you imagine. I was trained in magic that through fire gives birth to the very spirit, the true essence, of the rock and it is that which I craft into things such as these." I lifted one of my cheek-plaits to show him the shining sun-gold band that decorated and held it firm. "And small tools such as my knife here."

In the dull winter light, the blade of the knife was not shown at its flashing best, but still it gleamed with a reflection from the clouds and was so clearly something entirely new that it drew gasps from some of the warriors present. At his request, I stepped towards Thorachis and passed him the blade, and allowed him a closer look at my tress-grips. There was no doubt he was impressed, but it was in my mind he could still take my possessions and have us all killed or sacrificed to his 'River Lord'. But it appeared his mind was working along a different path.

"You make these out of stone?"

"Yes."

"Any stone? Is the same spirit in the rocks of this hill?"

"No. To both questions. Each stone has a spirit; this we all understand. Yet only a few will reveal themselves in this fashion, and in truth I know not if such rocks are to be found here, nor yet anywhere on this island."

He considered this. "How long does it take to perform this magic?"

"A day or two to prepare the fuel and build the hearth, another to build a mould and crush the rock, then half a day for purification and the rest to release the essence, and perhaps another half-day to shape and finish the object. But the balance is delicate and the spirits capricious. I cannot always be sure they will work for me – or anyone."

Another pause. Then Thorachis spoke again, frowning. "Very well. You have six days. If you can give me a blade for myself and one for the Lord Magh, you and your companions will go free. If not, a different sort of sacrifice may be needed; I may think it safe to ignore your curse, seer or not. Tomorrow my own seer Tennec will take you to our spirit house. There you can prepare and build your hearth. There will be spirits aplenty to assist you if you have need of them." He turned and strode away, several of his entourage in tow, leaving us with little option but to obey.

The next few days we spent busily preparing for our task. We were lodged in a tidy guest hut near the centre of the village and allowed to move freely, although always with one or two of Thorachis' men in attendance. We discussed making a run for it, but in the heart of their territory it seemed too small a chance and I counselled against it. If we ran, it would seem as if we feared Thorachis' threat. Besides, I felt I had been challenged and intended to show the man I was equal to any task he could conceive for me. Thinking like that surprised me a little until I realised that I was changing; I was no longer the disconsolate and uncertain youth I had been when my journey began. Was I beginning to believe my own fable?

Our escorts took us to a section of the river bank to collect several basket-loads of clay, which Kirah and I spent the rest of the day sorting to remove all the unwanted stones, roots and other impurities. Tokhan brought in a basket of coarse sand from one of the streams, and on the second day we carried our materials up the hill to the spirit house.

The House of Magh was certainly an impressive structure. Our first impression as we climbed the gentle slope towards it was of a great bank topped with a stout palisade of man-high posts within which a thin curl of smoke indicated activity. But as we entered the lower gate into the enclosure, we saw that the palisade stood well behind the bank and its great posts were in reality several times our height. Between the palisade and the bank was a substantial ditch, an arrangement I had never before seen on my travels. It was as if the enclosure had been turned inside-out, so that it protected the world outside from what went on within. Considering the power wielded in some spirit ceremonies, and the unpredictable nature of some of the spirits, I had to admit this seemed like a sensible idea!

The enclosure covered a vast area two hundred paces across to the opposite entrance at the top of the ridge, where the posts were, if anything, even taller than those near us. Inside, the eye was drawn at once to a small forest of tall posts, many of them carved and painted, set within their own circular bank, again with an internal ditch. Near the centre of the great enclosure burned a small fire, generating the column of smoke we had seen earlier. Beside it sat a lone seer, swathed in a thick buckskin blanket and watched over by his minder as he lost himself in the smoke and travelled who-knew-where in the other realms.

Another seer, one I recognised as having been with Thorachis on our first day, came to greet us. He led us to a space near the edge of the enclosure and perhaps a third of the way around from the lower gate.

"This is where the Lord Magh has decreed you may

perform our task. Gather together what you require and bring it here. Do not ask us for help; we have our own more worthy duties to perform."

I noticed it was about as far from the inner enclosure as it could be and well away from the prestigious zones in the centre or flanking the gates. Whatever Thorachis thought of us, his seers were leaving us in no doubt as to their view of our low status in this spirit house. Kefhan was annoyed and complained angrily to the official, but it was quite pointless. With a curt word to our escort the seer turned on his heel and strode away from us.

I set to with Kirah to dig the shallow pit and build the oval walls of the hearth, the ceremonial womb of the earth from which the essence of the ore would be born. Syllan hesitated a moment, then undid his cloak and took up a large antler pick.

"What would you have me do? I cannot just stand here pretending to guard you from our guards!"

"Syllan, my friend, we need water to mix with our earth. It would be a good gesture to take these water skins down to the river and ask Magh for a blessing on the water we take. Our prayer might carry extra weight if it comes from a chief's son. Will you do that?"

"Judging by the size of these skins," quipped Syllan, as he lifted the two bags up, "the prayer won't be the only thing carrying a lot of weight!" We all chuckled as he dutifully set off down the hill to the river.

We had no time to build a slow-burning stack to make the charcoal we needed for the smelt, so I sent Kefhan and Tokhan back to the village to begin collecting charcoal from the houses there. Each hearth might give us six to eight decent pieces, so that we would have to obtain lumps from every fire at least twice to have enough fuel for our purpose.

One or other of our escorts accompanied us on all our excursions, generally keeping in the background, but helping out with language or other difficulties in a friendly way. That they mistrusted the two plainsmen was apparent, but they were not mistreated, nor did our escorts seem to feel animosity towards the rest of us.

During the afternoon I took the time to take a better look around the House of Magh; the inner structure proved to comprise several circles of posts, each set within the next with a common centre, with the tallest in the central ring and flanking the entrance. I guessed this would be used on feast days for a weaving circle dance to aid the crossing into the spirit world, and was quietly sad that I would not be there to witness such an occasion. I walked on round to the upper gate, where I stood in silence awhile, impressed at the view.

The entrance faced out across the river valley, where below me I could see the several braids of the stream glittering in the weak winter sunshine. As I watched the light and the water flow, each to their own rhythms, I felt again that alteration in reality and seemed to drift down closer to the river. Before me, the glistening waters bent and shifted, and merged into a pulsing, one-eyed face that glared back at me as I stared in wonder at it. It all lasted just a few moments, but as the vision blurred and retreated once more, I thought for a moment the great eye closed briefly, and the glare softened into the slightest of smiles. I was in no doubt that I had just been granted an audience with Lord Magh himself and that I had somehow met with his approval. I remember I was puzzled and not a little worried at the increasing frequency of these little visions, which I suspected had begun soon after my walk in the spirit world at midwinter. I was also wondering if we could wrest any advantage from the discovery of this unexpected ally. I walked back to Kirah and resumed work on the hearth.

Another day was spent gathering more fuel and moving what we needed up to the spirit house. I began to appreciate the size of this village within which were gathered more than a hundred souls. The houses seemed substantial enough, although in most cases only the doorposts and a rear anchor post penetrated the soil to pin the roof to the earth. I was told many of them stood empty much of the summer as folk moved their herds around the territory. It also appeared that Syllan's assessment of the warlike nature of these people was accurate, for every adult man carried weapons; they looked ready for a fight if a dog barked. I saw many men making spears or arrows, including one weasel-faced runt I watched dipping his arrows in some brown syrup which I felt certain was poison. I shivered and hurried on with our task. Well before sunset we had finished our preparations and were able to spend the evening relaxing in our hut.

"One of Thorachis' wives told me she and the other women have prepared the sweat lodge for you for tomorrow," said Kirah. "They have scoured out the ditch around it in readiness. There will be a fire laid and started for us at first light."

"Thank you, Kirah," I replied. "But why do you exclude yourself from this? We need you cleansed and focussed for the smelt as well, little sister."

It was unusual at home for women to participate in birthing the rock spirit, but the process would require at least three pairs of strong arms, and Kirah was a gifted potter and as good with fire as either Kefhan or myself. After her initial surprise, she quickly saw the sense in my plan and seemed pleased to be included as an equal.

Syllan shook his head. "What will become of us, I wonder? If you fail, I fear that their sacrifice will be me and

Tokhan, as enemies of their people. And even if you succeed, will Thorachis keep his word? He may think to keep you, and rid himself of your guides by throwing us to his so-called River Lord."

I tried to reassure him with my vision of the previous day. "Be in no doubt that Magh exists, Syllan, but I think he favours us for some reason. I do not think he will allow us to fall victim to Thorachis' treachery, should it occur. And we will succeed, I am confident of that. Still, we should be ready for a rapid departure if once we are given a chance to go, and not give our hosts time to dream up new challenges or forfeits."

I did not add that I was already considering a way to ensure that chance presented itself. Better that nobody knew what I had in mind.

Early on the fourth day, the three of us who would undertake the purification of the ore entered the sweat lodge, cleansing body and soul in the hot steam. Before meditating on the task ahead, we rubbed our bodies with dried leaves and petals, crushing them to release the aroma and draw down the power to realise our magic. Because of the hot furnace, it was too dangerous to perform this rite in trance, so we needed to gain the support of the spirits without actually crossing over, just by calling them near and impressing them with our purity and power of mind. Without their help, the stone would never surrender its essence, and all our work would be in vain. But as the morning passed, I felt more strongly than ever that they were working with us and we would succeed.

We entered the spirit house, where Syllan and Tokhan stood guard on our equipment. Just before midday, we lit the fire and began the ritual. Kirah had never performed this great spell before, but she was familiar with the firing of pots upon which this ritual was based, and she soon picked up the way of it, adding her powerful skills to the mix. As I had foreseen, it went both quickly and well; by mid-afternoon we knew that in the small cups the ore had given up its essence and the golden fluid was ready to be poured.

While we were hard at work, a small group of onlookers gathered, held at a distance by our two sentries to prevent them learning our secret rites. Foremost among them was Thorachis himself, with two of his seer-advisors in his shadow as ever. Around them were several warriors, including some of our escorts, and four others whom I supposed from their dress to be seers or keepers of the spirit house. Once I had scraped the embers aside and assured myself we had pure liquid in our pots, I beckoned to Thorachis to come closer to witness the pouring. Tokhan, as we had agreed, made it clear that the others were not invited forward. I smiled inwardly. It was a small power play, but one that gave the Plainsmen satisfaction and showed the locals we were in control.

The pour into the blade-moulds went perfectly, with only a few drops of the essence falling aside. Then we waited a short while for the liquid to harden again before breaking open the clay moulds to reveal the shining moon-gold blades inside. Thorachis gasped in wonder and, taking a leather cloth from my hand, lifted one of them high above his head to show his fellows, who likewise showed their amazement with whoops and gasps. I carefully took the blade back from him, then Kefhan and I sat down to tidy and polish the two knives before attaching the wooden handles we had carved the previous evening.

The sun was almost on the skyline, setting the evening clouds on fire, when we formally handed over the finished knives, and once Thorachis had chosen one for himself and tucked it into his belt, they all turned to process down to the river for the sacrifice. At this point I needed to be left behind for a few moments and made as if I needed a little time alone, but the seers would have none of it and I was ushered off along with the others, my escape plan in tatters. As we left the enclosure, Kirah slipped off into the gorse for a moment to relieve herself, but the rest of us were hurried along to our destiny. Kirah was a woman, and clearly not significant in the eyes of the locals. I wished I had taken the chance to share my plan with her, but it was too late now, and I decided I would put my trust in the goodwill I had felt emanating from Magh.

The ceremony was relatively straightforward, with the two leading seers each calling the praises of the river spirit to attract his attention, after which Thorachis spoke up and in a sing-song voice recited the story of the gift they were about to give. We were pushed forward to be introduced as the makers of the offering, although Thorachis completely ignored Kirah in either the introduction or the story. I thought she might be annoyed at this, but when I glanced at her, she was smiling to herself, and when she caught my eye, she so plainly winked at me, I almost laughed out loud.

Then they began to chant, and Thorachis stepped forward so that the river came up over his feet. As the sun dipped at last below the horizon, he lifted the knife and shouted, "Lord Magh, receive this gift from your people! Receive this magic, this power, this wonder, and give us in return your grace!" With that he threw the offering well out into the stream where it splashed as it slipped from our world into the next, into the hands of Magh.

There was a long silence, broken at last by a sudden cry from one of the warriors. We all turned and looked up the hill where he pointed, and all saw in the twilight the thick-ening column of smoke rising above a red glow beyond the palisade of the spirit house. With cries of dismay, Thorachis' men turned as one and ran back up the hill. I guessed at once that what I had intended to precipitate had happened without my aid, and that sparks from our untended furnace had caught fire to the woodpile (to which I had added a good proportion of kindling and dry moss with this in mind), which would in turn now be starting to burn the palisade itself. I silently gave my thanks to Magh, wondering at the same time why he was so displeased with his own people just now.

"Quickly, there is no time to lose! Back to the village and let us be away from here before they notice we are gone!"

It was Kirah calling us to action, and once more I was impressed by her grasp of the situation and the opportunity it gave us. No guards had remained with us and when they returned, I guessed we would be in for a rough time for firing their temple. Or worse; for the thought of our becoming a sacrifice to Magh seemed even more likely now.

We ran; down along the river, across the small stream and up the path to the village. There were no guards on our hut, so we ducked inside and frantically began to gather our belongings.

"Lucky they left us our weapons!" exclaimed Syllan, slinging his quiver across his shoulder.

"The rocks! Kefhan, have you got your bag?" I looked nervously at him as we headed for the doorway. He just grinned back, patted his backpack and raised his brows as if to say "Really? You think I would forget them?"

"Hurry, there may be no guards, but there may still be warriors in the village," was all Kirah would say, ducking out in front of us.

We were in and out in less time than it took to draw five breaths, clutching our few bags and belongings in our arms in our haste to flee. We had no idea how soon they would spot our absence and come after us, and we had no intention of waiting to find out. Moments later we were running out of the settlement along the opposite way, with the dying day and the growing glow of the fire at our backs and the night in front of us.

,

CHAPTER FOUR

There had been little opportunity to explore this direction from the village; travel towards the sunrise had been actively discouraged. Even so, we had learned that the stream we had crossed on our journey in was just a tributary flowing into Magh's river at the end of the ridge. The main river lay well to our left, in a flat floodplain through which the water swirled in sometimes one, sometimes two and sometimes even three channels. The ground was marshy and treacherous; we had been advised to stay on established paths when crossing the floodplain. Of course, that meant any pursuers would know the way and be able to travel much faster than could we. So, we made haste, keeping to the top of the low ridge as long as we could, following a broad track across the heath. After perhaps half a march, running and walking by turns, we collapsed breathless beside a small copse of trees next to the trail.

"Still burning strongly!" Tokhan looked back along the river towards the spirit house. By now it was almost completely dark, and the glow of the fire was the strongest light we could see in the world. We were at once aware of how far we had come, and at the same time how little distance we had put between us and pursuit.

"Do you think they will follow?" asked Kefhan.

"Without doubt!" Syllan stared off into the darkness. "The only question is, how soon?"

"They will need to put the fire out first." I stood up, leaning on my bow for support. "We have a while yet, but we should keep moving."

But it was obvious that Kirah needed a little more time. She apologised, saying she just felt a little unwell; certainly, she looked slightly pale and waxy. A moment later she ran off into the grove, returning shortly afterwards looking flushed. I thought perhaps that the release of tension had made her ill; whatever it was, she indicated that she felt well enough to continue, so we hefted our bundles and began to trot down the path.

So far, we had been moving through heathland, with sandy soils covered with patches of heather and gorse. As we started now to descend towards the river, there were more stands of trees, joining together to form small patches of woodland with grassy meadows in between. We skirted round a small farmstead, then a short distance later we had to detour around a larger hamlet, with six or seven fields cleared around the houses. A few people were outside tending to their beasts or bringing in firewood, but no one saw us pass along the far side of the clearing against the dark of the woods.

A little further on we came to the first river channel, perhaps three paces across and waist deep, or more – it was hard to tell in the darkness. Syllan suggested we cut back to our right to regain the path, where there might be stepping stones or a ford. As it happened, the stock path turned and followed the river still further, but where we rejoined it, a huge tree trunk had dropped across the stream and we were able to cross dry-shod to the far bank. From there we followed a narrower trail that led on for more than two hundred paces to the second channel. Here we rejoined the main stock path at a fast-flowing ford. We were going to get wet anyway.

We had no idea how deep the water might be. The stream was swollen and flew hissing and clattering across the gravel banks. But with only half the stars and no moon yet, it was flinty black and quite opaque midstream: a shadow, showing none of the movement we could plainly hear. We stood uncertainly, trying to decide what to do next. But it seemed that Magh still favoured us, for the moon at last appeared from behind the clouds and gave us light to make our decisions. We guessed that the water was about knee deep and fordable with care, so we gathered our belongings together, rolled up our leggings, and, led by the stalwart Tokhan, began the crossing.

It almost went without a hitch. Almost. I was last in line, with Kirah in front of me. Halfway over, she stumbled and slipped. She recovered her balance, but I had already stepped forward to catch her; it was I who lost my footing and fell sideways into the icy water. I twisted to get my knees under me and put out one hand, jarring both arm and knees as they struck the cobbles on the streambed, sending a shaft of pain up my back. My move had saved my pack and my upper clothing from getting too wet, but my arm throbbed for some time afterwards and I could feel the bruises on my knees swelling as Kirah and Kefhan helped me to my feet and across the rest of the river.

I collapsed on the bank, shivering violently from the shock and the cold.

Gradually I brought the shivers under control and tried to ignore the aches in my back and limbs. Kirah built a small fire to warm us and dry our legs, while my brother pulled my sodden leggings off and wrung them to squeeze out the worst of the icy water.

"Here, let me put something on those bruises." Kirah dried my legs with a square of soft leather. "There are dock leaves here and I have a poultice ready mixed in my bag. Come, finish drying yourself while I get it for you."

As I dried myself and recovered, I thought again of the pursuit, trying to picture what was happening back at the village. I closed my eyes in concentration, trying to set off a vision, but I was no great seer back then, and my insights always seemed to come at random. Besides, my mind was still in turmoil from the recent fall in the stream. I was too distracted to expect to induce at will the dislocation I needed for a vision.

We pressed on up the hill, through thicker woods with a dense undergrowth of dry brown bracken. There were no side paths off our route, and we began to think that the land this side of the river was empty of habitation. Almost at the top of the ridge, we found a clearing where several trees had come down during a storm two or three winters before, and we dropped our packs and ourselves against one lichen-covered log to rest.

With the moon again in hiding, we looked out over a landscape of almost total blackness, only broken by a couple of faint flickers from outside fires, and in a few places by a distant wink of light as a farmer's door was briefly opened and shut. There was no longer a light from the burning palisade, so we guessed the blaze had been extinguished.

Syllan shook his head and pushed the hair back from his face. "The spirits must truly be with us tonight. Our kiln was a good few feet from the wooden wall; how could the fire have crossed that space and found something to catch on?"

"As for that," I replied, "I prepared some tinder and kindling in the woodpile with just this purpose in mind. But they wouldn't let me stay behind a moment, and I had no opportunity to carry through my plan. Thank Magh for that part of it, at least!"

But Kefhan turned a thoughtful gaze towards his wife. "No, brother, you had no chance to return to the fire. But *one* of us did."

Kirah looked up at her partner, gave him a momentary frown, then smiled innocently at the rest of us. It was only then that I realised just why she had been so ready to move back at the river; that it was *she* who had slipped back, and carried a load of embers over to the woodpile. Somehow, she had divined my plan, so that when I was prevented from carrying it out, she had stepped into my place. I threw back my head and laughed, sending another stab of pain through my rapidly stiffening body. Tokhan went so far as to walk over to Kirah and clap her on the shoulder, grinning all the while.

I lay back, trying again to penetrate the darkness with my sight to confirm whether any pursuit had been mounted yet, but without success. Then once again, the moon broke out to give us light, and as I stared into her spirit face, I felt the familiar tingle between my shoulder blades. Through a dark vortex, I found myself looking between the houses of the village as a party of armed warriors with hunting dogs trotted towards me, the lit torches in their hands glinting on the flint points of the spears and arrows they held ready.

There was at least a dozen of them, led by Granadh and two of the others from our first escort a few days earlier. Behind them came a man I had not seen before, followed by a short man with a small bow. With a shiver, I recognised the man I had seen dipping his arrows in poison in the village. Poison arrows were for game, not for warfare. Or at least, those were the morals I had been taught, but the look of this weasel made me realise that these people might have quite different rules, if any of what Syllan had told us was true. The shock brought an end to my brief trance, and I came back with relief to my friends on the ridge-top.

"They are coming, with torches and bows. They have dogs, too. And there is one among them whose arrows we would not wish to feel." I reminded them of seeing Weasel-face.

"We should be moving!" said Syllan, though his companion seemed inclined to stay and fight it out.

I fell in beside Tokhan. "Not here, this is not a good place. But I fear we will have to fight before the night is out, so keep your eyes open for a good ambush spot."

"I have been looking for some time. This was the best I have seen so far. There's cover, but not far enough from the trees."

"Just what I was thinking. We must keep looking!"

We crossed over the ridge crest and began our descent down the gentle back slope to the next river. Again, we saw no signs of life, confirming our initial feeling that this ridge was deserted.

"It must be neutral land between Thorachis' people and their neighbours," muttered Syllan. "In these parts that would be Chatka's clan, or perhaps the people of Trebhana. I'm not sure how far along we have come. But either of them would be preferable to Thorachis, and I expect neither has much love for him and his thugs. So, once we cross the river, we might be safe." He let out a sound half-way between a growl and a chuckle."Although I wouldn't be too sure of that!"

When we reached the river, we could see in the moonlight that it was, like the others, swollen from the rain, flowing fast and deep. It was wider than the other streams, too. Although usually this must be a shallow ford, I thought the waters would come over our waists were we to wade across now. The river was too broad to be spanned by a fallen tree, and with no settlements on this side, there was no likelihood of useable stepping stones or a slab bridge nearby. We held a short conference, but soon agreed we would have to cross on foot here.

I began to undress. "Strip off your clothes and tie them into your packs to keep them dry. We'll need a fire on the far side, but with luck *we* will dry quicker than our clothing."

There was a small shrine beside the path near the water's edge, just a waist-high standing stone next to a small quern which was itself resting on two other flat slabs of stone. I briefly wondered if the ridge we had just crossed was a sacred place but, if so, I had had no sense of it as we passed through. As I touched the upright stone, trying to attune my senses to the force acknowledged by the shrine, I felt myself drawn always to the water, especially upstream. From my pack I took a small handful of ground barley and a finger of dried meat, placing them in the bowl of the quern. While the others watched in silence, I drew forth my copper blade and used it to make a small incision on the butt of my hand. I held the hand over the bowl as I muttered a quick prayer to those unknown water spirits, letting four drops fall onto the flour, a blood sacrifice I thought well worth giving to secure a safe crossing.

We turned in silence from the shrine and stepped one by one into the icy stream. The chill spread in seconds up from our ankles to our knees, then as we went further in, up the thighs to the organs, already withered from the intense cold. Before we were half-way across, the icy stream drained the heat from our bodies, making us shiver uncontrollably. Despite the cold and the loss of feeling in my legs, I became aware of a presence in the water, of something almost solid brushing against my legs, pushing with a slight pressure against the current; something that seemed to swim, yet was so evidently not a fish.

Kefhan turned back to me."Can you feel them? I feel they are guiding my feet – but for good or ill, I cannot tell."

I nodded agreement.

He continued, "And the water is rising. Or going to rise. I feel it through my legs, directly into my head."

"This river is not a part of Magh's realm," I replied. " I know not who this spirit is – or if indeed they are many – but it or they are surely here with us. Take care where you put your feet and let us not dally in the water."

The moon stayed with us for most of the crossing, disappearing behind a wall of cloud when Tokhan was just a few feet short of the far bank. As it did so, I felt the vision-reality descend on me once more, and I saw clearly our pursuers, still in moonlight, as they came to the fallen tree across the first stream and began to cross over to the floodplain between the two channels. It lasted just a moment, but I knew this was happening *now,* and that they were no more than half a march behind us, so quickly had they traversed the familiar paths of their own territory.

This time, we all made it safely across, running one after the other into the trees beyond the reed bed. We rubbed our legs vigorously with handfuls of bracken and set about making a small fire to warm us through again. I told the others of the vision I had seen; they agreed we should make this a brief stop,then move away from the river as soon as we could. We did not want to give away our position by still showing a light when Granadh's posse topped the ridge.

"We need to find a place to make a stand," I suggested. "They may decide not to cross the river, but if they do, they will be on another's soil and perhaps not so ready to make a fight of it. If we can catch them unawares, we may be able to discourage them from chasing us further."

So, we doused the little fire and moved out, with Syllan and Tokhan scouting ahead for a suitable ambush where we could wait for our enemies. The roar of the river decreased rapidly as we followed the path up a slight terrace to the next level, walking towards a darker horizon I took to be another low ridge. As we reached it and the track turned to climb the slope at a shallower angle, we saw Syllan waiting for us, signing that we should follow him into the bracken. He led us to a small clutch of boulders and bushes a dozen paces off the path, with a sufficiently clear view back towards the river for an easy arrow cast.

"Tokhan spotted it. It's a perfect spot. He even found a place to light a fire that cannot be seen from the path."

There was our warrior, sitting with his feet in a hole left by a cast-down tree, with the hollow and the mass of earth among the roots completely hiding his little fire from the sight of anyone lower down the slope. We gathered round the flame and bathed a while in its slight but welcome warmth. The earlier cloud bank had moved away now; the moon was playing hide and seek among a great herd of smaller clouds migrating purposefully across the sky. Although it was still well short of midnight, we had been running for an age now after a long, tense day, so that even Tokhan was showing signs of weariness. I was exhausted and was soon nodding off, my eyes fighting to stay closed each time I blinked. In one of these moments I had another flash of vision, seeing our pursuers on the far riverbank by the shrine, looking out over the swollen waters, arguing amongst themselves. Then Granadh snorted and began to strip off; the others followed suit, grumbling and shivering as they wrapped their clothes into bundles.

"They are crossing the river. They will be here soon, but it seems they have left the dogs behind. We should make our plans."

We did not have long to wait. Our pursuers must have paused only to scrub themselves dry on the bracken before dressing and coming straight ahead. I remember thinking I had been wrong about their enthusiasm waning when they left their home territory, but then I thought of the dissent and grumbling I had witnessed in my vision and I felt reassured.

Our enemies were already over the terrace when the moon revealed their presence to us. We watched in silence as they filed along the track towards us. I counted only ten of them. I checked again, but with the same result. It was possible my vision had misled me or they had lost two of their number along the way. I wondered if they had been deterred or even washed away by the rising waters; then I remembered the dogs and realised the pair had probably stayed with the animals. Either way, it would not make the rest feel any better or braver, and that was a good thing. As they came closer, I could make out the Weasel, now third in line. I made up my mind to put my first arrow through him, before he could send his poison darts our way.

They were almost at the bend in the path when we launched our attack. Tokhan stepped from behind the fallen tree roots, hurling his spear at Granadh, who still led the troop. I took aim at my target and let an arrow fly, nocking another to the bow as fast as I could for a second shot before our pursuers could react. I saw Weasel-face stagger and knew I had hit him, but he didn't fall, so I loosed my second arrow at him too. Kefhan and Syllan had each sent shots into the advancing warriors, and Kirah had joined in with her small but deadly slingshot.

Our foes dived off the track into the undergrowth and sent a few wild arrows over our heads, although I doubt they could see anything to aim at, with our cover and the blackness of the ridge at our backs. I could see two bodies in the track, and we could hear at least one man moaning in the shadows. Then the moon did one of her tricks, following our enemies into hiding. Neither side could now see anything to aim at, nor be sure of the position of the others. I looked up at the sky and could see another bank of cloud bearing down on us. A few snowflakes began to fall, drifting unhurriedly on the slight breeze. I had no desire to sit through a snowstorm with the current stalemate upon us, so I made up my mind to move things along a little.

"Hear me!" I cried out, in as deep and oracular a tone as I could manage. "I am Weyllan, seer and stone-changer from the White Mountains! I have watched you following us, I have seen you fail to make an offering to the river spirits at your back."

A single arrow flew out of the darkness, aimed, I suppose, at the sound of my voice. It missed by a wide margin, and I continued with scarcely a break. "Be certain that I have also seen your return journey, with those of you who die amid the coming flood and the flying snow when you cross the water again. If you wait here, your fate is certain. If you go now, before the storm hits us, you may escape the wrath of the spirits. I have spoken!"

Well, I thought, a bluff had worked with these folk before, and what I said was close enough to the truth of what they could all see coming. If it worked, our troubles were over for a while. If not, we had lost nothing.

I could hear a whispered conversation down by the track. Then a voice called back, "We are leaving! Allow us to collect our kinsmen and do not shoot as we go. We fear the river spirits, but we do not fear *you.* If you shoot again, we will change our minds and kill you all!"

There was a roar of laughter from Tokhan. "Leave them to lie there. I would have my spear back, and see the face of my slain enemy. I am Tokhan, and there will never be enough of you to kill me and my comrades. Go now, before we cheat the spirits of their sacrifice and kill you ourselves!" He laughed again, in a way that had even me worried; it must have filled Thorachis' warriors with dread.

"We cannot leave Granadh," called their spokesman from the darkness. "We must at least try to return with his body. Allow us to remove your spear and go in peace, we entreat you!"

"Remove the shafts, then, and place them in the path," I called back. "Do no more, but leave at once! The river is already rising – listen, and you will hear I speak the truth." Indeed, I had myself just noticed the sound of the river, audible for the first time since we had left the track. Of course, it might just have been a subtle shift in the way the wind was blowing, as the snow began to fall more thickly.

A shadow appeared on the path next to one of the bodies, just visible in the faint light reflected from the pale snow-clouds. The figure knelt briefly beside the shape I now assumed to be Granadh, then stood and, grasping the spear-shaft, pulled the blade clear. He bent again, appearing to pull at a second object that I guessed was an arrow shaft. Another shadow appeared and performed the same duty on the other body, but a cry of pain revealed the man was not yet dead. As he was lifted across the warrior's shoulders, I could see he was the one we had nicknamed Weasel-face. Then the others came out of hiding and, carrying their comrades, they retreated down the path, two a little behind the rest, watching us as they went.

Kefhan and Syllan both stood to join Tokhan in a derisive victory cry that was instantly muffled by the snow. We watched until our foes went out of sight down the terrace before Tokhan ran down to the track to retrieve our weapons. Then we gathered our belongings and left the ambush to climb the ridge, glad to be on our way again.

I walked behind Syllan, lost in my thoughts. Now the action was over, I felt weak-kneed with relief that it had gone so well. I tried to use my new special sight to locate the retreating warriors, but I was far too exhausted. When there was need, the Kas flowed through me to power my visions, and I had to accept I had no need of it now. I chewed on some dried berries from my bag to give me strength, and tried to set my mind on the way ahead and the last stretch of our journey. Only once we were well away from the scene did we start to look for a sheltered place where we could at last make camp and rest until the storm abated.

CHAPTER FIVE

They stopped well after midnight and took shelter in an abandoned shepherd's hut that Syllan spotted just off the path. It was little more than a pitched roof set on the ground; there was no door and the thatch was worn thin in patches, but it kept out the wind and snow. Under a hide in the corner, he found a cache of firewood to light another fire to keep them warm through the night.

Syllan took the first watch, knowing he would not be able to sleep yet. He sat by the fire in the doorway, staring out into the night and the falling snow as he turned over the events of the last few days in his mind and tried to store them away to tell his family when he reached home. With a start, he realised that that might only be a few days ahead. After such a long journey, he and Tokhan were nearly home again!

A slight noise made him turn to look into the shelter, but it was only someone shifting position as they slept. He cast his eyes over his four companions, just bundles in the firelight with their boots projecting from beneath their cloaks. They had come a long way together. He had come to see the values and abilities of each, all of them combining to make this little group a surprisingly resourceful and effective band. He could not have hand-picked a better bunch if he had tried to. He smiled, turning again to stare out into the snow that flickered as it caught the firelight. There was no sound, nothing stirred. Eventually he grew tired and leaned across to wake Kefhan for the last watch. Then he rolled himself up in his cloak in the warm hollow left by the seer's cousin, and fell quietly into sleep.

Before dawn, the snow stopped. The day broke on a dull white world beneath a grey cloud that promised more foul weather to come. And it came; by mid-morning it had thawed slightly, then a fine sleety drizzle began to fall. Syllan led the party, slipping in the slush underfoot, away from the direct route home to follow the ridge towards higher ground. There he reckoned the going would be easier and the streams less swollen. After so long away, he was keen to see his father and brother again, and to relax in the security of his own village. Moreover, he was aware that the snow would have erased their tracks; if there were any further pursuit, Thorachis would expect them to head towards the Plain by the most direct route. By taking a slight detour, they might avoid any further danger and could even get home sooner if the bad weather set in for several days.

They walked until almost noon, descending into a deep valley to cross a swollen river, which lapped at the limit of its banks and spread in places onto the grassy terrace beyond. They searched for some time to find a place to cross, eventually locating a ford by following the numerous animal tracks leading to the water's edge and up the other bank. Even so, the icy water was waist deep; they had to tread carefully as they went to keep their clothing dry.

Syllan led the party out of the valley up a path alongside a small but voluble brook, where they drank their fill and topped up their water-skins. Right up until they'd crossed the last river, he had felt he'd been leading the way under false pretences. Never before had he been down to the coast in this area. He'd been guessing his way much of the time, basing the route on the descriptions of his father and uncle, who had raided this way in years gone by. Now they were away from the sea, he felt more confident, as he had travelled through this land as a boy with his father.

He was aware that when it came to a difficult or dangerous situation, the party always turned to Weyllan for leadership. As a chieftain's son, he felt a twinge of jealousy at this, but deep down he knew that the seer was a natural leader. Besides, it was logical that as the older of them, Weyllan should take the lead when experience mattered. And yet, even though he knew how much Weyllan had matured on their journey, how much more assured he had become – it was *he*, Syllan, who was the leader of the little troop, and it rankled that the seer seemed to put himself forward so often.

Weyllan seemed a true enough friend, but he would bear watching. Even as the thought formed in his head, Syllan felt guilty for letting his envy get the better of him, even for a moment. He shivered, coming abruptly out of his daydream; he could feel the cold creeping into his bones from the soaking at the ford. He began looking for a place where they could stop to light a fire and warm up.

Perhaps half a march further on, they found on a sheltered slope and stopped for a makeshift meal around a fire they allowed to blaze for a while, making their clothing steam as it dried. The sleet had stopped, so they sat with their backs to some trees where the cleared area of an old field allowed them a view of the land they had just crossed. Just below them, the ground dropped away towards the river valley they had crossed in the morning and between the trees, they caught glimpses of the swirling waters, reflecting the dead grey of the sky above. Their supplies were much depleted after the stay in Thorachis' village, and since they had seen several deer on the march that morning, Syllan and Kefhan set off to hunt for fresh meat while the others rested.

At the top of the ridge, the hunters came upon a long burial mound of the type built by earlier generations to house their ancestors. The mound would have provided a good look-out point, but neither man wished to insult the local spirits by walking over their monument, so they continued past it, muttering quiet greetings as a sign of respect to the spirits who dwelt there.

They re-entered the wood on the far slope of the spur. Syllan loved travelling through the woods in winter, drawing strength in some indefinable way from the stark harshness of the bare branches and the dead bracken. Even so, his attention was drawn to a few fresh shoots, as the first spring bulbs began to poke their leaves through the mud and snow. Another moon and they would be in flower, tiny spots of white and green among the brown. That thought pleased him and he smiled to himself.

"If we turn towards the hills now, we can swing back in a wide loop to the mound." Kefhan swept his arm in an arc to indicate the path they should take. Syllan nodded his assent.

"We should stick to the lower slopes where the woods are more broken – we will find clearings with better grazing there."

"Agreed. Any open spaces higher up are likely to be all bracken and bog. Even if there is game up there, we'll have a soggy time finding it!"Syllan laughed at the image that brought to his mind, as they swung left on the route indicated by Kefhan.

After only a short distance, they saw a small herd of deer

grazing in a clearing. Syllan elected to take a shot at a small doe on the downwind edge of the herd, and moved off through the wood to close in on the prey. To his chagrin, he now saw that there was a young stag grazing within a pace or two of his chosen shooting point and realised he would have to take a more difficult shot from where he stood.

Adjusting his stance, he took careful aim, trying once again to find the zone of concentration he had learned from Weyllan on the journey. He saw with his mind's eye the arc of light that the seer could create, held his breath and released along the arc. The arrow struck the doe through the shoulder and punched straight on through to the heart, dropping the poor creature in its tracks. The young buck jerked its head up, baying a warning that instantly sent the herd flying away into the woods. Kefhan ran up, and they trussed up the doe. That done, Syllan slung it across his back as they turned back along their tracks to rejoin the others.

Syllan was secretly very proud of his shot. It was his best in some time; he wished his friend Weyllan could have seen it. A hard shot between the trees and an awkward angle on the target, but he had shot so true, the animal must never have known she was dying. He smiled again, thinking back to other hunts where sometimes he had been less successful.

Inevitably, his thoughts returned to one day in particular. It had been back in the autumn, while the group was hiking through the hills on the mainland, a week after crossing the Great River. He had gone out hunting with Tokhan and Weyllan, leaving Kefhan and his wife to rest at the homestead where they had stayed the night. Kefhan was still weak after his fever, which had forced them to halt them at a village next to the Great River. They had been held up there for a twelve-night or longer, then as long again when Kefhan's fever had returned just after they made the crossing. And here he was, still causing them delays. Syllan smiled, remembering. Now he knew the man better, and was warming to him more and more.

On that particular day, Syllan recalled, he had been feeling especially annoyed about the frequent stops Kefhan's illness required them to make; it was pushing them ever closer to winter. There was a very real possibility of being stuck on the mainland until the fishermen could venture out again in the early spring. Syllan was eager to get home with his prize in time for the winter solstice celebration and, whilst Weyllan continued to impress him and win his admiration, he was beginning to wish they had never brought the young cousin and his wife along. He wasn't sure he even liked the potter Kirah, and Kefhan seemed more of a liability than even Dutehar had been.

At that moment, the hunters had heard a great crashing noise in the bushes to their left. A massive male boar burst into the clearing, charging straight for Syllan, screeching its malice at the intruders. Its little eyes glared at him above two wicked tusks that scythed out a long finger-length from the jaw, as its drumming hooves made the very earth vibrate. Instinctively, he had drawn his bow, with an arrow nocked ready to shoot, taken a hasty aim and loosed the shaft at the boar. The flint tip creased the animal's forehead, slicing through one ear. It had the sole effect of enraging it even more.

Syllan had no time to reload, or to do more than lift his bow to ward off the inevitable impact as he saw his doom flashing towards him. Yet even as the boar's head went down ready for the first tusk-slash to its victim, Weyllan had nocked an arrow, lifted his bow and shot in a single movement, taking the boar through the heart at no more than two paces.

Syllan was knocked flying by the tumbling boar as it careered into him under the momentum of its charge.

Miraculously, apart from crashing his teeth together and bruising his backside in the fall, a slight graze on his arm from a tusk was his only injury. As he sat, winded and shocked, gagging from the pungent odour from the carcass, he stared blindly at the flighted end of the shaft protruding just a handspan from its side. He blinked, considering with a shudder how close he had just come to being gored or even killed.

"I'm alright, I think." He flexed his limbs experimentally in response to his companions' inquiries. "Just a little shaken. I … Weyllan, thank you. I owe you my life."

"You owe me nothing, my friend. Your coming helped me come to my senses, and has set me on a path of adventure such as I would barely have dreamed of a moon before. It may take me some time to pay what I owe for all that, if owing and paying are needed between friends."

That was the first time Syllan had thought that Weyllan might consider him a friend. The thought had made him happy. Once the young seer had stopped moping over his girl – Syllan struggled to recall her name, then mentally shrugged and gave up – he had shown a quiet presence that warmed and mellowed anyone near him, and Syllan was no exception. He liked him, admired him and wanted to be more like him; but he had not considered he might be liked in his turn. He had laughed aloud and gratefully taken the hand Weyllan held out to pull him to his feet.

And now …. Syllan was suddenly aware that Kefhan was looking back at him with a broad grin on his face. It took him a moment to realise he had been singing out loud as he lost himself in his reverie.

He grinned back. "Spring will be with us soon. And I am nearly home again!" He spread his hands out, palms upward.

"Spring can't come soon enough," was the reply. "And a

home is something I feel the need for after so long on the road."

Syllan nodded, understanding the emotion perfectly. He was surprised to reflect how much his relationship with Kefhan had improved over the last few moons. He actively enjoyed the man's company, his commonsense practicality and his ability to plan, to anticipate what was needed in pretty much any situation. He was also someone who was not better than Syllan in any way that mattered to either of them. With a shock, he realised he was comparing the man to Weyllan. Did he believe that the seer was a better man than he? Was that the real source of his doubts? Simple jealousy of the man who had saved his life and called him a friend? Feeling guilty once again, Syllan shook his head to clear the thoughts and forced himself to concentrate on the trail and the country through which they were walking.

By the time the whole party was moving again, it was late in the day and the wind was rising. They continued up the ridge, with the low sun almost behind them, past the barrow he and Kefhan had seen earlier, following a faint track that headed in the direction they wanted. As the twilight intensified, they dipped through another valley and climbed another hill to come upon not one, but two great burial mounds less than fifty paces apart. Next to one of them was a bank which at first Syllan took to be another barrow, but as they came up to it, he saw two banks with side ditches running off into the gloom ahead.

"This is a place for spirits, not people," muttered Weyllan. "It's got the hackles rising on my neck. We should not linger here. I do not like it at all!"

"No arguments there, brother!" said Kefhan. "But we can't go much further. There was little warmth in the day; what there was is already gone and there will be frost or more snow before midnight."

Syllan conferred with Tokhan, then led the group off up the slope following a path visible despite the dying light. They had not walked far before Tokhan grunted and pointed ahead. For a few breaths, the flicker of a fire could be seen through a doorway, but its light was abruptly cut off when the door was shut against the weather. The fire indicated a homestead and promised a dry, warm shelter. There was no opposition when Syllan suggested they make for it and request hospitality from the occupants for the night.

Snow fell again as they slept in a rickety guest hut, but by morning the sky had cleared and the sun created a dazzling reflection off the white landscape. From the homestead, the party could see much of the great spirit path laid out across the land before them, stretching from the barrows they had seen the night before for a full march across the fields and through the woods. The shadows of the banks and ditches were clear in the low morning sun.

Syllan had seen it once before, but for the others it was a new experience, and one that impressed even Weyllan.

"I have never seen its like before," he said. "It looks like not one, but two or three spirit paths, joined end to end. It is hard to believe that nobody knows who had it made, or to what end he did it!"

"As our host told us at great length, there are several conflicting legends about it, and no one knows which, if any, are the truest tales. We have a similar pathway near us on the Plain, but it is less than half as long as this. Much less. And even there, the exact purpose of the path is obscure, though the legends link it to a seer called Urda, many, many cycles ago."

"I look forward to seeing it," replied Weyllan. "Shall we hasten our way towards more familiar spirits?"

Syllan chuckled. "The very words I was about to utter. We'll make good progress if this weather holds. We could even get home tonight, with luck."

As it came to pass, Syllan and his companions were to spend one more night on the journey. They continued on, passing a dozen or so burial mounds, and rested beside one around noon where they could look down across a slight saddle in which the great spirit path ended amid a group of three or more barrows. The day remained cold but bright, and towards its end, they crossed an escarpment before dropping into the river valley below. Rounding the end of yet another ridge, Syllan found himself standing above a broad valley through which several river channels ran, and into which at least three other streams flowed from the far side. There were marshy meadows everywhere along the valley below them, so he suggested they camp above the night-flies and insects, and find their way across in the morning.

"How far is it now?" Kefhan inquired, with a comforting arm around his wife. Kirah had been unwell all day and was clearly exhausted by the long marches. Syllan wondered idly what the problem was, as they had all shared the same food and water along the way. It would be some time before he found out.

"We are on familiar ground now, have no fear. You see the river flowing from the north, on the right over there? That is the Ayn, our River, the one that flows past our home and down which the ashes of our people pass back to the earth. Once we cross the valley, we will be little more than two marches from home. We will be there well before sunset."

The next day, once they had at last picked a path over the marshes, they crossed a ridge and dropped into the valley of one of the three tributaries. Syllan was confident here, recognising specific features in the landscape and pointing them out to the others.

They followed the valley until noon, then cut a short way inland and angled up onto higher ground, leaving the riverine woodland behind and passing into open grassland. Syllanclimbed to the crest of the ridge, then waited for the others to catch up. The grassland extended with only occasional trees and copses as far as the skyline, but a short march away was a low ridge. Syllan indicated what lay beyond.

The great Spirit House of the Plain was now in sight. Even from this distance, it was clear that this was no mere circle of stones, but a complex construction of stonework such as none of the Mainlanders had seen before in their travels. There were several burial mounds visible, but no house, field, or garden was to be seen.

Weyllan shivered, perhaps at the sheer scale of the sacred landscape."A dead land," he murmured.

"I had imagined something ... well, larger," remarked Kefhan, adding a little lamely, "The setting is ... impressive, and the structure too! It's just ..." His voice tailed off, as he became aware that any words were inadequate.

Syllan bridled a little. "Wait until you see it close up, or approach the Spirit House as the midwinter sun is setting. You will have no doubts then."

He led them on across the ridge, back to the edge of the river valley. They lost sight of the sacred land, pressing on as the sun began to dip towards the horizon. They traversed a last valley and one more ridge. Then, spread across the slope before them, they saw at last the houses and the smoke of Syllan's home, and came to the end of their long journey.

PART II
THE SEER'S PATH

CHAPTER SIX

I was relieved at last to have arrived, and glad at the prospect of not having to travel anywhere for a while. Not that I was able to rest much; the first few days after our arrival blur into one another in my memory, with one introduction following another as various seers and leaders came to view the stranger who had come to live with them. Kefhan, Kirah, and I were housed in the guest-hut of an elder seer, Turac, who was to become my guide and mentor as I learned the ways of the Children of Hatha.

On the first evening, I recall, we were taken to meet Syllan's father Atharon. I was impressed by his powerful stature and confident leadership. Grey of hair and past his prime he might have been, but he still had a towering presence that dominated the room. He had clearly been briefed by Syllan, so from the outset his welcome was warm to all three of us; he seemed quite satisfied with the result of his son's quest. To Kirah specifically he extended his welcome, saying the Plain's potters would be glad of the chance to exchange ideas, whilst the women would be happy for news and views from afar, of which we men would likely be inadequate bearers. He took me aside for a moment to brief me.

"I chose Turac to be your host and guide because I know he is of one mind with me, in that we need some outside thinking to solve our problems. And, I admit, because I was expecting someone rather older to return with Syllan!" He gave out a hearty laugh at this. "But there are others who will oppose any contribution you offer simply because you are an outsider. Be wary of them, but be certain you may speak freely to Turac or myself. Even if we disagree, we will listen and consider your words as friends and allies. I am glad, too, that you have made a firm friend of my son. I hope that friendship lasts you both a lifetime."

I was to meet some of my opponents quite soon, as Atharon arranged a small feast in my honour, to which many of the seers and leaders of the tribe were invited. My memory is a little vague, but I think there were about a dozen men and women at the meal. All three of us Mainlanders were kept busy answering questions about our arts and our background. Syllan joined in, regaling everyone with tales of our adventures (and his own) on the journey. Dutehar's uncle roared with laughter when he heard the story of his nephew's antics and eventual marriage.

There was an elder called Ursehan, there with a seer, Reirda, from the same clan. Their antagonism towards me became apparent when we spoke before the meal.

"So, Syllan has put it abroad that you are a great seer as well as one gifted to control the spirits of rocks." Reirda's lip curled into something between a sneer and a snarl. "It is just as well. I see no advantage in separating anything from its spirit, and when last I saw a blade made from this new … stuff, it was no better than a good polished flint edge."

I tried to make light of it. "A seer – that is something the Matriarch of Ashila's Children called me once, on the mainland before we arrived here. She may just have flattered me to get me to join their Solstice healing." I smiled. "But only time will tell, and I will not judge myself."

"We have enough gifted seers of our own," put in Ursehan. "But then, old Atharon didn't bring you all the way here to dance about among the stones, did he? He wants you to fix them, to make them work again. He has some mad idea that your kind can see a solution to it all, but you have no more chance than the last one who tried."

At that point Turac cut in, drawing me away from the pair. He warned me not to expect support from them, or any others of their clan. They were related to the original leaders of Hatha's Children, and had a long-standing feud with Atharon's kinfolk, one going back many generations, so that they were always opposed to any ideas from the current leadership.

As he spoke, I was piecing together a thread from the short conversation. If Reirda had seen copper tools, and Ursehan thought my 'kind' had tried to fix whatever was wrong with the stones before, they had evidently met at least one of the 'visitors' Syllan had spoken about. Also, were they suggesting I was not the first stone-changer to attempt to 'make the stones work'? I immediately thought about my grandfather.

Turac must have overheard. "We have had one or two visitors before," he explained. "One may have shown them a blade, who knows? I met one myself, once, when I was a child. I do not remember the man's name now, or how long he was here for. But I'm sure no one stayed long enough to find a way of 'fixing' the stones."

I could get no more out of him, except that Atharon would probably speak to me about the stones once I had seen them for myself. The idea seemed to want to stay in my mind, despite his assurances. I resolved to ask Atharon directly, when we finally did have our meeting, just what he wanted from me and whence came the idea that I – or more accurately, Orelac – could help. But first, I would like to see the stones up close.

I have never forgotten my first experience of entering the great Spirit House on the Plain. The weather had turned cold again the night of our arrival, and fresh snow fell for the first two days or so, covering everything in a white cloak that froze as hard as ice. Turac took all three of us as soon as the weather eased a little. The sky had cleared, bathing the land in soft sunlight that made the snow sparkle, steaming as the day warmed up.

We walked from the settlement over the ridge back into the sacred landscape and saw the Temple in the distance, golden and benign in the sunshine. As we descended into the boggy bottom of the little valley, we lost sight of the stones and could see only the top of the guide-stone, but as we climbed up the slope towards them, they came back into view, suddenly much closer. The sun lit only one side of the enclosure, giving it a much more forbidding air. On the shaded slope I could feel the cold again, my breath coming in small clouds of steam from my mouth and freezing on my beard where it settled. Apprehensive, or just cold, I shivered under my cloak with its fresh straw lining, wondering for a moment where I had brought myself and my friends.

At the top of the slope was the single, great, guide-stone, easily twice my height, that drew us in to the main enclosure. The entrance was flanked by two more stones, almost as big as the first, between which we must walk to enter the circle. Each one bore a face that watched our every move; I wondered if arms would suddenly appear to keep us out if they disapproved of us in some way. But we passed through without incident, so I suppose we passed their test. On either side of the entrance was a ditch with a chalk bank, still reasonably white after having been scoured for the midwinter celebrations.

There, within this enclosure, stood the most amazing stone structure I had ever seen. Talking to those who have grown up with the great Spirit House as an everyday sight, it must be hard to understand just how overwhelming was this grand marvel. Thirty upright blocks (I counted them some days later) formed the circle, each one chipped and ground into a regular shape. They were capped with equally well-shaped lintels, each supported between two uprights, and each fitting tightly against the next so that no light could pass between them. Later, Turac told us that the stones were jointed together with great studs that fitted hollows in the lintels and that similar joints had been used to lock the lintels together to complete the circle. My jaw fell open in amazement; not once, but three or four times, as I saw or heard more details of this wonder.

Inside the circle were many other stones, some much smaller, but the space was dominated by an arc of five great doorways of stone that towered above us, each made of three giant blocks, with the greatest of the five in the centre of the curve, directly opposite the entrance. My eyes filled with tears, and though I blamed the icy wind that had sprung up, it was in truth mostly emotion as I gazed at the great stones, feeling their brooding presence press in on me.

We passed through multiple rows of smaller stones into the inner space before the great doorway, and the hackles rose on my neck as I felt the power of the place settle about me. I whispered a quick prayer to greet the spirits that dwelt there and express my awe at their fine house, then took a deep breath and tried to bring my emotions under control.

Turac told us about the various features of the Temple,

the symbols and the significance of different parts of the edifice. I was listening at first, but soon I began to drift a little in my head until suddenly I was aware the stones had faded, and I stood again on the grey sands of the spirit realm. I knew without turning that I was surrounded by a dozen or more human-like spirits who I took to be some of the ancestors Turac had been telling us were buried around the Temple.

"Greetings to you, Seer and Stone-changer!" said a hissing voice in my head. "We have been awaiting your arrival for some time."

"Though not with any eagerness, Outlander," interrupted another. There was an outbreak of voices, a whispered argument.

The first voice continued as if nothing had been said. "And we welcome you to the Heart of the World, where all power lies, if you can find the means to release it!"

"He has no blood links with any of us. He can do no good here. Do not give the Outlander ideas about his influence," snarled the dissenting voice, causing more whispers at the edge of my hearing.

"This man needs no blood ties. He has a gift rare among men, that he can hear and work with any spirits he chooses. We will welcome him and work with him when the time comes."

The first voice sounded calm and reasonable. "And you, young man, should pay no heed to Urda's kin. You will do great things here in your new home; we will see what unfolds in time."

I could sense the vision starting to fade, and I blurted out, "Wait, please, who are you?"

"I am Tyris, a child of Hatha, she who called this Temple into being so many generations ago. It was I who …"

"You lie, Tyris! It was *our* kin who brought the stones over and set them up! We raised the first temple here. You and your kin can lay no claim …"

But already the spirits were dissipating, and the sand faded as the stones came back before my eyes. I roused to find myself on my knees, supported by Kefhan.

"Is he all right?" Turac looked nervous.

"He will be. It's just another vision. They have become more frequent since we landed on this island."

The old seer shook his head. "A vision? On his first entry? He must be favoured indeed!"

"I am fine, now, really. Just a little overwhelmed by this wonderful place. I'm all right." And to prove my point, I rose groggily to my feet, only staggering slightly in the firm grip of my cousin.

"Now that you have walked among the stones, you will appreciate that this Spirit House is unique," said Atharon, when we met again a few days afterwards. "Both in its build and its location, as you must have seen."

"I saw the landscape. An image of the whole of existence. The great circle of the world of men, with the Spirit House at its very centre. The wide arc of the heavens above, with sun and moon clear from horizon to horizon. Tyris called it the Heart of the World, and I can easily believe her."

"Yes, I heard that you met Tyris. She is one of our greatest ancestors, the first matriarch of our line. You were honoured to be greeted by her. She is remembered as the one who first stood by the guide stone and understood how that place is the very centre of the cosmos, with the circle of the firmament around her, the realms of the sky spirits above and the underworld below, just a hand span beneath the surface. Such a perfect model, she realised, that it would, when needed, become the very thing it modelled! She it was who divined the centre point of the Temple, the very centre of existence, she who called for a circle to be put up around it to draw the power of the world-circle down into the Spirit House inside the banks."

"But the spirits of Urda's clan thought otherwise. Who was Urda, and what had she to do with it all?"I asked.

"Urda was once matriarch of our people, chief seer in an age when homage was still done to our forebears at the long mounds. She built the great spirit path near to the Spirit House, leading to and from the mound where dwelt her ancestors. But by Tyris' time, *our* line had taken the matriarchy from Urda's kin, and deservedly so, for they were great seers. Yet one of Urda's people married a traveller from far off, at the edge of the land before the Sunset Sea. This man, Myradoc, knew of a great circle of powerful stones in his homeland and persuaded Urda's kin to bring them here to place around the circle of Tyris in place of the wooden posts she had first proposed. With them came many from his homeland, come to dwell at the Heart of the World. They brought with them the ashes of some of their ancestors to be buried here with some of ours to bind them all, spirit and stone, to serve us." Atharon paused, his eyes focussed somewhere off in the distance, as if he was recalling the actual events from experience."Thus Myradoc and his wife Leca took back the leadership of our people from Tyris' clan, and for many generations thereafter the kin of Urda once again led the children of Hatha in all things, until at last the line died out. Our people split apart, as so often happens, when it seemed the ancestors had forsaken us all. But in the time of my thrice great-grandmother, my line – kin to Tyris herself, was once more chosen to lead our people."

The old chief shifted his weight and changed his staff to his other hand, drawing himself up proudly."It was my great-grandfather Myrthis who directed our people to build the new Temple." He shrugged, then sighed."That led to the moving of the original stones, the cause of much contention among us, and indeed, among the spirits of our ancestors Ursehan and Reirda, whom you have met, belong to a line that was closely related to Urda's clan and mixed with the newcomers from the Sunset Sea. They see no good coming from the Spirit House until the stones of Myradoc are replaced in their original positions."

I chewed this over for a while, wondering why they had not then undertaken the obvious move. "So where are the stones now? And why not move them back?" I asked, still puzzled.

"You have seen them." Atharon moved to the doorway to stare out towards the stones. "They were the arc of smaller stones inside the walls of the Spirit House. The old circle was damaged and rarely used for burial anymore; our seers felt little power remaining in it, so it was decided to create a smaller circle, a spirit house, in the middle of the enclosure for the old ones. Most of the stones had been pulled up, and a few were broken before opposition mounted in our councils. The work stopped. The old stones lay where they had fallen for nearly two great moon cycles until Myrthis tried to reshape the Temple using them, then trimmed the stones and attempted the first lintels. They are changed now, for good or ill. I see no point in returning to a form that no longer holds power."

He did not seem keen to tell me more, so I began to talk of other things. It was a while before we came at last to the main reason for the interview. We were speaking of the power of the circle and of stone circles especially; how they could help to focus or concentrate the power we seers needed to travel among the spirits and, most importantly, to return again with the understandings we had gained. It was not knowledge we used much where I had grown up, where such circular spirit houses are rare, but I had learned a little on our journey and experienced it for myself at the solstice dance I had joined with the Children of Ashila.

Atharon said, "Our Spirit House has great stones in a circle, all interlocked and awake. It has all the requisite features to call down great power; it even incorporates the ancestor-stones of the old circle. Yet for three generations now our seers say they get little more enhancement of their abilities than if they were working at home. There *is* power there, though, and great energy, I have felt it myself."

I nodded as I heard this. I had felt it too.

"But the power seems blocked within the structure and is not accessible to our seers. It should be the greatest place of power in the land, where it sits at the very heart of the world, but the power it contains surges and dies again without helping us much at all."

"And you think I can help? I, who have so little prior knowledge of this place?"

I was amazed, but Atharon spread his hands wide and cocked his head to the side as he looked at me, as if to ask why it was so unlikely.

"You have heard you are not the first stone-changer to pass through our land. One at least thought he saw a way to 'clear the blockage' as he put it, but he left before he shared his idea with us."

"Was this not my grandfather?" I queried, my scalp suddenly tingling as a shiver ran up my neck.

"He told us very little about himself, Weyllan. Who can say if he was your kinsman or no? But certainly, *one* of our visitors told us your homeland was famed for its powerful seers. Only when he came into the region in search of one, was my son Syllan pointed towards *your* village, and your uncle as the best man. I assumed he would have explained this to you."

He had not. It had seemed to me that Syllan had known *exactly* who he was looking for from the very start. But I had no reason to doubt my new leader; I had to be content with Atharon's explanation for the moment.

Soon afterwards, he indicated that he had other things to do, and our meeting came to an end. I walked back to our hut, deep in thought about the Spirit House, wondering how it could be made to work again. It was obvious that I would have to use it, and experience the power flow before I could form a plan, so I put my ideas to one side until the time was right to take them forward.

The days passed quickly in exploring our new home and getting to know its people. Spring soon took hold of the world around us. We were settling in, starting to feel at home in this foreign land. Kirah made several friends, so in the spring she had them help her build a house for her and her family. For it was now public knowledge that she was with child; both Syllan and her husband had shaken their heads in disbelief that they had not seen the change in her shape and demeanour sooner. *I* had known since our last day's journey; I had a flash of vision when I held her hand to help her across a stream, in which I saw the babe in her belly. I had questioned her with a look, but she had smiled in such a way as to acknowledge the shared secret, so I held my peace and let her choose the time to tell us together. All those bouts of illness she had suffered along the way were no longer a mystery.

They chose a spot for the house on the ridge overlooking the River, where her trips for water would be quite short, with the door set facing the morning sun in winter. Kirah chose to have a round house after the fashion of our own people; I amused myself for a while, pondering the diversity of humankind. On the island, they build their houses with straight sides and their spirit houses in circles, while we Mainlanders built our homes round and our spirit houses in long rectangles, after the manner of our ancestors' houses.

Atharon's village, unlike that of Thorachis near the coast, was little more than a collection of homesteads scattered along the lower slopes of the ridge, itself just one of several similar, if more sparsely occupied, hills projecting towards the River like stubby fingers. There were perhaps twenty households on this ridge, each of two or three dwellings with some storage huts. Atharon's hut was recognisable by its central location, a larger house with ground-set posts and low walls. It also possessed an extra guest hut. The village had no palisade, and no guards, not even at Atharon's house.

The houses varied from portable mat or hide-walled summer shelters – with thatch added under weighted nets for winter insulation – through to simple A-frame dwellings, and there were a few solid-looking houses – like Atharon's – with chalk-daubed walls and hurdle doors. Turac's home-stead was just below the crest of the ridge, with a view down across the woods towards the old midwinter complex surrounded by its massive irregular grassy bank. Beside it, the small spirit house of tall wooden posts, used now in its stead, stood in a second clearing.

Each day I tried to walk a different piece of the territory, although some days the weather was too wet and windy to do anything much but feed the fire while we talked to one another. Whichever route I took, I came across farms or houses scattered across the slopes between the grassy hill-tops and the wooded valleys, occasionally clustered together for company, all with their doors towards the morning sun and their backs to the ever-present wind.

Not far from the old banked enclosure was a busy flint mine, run by two families affiliated to Ursehan's clan. They were rather more sociable than their kinsman, and invited me to share their meal one day. We talked of flint knapping, the properties of rocks, and the spirits within them. They showed me some finely-polished knives and gave me one as a gift. I took some flint with me when I left, promising them some of my arrowheads, for I was quite proud of my skill at making these little implements. I took them around the next time I went over that way and gave them the first of my little triangular barbed heads. They had never seen any quite like them; they expressed their pleasure openly and, I may say, loudly.

Sometimes old Turac would accompany me on my rambles, guiding my footsteps to places he felt I should know. He was always teaching me the ways of his people or a little of the huge store of knowledge he held in his head about the spirit world, and in particular about the heavens. I began to learn the local names for the great elemental spirits that ruled the destinies of us all: Lukan, the sun spirit, his sister Lena, the moon, and the Turashya, the sky spirits after whom my new teacher was named.

There were others I'm sure you know; of course, I knew them too, but by different names. Although I am sure they heard me and sometimes responded when I used the names I learnt as a boy, I needed these names to follow the rituals and to communicate my experiences. There was so much to absorb it seemed at times I had gone back many years to the start of my training, but in truth there was one major differ-ence; I now understood what was being said, what was behind the words. It was something I had often struggled with in my youth.

We visited the Spirit House several times. I was shown some of the secret alignments built into or added to the structure to acknowledge points in the passage of the heavens and the turning of the seasons. Each year a chalk image of Lena was moved another place around the circle of hollows inside the bank to mark our progress through another great cycle of fifty-six summers. The hollows also helped measure the time between the six festivals of the annual cycle, acting as a check on the counting of days and moons by the seers of the community.

I had a recurrence of the fever I had suffered the previous autumn, when we crossed the wide river valleys of the mainland. Although it was far less severe this time around, I lay in my furs and shivered for three days, missing the mid-point celebrations, the first of the new spring season, when day and night were thought to be equal in length. When I went forth again from the safety of the guest house, the change in the seasons was apparent. The wind still blew across the plain with its customary vigour, but the sun was warmer, and there seemed to be more of it than before, although this was perhaps just wish fulfilment after the rigours of our winter journey.

As among my own people, the mid-spring rites forty days later involved two or three days of celebrations with cere-monies to mark the start of the growing season. There was dancing where young men and women looked for partners. Most of the festivities took place around the homesteads and there was only one ceremony at the Spirit House where liba-tions were placed for the ancestors and where any new couples who chose to could receive the blessing, or other-wise, of their forebears. I was largely a spectator at this event, although I acted as a go-between for Kefhan and Kirah when they came to ask for the blessing of our new local spirits on their unborn child.

I decided I should demonstrate my real art to my new hosts and neighbours. With Kefhan, I built a small furnace in a sheltered spot near the base of the ridge. A few days after the hawthorn blossom began to open, we fired it up, using two of Kirah's fire-pots to hold the rock. We produced a small portion of sun-gold from which I made a pair of gold tress-rings, like my own, to offer to Atharon. I also made a batch of moon-gold into two knives for him and Syllan to keep as thanks for their guidance and hospitality. A tiny pellet of moon-gold liquid I had left over I cast into a leaf-shaped pendant for Tokhan.

Whoever had visited them before, it seemed none had left them gifts of our stock in trade, our essence of rocks. I found that surprising, but held my peace and stored my questions for another day.

Then, as spring metamorphosed into summer, three things happened that at last gave a sense of purpose and direction to my new existence, pulling me inexorably into my future.

CHAPTER SEVEN

The yellow flowers of early spring were already giving way to the blues of transition into summer when, a dozen days after the blessing of Kirah's child at the mid-point celebration, I borrowed a small boat and poled myself across the Ayn to climb the Sacred Hill on the other side. The idea that any peak not covered all year round in snow could be sacred was still hard for me to take seriously, despite having encountered a number of them in my travels. But I had learned to respect local ways when staying anywhere, and I intended to climb the peak in an attempt to contact the hill-spirits who dwelt there.

I spent a fruitless afternoon meditating on the summit, seeking a vision and transportation to the spirit world, but all I received was a wind-blown glow and a raging thirst. If there were indeed spirits on this mountain, they were in no mood to speak with me. I rolled up the reed mat I had sat upon, slung it across my shoulder and started down again, angling a little towards the sun in the direction of a small farm from which rose a curl of smoke. As I came nearer, I could see there were only two houses here, with a covered wood-store, a small fenced garden and three goats shut in a pen big enough for a dozen animals. The huts were sturdy, permanent structures, recently thatched; the yard was freshly swept and tidied as if for an expected visit.

Then my attention was drawn to a tall, thin pole beside the door from which dangled a small bundle of animal pelts and feathers, the sign of a wise woman or healer. The hackles rose on my neck as I considered it might be me for whom she had prepared. But I was, I told myself, a seer in my own right – if she had foreseen my arrival, what of it? I hoped she might have already chilled a little barley-beer for my thirst, with some goat's cheese to fill the hollow that I could feel in my stomach. I laughed out loud to dispel the feeling of disquiet that had settled on me. Yet my scalp still tingled. I tried to compose myself as I continued down to the homestead.

As I stepped into the yard, she came to the door to meet me, and if that was unsettling in my current mood, she did her best to counter it with the most welcoming smile I had seen in some time.

"Well, hello!"she called across the forecourt. "I saw you going up the hill earlier this morning, then when I saw you approaching, I thought you must be thirsty after so long up there. Come in; I shall make you a restoring drink to quench your thirst and see you home."

"Thank you. My name is Weyllan and I ..."

"Oh, I know well who you are, Stone-changer and Seer! I have seen you a few times at the Spirit House and about the landscape. Quite a wanderer you are, it would seem."

"I have been trying to learn my way around, and meet some of the people among whom I have come so far to live. I climbed the hill today for the same reason, to pay my respects to the sacred spirits there."

"And I'll guess you had but little luck there. They rarely

communicate with us mere mortals, and when they do, it will be at a time of their choosing, not ours. I live next door to them; I make regular offerings, but sometimes I hear nothing in reply from one year to the next. When I saw you this morning, I had an inkling you would stop by later, but whether that came from them or was just a tickle of a vision I couldn't say. But you are welcome either way. I get little enough company that has not come with some anguish or ailment, and talking to one who isn't in awe of me will make a pleasant change."

I made an instant mental effort to relax, ceasing my corner-of-eye peering into the darker shadows of the hut. I had always shared the common person's unease around healers and wise-women (despite my kinship with Kirah), but I thought out of deference to my current host, I should try to behave as if this were an everyday occurrence. As if she read my thoughts, she laughed playfully, then turned away to prepare my drink. When it came, it was an infusion of some herbs in cold spring water with, I thought, a little apple juice added for sweetness. It was quite pleasant and, as she had predicted, restorative.

Her name was Aslena, but I found it hard to guess her age as we talked, for though she had the weather-beaten look of an old crone, she walked easily and with a straight back, like a woman in her prime. She caught me studying her, and smiled a disconcerting smile as she again answered my unspoken thoughts.

"I am older than I look and younger than I feel, although sometimes it's the other way around."She paused before changing the subject. "You are not the first stone-changer to stop at my door, you know. Indeed, when I saw you the first time, I thought he had come back for me at last! But he must be dead by now, and I am sure he never took my childish adoration seriously enough to return for me even when he might have."

Again, I felt the hackles rise on my neck, but I kept my voice steady as I queried how long ago this had been.

"It must be nigh on forty summers ago now, dear. I was a young lass of twelve or thirteen summers then, and he was a man in his prime. He sometimes visited my father here, and I took a great shine to him. I'm sure he liked me well enough, but as I said, he was much older. Then he went off on his travels and I never saw him again."

"Do you remember his name?" I asked, hardly daring to breathe.

"Of course, I do! He was Kefhan, just like your friend! He went off to the great spirit house north of the plains, where the Aynash rises; when he returned, it was for a few days only before he took off to the sunset land and never returned."

I was stunned. My grandfather had been here; stayed here for time enough for Aslena to fall in love with him, then disappeared on some journey. Why had Atharon and his sons lied to me? Where had he gone, and what had his disappearance to do with this Spirit House beyond the Plain? I remember but little of the rest of our conversation. I think I told her then that Kefhan was my grandfather, and that our family had wondered what had become of him. I left soon afterwards, with the thought settling in my mind that I would have to speak with my hosts again about all of this.

When I went to talk to Atharon the following day, his first wife informed me he had gone hunting with his brother Athlan and might be away for several days. Syllan, too, was away but was expected back in a day or two. Frustrated, I stalked off, heading without any real aim in mind towards the Spirit House over the ridge. Already the ridge was more sparsely populated, with many of the summer shelters gone. The herders and their flocks and families had left for the summer pastures on the inner Plain or to the wide valleys to the north. They would return from time to time to weed their garden plots but would remain mostly away until the harvest.

I passed the ancient enclosure where, in times long past, the dead were laid out to be cleansed by the birds before their bones were sent down-river to the spirit world. Then, as in my homeland, it became usual to cremate the dead to release their spirit, and enclosures such as this one were left to decay. Some people feared to pass near them and would walk in a great arc to avoid them for fear of meeting an abandoned, vengeful spirit, but I have sat in meditation in several such enclosures over the years and never met or even sensed any lost souls. It was, I suppose, not an overnight change, so it seemed likely that all the rites were completed to send the spirits on their way before such places were abandoned as the new rites took over.

Thinking about this calmed me somewhat. When shortly afterwards I came to Urda's spirit path, I sat down a while on the bank to rest and gather my thoughts before continuing to the Temple on the next ridge. As I sat lost in my thoughts, I failed to notice the greying of the light or the shifting shadows around me. Suddenly I became aware that I was no longer alone, and no longer where I had been a few moments before. A small clutch of spirits stood close by my left side and it was clear that they were discussing me.

"Are you sure it is he?"

"Quite sure. He was being lied to by that charlatan Tyris! But I gave her a piece of my mind."

"Well, Leca, that must have scared her back to life!" broke in a third voice, clearly unimpressed by Leca. "With what's

left of your mind, I am always surprised we can even understand you."

"Enough!" came a voice that expected – and received –
instant obedience. "So, this is the one who they hope will
unlock the power of the Temple? He does not look to be
much of a challenge. I predict he will have no more success
than the other one, and if he even gets that far, we will
arrange another little surprise for him."

"I feel this one is stronger than his kinsman, Mistress,"
came the third voice again. "We should watch our words and
ways with him. Ah, in truth, you may already have said too
much – see, he is here with us!"

I was aware of four spectral faces turned towards me, and
I twisted to look directly at them, although there was no
great detail to be seen. The leader spoke again.

"Then let him know we will oppose him at every turn and
let him feel the power we hold still over this place."

"But now is not the time. Let us be away, Mistress."

"Agreed," finished the one they called 'Mistress'. I watched
as they faded into shapeless wisps of mist that dissipated
slowly in the still air until I was alone in this colourless half-
world. I waited for a while to see if anything else was stirring
there, managing for the first time to hold myself in the trance
until, certain there was nothing more to experience, I
allowed myself to slip back into the late morning sunshine of
the real world. Then I rose and walked on, reflecting that
here was yet another witness that my grandfather had been
here and stayed for some time. I was both intrigued and
worried by the other reference, that these spirits had had
some dealings with him and had arranged some form of 'surprise' for him. I was prepared to wager it had not been a
pleasant surprise; it seemed I still had more to learn from
Syllan or his father.

· · ·

I returned to Atharon's homestead the following day towards sunset, and although the chieftain himself was still absent, Syllan had come home. We walked out along the ridge together to talk privately. I had decided not to mention the comments passed by the spirits just yet, restricting myself to Aslena's account of my grandfather's visit. My friend listened, then walked on in silence for a while, considering his reply, I suppose.

"Weyllan, remember that I was not yet born when all this happened, so I only know what my father has told me of it. I believe there *was* a stone-changer who came here when my father was a young boy, while my grandfather Yrthyn was still chief. He stayed a short while – by the account you heard, perhaps it was longer than I understood from my father's telling – and then he continued his travels. Grandfather talked with him about the Spirit House. I believe he claimed to have an idea that the flow of power was being blocked in some way by the stones brought from the old temple near the Sunset Sea. If he said more than that to my grandfather, I cannot say, nor whether my father remembers anything more."

I recall I was still angry, still scowling at my companion, as we sat on a low bank to watch the sun go down. I was trying to find a way to ask why they had chosen to lie to me before without forcing a conflict in his loyalties.

In the end, I just lowered my head sadly and asked outright, "Why then, did your family tell me that no such visit took place? Did they lie, or just forget? And if he had some ideas about the stones, I must suppose there is a connection with your journey to employ his son's skills. But again, any such link was denied. It sounds as if there is something I am not being told, so I ask you again, as my friend; if you know more, tell me what you know. Please!"

He shook his head. "I know nothing more. But I promise

to ask my father and get him to tell you whatever else he can remember."

"My thanks to you, Syllan. I would truly like to know what became of my kinsman. I will wait to hear what you find out before I ask him anything more."

Our conversation turned to more mundane matters, and as the sun disappeared below the next ridge, we turned back to his house to share a pot of barley beer in the twilight.

The days passed while the moon completed another cycle; still I had no response from Syllan. Indeed, I thought he was avoiding me, as we only ever seemed to meet in the company of others before whom I did not feel I could discuss such a sensitive matter. Even the spirits were avoiding me, for I went three times to the Spirit House to seek counsel, but without any success. Then finally, on a day just before midsummer, I saw Syllan walking by. I hurried after him to catch up, hailing him. He stopped to wait for me, and soon I was able to ask him for news.

"Ah, my friend, I see I should have come to you sooner, but in truth what I heard from my father seemed of little import and not worth passing on."

He managed to sound offhand about it, but I was unconvinced and wondered if this had been a reason for avoiding me. "My father told me what we already knew, only adding that shortly after their discussion, your grandfather, assuming it was him, left to travel to the Sunset Sea to seek the source of the first stones. He never returned, and my father forgot even his name in time. When the seers here told my father that the Spirit House seemed to be losing its power, he began thinking of sending for Kefhan's son to see if he, too, might know how to unlock the power of the stones. You know the rest of the tale."

And that was all I could get from him. He soon changed the subject, asking if I would join the summer celebrations.

We talked of what it would entail and what we thought it meant. I went home brooding, wondering if I would ever find the answer in this place.

The third event occurred almost a moon after midsummer, when the whole region was in the midst of harvesting the wheat and barley crops. A messenger came running to Atharon's house; a large raiding party was stealing cattle and goats from our allies on the northern edge of the Plain. The word spread like a grassfire through the village; Kefhan and I scooped up our weapons, trotting towards the chieftain's homestead with several other men. Atharon quickly told us what he knew then, led by Athlan and Syllan, we set off at a fast trot towards the north.

In those times such raids occurred every two years or so, whenever our rivals felt strong enough. There was a long-standing feud between the people of the Plain and the tribes who lived around the downs centred on the great spirit house at the source of the Aynash River. A small party of young hotheads from one or other side would get it into their heads to head off a few dozen cows and whatever else they could lay hands on before retreating to their own territory. There was no time to be lost if we were to intercept them and punish them for their audacity. Such raids only lasted a day or two at most.

There were perhaps fifteen of us in our party, but as we passed across the Plain, others joined us, picking up whatever weapon they had to hand. We kept up a fast pace, covering a full march in a little over half the normal time. We were staying where possible on the high ground for easy running and to keep watch in case the raiders had turned southwards. Even so, it was a steady climb up to the long ridge, then along it to the long mound at the highest point on it. It appeared this was a traditional gathering place, for when we arrived, there were already several others waiting for their chieftain.

I remember standing to the side to catch my breath and being struck by the view of the grassy plains on every side of me. This was clearly a populous area, for I could see many homesteads dotted across the downs. Looking back the way we had come or towards the sunset, it looked peaceful and idyllic, but to the north I could see two or three columns of smoke rising from burning huts. For a moment I could not place what was wrong with the picture before me, then I realised there were no animals penned or grazing on the slopes between the homesteads. I had walked out this way a few times over the preceding moons, meeting many good people and making a few friends here. I was surprised to learn how much I felt both injury and outrage for my adopted countrymen.

Then we were moving again, thirty-eight armed and angry men, spoiling for a fight. The raiders had turned back to the north; it seemed the others knew where they were headed. Now we swung wide along the ridge again to make better time and trotted in an arc that made the distance much greater.

It hardly mattered. Encumbered with a large herd of unhappy cattle and an even more unruly herd of goats, the raiders were moving very slowly; we would soon overhaul them. We came at last to the edge of the high plain, higher even than the ridge we had gathered on earlier. Here the passage of the herd was evident, and I realised there must be few places along this ridge where it would be safe to descend with livestock. My companions must have known this would be the route the raiders would choose.

One man cried out, pointing down the hill. There, just a short distance from the base of the escarpment, were the herds, trotting across a clearing. I could not make out individual men or goats, but the cattle could be distinguished; I thought there must be at least a hundred head. If the thieves could get them safely home, it would give them all more prestige and wealth, but our response had been swift; I doubted they would get much further before we caught them. We took off together, running as fast as we dared down the steep incline, elated now at the prospect of catching and punishing these upstart intruders. As we reached the lower slopes the trees became more densely packed; we were soon running through close woodland dotted with broad oaks and cluttered with saplings and brambles. Yet such was the flattened track left by the livestock that our pace was undiminished despite the close vegetation.

The raiders must have realised we were following close behind, for their pace quickened and we encountered several abandoned goats along the way as the men strove to keep the cattle together. They soon saw even that was in vain, for a short time later, as we came out of the trees at the bottom of a low hill, we saw our prey waiting for us at the top of the slope. I was surprised, even alarmed, to see that they equalled us in number and their line appeared to bristle with spears. We stood on the edge of an old field, now somewhat overgrown, about seventy or eighty paces from them, but outlined against the sky they looked like giants come to trample us into the undergrowth. It was an intimidating sight; we fell into a breathless and uncertain silence.

Seeing us halt, the raiders cheered, then began to shout abuse and insults at us. We stood to regain our breath for a moment, but then one or two braver or fitter souls started to respond in kind and the air was thick with insults flying in all directions. In a part of my head, I remember wryly thinking that it was lucky such words were not arrows or we would all be lying wounded by now. That brought me to my senses and I bent my bow to the string, before selecting a couple of arrows from my bag. I saw Syllan, Kefhan and a few others do the same, as I wondered how many bows the other side held.

I had an answer soon enough. From up the slope came a sudden great shout, and as our foes began to charge down the hill towards us, some of them stayed back to shoot a few arrows each. We ducked aside from the first volleys, although one fellow to my right cried out and sat down heavily on the track with a shaft quivering in his thigh.

Then we answered in kind, except that we shot directly into the charging mob, with rather more effect, as several fell from the line. Some now broke stride to cast their spears, but with a shout, our men charged the slowing raiders, ducking under the spears. I was almost left behind, but broke into a run as a spear hit the earth half a pace from me. I shot a final arrow into some large lout about to swing a heavy stone mace at one of my comrades, and he fell back with a sharp cry. I swopped my bow and spear between my hands and ran at him, but my comrade was quicker, clubbing the man hard on the temple, laying him low in a moment.

Then the raiders were running back up the hill, with our side in hot pursuit. I saw one of their bowmen taking aim, and threw my spear with all my strength, only to see it pass harmlessly by between bow and body. Still, it shook his aim. His shot went wide before he turned away, joining his fellows in flight.

Another man twisted round to swing a club at Athlan, but the chief's son parried it easily with a fighting stick and stabbed with his spear into the man's extended arm. As they struggled, Syllan reached them and, timing it perfectly, thrust his spear into the man's side. He fell silently as both brothers rained blows down on him.

I ran past, collecting my spear as I passed it, on towards the now scattered and abandoned herds, where our warriors were stopping around me, hurling a final volley of taunts and insults after the fleeing raiders.

One of our men had a broken arm from a stone axe blow, a couple had arrows embedded in an arm or shoulder, whilst several had cuts or massive bruises forming from club blows. Six of the raiders lay or sat dazed where they had fallen. Syllan and Athlan's opponent lay near death, close to another slain by an arrow to the throat.

With a shock, I recognised my own shaft, and looked upon the anguished face of the first man I had ever killed. I felt suddenly weak and dizzy. I fell to my knees beside him, reaching out a hand to close those staring, accusatory eyes. Then the world darkened into grey, while the noise around me faded and I rocked back onto my heels as I passed into a vision-trance.

From the warrior's open mouth, a wispy grey steam issued as I watched, taking form into a faint likeness of the body. The eyes were open, and although turned towards me, were sightless and opaque. I mumbled something that was half an apology, half a blessing, but I could not tell if he heard anything as his wraith turned blindly away and faded with the trance. I sat in shock for what seemed an age, before Athlan came to my side.

"Cut out your arrow and come to help with the cattle. Syllan told me you were a fine bowman, Seer. That was a good shot, one to be proud of. Waste no tears on this fellow. He must have known the risks of going on a raid, and of joining battle."

He was right, of course, but it was still a great shock, both the knowledge that I had killed a man and the sight of that lost wraith fading into oblivion. I shook myself, standing to follow Athlan's advice. I stepped unsteadily past the brothers' opponent, now just another corpse in a puddle of blood, then walked on up the path to help gather together the herds.

The four surviving raiders had their wounds roughly tended, then their hands were bound and they were tied together on a long rope to be taken home as hostages or slaves. As we worked, I looked around me at this new landscape, noticing a short walk away a high earthen bank, now grassed over, running down the slope to a stream. Another bank was just visible some way beyond the first where the woods had not yet reclaimed the land; it looked as if quite an extensive area had been cordoned off at some time.

Syllan came up beside me and followed my gaze. "An old spirit house and feasting place, like the one near the River at home, although I know not what happened here to cause it to be sealed off this way."

I had heard that something bad had occurred in the valley near our village, but so far no one had seen fit to tell me the story. I made a mental note to ask again, and to ask some of the older folk if they knew of this place as well. At last we finished searching the fields and the edges of the wood around them, content we had most or all the livestock together again. Then as the sun sank towards the horizon, we turned the animals back towards the escarpment to begin the long climb back to the Plain.

CHAPTER EIGHT

When he entered his father's house the following day, Syllan was limping slightly from a spear cut he had received during the fight. He was surprised that he had been that close to a serious injury without seeing it, or being able to recall afterwards when it had occurred. His heart still raced when he thought back on the battle, so he made a special effort to compose himself for the audience. His father and brother were both there, as were some of the tribal elders, including old Witlan from the northern valley where the raid had taken place.

"I thank you both for your assistance in defeating the raid yesterday," began Atharon warmly, addressing Weyllan and Kefhan as they stood before him. "You are still newcomers here, and not under obligation to join in our ancient feuds, so your aid was appreciated by us all. We returned all the stolen cattle and most of the goats to their owners, whilst the raiders lost everything, including several of their number."

"Aye," interjected Witlan. "You can add our especial thanks, from those of us who lost animals and friends. You are both welcome to share our meals and company whenever you are in our valley."

Atharon smiled indulgently, nodding to the elder."You know we took four men captive yesterday. Two have been given as compensation to families who lost someone in the raid, and one will serve me for a time. The other we all feel should go to you, Stone-changers, for your service. He shall be your slave as long as you choose – when you tire of him you may dispose of him as you wish, as is the custom. Witlan here also gives you a fine milk cow to add to your herd, and three goats for Kirah and her child."

This was generous indeed. Syllan watched his friends' surprise and pleasure at this unexpected reward, feeling a mixture of emotions, of pleasure tinged with envy for their good fortune. But he told himself he was the son of the chief, so that where *his* courage and commitment were expected, the stone-changers had acted out of goodwill and friendship. He swallowed his jealousy, joining the others in congratulating the two young warriors.

Syllan's mother came in, bearing a pot of barley beer to complete the ceremony. He noticed as they sat down that the pot was one of Kirah's making, in the newer style, thin-walled with a rounded belly and a long, flared neck, and marked with rows of impressions all down the body.

Kirah was a talented potter and a good wife. He wondered, not for the first time, why she had chosen Kefhan for her husband over the more talented seer. Then he remembered what Weyllan had been like when they first met and understood her choice rather better. Kefhan rarely displayed the quiet strength and resolve he possessed, but it was there nevertheless, along with a compassion rare in a man so young.

As the pot came round for Syllan to drink in his turn, he

realised it was a good shape for a drinking pot, delivering the beer smoothly to one's mouth and not in a great surge to the whole of one's face. He took a second mouthful to quench both his thirst and his curiosity, finding his theory held up well to a repeated test. He passed the pot on to Witlan, then turned his attention back to the meeting.

They were talking about the feud with the people from the downs, which one of the elders said had been going on for generations since the raising of the stones. Many of the larger stones had come from the downs near the great circle there, Witlan told them. It was felt that some agreement had been broken by their removal or in the way it had been done. There had been an argument. Someone had lashed out with a spear, wounding somebody and starting the feud. It seemed that now neither side could remember what they had been arguing about or who had struck the first blow, but the feud continued, feeding on itself. Weyllan shook his head in sympathy, but Atharon muttered about the savage nature of their enemies. There was a murmur of assent from Witlan and others in the house.

The meeting broke up soon afterwards, leaving Syllan alone with his kinsmen. They sat in silence for a short time, until Athlan uncrossed his legs and stood up.

"So, my father, are we now to make these stone-changers a part of our clan? For if we do, we must surely tell them the whole sorry tale of their kinsman's stay here. I admit they proved handy in the little skirmish yesterday, but the outcome would have been the same without them. I say they have brought little to us that we did not already know or possess. The man Weyllan has yet to show any under-standing of either the Temple or his power, and will only cause trouble between our clans if he continues to delve into his grandfather's fate."

Atharon looked at his elder son, shaking his head."No, my son, I had no intention to invite them to a closer bond. I agree that Weyllan has yet to prove his worth as a seer and may yet cause trouble, but I hardly think we can send him home after yesterday. He has made many friends on the Plain; I suspect we would do ourselves more harm than good to act against him."

"You are showing your age, father! We should act now, before the harm is done, for afterwards will be too late. We can say what we like to our people. Tell them he was home-sick, that he wanted to leave. Say he admitted to having no idea how to fix the Spirit House and felt it was time to go. They will not be able to gainsay our views once he has gone."

Syllan flushed with anger."Athlan! How can you speak so of friends who gave their aid so willingly and risked harm to themselves for our people? It matters not that they did not affect the outcome of the fight, but that they participated without stint or fear!" He hammered one fist into his open palm for emphasis, his earlier twinges of jealousy forgotten. "Weyllan has just begun to grow as a seer and a spirit-traveller. It may yet take a year or two, but I think he will prove his worth, and more!"

The argument continued this way a little longer, with Athlan refusing to give ground, and their father barely able to make himself heard, until, with a loud clap of his hands, he caught their attention at last.

"My sons, your concerns are noted! Athlan, we cannot ask our friends to leave so soon. Your brother is right; young Weyllan is growing in power and wisdom, and may still provide the means to heal our Spirit House. It is also not our custom to refuse hospitality to travellers, and I have a feeling that these three will not be the last of their kind to come here. In the meantime, his skill with these new materials is something not available to our neighbours or our friends, so our control of that commodity enhances our status and our power. We will not offer them any more details of their ancestor's fate, but my decision is clear. The stone-changers stay!"

Kefhan and Kirah's new cow was a sturdy beast with a fine pair of forward-pointing horns. She was red-brown all over except for a single patch of white on her left haunch and two white socks on her forelegs. Kefhan had named her Duana, which had drawn derisive hoots from the others.

"Well, brother, we won't forget such a distinctive name easily! You could have called her 'Gift of the Aynash' or 'Booty', but no, you decided to name her 'Red One'. What about the white legs?" Weyllan had chuckled at his own humour.

"She is 'Red Lady' you idiot. How did you ever become head of the family, with language skills like that?"

"Can we be clear from this moment onwards, you are not going to be choosing our child's name, dearest husband?" Kirah's comment had caused everyone to laugh as they imagined similar names for her baby.

Kefhan smiled as he remembered the friendly jibes he had received. He had had the last laugh though, because seven days later, the cow was still Duana and nobody thought of her as anything else. He was now accepted by them all as master of their 'herd', on the grounds that it was a man's job - or more properly a boy's, but as yet they had no sons to call on. Weyllan? Well, love him all you might, but he was just too unreliable to do it. He looked at the four cows plodding in front of him, occasionally being hurried along by the new slave Enthis when they stopped to graze. It was hardly a display of great wealth for three people, but he thought they had done well for their first year in the new home.

Atharon had given them a pair of cattle when they arrived, to thank them for coming, whilst Kirah had earned another, named Tobah, when she had successfully set a broken leg for a patient earlier in the summer. She had also earned them three of the five goats they had owned prior to Witlan's gift; the other two had come to the men for a moon-gold knife they had fashioned for Turac.

Kefhan's grin became rueful as he considered his worth as a provider for his little family. His wife was making twice the contribution the men managed between them. At least all was fair with the four pigs they currently owned; one had come to each of them and one was a gift to all. Ah well, they were still settling in, and who knew what the future would bring? Another chuckle, as he thought that a seer ought to be able to find out. Despite always seeming happy to see what would come to pass for others, they were all understandably wary about looking into their own future.

He was taking the cattle away for a few days to allow them to feed on the lush grass of the inner Plain. It would give them a change of scenery while the grass around the homestead recovered before the winter. Enthis came with him, mainly because they were unused to having a slave around the house and had not yet found a suitable role to fill his time. Their father Orelac had had a slave for a few years when they were younger, but in adulthood all three of them had been used to dividing the duties between them, and found it difficult to order another person to do their work for them.

In this land, as in their own home, men and women taken as captives or made destitute through the loss of their herd or crop might become slaves for a season or two, doing the harder, more menial tasks of their hosts in return for food and support. Voluntary slaves could barter their way back to freedom as their fortunes improved, whilst captives were generally exchanged after a short period of service to punish them, or to assist those who had lost kin in the fighting. No one ever kept a slave for long, and it was considered dishonourable to abscond before being freed in an exchange. Enthis had settled in for the duration with a good heart and no apparent ill-feelings.

Caring for the herds on the summer grazing was an easy task. There were few if any predators up here; wolves rarely strayed up on to the Plain, where the herders' dogs tended to discourage them from approaching the animals. The hardest part was coping with the wind and the rain when it fell.

Kefhan had brought a few hides along, strapped to Tobah's back; on the way he and Enthis cut poles from the low stands of wood that grew in the few more sheltered valleys of the grassland. These were used to build a rough shelter; there was just room inside for themselves with their bags. Enthis gathered in as much dry firewood as would fit to supply the cooking fire; an easy task as there had been no rain for fifteen days or more, and the wood he brought in was tinder dry.

They were not alone on the Plain. Kefhan counted seven other shelters in their little valley alone. Grazing in the centre were more than fifty cows, with Atharon's bull supervising the combined herd. Everyone knew their own beasts, so there was no need to keep them apart; it would be a simple task to separate out their stock from the rest at the end of the season. With the herds combined this way, it was a simple task to watch over them, and only a few of the dozen or so strong young lads out there were actively herding on any given day. The others hunted nearby or more often lay outside in the sun, talking or playing a little music. There was always the thin piping of a bone flute playing somewhere; it seemed to calm the cattle as well as entertain the herders.

Kefhan did not intend to stay with the herd very long but he felt that they should at least show willing and share the task for a few days, before he slipped one of the lads a couple of arrowheads to keep an eye on their animals.

That evening, he rigged his bow with an extra cross-string and, using his mouth as a sound box, he began to tap out a tune with an arrow. With only a few tones, it was a simple tune, but the rhythm caught Enthis' attention and he joined in with some competent drumming on a piece of fire-wood. It passed the time and helped the two to bond a little as they sat by the fire in their new role as herdsmen.

They had been there just four nights when the fire broke out. One of the boys had left a cooking fire unattended, and the ever-present wind had fanned the embers until they jumped the gap to a nearby stand of grass. It began to spread at a fast walk into the dry grass near the campsite. Kefhan woke to the worried lowing of the herd and cries of several lads shouting as they ran about to little effect. Seeing the widening arc of the flames, he turned to Enthis who had like-wise woken to the noise.

"Quick, tear a couple of the hides off the shelter. We need to get over there and beat the flames out!"

Enthis obeyed, and they hurried along the slope to the fire, a few hundred paces from their camp. Kefhan called to the boys nearby to do the same from their own shelters, then join him in attacking the flames.

Two of the larger lads, he sent down to the herd to calm the animals. "Sing to them, walk among them, talk to them. You know what to do!"

Others soon came to join them or to tend to the cattle and prevent them from milling, the first sign they were considering a stampede to escape the danger. The hide beaters, and the leafy branches of two nearby bushes soon proved effective; before too long, the last of the flames were out.

Kefhan set a number of the boys to patrol the burnt area, by that time almost halfway to his campsite, to beat or stamp out any embers they saw. They would know to keep watch until daylight, so he and Enthis returned to the remains of their shelter, laying the scorched hides out on the grass to air for a day before they patched them back onto the brushwood frame. They would be all right as long as it didn't rain.

It rained. By dawn, the clouds had rolled in until the sky was full of dampness and drizzle. He and Enthis repaired their shelter, lighting a fire near the doorway to warm the inside and dry the hides.

Kefhan stared out into the grey morning. At least the rain would prevent the grassfire from starting up again. They would check their cows were well and head for home as soon as it dried out.

In the event, they stayed two more days. The rain fizzled out the following morning, leaving the sky a uniform sheet of grey cloud, too thick to let the sun through and too thin to hold rain. In the evening, the tedium was relieved at last by the arrival of Syllan and Weyllan, who had walked over on hearing about the fire. Kefhan told them the story, accenting the humorous angles.

Syllan's face was sober when he had heard the whole episode."We were lucky indeed that you were up here when it happened, my friend. We could have had to spend days rounding the herd up again, not to mention having perhaps to deal with one or two dead sons as well. Once I had doubts about you, Kefhan, but time and time again you have proved your worth, and we value your presence here as much as we do your brother's. Thanks from the heart to you from all of us who have our cattle here today."

Kefhan's heart swelled with pride at the praise. He

glanced at his brother who flashed him a wide grin and a wink, as if to share his pleasure and agree with Syllan's judgement.

"Where would we be without you, Kefhan? Next thing we know, Atharon will want you as one of his advisors if you handle every crisis this well!"

CHAPTER NINE

In the last moon of that summer, the wind roared and the rain fell so often that it seemed we went the whole time with neither a clear sunrise nor a sunset at the day's end. Yet sometimes in the evening, the clouds put on such a display of reds and yellows, shifting and billowing as one watched, that it seemed the very sky was on fire, the water in the clouds boiling and swirling, until I became transfixed by the sight, having more than one vision as I stood thus between realities.

Our new slave, Enthis, proved himself a willing and useful helper as Kirah neared her time, often volunteering his help without being asked. We began to regard him more as one of the family than a captive servant.

As the next moon grew to fullness, Kirah took to her bed and with the help of some of her new friends, gave my brother a child. The storms withdrew as we entered a short interlude of mild warmth when the leaves that had not already been stripped from the trees ripened and reddened, falling gently to the grass.

The birth of Ulrac was in every way the antithesis of the

weather; Kirah cried and screamed for most of the night and into the following morning. Kefhan and I offered prayers to Lukan when he rose into an unusually clear sky; we were answered with a dawn flight of starlings, who wheeled about the sunrise in a complicated display that I felt must be significant if only we could understand its meaning. Then we noticed the silence, soon broken by a new voice wailing for the first time in the cool morning air.

Kefhan gave a whoop and took me in a bear hug that nearly broke my ribs. Grinning like a maniac, he ran into the hut to greet his son and be with his wife. I stayed a moment, bowed my head to acknowledge Lukan's gift, then followed him inside to see my new kinsman and to offer Kirah a little of my strength to help her through the day.

I well remember laying my hand on her belly, channelling the power through me into her to heal and strengthen, and the gentle smile on her face as she accepted my gift. Looking back on it, I wonder whether she needed my help at all, for she showed herself yet again to be as resilient as any of us and quite able to draw down power for herself. But I felt the need to contribute, to have some part in the process. She understood me perfectly, just as she always has. She put her hand on mine, looking from me to Kefhan and back.

"We will call him Ulrac, Leaf-blower, to honour both the season and his powerful breath!" She smiled weakly at her joke. "And with the two of you as his guardians and guides, he will grow to be greater than any of us. This I saw in my pain and my transports. It is for you both to make it come to pass."

As the balmy autumn weather continued, I crossed the River again to visit Aslena. I had planned to ask her more about my grandfather's visit, but we soon fell to talking about Kirah's son and the changes it would make to our lives.

She put a bowl of beer in my hand and looked me in the eyes. "You have put down a root in this land, young Weyllan; it has gifted you a strong child. He should be raised here, at least long enough to accept it into his heart as home. You must plan to live here for quite some years now and you cannot continue your calling for that time as an outsider. The time has come for you to join our people, or at least to join the fellowship of the Spirit House."

"He's not my son." I bridled in response. "If there is a burden to be borne, it falls to Kefhan, not me. And what is this fellowship you speak of? I ..."

"Do not interrupt me," she admonished, albeit with a smile on her countenance. "I will explain about the fellowship. Of course, you have not heard of it; it was not for you to know! But I have spoken to Turac and others. They think it is time you were brought into the group. As for the child Ulrac being your son, you are his guardian, and if you continue to keep your distance from any woman, he is as close to a son as you are likely to get. I have seen the two of you together as he grows up, as close as any father and son, so heed my words and know the burden lies on you as much as it does upon your cousin."

I was silent for a while, absorbing the fact that she had been speaking with Turac about me as if she was a part of this mysterious group. And she had been having visions about my future, ones *I* was not seeing. That worried me even more. I finally said as much to her face; she laughed.

"We are often not gifted to see our own futures too clearly; it is what keeps us whole and sane. If you foresaw every bad thing that might happen to you, if you spent all your energies trying to avoid them, you would soon twist your mind into a cord so taut it would take but a small mishap to break it in two."

"And you are wondering whether I, a mere woman, am a member of this secretive fellowship? Well, yes I am, and a few other women too. But it is not some warrior society with secret signs and spells in the darkness. You must simply prove yourself worthy before your peers for the right to take part in all the ceremonies at the Temple.The winter festival will soon be on us, and Turac felt it would be best if you wereinitiated into the brotherhood – such as it is – before then. It means you will have a full part in the rites and your experiences will be accepted by us all."

She went on to explain more about the initiation they thought I should undertake. There would be a purification near the Spirit House to prepare me for the rite. Then I would be taken among the stones blindfolded and presented to certain places without being told what they were. I was to be taken on a journey, still blind, to a special place where I would be left to seek a vision for three or four days.

"But I have visions already. I have been shown the Spirit House and participated in the Summer ceremonials," I protested, but she only put her head on one side and asked what I had seen of consequence.

The answer, of course, was very little. I tried again. "If I agree to this, how will anyone judge me worthy or not, should I fail?"

"If you are to join us, you will see what we have seen, or something close to it. All who practice their craft here have seen it, and we will know if you are worthy."

I protested a little more, but in my heart, I knew she was right. If I was to live among these people for the next few years, I would need to be accepted as one of them, as a man and as a seer, if I could pass their test. In the end, Aslena said

I must make the arrangements through Turac. I returned home feeling not a little apprehensive.

So it was that some days later I found myself with Turac and two other men dragging poles up from the woods by the River to the ridge a short distance on the sunset side of the Spirit House, helping to build a place of cleansing for my initiation. The shelter was a dome, built of tightly woven branches covered with turves for walls, and straw rammed into the weave to serve as a roof. Inside was a large hearth surrounded by selected stones to be heated in the fire. There were three low turf benches for seating. The whole structure was surrounded by a ditch dug into the chalk to enclose the sacred area.

The rites began on the second night following the completion of the sweat lodge. Three men in animal masks pushed open the hurdle door to my hut as I slept, bundled me up unceremoniously in some smelly hides, and dragged me out into the night. Confused by sleep, I had just enough sense not to lash out at my abductors as they carried me some distance from the settlement. I was at last dropped onto the grass while one man placed a blindfold on my face as another tied my hands, quite loosely to show it was only a symbolic bondage. They whispered incantations as they did so. With a brief word of warning, I was then taken by the hand and led the rest of the way to the sweat house, where they stripped me of my clothing before I was allowed to enter, still blindfolded. Inside, my bonds and blindfold were removed and my captors welcomed me to the initiation.

I remember there were six others in the hut with me, most of whom I had seen at the midsummer celebrations or at other times at the Temple. There was Turac, of course, and an old, half-blind seer known as Tefakin, as well as a young man no older than me, Dobris, who was to become a good friend in later years. With the fire already set and water heating in two pots, we were arranged around the hearth by Tefakin, who seemed to be in charge of the ceremony. He spoke at length of the history of his people and of the building of the Spirit House while the stones grew hot as we spread fresh embers across them whenever the last spread grew grey.

At last there was a pause, and Turac, offering a prayer to the spirits, splashed a little hot water on the stones in front of him, creating a dense puff of steam. The others followed in turn, finishing with me. The room was filling now with steam; the air felt close and cloying. Then Turac began again, wiping aside his latest spread of hot charcoal to dash more water on the stones while he told me a tale about the deeds of Tyris, the seer who built the first spirit house on the plain, ending with a prayer to his spirit to accept me as a brother. Again, each man did the same, with different tales of the ancestors and prayers to their spirits. Outside, someone was beating a soft rhythm on a hand drum, adding to the increasingly hypnotic atmosphere in the hut.

I began to drift off into a half-visionary state as time went by, but was brought back each time it came to my turn, when one of them would ask me a question about my motives or my abilities. Finally, Tefakin began to sing, and they all took up the chant. I was encouraged to join in as I learned the words; together, we sang our way through more tales and prayers, while I became more detached and more sleepy as the sky began to lighten. The singing slowed to a hum, then faded to silence as we sat absorbing the moment, until an unseen hand gently pulled aside the hide screen at the doorway. We watched the sun break over the horizon to begin the new day.

As we stepped out into the cold autumn air, some young

attendants put fur cloaks around our shoulders and we were handed our clothes to put back on. Then we sat in a circle as a bowl of warm sour milk fortified with a liberal dose of cow's blood was handed round. We were each given a small bowl of mashed-up plants that tasted foul but filled the stomach most comfortingly. More prayers were offered, and Tefakin warned me that in my purified state now I should look upon no one, nor think of anything beyond the purpose of my quest, while they led me over the hills to where I was to seek my spirit guide, who would help me complete the quest.

I was blindfolded once more, and they led me away. I felt the presence of the Spirit House where prayers were offered to the spirits; then we walked in a long arc down to the Ayn, where we waded through the waste-deep, icy water to the far bank. By now, I felt certain our destination was the sacred mountain I had visited already, and my heart sank as I remembered my lack of success on that occasion.

And so it proved to be. They removed the cloth from my eyes when we were half-way up the hill, then released me to find my quest seat and my visions. I had a little water, but no food, and Turac's last instruction was that I should remain here until I had the vision that would show I was accepted by the spirits. It was all so long ago, yet I recall it all as if it had happened this autumn past, such was the feeling of separation and dislocation I felt.

I turned away with hardly a word, setting off around the sunny side of the hill until I came to a flat shelf of stone, of the same type as that used to build the Temple. I felt that if I were to connect anywhere, it would be on such a surface. Besides, from it I could see both the sunrise and its setting, if I was to be blessed with any sun during my quest.

And there I sat for three days, in the sun and the rain, without food and, much as I tried, without a vision of any sort. Despite all my efforts, I slept twice, waking without any memory of my dreams, until I began to think I would fail altogether. Then, as the sun set behind a thick bank of cloud for the third time, I was surprised to see a vixen approaching me through the grass and bracken.

She looked directly at me as she stood just a pace away, seeming to speak directly into my head."I am Reya, and I am come to help you tonight. Gather your cloak about you and follow me."

"Are you real, or are you some spirit?" I should have known better than to ask, really, but I was weak with hunger and despair and not in a state to think this encounter through at all.

"Do you think then that a spirit is not real? Have they misjudged you to that degree?" The fox shook her head, looking at me again with a hint of pity in her eyes. "If you touch me, you will feel me solid enough beside you, but when we walk together, no one else will see either of us as we pass, for we will walk in the spirit land. Follow me now, and speak only when I tell you to."

It was my first meeting with Reya, who has since been my guide many times. I did not feel I had made a good impression, so I followed without protest as we moved deeper into the bracken. The sun was soon gone, but the darkness that closed around me within a few dozen steps was not the darkness of early evening. It was impenetrable, seemed to press in on me from all directions, and it smelled of damp earth or rotting leaves. I could not see Reya before me, but I could hear the clicking of her claws as she walked, and she spoke to me all the time to keep me with her.

It seemed that for a long time, Reya led me downwards through the darkness until at length I felt it no longer pressed in on me. It was somehow thinner, more airy, and I had an uncanny sensation of emptiness stretching away from me in every direction. I stopped, putting out my arms to feel for the edges of the void, but to no avail.

Remembering what I had been told, I said nothing, but Reya's voice came out of the darkness to answer my unspoken question. "In your world, we now stand deep beneath the hill on which you have been sitting for the past few days. In this realm, there is no hill above us, nor indeed anything but darkness. Ahead of us lies a great ruin, a huge house such as you have never seen before, wherein lies that which you seek. Speak now," she said.

"Is it far? It seems to me there is nothing anywhere except the ground on which we stand."

"Not so far as you might think, Seer. Distances here are not as they appear at first, nor indeed is much else. Shall we go on?"

I nodded and was aware of her moving away from me, angling a little to the left. I followed, more confident now that there was something to aim for, however strange it might seem when we reached it. As my eyes grew more used to the darkness, I was able to discern several shades of shadow before me, resolving into a wide scatter of boulders across the surface,and I could just see the darker shape of the vixen moving ahead of me, in silence now, the pale tip of her tail rocking from side to side as she trotted along.

Then before me there loomed a solid wall of black stone, broken only by a small doorway formed by three huge stones. They instantly brought to my mind the five great gateways of the Temple on the Plain, although the passage between these stones was wide enough for me to walk between the uprights with my arms stretched out, still barely brushing the walls on either side.

We passed through, crossed a flagged stone floor and began to climb a broad flight of steps. I don't think I had ever seen more than three steps together before, but here there must have been twenty or so, each two feet wide and several paces across. At the top was another, larger, doorway with an angled lintel made from many courses of stone, each jutting out from the one beneath until they met at the top.

Reya had been right. I had never seen a structure like this in my world, and I stared off into the darkness to either side trying to make out more details, but without success.

What lay beyond this doorway was hidden from view by a blank wall which, however, did not extend more than a few paces to either side. I was able to see this because the ends of the wall were lit by a faint bluish glow from behind. Reya led me through and around the wall beyond, where I stopped short in wonder at the scene before me.

I was standing on the edge of a vast chamber with walls of chalk or some other white rock, with the floor almost covered in massive heaps of stones and crystals that glinted and glittered in the pale light emanating from several large orbs mounted on the walls.

Reya sat down, turning her head back to face me. "From here, you must go ahead alone. What you see here you should report back to your brothers in the other world. I will wait here a while in case you need my assistance to return home."

I gave a sign of thanks, walking uncertainly forward to the nearest pile of stones. I passed around it, penetrating further into the chamber. The crystals, as I recall, were mainly of pink or clear quartz, though here and there I saw clusters of blue or purple ones like gems I had seen at home among the mountains. The stones were of all sorts and colours, all tumbled round like pebbles from a stream or the seashore. Some I had seen before: the bright red of jasper, the shiny greyish black of star-stone; there were both blue and green ores of moon-gold. I even saw nodules of true gold amongst the piles. I was sorely tempted several times to pick some up, but I restrained myself. This was so clearly a collection, a hoard, made by something sentient, that I felt it would be bad manners, not to mention bad luck, to touch it without consent.

And so it proved, for as I rounded the end of a long ridge of quartz, I saw on the other side what looked like a colossal adder, loosely coiled around a single great pillar of stone that soared up into the darkness overhead. Like an adder's, the great blue head was triangular, a full pace long and more than an arm's length across, with eyes the size of a child's head, each one banded in different coloured rings like an agate. It turned to look at me, uncoiling slightly from its pillar, and to my surprise unfolded a jointed scaly leg to support its weight. The body, in contrast to the head, was covered in green and yellow patches except beneath the neck where the paler skin was flecked with warning red.

"I greet you, Seer! How are you called in your tongue?"

As with Reya, the words formed ready in my mind. What I actually heard was a series of hisses and growls that conveyed neither emotion or meaning.

"I am Weyllan, a stone-changer from the great White Mountains of the mainland. I am on a vision-quest to gain entry to the fellowship of seers at the Spirit House on the Plain. To whom do I speak?"

"Fairly said, young Weyllan. I am Brwslyi, and you have stumbled unbidden into my house on a very different plain." He rumbled contentedly at his own humour. "Why have you come here? I do not, as a rule, give out visions to anyone who crosses my doorstep. I am more inclined to take your soul for my supper!"

I found it hard to take this reply seriously. It sounded so much like a childhood tale of terror that I wondered if the beast was joking again. But then again, I did not know much about this great lizard creature, least of all what it ate. I decided to remain respectful but to make it clear I was not frightened by the threat.

"I think perhaps *you* are my vision," I replied. "Since I knew nothing of your existence and you nothing of mine, I cannot see how either of us could bid the other come to visit. But I mean no harm nor disrespect; if you do not wish to speak further, I will leave you alone. Yet I feel that more should come of our meeting, for I will be a seer of the Spirit House. I am certain you are linked to the Plain and its people in some way. I have little enough to offer as a greeting gift, but I see among your stones and gems here you have metal ores. I have here a small blade made from the very essence of the rock, such as I'm sure you have never seen before."

So saying, I drew my small copper knife from my belt, offering it up for Brwslyi's inspection. The beast uncoiled another leg and reached out to take the blade from me, hissing expectantly as it drew the object closer. The deep rumbling came again, as Brwslyi opened his jaws in what was probably his best attempt at a smile.

"That is a kind gesture, and a brave one, since this would have been your only defence against me had I chosen to … eat you, perhaps. This is indeed the first such piece I have seen made by your kind, though I am sure it will not be the last. Now I should return the kindness and bestow upon you a good gift. Let me think a moment."

He closed his eyes, tilting his head steeply to one side as his thin tongue flicked out to inquire of the air around him.

"Ah, yes, I have just the things."He placed the knife on the floor beside him and again reached forward with one clawed limb, opening itin front of me to reveala small, perforated oval of jet. "This talisman will offer you protection against-many ills, and guard you against the curses of the spirits of your kind."

He reached down and plucked a single scale from his

chest. "And this will be a mystery to you for many years, but when its time comes, you will know how to use it to give you power over a great evil. I am aware that you also desire some of the rocks in my little collection. You are welcome to take away with you whatever you can carry in your hands, but be warned; we are not of the same world, and all may not be as it was here when you return with it to your own land."

With that he turned away, picking up my knife and turning it over and over in his claw, evidently quite taken with it. I bowed low as I began to walk backwards away from his presence.

"You are a sensible man. I can tell you would not want to know your future too soon, but I will say this; you will wield great power and achieve many good things in your life, Seer. But there is always a price. Remember, the price for such power is often high. Rise above misfortune and you will come to your destiny in good time. I hope we do meet again before then, but if not, I wish you well. Go in peace, Weyllan of the White Mountains."

Again, that chuckling throaty growl showed that he was expressing humour. I hoped that it was a friendly joke and not just mockery, but either way, I had little to give in return. I repeated my bow, backing away before turning to make my way back to the doorway, collecting a small handful of gold nuggets and gemstones as I passed. I was also taken by three large and almost identical crystals of quartz and added them to my little haul. Then I rejoined Reya, who wagged her tail with pleasure at my reappearance.

"That was quick," she said with a slight yap. "You could have been lost for an age in that maze of rocks."

I laughed. "I have always been able to find my way home again, have no fear."

"Ah well, then you will have no further need of me!" And with that, the vixen disappeared before my eyes.

. . .

I stood in shock for a long while. That was not at all what I had meant, forI had no idea how to return to my world without Reya. Whenever I had had visions before, I had simply lost consciousness, then woken up again a few moments later. Somehow, I had the feeling that I was not going to just awaken from this dream without some specialist help.

"Reya," I called repeatedly, "Come back! Of course, I need a guide to get out of here!" But there was no response to any of my pleas.

I thought I could probably find my way back across the plain and, hoping that Reya would return if I made an effort on my own, I set out to retrace my steps. My eyes soon regained their night vision after the glow in Brwslyi's hall, so that once out of the building, I could see our tracks still clear in the dust. I followed them quickly back across the plain, expecting at any moment to see Reya sitting in the path before me, grinning from ear to ear. But I reached a point where the darkness ahead became impenetrable, and the tracks we had made on our inward journey were no longer visible, even when I crouched down with my face close to the dirt.

Almost in despair, I reached out with my free arm, trying to find my way into the dark wall, but felt only the dense blackness I had sensed all around me as we came through before. I tried to think, but could find no way to overcome the obstacle, until I closed my eyes in surrender. Then, in plain sight on the inside of my eyelids, I could see a paler oval, like a narrow opening into a cave or tunnel. I stepped towards it and entered the darkness again.

I realised then that I needed my inner vision, my seer's sight, to follow the way; so keeping my eyes shut, I followed the pale line through the division between the worlds until I sensed once more the presence of the bracken around me and felt its fronds brushing my leggings.

It was almost daylight when I opened my eyes. A paling sky and a broad orange glow showed how much time had passed. I could see the bracken around me and judged I was about fifty paces from my earlier station. I set out in that direction to find my cloak and water-skin again. Then as the light grew, I emptied my booty on to my cloak, only to find I had an armful of common grey pebbles.

Only the three crystals were the same; the quartz had crossed between the worlds unchanged. It was the only treasure I had brought back. Then I remembered the gifts from Brwslyi and dug into my pouch. They too had survived the journey; they were the proof I needed that I had indeed made the journey and had not merely fallen into a half-starved dream. I returned everything to my pouch, shouldered my water-skin, then put on my cloak before turning away from the sunrise and heading back off the hill to the Spirit House again.

CHAPTER TEN

For the past few days, we had taken turns to observe the setting of the sun from within the Spirit House. This was no great secret of the fellowship of seers on the Plain; it was knowledge almost everyone possessed and could use to calculate the passage of time through the seasons. You could stand in the doorway of your house to watch the sun rise and set, marking its movement across the horizon, knowing by its progress how far advanced was the season. Twice a year, it would reach the limits of its traverse and pause for a few days before moving back along the horizon to its other limit. That being so, once I became familiar with the skyline as we saw it from the Temple, I could watch the sun set through a sheet of finely split hide to calculate how long it would be until Lukan ceased his movement, standing still for days to mark the beginning of the dead moons of winter. And as I marked where the last sliver of the sun fell below the hills, I knew that the Soul Days, when the ancestors came back through the long darkness to be with their offspring again, would begin within the next two days or so.

During these watches, my mind often turned back to the

moment when I became a part of this community, when I came down off the sacred hill and recounted my experiences to Turac, Tefakin and the others who gathered to hear my testimony. They had nodded in an accommodating manner when I described the cavernous space beneath where the hill stood in our world; they had been mildly impressed when I described the beast's house with its hoard; they had definitely raised their eyebrows when I recounted my conversation with Brwslyi. But they seemed awed, nodding to one another, at the news that he had given me one of his own scales, and that I had subsequently found my own way back between the two worlds without the aid of my spirit guide. As we walked home afterwards, Turac's restrained chuckles had finally broken out into guffaws of laughter.

"Oh, to see the looks on their faces when you held out that scale! That was worth my whole lifetime of dealing with those self-important shysters! Oh, by the sun and moon, I shall laugh on that for years to come! I received only a good day and good wishes from Brwslyi when I was initiated; Tefakin, like you, got a powerful talisman, as did one or two others. A few of us were offered a choice from his rock pile or some worthy advice for a future need, but none of them – not one of those living – has received two gifts, let alone a scale from his own body. You are truly honoured!"

He slapped me on the back, shaking his head in disbelief at my good fortune."You may rest assured there will be several who will be most jealous of your achievement. Take care in your dealings with the brothers for a while, in case one of them should try to discredit you in the eyes of the others. But, oh, how glad I am I lived to see today! And to live at the dawn of what promises to be a most exciting time."

We went home to Kefhan and Kirah, where we sat long into the night going over the tale again and again as we drank our way through two full pots of beer, even though I knew that the next day I would have to begin training all over again to learn the secrets and the order of rites that were performed at the Great Spirit House on the Plain. Every day from then until the day of the midwinter ceremonies, I would be given instruction in my role and the ways in which we were to reactivate the sun spirit to bring the ancestors with us through the darkness into the new day and the new year.

Some of the things I learned then cannot be spoken of here; they were secrets of the initiated and only if you become one of the fellowship will you learn them. But much of it is known to everyone with the will to listen; so all of us know of the procession that occurs, bringing the spirits of our newly departed kinfolk from the spirit house by the Ayn, along the banks to the landing-place, and over the ridge to the approach to the great Spirit House on the Plain. This is a rite we all understand, when the spirits of those who have died in the year are gathered together during the Soul Days, then taken to meet their fellows at the Temple, where they are admitted into the great host of the ancestors.

Of course, only the very few chosen will have their ashes interred within the banks, and more often than not, none will be chosen. The remainder of the dead will be carried back along the path to the landing place after the ceremony, to be scattered on the waters to float or sink as chance dictates until they are returned to the earth whence they came. Their spirits, however, will remain forever near the Spirit House to help their children and their children's children in the times to come.

And we, the seers of the fellowship, will walk amongst them, speak with them to tell them our needs, and ask their assistance. They, in turn, will give advice through us, taking our messages to the spirits that rule our lives. This is the way of the world everywhere, on the Plain as beside the sea or across it to the White Mountains where I was born. Everyone understands all this, and is a part of the whole, each as much as every other living plant and creature.

But I was now a part of something else, a band of seers, both men and women, who exercised our skills at the very centre of the world. For the longer I spent on the Plain, the more I came to realise that our Spirit House stood not just at the centre of our little world, but at the symbolic heart of everyone's world, from the plains beyond my homeland mountains to the shores of the Great Ocean and even to the islands that lay scattered on its waters.

In the days between my vision and midwinter I also learned many other things, such as which local plants could be eaten or inhaled to bring on the fainting visions on demand. I also learned which incantations would influence which spirit realm I would visit in my vision to obtain the specific answers I sought, rather than the almost random experiences I had had previously. Had I paid more attention to my teachers when I was a youngster, I would probably have known much of this already, but I had only ever been interested in the world of rocks with their essences and spirits. My tutors had given up teaching me the special skills of the seer when they became convinced I would never develop this side of my abilities.

Now, I had a great deal to learn in a very short time, but I was an eager student, and it all fell into place inside me so that most of it I had only to hear the once and it became a part of me to use my whole life long.

As it was, that year rainstorms and high winds marred the first of the Soul Days; the weather seers among the fellowship agreed that we should wait for the third day of the five to allow the storms to pass before we began our ceremonies. They were proven right; the rain and wind both died away during the night of feasting in which folk said farewell to their kin, preparing them for the transition of the following day.

Those of us who were to participate in the ceremony and the vision dance the next day did not feast. Instead, we ate lightly and retired early, to be woken at midnight when we entered the sweat house to purify ourselves for the events to come. I have always enjoyed the cleansing sensation I get from the sweathouse, the light-headed sense that not only is your body clean and purified, but that the world you walk in afterwards is likewise a purer place, with sharper colours and clearer air through which so much can be seen that is not normally presented to the eyes.

We emerged into a grey dawn with dull, baggy clouds stretching from one end of the sky to the other. Those who wished to, myself among them, applied spirit pigment to our faces and bodies, both as barriers against harm and to identify each other should we meet on the other side. Then, as we made a prayer to the morning, it seemed the Turashyi answered us as a band of clear sky appeared to the south, widening rapidly until the first glow of the sunrise could be seen behind the sacred hill where I had so recently spent such a precious time on my vision quest.

We broke our fast with a meal of venison and choice cuts from a sacrificed bull, both cooked with a heady mix of herbs prepared by Kirah and her fellow healers, washing it all down with a fortifying beaker of warmed mead. Some of the older folk complained about the pot we used, but when they learned it was one of Kirah's "new" pattern vessels (new to them, if not to those of us from the mainland) given in honour of my initiation, they acquiesced and swallowed the sacred drink happily enough.

Then we built a fire before the entrance to the spirit house near the chalk banks that enclosed the abandoned builders' village to wait while the people awoke and brought over the ashes of their kinfolk to be placed in the house. Around mid-morning, a small group of men and women walked up from the River bearing three leather bags of ashes. They were people I had not met before; I guessed they came from the community scattered across the down the other side of the sacred hill. They were hardy looking folk, shorter and more wiry than the local Plainsmen, well-dressed in thick fur cloaks with hats of soft pelt that they could draw down to cover their ears in icy weather.

One of them approached me and placed his hand to his breast in greeting."You must be Weyllan, the stone-changer. I have foreseen your coming for some time, and am saddened that you have not yet graced our homes with a visit. I am Jahrain, a seer of the small community of Northerners who remain here. You have a part to play in our lives, too, so now that you have joined the fellowship, you should seek us out as soon as you might."

I was a little perplexed at this prediction, but the sweath-ouse and the morning mead had relaxed me as it opened me up to every new situation, so I smiled warmly at him and returned his greeting, promising to visit in the new year.

"Are you coming with us to the Spirit House?"I asked, but he shook his head.

"We are not permitted anymore. Though we helped to build the Temple, since the events that occurred behind us," he nodded his head towards the massive chalk bank nearby, "We may not participate in the ceremonies there. But I will bring our dead with me and if you will carry them within, I will wait outside with my people to collect them in the morning."

I was reminded again that I had yet to find out what had happened to bring about the closing off of such a large area and made my mind up to ask Turac for the whole story. It sounded as though it might be wise to pay the promised visit to Jahrain's people to hear his version as well. I stored the thoughts away for retrieval after the ceremonies were done for the year.

At midday, a horn sounded and we gathered for the procession. We stood together in the spirit house, the tall timber posts towering above us as Tufakin led the chant to sing the praises of the departed, and to warn the ancestors of their coming. A libation of mead was made before each of the stones representing the different clans who made up this community, beside which the bags and urns that held the ashes of their dead had been placed.

There was no stone for the Northerners, but young Dobris, who had been chosen to perform this part of the ritual, poured a small portion of the drink in front of the three bags just as solemnly as he did the others. Then Tufakin made a clear reference in his song to the "sons of the stone-makers", calling on his ancestors to honour them and accept them. I hoped Jahrain could hear his song from outside the spirit house and that the praise-words pleased him. The short service over, we carried the ashes of our people out to their waiting kinfolk, then with them behind us, we marched out towards the River.

The procession led us down the Ayn, alongside the sacred waters, the gateway to the afterlife, around several bends to the old landing place. There had once been a spirit house here, too, in years gone by; you could still see the disturbed earth and the remains of the banks around it. Syllan had told me that at one time the procession had begun here, but the stones were dismantled when the new Temple was being built, although they were never moved to the new site as planned. Then the wooden spirit house we had started from today was set up in its stead. Now only the scar of the structure marked the traditional point of departure from the River, the place where the ashes of the departed would tomorrow be spread upon the waters.

Turac and Tufakin led the congregation up the slope away from the River, walking in a long arc towards the Spirit House on the Plain as the wintery sunlight began to fade and the chill of the evening settled on us as we walked through the long grass up over the ridge.

A small stone cairn marked the start of the final climb to the Temple; we paused there to eat a light meal of cold meat and herbs designed to enhance our sight and our visions. From the combe, the Spirit House was largely hidden from view, with only a few lintels and the top of the marker stone visible. When the elders judged it was the right moment to begin the ascent, we lined up again and commenced our procession with one of the chants I had recently been taught as we climbed.

The timing was perfect. I was quite literally staggered by my first sight of the circle, with the lintels all afire and glowing as the sun descended amongst them. As we continued up the hill, the uprights appeared, all dark and desperate shadows, whilst radiating from between them the golden beams of Lukan's light added to the other-worldliness of the scene. There was no doubt in anyone's mind that we were entering a place of active power, where wonderful things might happen.

Those who were not to enter the precinct turned off before the white chalk bank, handing their bundles of ashes and cremated bone to one of the initiates, who would place them in the Temple during the celebrations. There were others there too, men and women who had not joined the procession but had come ahead to witness the year's end with us. This would be my first Soul Night at the Spirit House, and every moment is painted starkly on my mind.

As we entered the circle, Lukan had still not quite departed; his light shone on us through and around his great gateway, illuminating the interior of the Temple as our torch-bearers circled round to light the torches set among the stones. As the last of the sunset flared briefly between the uprights of the gateway, two bowls full of wood were lit upon the lintel to hold the spirit light there through the night and keep it alive until we brought the sun back again with the dawn.

The horn was blown again, joined now by two others as the drummers began a slow beat to mark the funeral of Lukan. We sang a different song to the new beat, singing the praises of the sun spirit, calling on the ancestors to awaken and carry our words to Lukan as he journeyed through the underworld. Niyvash, the first and brightest of the star spirits, appeared, then Lena rose from her bed to watch us dance. More mead was passed around, and the drums began the dance rhythm in earnest.

I had not intended to join the travellers who went on to the spirit realms during the dance, as I had no special task appointed me, but I was not in control of my soul that night. I danced, feeling the rhythm swell and fall within me like waves upon the ocean, and soon I was a wave, rising and tumbling, pulled along by the flow of the current. Without thought, I spread my arms to receive the Kas, the life-force, and felt it flow into me between my shoulders, felt the warmth spread across my back and chest to burst into my head, causing me to stagger. I fell from the dance in this world to join the spirits as they swayed in a great circle alongside our own. I could feel the familiar sand under my feet, soft andsparkling, thrown up in sprays by my boots at every step. I could see the grey gloom around me, and the ancestors – so many ancestors I could never count them all – sweeping along with me in the current I could feel but could not see.

I saw also lines of upright stones, not in a circle but on each side of me, moving with me, always standing between me and the ancestors. When I tried to change direction, or tried crossing the lines to reach the spirits, the stones moved with me while the eddies swirled the sand and the spirits away. I saw briefly the women I had seen that day I rested on the spirit path, two of whom I now recognised as the shades of Leca and Urda. And Urda saw me and laughed at my discomfort, pointing it out to her companions before she swept towards me on the far side of the stones.

"See!" she cried. "These are my stones. They will block you at every turn, to keep from you and the others the full power that is in this place! I have cast a spell on them, so they will obey me always. You will never achieve your ambition to have your friends control the spirits here or unlock the secrets I have hidden from you all. And now I have you trapped among my stones; there you will remain while your body fades and rots back in the world of the living!"

She laughed again as she swirled away. I tried again to burst through the lines of stones, first on one side and then the other, but could not free myself. I felt panic rising in me, but I pushed it down, tried to sweep it away. All I had to do was return to my reality, to my own body, to wake myself up on the other side.

But it was one thing to think that and quite another to achieve it. I could not believe I was unable to break free; I turned to look backwards, but in that direction, all was darkness. There was no *before* here, and no *after,* just the never-ending *now.* I could expect no help from outside. I could change the nature of stone, I had faced a serpent-lizard and made my way home, yet I couldn't find my way back from this sandy wasteland. I began to wish Reya was here to guide me and I tried to imagine how I would get out if I were her. Then I heard the swish of wing-beats and looked up to see an enormous kite hovering behind my shoulder. I turned, and I swear the bird winked at me.

"You ask for me, and here I am," said a familiar voice.

"But you are not Reya; you are not a fox!"

"Yet again, you astonish me! Did you learn nothing when they taught you as a child? I am indeed your guardian, Reya. I am a spirit guide; I can change my form as I need to so that I may better perform my task. Although I confess, I am partial to the fox shape – it gives me speed and cunning, courage and beauty. But this form has its uses, too; on this occasion, there is only one way out from those stones, and that is up!"

At last I began to understand; I raised my arms above my head as Reya positioned herself above me. Then I reached up to grasp her ankles as she beat her wings in powerful sweeps that lifted us both clear of the ground, then above the stones and the spell cast by Urda.

Almost in the same moment, the scene began to fade before me. The great stones of the Spirit House drifted back into focus as I came back into my own body, now sagging against one of the inner stones and supported by another seer who was acting tonight as a guardian of the bodies of those of us who had travelled through the doorways. He half-carried, half-walked me to the outer ring of uprights and sat me down, returning a moment later to give me a cup of icy water to revive me.

I had not the strength to rejoin the dance, so I sat and watched as I pondered the meaning of my latest vision. I think I also slept for a while, for it seemed soon afterwards that the sky began to lighten and the night drew to an end.

Turac came across to speak with me, having recently returned from his own journey after enlisting the aid of his kinsmen on the far side to get good weather for the crops and fine days for the harvest. The drummers had long since stopped their beating, and the dancers had all collapsed after their journeys or given up the attempt.

We both stood up, strolling over to join the others, as I told him of my short visit to the spirit world. He shook his head in worry, saying I was lucky to have escaped so lightly, and wondering why Urda should have singled me out for her mischief. As the light strengthened, we all stepped out of the stone circle; the drummers struck up one last rhythm, and we began the chant to welcome back Lukan to our world with us. We gave no more thought to Urda's machinations, though as we were to learn, she was far from done with me.

CHAPTER ELEVEN

In the weeks after the turning of the year, Kefhan stepped up quietly to take on the role of leader of the family. He saw straight away that his brother needed time to recover and to understand the meaning of the experience he had had, so he drew Weyllan under his wing for as long as the young seer needed. It was Kefhan who went hunting to bring home a small deer or with luck one of the few boar left in the riverine woodland; it was he who tended the family herd, now comprising five cows, with more than twice that number of pigs and goats. He bled or milked the cows when required and chose a piglet for slaughter when game was scarce. He also found time to go out with Kirah to collect clay from the riverbank for her pots, sometimes sitting with her as they sorted the clay to remove the larger pebbles and rootlets that would make fine pottery harder to create. The frosts in the winter months also helped to break down the clay so that it was easier to work when Kirah chose to start her craft in the spring.

His brother's rise to prominence was evident for anyone to see. He had arrived as a friend of the chief's son, but had soon made numerous other friends across the Plain. He had shown his skills as a stone-changer and brought back unheard-of gifts from the spirit under the sacred hill. The group had been there a year, and already Weyllan was a respected member of the Temple fellowship, whose advice was sought by more experienced seers in the community.

Kirah had quietly been making a name for herself as well, producing new styles of pottery in addition to well-crafted examples of local shapes for barter when she wasn't busy treating patients for every known ailment. There were other successful wise women among Hatha's people, but Kirah had still forged herself a place among them in a short time, a clear sign of her skill in this field.

It was not that Kefhan was without power of his own, for he was an expert hunter and a good stone-changer in his own right, with the ability to see to the heart of any person within a few moments of first meeting them. But he was forever overshadowed by the powers of his wife and his brother; he knew that his role was always to support them and watch their backs, to make sure that normal life flowed on around them. He was the pivot around which their little cosmos turned, or as Weyllan had once put it, "the rock that holds us all steady". And he was well content with that role, enjoying the experience without having to perform miracles himself. Or perhaps, if they all rode the River in a boat representing his family, he saw himself as the one sitting in the stern with the steering paddle, keeping the boat and its crew steady in the current.

Both Turac and Syllan were regular visitors to the little homestead. Syllan had donated two large pelts, a cowhide and a bearskin with the fur still attached, to keep the family warm through the winter. On fine days, they would all sit around the fire set just outside the house, talking, while Kirah kept them all supplied with beakers of barley beer as they put the world to rights. Naturally, they talked about Weyllan's vision and the malice of the spirit Urda.

"Perhaps it is just that she objects to any change brought in by my family," said Syllan on one occasion. "Her hatred of my lineage for what she sees as our usurping of her family's destiny, however inaccurate that may be, is still apparent in the deeds of her remaining kinsmen and her actions in the other world."

"There is more to it than that." Turac shook his old head sadly. "Whatever happened to her to trap her in the spirit world, whatever became of her body in that burial mound, it has turned her from the revered leader that she was into a bitter and unstable demon bent on evil in both worlds."

"I have heard a little of this tale, but never the whole story at once." Weyllan looked at his mentor, his curiosity aroused. "Will you tell me what happened to create the demon? I may need the knowledge if I am to face her again."

So Turac related the story, with occasional interruptions or questions from the chief's son, of Urda's decision to build the spirit path and use it to travel into the other world to where her ancestors dwelt.

"When Urda was the matriarch and leading seer of our people, there was no Temple on the ridge here. Indeed, I am not sure that the guide stone was even raised in those days. They already knew that this was the centre of all things, but I think perhaps they avoided the site except as a powerful place for seers to come on vision quests. The great long mound at the sunrise end of the spirit path houses the bones of Hatha with her family and kin from the beginning of our life here on the Plain. Urda could certainly trace her line directly back to the founder. But there was discontent among the Children of Hatha; Urda felt they were about to split again and perhaps fight among themselves. So, she called for the spirit path to be built to channel her power to take her spirit from the long mound to find the dwellings of our fore-bears on the other side."

"But I thought the ancestors live in the long mound, only in the other realm?" queried Syllan.

"No, Syllan, for although the mound exists in both worlds, it would be a most uncomfortable house for such revered spirits. On the other side, Hatha's kin set up their shelters beside a beautiful stream that drains into a lake in the – well, directions have little meaning in the spirit world – which in our world is at the sunset end of the spirit path."

"Have you been there?" Weyllan wanted to know.

"I am not sure." The old seer shrugged, shaking his head once more. "No one has been there in generations. When I first began having visions, I travelled to my father in a green land with water - but if it was Hatha's home, I never saw their spirits about the place. Nowadays, all we get to see are the endless sands of the twilight world that stands before and above the ancestors' home, where the lesser spirits dwell with those that have yet to pass beyond. They meet us there, halfway between the two if you like, but sometimes they refer to the beautiful land beyond."

"I wonder," muttered Weyllan. "Perhaps even the spirits have their dreams and imaginings."

Turac shrugged as if to dismiss Weyllan's cynicism.

Kefhan quickly moved the conversation away from conflict. "And why did she need something so strong as a spirit path to aid her?"

"It was a long time ago, but as I have heard it told, she planned to gather up all the woes and sickness that were tearing her people apart, then to lead them along to the stream, where, with the spirits, she could cleanse them or drown them, thereby healing the rifts among Hatha's people. The spells that bound power within the banks of the spirit path were to help her control all these ills and prevent them escaping back into the living world. Whatever Urda's intention, something went awry. She entered the long mound in a spirit-walk, bearing as she thought all the ills and woes, but she never made it to the stream at the other end. Nor did they ever find her body in the chamber of the mound. She had somehow been trapped in the spirit world, just as she in turn tried to trap you." Turac nodded atWeyllan. "But whilst many of the ills she bore slipped back into our world, she must have held fast to others, and I wonder if it was those that poisoned her spirit."

Syllan finished the tale for Turac. "It was many generations before anyone living even encountered Urda's spirit. It was lost in limbo, perhaps, or gone off on a journey to rid itself of the curse. Not even seers of her clan ever got the story from her, and to this day nobody knows what happened to her on that fateful crossing. It seems that the divisions continued to plague our people, growing into the enmity between my family and Urda's descendants today."

"And it was *her* kin that brought the stones from the Sunset Sea?" Kefhan turned back to the old seer.

"It was. Syllan's kinswoman Tyris decided, in the end, to take some of the bones from the long mound and add them to a new circle she was building at the Heart of the World. She planned a ring of wooden posts, but Urda's kinswoman Leca and her man took over the plan and brought his stones from his old home. Not that it was a bad idea; these stones came from a place of power. They had been among the first in the world to be made into a spirit house using the power of the circle. Once here, they were used for many generations to focus the power the seers called down, binding the spirits to heal the ills in our community. It was we who failed as a people, not the stones. That failure was what brought about the decline of Hatha's Children in the dark cycles."

Kefhan watched Turac retreat into thoughts of his own,

and for some time the company sat staring into the fire, drinking mechanically from the beer pot as it passed from person to person. There was a lot to think about, and Kefhan looked across at his brother, wondering if his power had helped give him any insights into the conundrum that was Urda's story.

Although the winter was cold and the wind bitter, there was little snow on the Plain. The moon of white flowers came and went, the first of the optimistic yellow daffodils and purple crocuses shot up their stems, the buds grew and opened for any available sunshine. It was going to be a good year for daffodils, which presaged a good summer to come.

Kefhan and Weyllan both put their shoulders to the plough to break some frozen ground, turning several rows of earth for the spring sowing. Kefhan planned that they would plant enough to provide all their own bread through the next winter, with enough left for Kirah to brew some dark barley beer to comfort them in the evenings after the harvest. Until then, they would have to barter for grain, for they had had no seed to sow the previous spring. This was no great hardship, and the two men made a good trade in their new barbed arrowheads. Within a year or so, the rest of the men would have worked out how to make their own, but for now, the new points were much sought after, and they had no shortage of customers.

In the fourth moon of the year, a little before the equinox, Kefhan set off with Weyllan to visit the settlement of the Northerners across the Ayn, in response to Jahrain's earlier invitation. It was a fine, if blustery, day, and they made good time to the River, borrowing a boat to cross over, as the water was still high from the winter rains.

A short march beyond was Aslena's farm, south of the

Sacred Hill, where they stopped for a while to make sure all was well with her, and to make her a gift of a haunch of venison they had shot the day before. She was pleased with the meat, and offered to take them to the home of Jahrain.

The man was out somewhere with his brother, Maklyr, when they arrived. Kefhan handed Jahrain's wife another cut from the deer, for which she thanked him politely before going inside. She then emerged with a small pot of beer which she passed to her visitors to refresh themselves.

Then Jahrain and Maklyr strode up, she took the pot back to refill it, then left the men to themselves with the beer going from hand to hand. Aslena stayed, performing the introductions and partaking of the beer with the men without the slightest hesitation. Clearly, the Northerners knew and respected her, for they seemed to treat this as quite normal.

"I am curious to know more about your people here," said Weyllan, once all the pleasantries had been exchanged and they were seated on the ground looking out at the view. "Why have neither Atharon nor his sons, nor even Turac, my mentor, mentioned your existence?"

"That does not surprise me at all. They banished us from the stones and they try most of the time to pretend that we no longer dwell here – or even that we were ever here to begin with." Jahrain chuckled. "There were once more than two hundred of us, but some died and others went home. These days there are fewer than half that number scattered across this ridge. We came here in my great grandfather's time, from a land of lakes and mountains, after a seer named Tamakis had a vision that the circle here was to be rebuilt; the spirits instructed him to come south to lend a hand with the process. He brought with him his kinsfolk, and several other families, my own among them, who wished to see this place that claimed to be the Heart of the World."

Jahrain looked around at his audience, then continued, "At that time, Myrthis was trying to build a new spirit house using the ancient stones from the great circle. He had an idea to construct a double circle in which the dances and ceremonies would take place at the very centre of the great circle, but from the start, he had been beset with difficulties. Many of the stones had cracked in the ground and fell in two when they were lifted out of their holes. It was clear that there would never be enough to complete the spirit house, so he planned to take apart the lesser house down at the landing-place, although as it came about that never happened. The spirits were in turmoil over all this change even then. When Myrthis made up his mind to shape the stones to build a stone house like the timber ones, with lintels and screens, the spirits were furious! They interfered at every stage of the work, to halt it if they could. Chief among these were spirits from Urda's clan, who laid a special claim on the ancient stones."

Jahrain paused to wet his throat with a noisy gulp of beer. "That was the point at which Tamakis arrived with my people, and shortly afterwards came a smaller party from the mountains by the Sunset Sea, whence came the stones in the first place. Among both groups, there were experienced stonemasons, and together they managed to persuade Myrthis to change his plans. They outlined a design for a larger temple which would have elements common to other great circles, whilst still reflecting the local beliefs of the Children of Hatha. The story goes that there was endless argument over the source of the stones for this new design, and the degree to which shaping them and building a lintelled stone temple could be achieved. In the end, Myrthis held to his vision, and they all agreed to build the Spirit House you have seen and worked in."

"Neither Tamakis nor Myrthis lived to see their work

completed," interjected Maklyr. "The people from the sunset sea and our forebears knew the tricks of moving and raising the stones; they were soon able to improve the joints required to lock the stones together. None of them, though, realised just how long it would take to shape the stones while allowing each to keep its character and spirit."

Jahrain shook his head, ruefully acknowledging the considerable task their ancestors had taken on.

"There was also the continued opposition of the ancestral spirits dwelling there," Maklyr went on. "Although we are told it was greatly reduced by the idea to use local stone for the build. Nobody dared move the older stones again, except for a few that had to be removed for a while to allow the setting of the great portals. In the end, however, it was all finished. Then there followed months of celebration, culminating in the first ceremonies within the completed Temple."

Kefhan was fascinated by this account of the building of the Spirit House, but Weyllan was concerned with why the Northerners had been exiled and expunged from the people's consciousness. He put the question to Jahrain, who indicated that he should have patience as all would become apparent as the tale continued.

"After Myrthis' death, the elders chose a new leader, the best seer among them, a woman named Dersa. The following summer, the fever claimed our own seer, Tamakis, and he was replaced by his nephew Tamhain, who, whilst he was a charming talker and a handsome young man, was neither a mason nor a particularly powerful seer; he was ill-equipped to take the lead at such a difficult time. Now, two things happened that began the slide to the exiling of our kinfolk."

Jahrain paused for effect. "The first was that young Dersa fell in love with Tamhainso that the two joined together as man and wife. That should have been a good omen, but from the outset, they could not get on under the same roof and fought over everything. The second thing was that, try as they might, the seers could not harness the energy contained in the Spirit House. If anything, they felt it was working against them, blocking their movement through the spirit realms."

Weyllan sat up straight at that. He turned to Kefhan, jutting his chin forward, eyebrows raised in a gesture that clearly said, "You see? That is just as it was for me!"

Jahrain chuckled again. "Tamhain had the double arc of the old stones repaired and put into balance, but it made little difference. Some were able to draw a little help from the stones, but for many seers, they found they had better visions in the ring between the stones and the ditch, outside the Spirit House itself."

Maklyr took up the tale again to give his brother a chance to get his breath back."Now, Tamhain blamed Dersa, or at least her people, and she, in turn, blamed him for his lack of direction. The Children of Hatha followed their leader while we supported ours, and the poor folk from the Sunset Sea were blamed by everyone until they had had enough. Just a few summers after the completion of the Spirit House, they packed their belongings and left without a word. The very next year, after a particularly unsatisfactory Soul Days ceremony, when the omens for the following summer looked bleak indeed, Dersa and Tamhain separated after a heated row. Tamhain stormed off into the night. He was found late the next day, in the Temple at the base of the sunset doorway, with his head split open. Had he fallen? Was he murdered? Feelings were running high.

"The following night, when a group of Hatha's children were offended by an accusation one of our kinsfolk put out, they turned on him. Within a short time, there was a bloody battle running all across the village, with more and more local men arming themselves to aid their brothers. By daylight, our people had pushed the locals out of the village but were now surrounded, outnumbered many times over by Hatha's Children and their allies. In the cold light of the morning, everyone looked about them at the carnage and felt sick about what had happened in the darkness. Truly, the spirits had turned against these people and this land."

The Northerner shook his head sadly to emphasise his words."Well, along came Dersa, grieving for her husband despite having fought with him at their last meeting, and called out the war leaders of each side. 'There will be no feud!' she declared, laying down the law to both sides, with all of them in disgrace in her eyes, to fight so when they should have been mourning. Then she went into the village where her anger turned to despair and horror at the sight of the slaughter. It was said that more had died that night than there are stones in the Temple; many more were crippled or maimed. It would take the healers through until the harvest to repair their injuries and bring balance back into the people and the land they had spoiled."

Kefhan was silent, shocked at the image of carnage he had just heard. Weyllan gazed at the ground as Kefhan rested his head in his hands. He felt disbelief, unable to come to terms with what had happened between these erstwhile friends. He thought he would never understand the violence of an angry mob, nor how they failed to see the suffering they were causing. He could not look up, even when Jahrain continued his tale.

"Dersa came out to address the gathering. 'This is not a blame laid upon either side, but a curse upon us all. There is no easy solution. But to reduce the chance that this will happen again, this village will be abandoned and razed, with a great bank built around it to hold in the ill-fortune that has bred here today. Now the North folk must take their belongings and move across the River to the far side of the sacred hill where they will live in seclusion if they chose to remain here.' Dersa was effectively exiling us all. We were allowed to continue to share the Spirit House at the four seasons' ceremonials at first, but it was obvious we were not welcome. When Dersa died a few summers later, our seers were prohibited from entering the Temple, even to bless the dead at the year's end. Many of the survivors left to go back to our northern home, or to move elsewhere where they were more welcome, and those of our parents that remained did so in the hope that something would happen to heal the rift. Your vision in the Spirit House, Weyllan, is the first sign we have heard that there may have been forces at work deliberately trying to damage the harmony of our village and the work of the Spirit House."

Kefhan noticed Weyllan was quiet for the rest of their stay. He said little even on the journey home, beyond a fond farewell to Aslena when they passed her homestead as the twilight deepened.

Before they reached home, he caught Kefhan's arm. "This has been a revelation indeed. For the first time, I begin to understand what I experienced, that it was not some petty personal vendetta aimed at me alone, but rather part of a much broader campaign of hatred and interference being waged by Urda and her cronies on the other side. As she said, *they* controlled the stones; *they* could choose whom they allowed to access the power therein. I would lay odds that seers like Ursehan and Reirda, who claim kinship with her line, can get much easier access than Atharon's kin."

It was fully dark by the time they reached their home again. Interested as Kefhan was in Weyllan's new insight, he had no time to absorb it, as his young son greeted his return with a mighty howl, taking over all his attention and his emotion from that moment on. His wife watched him from the fire-side with a benevolent half-smile for a while, then turned suddenly to where Weyllan had seated himself across the fire from her.

"I forgot for a moment; there was another raid today! Or at least, there was some fighting up to the north of the Plain. I heard that one man was killed, and another is likely to die of his wound."

Kefhan looked up sharply as Weyllan responded, "When did this happen? And do you know more details?"

Kirah shook her head. "I know very little more. I heard the story around midday, so I suppose that it happened early today or even yesterday. Atharon's youngest came by to fetch you. You should go across and see him, I think."

Weyllan nodded his agreement, at once putting his cloak and cap back on. Kefhan offered to go as well, if he would wait a short time, but Weyllan replied, "No, brother, stay here – enjoy your son's company a little! There cannot be anything we can do at this stage, so I go out of courtesy and to hear the news in more detail. I will return shortly to tell you both what I learn."

Kefhan and Kirah heard the story from him later, on his return. Weyllan, it seemed, had arrived just as the chief's family were about to eat, so had accepted a small bowl of stew while he listened to the story of the latest episode in the ongoing feud.

"Atharon told me that a runner came to them late in the morning, to let them know that a hunting party had been ambushed down on the valley floor just off the Plain; not far in truth from where I and his sons fought our little battle last summer. There were five of our men from two of the home-steads up on the edge of the Plain who were involved. Appar-ently, they were following a deer trail late yesterday and had their attention set on their quarry when out of the woods came a shower of spears and arrows, followed by a ragged charge by nine or ten warriors bursting forth before even the spears had landed! With two of them hit by arrows, our fellows had little choice but to flee, but the others caught them. In the skirmish that ensued, young Tarohan was stabbed and fell dead. The others broke off, having wounded a couple of the enemy, so they said, and managed to make it away with both their injured comrades."

"Have you ever met this Tarohan?" Kefhan asked.

Weyllan thought he had met him once but had only a vague recollection of the young man's face. "I feel anger and grief for the Plainsman, almost as if I were kin to the poor man. Atharon says one of the wounded men will recover, but the other took an arrow in the gut. He looks set to die, if he has not already done so. Sadly, he was Withan, the son of Witlan, whom I helped the last time, and the old man has again been hard-hit by this feud."

Kefhan frowned. "If all this happened yesterday, it would have been too late to send out a war party with any hope of catching the culprits, so … well, I wonder why Atharon sent for you so soon after he heard the news?"

"Apparently, it was Syllan who sent for me. He had travelled up there to see what might be done for the families, and he thought it would be good if I could go with him. But we were visiting Jahrain, so Syllan went on alone. I was thanked for coming over to answer the summons anyway, and told that Atharon appreciated my growing loyalty, even though by that time, there was little more that could be done to help."

"Did you tell Atharon about the visit to the Northerners, Weyllan?"

"I will talk to Syllan about it next time we meet. My loyalty is not as total as Atharon believes. But then, I'm still not convinced that the chief's family have told us everything they know concerning our grandfather, and I took Atharon's protestations of appreciation with a little salt as well. And then there was the further injury to Witlan's family. A warrior's first instinct is vengeance, but as a seer, I have doubts about the usefulness of that strategy."

"Then, brother," offered Kefhan, "we must mull over what can be done to gain a better outcome."

Weyllan was not the only one thinking about vengeance that day. Far off to the south, Mikhan hobbled through the village to the compound where Thorachis lived. He was answering a summons from his chief and thought he knew what it would be about.

"I am glad to see you are recovered from your wounds at last, Mikhan. You *are* better now, I assume?"

"For the most part, Lord, I am. I cannot yet put much weight on my leg and I still have twinges of pain at times from this shoulder, especially when I think of those cursed stone-changers!"

"I have not forgotten them either, or their responsibility for the death of my son. I would have my vengeance on them all, but most certainly on that great ox that cast the spear into Granadh. It is about this very thing that I wanted to speak with you. A trader came through a few days ago, as I am sure you know. He told me that the stone-changer Weyllan and his kin now live with the People of Hatha on the great Plain. Had I known that was their destination, I would have had them killed as soon as they were taken, but the devious animals kept quiet about it!"

Mikhan smiled to himself. How little this said for the skill of Thorachis' own seers! They couldn't foresee the corn husks in the dregs of their beer, let alone the future of visitors and potential hostages.

"I would dearly like to be a part of that revenge," was all he said aloud.

"That, too, is why I called for you. I know you to be a man who can think and plan ahead, a good hunter and a determined pursuer. I wanted to ask you if you could think of an appropriate way to take our revenge and whether you would oversee its outcome for us both."

"One of my arrows would surely be the right end for such a hunt. But I think that would be too obvious; I would need a strategy that would get me out of there alive. I accept your commission, Lord, and will travel inland to the great Plain to see what transpires there. I will make my plans once I know what will succeed. But rest assured, Lord, the stone-changer will die. And as many of his friends as I can send with him."

"I leave this with you, then, Mikhan. If you are triumphant, you will become my most trusted aide and advisor, with all the rewards that go with that role. Take a slave with you to act as messenger and send him home to me when you have good news for him to carry."

Mikhan bowed his head to his chieftain and backed out of the house, well pleased with this development. His plans for revenge had been well advanced before the interview; he had intended to carry them through without any promise of reward, but this now meant that he was acting for his chief and would be well rewarded for paying his debts to the foreigners. He returned to his own home deep in thought.

He was not yet well enough to travel such a distance. So, despite his desire for revenge and the added impetus of Thorachis' offer, he decided the journey would have to be delayed until late in spring. That gave him ample time to choose which route he would take and what he would do when he arrived. He would need a story to tell; saying he came from Thorachis' tribe would hardly open doors for him. He made up his mind to say he came from the lands near the great spirit-path and that he came to consult the spirits at the Heart of the World. He was happy he could act the part of a seer well enough to fool those Plains-dwellers for a moon or two. He would be there and back before next winter set in.

CHAPTER TWELVE

Ever since the first raid, I had been feeling a desire to visit the Great Circle where the Aynash sprang forth from the earth, in the territory of the Children of Ayena, but had been put off by the risk of visiting as a friend to their enemies. Gradually, however, it came to me that I was ideally placed to try to broker an end to the feud, if indeed it was true no one could remember quite why it had started. Despite my initiation into the Temple, I was still considered an outsider, only a guest of the people of the Plain, and I thought I could use that ambiguity to offer some neutrality in any negotiations. I decided to discuss the idea with Turac.

"The role of peacemaker is best given to an outside visitor, so as a seer and part of the Spirit House, you will command respect from their elders. I think it a good idea, but I do feel you should have a plan in mind for ending the feud before you go; trusting fate to inspire you when you are there seems to be courting failure and our possible deaths," was his reaction when I proposed the trip to him.

I raised my eyebrows at this. "*Our* possible deaths? Does this mean you wish to come with me?"

Turac grinned. "Do you think I would miss witnessing this? Anyway, you need a representative of our people with authority to accept a deal if you can make one. I think your brother should come too. Three is an auspicious number. But please try to put together a few ideas to propose when we arrive."

We talked a little further about the journey and when best to undertake it. The planting would be over in a few days; once the fields were raked and the herds moved to their summer grazing, everybody would have more free time for travelling and talking. Turac went directly to seek approval from Atharon while I walked back to persuade Kefhan to come with us.

We decided to wait another full moon while the winter streams subsided. When they did, we had to wait again while the moon waned and darkened, then a few more days until it was again swelling towards the half-circle. Turac and the others felt we would have the strongest chance if we were to petition under a fertile, growing moon, always a time of good fortune and good omens. Kefhan and I were in total agreement with this strategy, having the same beliefs ourselves.

So it was that on a particularly hot morning at the very beginning of summer, we three set off across the plain towards the wide wooded valley and the downs beyond. We took a different route this time, keeping to the high ground along the edge of the valley of our sacred Ayn for a full march, then dropping down to the riverside to rest beside a wide reed-bed that whispered to us and the waterfowl throughout our stay. From then on, we followed the River, cutting across the meanders to maintain a straight line of travel.

The line of hills fell away to our left as we passed out from the Plain and into the broad valley, fording a small stream before angling away from the River to traverse the valley. The day grew hotter as the sun climbed to its zenith, and we stopped several times to rest, splashing water from the streams we crossed over our heads to cool us down. Ahead of us, we could see a pair of hills standing high above the valley floor, while behind them a line of hills ran across our path.

"What is that on top of the ridge?" asked Kefhan of our guide as we crested yet another low rise. "Is it a great mound, or a natural feature?"

"That is a great barrow, the tallest I have ever seen," said Turac. "It overlooks a pass up on to the downs behind those hills, which we will follow up to a ridge path beyond. That will lead us directly to the Great Circle and the Children of Ayena."

We aimed directly at the gap between the two hills, stopping in the saddle between them for a rest and a quick meal of dried meat and fruit. Then we pressed on along the side of a lower hill that joined our twins with the ridge behind. The woods were more open here, so that goats and cattle grazed on the rich grass, looking up with curiosity as we walked by. We saw several homesteads and a few other people on our way, but none showed any signs of aggression, or even interest in our passing. As we climbed the ridge along the little valley that cut into it, I could see the true size of the barrow that dominated the crest.

From our route, it looked like an easy climb to the mound, and I suggested we took a little time for a closer look. Turac had no objections, and a short while later we were seated on the grass by the forecourt of the barrow, looking out across the way we had come, with a view clear to the escarpment on the far side that marked the edge of the Plain. Turac indicated a point on the horizon to our right, saying that was where we had followed the herd down into the valley almost a year ago, and behind the trees was the place we had fought the raiders and recovered our property. To our left, almost hanging off the ridge on the far side of the valley we had climbed, were the remains of an enclosure, one of the oval spirit-rings of the ancestors long ago.

I turned back to our present location and asked Turac about the occupants of the mound.

"No one now living knows who lies buried there," said Turac. "It is even said that it is not an ancestral barrow at all, but the grave of one of the giants who roamed this land before ever we came to farm here."

I moved away from the others, and stood between the horns of the forecourt, facing the earthen wall blocking the tomb entrance. The place still held power aplenty; I felt the now familiar tingling of my spine and neck, but try as I might, I could make no contact with any spirits, nor was I rewarded with even a momentary vision. The day was hot. I was tired. I produced several reasons to myself for my lack of success, but I could not shake the feeling that the spirits were deliberately denying me access. When I returned to my companions, we set off again to walk the ridge path across the downs.

A small cairn marked the place where the path reached the top of the ridge; Turac paused to pick a flint nodule from the ground and add it to the pile, whispering a quick prayer as he did so. We followed his example, asking the spirits of the ridge to grant us safe passage and to lead us also on the path to understanding. Such shrines and cairns were common across the landscape, but I remember this one because, as I spoke my request, a brightly coloured jay flew straight towards us, swooped around our party, rolled once before us, then flew off in the direction we were to take. I had rarely seen anything I could be certain was an omen or sign before, but there could be no question here that the spirits had heard us and given us their blessing. I took a small button of rock crystal from my pouch and placed that beneath my flint nodule in thanks before we went on our way.

About halfway along the path, we had first sight of our destination. A little to our left, a thin column of smoke rose into the sky, whilst further towards the afternoon sun was a massive mound of earth and chalk, raised up from within a natural hollow to touch the horizon. As we came closer, I stopped to examine them both more carefully. The earth mound, already partially grassed over, had a flat top, and there seemed to be a faint path winding around the hill to the top. Turac did not know its proper use, although we reckoned it must be something connected to summoning sky spirits, or perhaps the sun spirit Lukan. It would also make a splendid signal hill, visible from a wide area across the territory, as Kefhan, ever the most practical of us, pointed out.

The smoke we'd seen was issuing from the central vent of a large, circular house, surrounded a few paces from the walls by a circle of stones. From the far side, we could see a double line of standing stones running down the hillside, reappearing some distance beyond, passing out of sight along the other side of a small hill that stood between it and the earthen mound. The ridge path passed close to the large hut, and Turac confirmed it was to this place we were headed first.

Close to, when we arrived there, I could see the sides of this house were not solid, but instead were formed of alternate wooden posts and standing stones with gaps between them, through some of which a man could step without hindrance. A larger circle of posts, each about twice my height, surrounded the structure. Most of these supported woven hurdles that blocked the way through to the building. The stones of the wall and of the outer ring were all of the same gritty rock that our own Spirit House was made from; I supposed that they had a nearby source of the material. The roof, too, was less substantial than it had at first seemed and was really little more than a thin layer of reeds tied to the ring lintels to provide shade inside.

There was no one about, so we entered the circle and the house through the nearest convenient gap. I was aware of an instant presence of power inside; a glance at Turac showed he had felt it as well. The hair on my neck tingled and my scalp was stung by a hundred tiny prickles as I looked around. There were two rings of posts inside supporting the roof and in the centre was a small fire set on a large potsherd, the smoke from which twisted up through the wide vent in the thatch. To the side of the fire, partly hidden by the roof-shadow, sat a hooded female figure. I could not see the eyes, but I knew they were set on us as we stood uncertainly to one side. The woman tossed a handful of dried leaves on the fire, which thickened the smoke and gave off a pungent, heady aroma.

"As strangers, I suppose it is fitting you should enter this house the wrong way. Approach the fire and let me see you clearly."

The voice was that of an old woman, although when we came nearer and could see her face, she looked to have fewer than thirty summers.

"Welcome! I am the keeper of the flame here in this house upon the ridge, at the beginning and the end of life's journey. What brings you here this day?"

We explained that we wished to speak with the Mother of her people, but we thought it better not to tell her why at this time. She cocked her head to the side a little and regarded us solemnly for a moment, waiting for us to continue.

When we said nothing, she tutted."So, you do not wish to tell me you come from the high Plain to talk about the feud that exists between our peoples? So be it, but now you see that I do not need your words to hear your hearts. This is the House of Truth, and all truths are revealed to the flame-keeper. Remember that if I have cause to question you again."

I bowed my head in apology. "We meant no rudeness, but we were not sure how much to say now. If you see our hearts, lady, then you will also know my brother and I are visitors. We have come to see if wounds can be healed, not to make demands."

"Indeed, I can, and you are welcome with your good intentions. I will pass word to our Mother that you are on your way and wish you well in your endeavour, young seer. I would take it as a kindness to hear how you fared when you return past this house again."

We left by the proper entrance this time, although to be fair to us it was barely bigger than the one we had used before, but was marked from the inside by two larger carved and painted posts. On them, I saw panels of spirals between diamonds or zig-zag bands, all reminiscent of images I remember from my times of crossing to the spirit world. On each post was a face, one a hideous, grimacing crone, the other a smiling child.

We walked down the slope along the avenue of stones, each pair set to be the opposite of its partner in shape and character, in constant reference to the forces of balance in the universe, between life and death, light and darkness, good and evil, and many others besides. We strode then on the path of life, constantly having to navigate our way between these oppositions to keep the balance as we progressed along the path. I was so occupied by my thoughts that I hardly noticed the looming banks of the enclosure ahead until we were hailed by two warriors who barred our way with their spears.

. . .

Our guards escorted us around the outside of the massive bank, across a track leading back up to the ridge nearby, then on up a valley towards a distant cluster of houses. They turned out to be a scatter of homesteads and small field gardens extending on along the valley and the lower slopes of the ridge, not unlike our own adopted home on the Plain. Dogs barked at our approach; a few goats and pigs looked up to see what was coming, but we saw no one except two small children, who ran out to the track to watch us pass.

Among the broadly rectangular homes and shelters, there was a slightly larger round building towards which we were taken. One warrior entered, and the other indicated that we should follow whilst he brought up the rear. Like the much bigger spirit house on the ridge, this one was lit by a central opening in the roof above a large hearth in which, however, no fire burned on this warm summer day. Near the centre of the room was a group of people sitting or standing around a seated woman wearing a rare woven dress, with ravens' feathers plaited into her hair. Around her neck she wore a string of seashell beads and a flint knife on a leather thong. Without doubt, this was the matriarch we had come to meet. She beckoned us to come forward and stand before her.

"Be welcome! I am Lomara, matriarch of the Children of Ayena. My sister Miranis has told me of your arrival and your mission, but not who you are. Please introduce yourselves."

I stepped forward. "I am Weyllan, a stone-changer from across the sea, visiting the Children of Hatha with my brother Kefhan here. This is Turac, a seer from the Plain and our guide during our stay here." I bowed my head in respectful greeting. "We come on our own initiative, but with the blessing of the leader of the Plain's people, and bring you greetings from Atharon himself, with the request that you hear our embassy."

She gave a curt nod, so I continued. "It seems to be in the nature of men that they will always find something over which to fight. Certainly, there are long-running feuds just like this among my own people, and I have heard of others on my travels. All too often, the hatred and anger continue long after the original cause has been forgotten and perhaps avenged. So that when we asked on the Plain what caused this feud, we were met with shrugs or puzzled frowns. I wondered if the people of this valley remember why your people fight my hosts generation after generation?"

Lomara frowned, leaning forward, her eyes narrowed and hard. "People have short memories when they are at fault. It all began with the building of that unnatural *thing* you call a spirit house! Your seer Myrthis asked for a few of our great boulders from the downs to rebuild the old circle but ended up taking every large stone in the fields! Then he put it about that their stones now held all the power and managed to get help from all over the land to build his temple. We were left a backwater, swept aside and insulted. To make matters worse, you could fit hisentire construction inside one of our inner circles!" She shook her head in annoyance and disbelief.

Turac took a small step forward."If I may speak; it is also said that when your great spirit house was built, your ancestors drew the power from our circle at the Heart of the World. Please understand, I am not trying to light fires here, but the source of our quarrel may be older than you suggest; both sides may have valid cause for calling insult or injury by the other. And yet..."

He got no further. One of the others in the room spat out, "That is a lie! Mother, how can you listen to this and not strike the enemy down?"

"Lomhan, my son, calm yourself and step back," replied the Matriarch, turning back to Turac. "It is our belief that the old circle on the Plain was dead or dying before ever we began our spirit house. The fault is with your people, Turac, not with mine!"

I opened my mouth to interject, but Turac was quicker. "So, you deny any injury on your side? I might have known! I remind you of your first remark about short memories; it seems to work both ways. Even so ..."

Again, he was interrupted, this time more forcefully, as Lomhan suddenly lunged forward with a long flint knife in his hand and an obscenity on his lips.

Turac started back, stumbling as the blade approached. I stepped towards them and swiped at the weapon, though I was still a full pace away. We all stopped in mid-stride as the knife spun from Lomhan's fingers, shattering even as it tumbled to the floor. There was silence for an instant.

Then Lomara spoke, quietly and forcefully. "Lomhan, return to your place. We will speak further on this later. Seer – Weyllan, is it? Thank you for preventing what would have been a terrible offence. Know that all of your party are here under my protection whilst in my territory, and this *will not happen again*!"

She turned to the others in the room, indicating us with her hand as she spoke. "Turac, my apologies. I hope you are unharmed? Good. I see no point in continuing this discussion when we are all so heated. We will speak again tomorrow at sunset. In the meanwhile, I am sure our visitors would wish to see our spirit house. Afron, I put our guests in your hands; please provide them with shelter and food. You can show them the Place of Balance in the morning."

I was inclined to agree with her about breaking off the negotiations, for I was still a little stunned and confused by what had happened. Had *I* caused the blade to deflect and shatter? That certainly was what Lomara seemed to be saying.

We bowed to the Matriarch as we followed our new host,

Afron, out of the house. He was Lomara's elder son, a man of comparable years to our companion Turac. He was well dressed in soft deerskin leggings under a smock decorated with shell beads, and walked with a distinct limp from what looked like a badly broken shin many years in the past. He led us along the hillside a short distance to a pair of huts, with two cleared circles where I guessed there were two shelters in winter. Afron saw my glance and explained that his sons had gone with their families to follow the herds, but that he usually stayed behind these days, with his wife and two young daughters.

As he spoke, two women emerged from one of the huts, coming forward to greet us. The older woman was his wife, Sekerta, and the other, his young daughter Kerta. Both, as we discovered during the course of a good meal served with a deal of barley beer, were well mannered and intelligent. I began to develop the germ of a plan as we talked and laughed the evening through.

We set out early the next day for the short walk to the temple. Afron was amicable, joking that this time we would be taken in through the 'proper' entrance. We walked along another way lined with stones, paired in oppositions just like the one we had come in by the previous day. This path led from the spirit house to two much older structures, a small banked enclosure and one of the old long burial mounds. Afron explained that this was the way the seers went to visit the old spirits of the departed, or to draw them in to the great circle to participate in the major celebrations and dances.

By contrast, he told us, the way between the circle and the House of Truth was used to take newly chosen spirits from the temple to be shown the correct pathways to the spirit world. The old and the new; sending them home and drawing them back; more oppositions built into this sacred landscape.

Beyond the pathway, the land was kept clear of trees for at least thirty paces, presenting a mosaic of grass pastures and bracken. Further back the valley was covered with scrubby woodland with a dense under-layer of bracken and brambles. It was quite unlike the countryside up on the Plain, and more akin to the coastal landscape we had encountered when we first landed.

I was taken aback by the sheer size of the Spirit House when we entered. The towering banks we had seen already looked twice as tall against the great ditch inside; together, they stood many times the height of a tall man. Within the ditch stood a ring of massive stones, with the greatest ones near the entrances, larger even than the stones of the Temple back on the Plain. Before us was a clear area roughly the shape of a crescent moon, beyond which stood two more stone circles, each as wide as our own Temple and each with a central feature: a dark cave or door to the underworld in the one; an enormously tall monolith pointing to the stars in the other. Heaven and earth, light and darkness, female and male, good and evil; the longer you thought about them, the more the oppositions multiplied, each new pair giving rise to another until your head spun.

The moon arena, we learned, was used to stage recitals of great deeds for the people and the spirits gathered there, for a winding-unwinding dance that told of journeys to the other realms. People also sat there to watch the seers dance in the inner rings.

It slowly came to me as I walked around this amazing place, that if our own Temple was the very heart of time and the world, this one formed the still point at the centre of all the opposites that gave balance to our existence. It was the fulcrum of the universe. I saw then that this was the sense in which Lomara had titled the place the previous day.

I sat on a small stone to contemplate for a while, and as had happened sometimes before, I gradually became aware that the colours of the world were darkening, fading into the monotone of the spirit world. This time, however, I seemed to rise high above the sandy plain, close to the stars of the night sky. They were scattered around me in the darkness, shining as bright orbs the size of the moon herself, each one aware and conscious. All of them were looking at me.

I saw no faces, no eyes, no signs of humanity; these spirits seemed beyond that. Thoughts formed in my mind without words, images and concepts I had no words for, weighing my soul as they pierced the darkest corners of my heart. There were my fears, my pride, my self-doubt, my vanity, my desires and my arrogance; all were caught in a wind, swirled up to be blown away, leaving behind sensations of fire and water, earth and air, the very essence of my being, all there within me in my own unique balance.

It seemed to me as I floated there that I could reach out to touch the nearest star. So, I did, cupping my hand beneath the sphere as if I were giving it support. The weight in my palm both surprised and unbalanced me, causing me suddenly to tip sideways. I thrust my other arm out to catch another star for balance. That seemed to help, and for a moment I thought all was well until I noticed I was slowly tumbling relative to the other spheres around me. So, I reached out with another arm, and then another, for it seemed I had as many arms as I needed, until the sky was again still. I was balancing ten or more shining spirit orbs in my hands; I could feel the currents flowing through my body between the stars as they used me as a bridge between their consciousnesses. I had never felt anything at once so strange and yet so fulfilling; the thought grew in my mind that I hoped this would continue forever.

It could not, of course. I knew it, even as I looked into one bright globe and saw a scene begin to resolve itself within the glow. There was green grass, and people dancing in a swirling, laughing spiral, closing in on a young couple at the centre of the space, skipping around them chanting and calling blessings upon them. I thought I recognised the couple, but whenever I tried to look more closely, their faces blurred, changing even as I sought to identify them.

Then the scene faded and I was back among the stars. I felt the balance again, stronger now, so I tried removing first one and then another of my supporting hands, without causing the tumbling to start again. As I released the final pair of spheres, I thought I began to comprehend the meaning of the vision and of my role in the events unfolding around me. Reality flooded back from the edges of my view until I was back once again in the great circle with the others.

They were the same, but I had changed forever. I knew that I was to be the bridge between the centre and the fulcrum, that the balance would flow through me to steady this world in the times of upheaval that were to come, and that the first step was to propose my solution to the feud between the two peoples who controlled these places at the heart of existence.

By the time we returned to seek counsel with Lomara that evening, I had settled on the plan I would offer. After the formal exchange of greetings, the Matriarch apologised for her son's behaviour previously. Turac nodded acceptance.

I agreed."It seems that as with so many of these long-running disputes, there is blame attributed by both sides, right or wrong, and I cannot see that you can end this by one side apologising for one slight whilst still nursing anger and distrust from another. There will always be imbalance, and the feud will rekindle. It seems to me that to regain the balance you all need, both leaders should meet to agree that *all* past grievances should be considered forgiven and void; that we should all settle on a simple reparation that will benefit both sides."

Lomara and Turac both raised eyebrows at this but absorbed it without obvious rancour. Lomara cocked her head to the side a little, regarding me with curiosity. "I am guessing that you have some form of reparation in mind, young Stone-changer?"

I smiled. "Of course. Although it is less a reparation than a reconciliation. Each of your spirit houses can channel great power and the great stones of each are a part of that process. Both are huge achievements, symbols of the prowess and strength of your peoples. To continue squabbling is to reduce the power of both tribes; it will lessen the impression your ancestors can make upon the spirits. So, I propose not just an end to the feud, but a union between the two peoples. I have already spoken to Kerta and obtained her consent to try this; I suggest a marriage between your grand-daughter and the second son of Atharon, my friend Syllan. He is a good man, a chief's son in every way. He will make her a fine husband. It will link your peoples at the highest level, and provide a good reason for everyone to refrain from further aggression."

"Are you suggesting we send Atharon a hostage? Because that will not be acceptable to my people at all." Lomara's voice had developed a distinct edge.

"No, not at all. I think these two are of similar temperament and may well become firm friends. It is for them to decide if they accept the match; I would not have it any other way. Kerta will be free to come and go without hindrance, as will all other members of both tribes. I suggest it as a symbol of the future friendship between your peoples; one which everyone – on both sides – will want to support."

"And, of course, there is the question of a settlement for the bride?"

"I thought of that. On my travels to this island, I came across many different ways of making this payment. Some depend on where the couple dwell after their marriage, to compensate for the loss of a son or a daughter. Others seem to give the husband wealth to keep the bride happy, whilst still others have no arrangement at all. My uncle used to tell me that raiding for cattle mixes up the bloodlines, and strengthens the herd by this means. So, I propose an exchange to replace the raiding, going both ways equally. Perhaps a dozen animals each, every two years or so? I do not think it is for me to pronounce on a final figure."

There was a short silence. Then Lomara addressed her son. "Afron, we are discussing the betrothal of your daughter. Do you wish to speak at this time?"

"I …I am quite stunned, Mother. I would wish to consult with my wife and child first. However, if Kerta understands the proposal and has truly given her consent, I will not oppose it. This would be a good way to heal the old wound. It may even, as Weyllan suggests, improve our hand in dealing with the spirits."

"Very well. I, too, think this is a sound idea and may be just what we need to end this feud. But whether Kerta or another is offered, I will not say until we have spoken with her ourselves. You should return to Atharon – and Syllan – now, to tell them your plan. If they accept it, I will come with Afron in ten days to discuss the details with them. I hope I will see you again then, Weyllan, and wish you a safe return."

We were dismissed, so we made our farewells and withdrew.

. . .

We were now faced with a new problem. It was growing dark, and we had had no renewed offer of hospitality from Afron, nor any indication that any was intended. I remember we stood looking down the valley towards the spirit house, a little bemused until Kefhan suggested we walk up to the ridge path before we lost all the light, there to look for a safe place to sleep. So, we set out up the slope to the ridge path, turning south along it towards home. We walked for a while, but the land was very open, and we saw no shelter until we came again to the strange House of Truth, where we had met Miranis. As we approached, she was standing at the edge of the outer stone ring watching us. She waved when she saw we had spotted her.

"Greetings again," she said when we arrived."I think you seek a safe place for the night. There is none safer than this, so be welcome as my guests and keep an old woman company with your stories."

So, we entered the temple for the second time, through the right entrance as befitted our more familiar status. A young girl, introduced as Miranis' granddaughter, brought us food and water from their home across the ridge path as we sat talking well into the evening. The keeper laughed a good deal, telling us a little about her people, whilst Kefhan and I in return told her of our home far away, and why we had undertaken this great journey to the Temple on the Plain. I felt relaxed, totally at ease, and despite the dormant power I sensed from time to time, I had no visions or portents.

As I was thinking this, Miranis looked across at me, smiling. "The House knows you are guests here in need of sanctuary, so it will not engage with you unless you will it to do so. Most days, this is a place where life meets death, and they exchange views and knowledge, the spirit world with the living. They are here with us, but tonight the spirits can just listen, enjoying our stories, as we ourselves are doing."

As we began to think of sleep, a light drizzle started to fall, spitting on the embers in the open hearth. The thin layer of thatch was enough to keep most of it out, so we lay down on the beds of hide-covered straw that were put out for us, wrapping our cloaks about us to deflect any rain that came through, and slept soundly until daylight. We broke our fast with some warm bread with goat's cheese and a handful of early strawberries to share as we made ready to leave.

Miranis came over with an armful of logs for her fire, and stopped to say farewell."You have chosen a long road to travel, Weyllan; I see it will not be an easy one. I wish you good fortune in your work. Whatever comes of this attempt to end the feud between my people and yours, be certain you will always be welcome here under my protection. I hope you will return soon to lighten another evening for me, my friends."

I smiled back at her, thanking her warmly for her hospitality and friendship."I have high hopes for my solution. I feel certain that Syllan and Kerta will make a fine match. Know that you will be most welcome to stay with us should you come to visit your kinswoman, if you can entrust your flame to your granddaughter for longer than a night, that is."

So, we parted on the best of terms, and despite the persistent drizzle, our spirits were high as we hiked off back along the ridge path to the distant Plain.

CHAPTER THIRTEEN

Over the next few days, Kirah heard the story of her partner's mission to Lomara and the Place of Balance many times and found herself fascinated by the simplicity of Weyllan's solution. She had made many new friends on the Plain and knew most of the women were tired of the ongoing feud and the disruption it regularly brought to their lives. That being said, she also acknowledged that they almost all blamed the Children of Ayena for the hostilities, and it would take something extraordinary to overcome that bias.

Weyllan assured them that the young Kerta was just the person to achieve this; with her beauty, her warmth and her outgoing friendliness, she would melt the hearts of all the men and most of the women on the Plain and put them in a mind to forgive and forget any slights by her people, real or imagined. His confidence was infectious, and Kirah found herself awaiting the arrival of the bride-to-be with eager anticipation.

When word finally came that they were about to arrive, she and Kefhan hurried along the ridge to the chief's house to witness the first meeting of the two leaders and the betrothed couple. She struggled to keep up, with the child in her arms trying to unbalance her at every step, but she made no complaint; she had found, to her surprise, that she enjoyed motherhood so much, there was little that the wriggling bundle she carried could do that upset her. She was quite happy to divide her attention between the rough path and her rapidly growing son, who smiled endearingly back at her, blissfully unaware of the danger he was bringing to them both by taking her attention.

When they arrived, Weyllan was already there beside Atharon, his wife Sylwa, and their sons. Syllan looked nervous and uncomfortable in his newly-painted and beaded tunic and unpainted face.

Enthis had come with them; he and his three fellow captives were to be given their freedom that day as a sign of goodwill. Kirah received his warm farewell with a smile, and Kefhan took his hand before the slave crossed the yard to join his fellows awaiting the arrival of their matriarch. He seemed at ease, but Kirah suspected he would be far more emotive and much happier by tomorrow night, when he and his comrades returned at last to their own homes and families. She silently wished him well, and sent a blessing ahead of him to his wife and children who waited for him among the Aynash who had remained at home.

Among the crowd gathering in the forecourt of the homestead, Kirah saw familiar faces everywhere and was again reminded of the extent to which they had become a part of this community in the past few months. There was Aslena, who must somehow have foreseen the event to have arrived all the way from her home over the Ayn. Across the clearing stood Tokhan, his arm familiarly around the shoulder of a tall, black-haired woman who leaned towards him to complete the embrace.

Kirah had heard that Tokhan had found a girl at last, one

who worshipped her heroic warrior with an unshakeable love, but this was her first sight of her. Kirah cocked her head slightly and smiled warmly at Tokhan, who, sensing her attention, returned a shy smile, and nodded in greeting.

Then all eyes turned towards the small party approaching along the ridge, watching intently as they came close enough to see their expressions. Lomara stopped them about four paces from the reception party and made a slight bow to Atharon and his sons. She wore a long gown of soft doeskin, stained a dark brown and richly painted with spirals and scenes of hunting and dancing. At her neck was a string of beads, alternate amber and jet, light and dark, with a single, massive, bear-tooth at its centre. Her hair was woven with raven feathers just as the men had described; they gave her a wild and rather frightening countenance that commanded respect without a single word spoken.

Greetings and honorifics were duly exchanged and Atharon, returning the bow to Lomara, ushered them all into his house. Kirah was aware of these events, but her attention was on the two young protagonists who were sizing each other up for the first time. Kerta looked relieved and smiled a silent greeting to Syllan, who on his part seemed quite taken aback at his betrothed's comely appearance. He glanced behind him to see who she was smiling at before he realised that he was the target, then grinned sheepishly back and raised an awkward hand to wave at her.

In deliberate contrast to her grandmother, Kerta's gown was bleached to a pale cream colour and enhanced with rows of tiny white shell beads. Her hair was tied back in a broad plait that hung down her back, and decorated with a garland of green wheat and daisies. Syllan's eyes were fixed on her and followed her as she entered the house.

Then, as he turned to go in, Kirah saw him look wildly up

at the sky and shake his head as if to clear it. She laughed to herself and thought it as promising a beginning as anyone could have wished for. Young Syllan was clearly smitten with his intended, and she was, it seemed, prepared at least to consider him. It seemed unlikely that either would raise any further objections to the proposed union. Kirah turned away and left them to it, walking as far as her own house talking to Aslena, whom she had found she both liked and respected.

They were back at Atharon's compound three days later for a feast in celebration of the marriage and the proposed peace. There must have been ninety people there, the heads of lineages and senior seers of the Plainsfolk, and Lomara's entourage had been swelled by around twenty of her people who had walked over to join the party.

It had taken Atharon's kinswomen two days to prepare everything. Kirah, with other brewers, brought along pots of barley beer to help wash the food down, but the mats filled with food and the three pigs roasting over three fires around the compound had all been arranged by the family. She remarked that there were, after all, drawbacks to being a hereditary chieftain, and was rewarded with a broad grin of appreciation from Kefhan.

The feasting went on from around midday to well after midnight, although only a few guests stayed for the entire event. They came to witness the union of the two families and the healing of the rift between the two peoples, so for many, once they had eaten their fill, there was no reason to stay and plenty to do at home.

Two more pigs and a pair of deer were roasted; there were stews of hare and bustard, pigeon, and even badger from setts near the River. It was too early for nuts or fruits, and the winter storage had long since run out, but the cooks added flavour and bulk with greenery and a few edible tubers. With a constant fresh supply of beer as newcomers dropped in, there was plenty to go around; the spread Atharon provided would be remembered by everyone for many years to come.

There was no ceremony, either. Among the people of the Plain and for some distance to the north, the statement of intent was the bond, alongside any exchange of gifts. In this case the Children of Ayena had brought a small herd of cattle, including six which were given directly to Witlan, for distribution among his neighbours affected by the recent fracas. Atharon in turn presented Lomara with four hides ready for tailoring, two fine stone axes and a small copper dagger with a decorated hilt made by Kefhan and Weyllan for just this purpose.

Syllan led his bride to join the stone-changers as the light began to fade, sitting to talk with his friends for a time. There, Kirah was formally introduced to Kerta before the men started discussing a recent hunt, leaving the women to become acquainted. Kirah soon found herself warming to her young companion, being reminded of Weyllan's prediction that she would melt hearts wherever she went. She had a generosity of spirit and such strong empathy that she seemed at once to offer support and friendship to whomever she was with, whilst being totally unaware of the gift she wielded so easily. Before long, Kirah found herself entertaining the new bride with the saga of their journey from the White Mountains to the Plain, of the adventures they had had and the people they had encountered along the way, with Kerta gasping and laughing by turns as the tale unfolded. When Kirah moved back from the heat of the fire to feed an increasingly demanding Ulrac, the talk moved to marriage and motherhood. There, too, Kirah kept her new friend in good humour with both her story and her advice.

Kerta asked at length about Weyllan, the architect of all that was happening. "Is he really a powerful mage, an extraordinary seer? I was so in awe of him when he stayed with my parents; he carries such a powerful aura about him and seems to see right inside the people he talks to."

Kirah smiled. She could easily recognise her kinsman in that description, yet there was so much more to him than that.

"I think he is still growing into his power," she replied. "With every new crossing he makes, he gains more control and sees further. Already he has outstripped his tutors, but he remains humble. I worry that his power may one day cause jealousy between him and Syllan, but I am also sure that he will be unaware of it and quite at a loss to explain it if it ever happens. He is a thoroughly good man who seeks only the best for others. He cares very little for his own comfort on the way." She smiled absently to herself at this unexpected prediction. "I don't know where that came from. Please don't think I meant to suggest that Syllan isn't a good man as well!"

It was Kerta's turn to smile and to reassure her new friend that she took no offence. "You like Weyllan a great deal. To hear you talk, I would think he was also your husband …" Then she realised the implication of what she had said, and in her turn, began to stutter a rapid apology.

Kirah collapsed laughing, almost upsetting the child in her arms, causing him to stir into wakefulness for a few moments. She pulled herself together, but sat for a while turning the girl's assertion over in her head. She was really fond of Weyllan, who, after her husband – and now her son – was the most important person in her life. She admired his skill, his power and the way he cared for his little family. For there was no doubt in her mind that he was the head of the family, not her slightly older husband.

She looked across the fire at the two men in her life, and felt glad that she had both of them at her side on this great adventure. She thought almost for the first time about her decision to come with them on this odyssey, deciding she was glad she had made that choice, too. If she died of a fever in the next summer, she would still have lived a fuller life than ever she could have expected at home; although having cured more than one fever this summer already, she felt confident she had the skills to keep herself alive rather longer than that.

The moon waxed to full and faded away to nothing again. The crops by now were well up, with the grains on the wheat and barley swelling in the summer warmth. Kirah walked through the field, testing occasional grains between her fingers. Another moon cycle, she thought, until they would be ready for harvest. In the meanwhile, there was little they could do. Like many other women at this time, she took the last of their reserve of barley to brew a final batch of beer, keeping back the wheat to bake bread. They would run out well before the harvest, but they had lived without bread for longer periods in the past and would come to no harm.

Kefhan went with two younger men to take their combined herds to fresh pastures on the plain but, with Ulrac still at her breast, Kirah decided to stay where she was to continue her healing and potting around their homestead. Weyllan was out much of the time, with Syllan or Turac, or visiting his cousin in the summer pastures. He had told her that he had tried to broach the subject of the Northerners' status with Atharon, but the chieftain had changed the subject, and had refused to be drawn when Weyllan brought it up a second time.

One day, after a few days of unseasonal rain and whipping winds, a stranger walked up from the River ford to their house...and opened a new chapter in their lives.

His name was Nyren, and he travelled with his wife Wheris and their young son Nykhin. He had spoken with Jahrain across the River, who had directed him to come directly to their homestead. Kirah greeted the newcomers and after hearing their introductions, she led them out past the herb patch to where Weyllan was tending Ulrac, and trying to sharpen his worn-out metal knife.

The introductions over, Nyren opened the conversation. "You look as if you need a new blade. Do you have any more of the ore stone you need to make one?"

"A little," Weyllan replied, cautiously. "What is your interest in stone-changing?"

Kirah took charge of her son to allow the seer to concentrate on his visitor, but lingered to listen to the conversation.

"I, too, am a stone-changer, which is why I was directed to you and not to your chieftain. We live over yonder," Nyren indicated the direction of the sunrise, "about three days' walk. I have long since run out of ores, but then I heard from another of our kind that the right rocks are to be found scattered in the hills between here and the Sunset Sea. I decided to travel there to seek them out. If we can find a source of the ore on this island, it will change our lives, and those of our hosts, forever."

Weyllan was silent, but Kirah saw his eyes scanning his visitor's face, trying to assess the newcomer. Nyren was a wiry little man, easily a hand-width shorter than Weyllan, with a lined face that suggested he was also many summers older. But the wide-set eyes were clear and open; his face spoke of an honest and straightforward character. She watched a smile lighten Weyllan's expression as he held out his hand in welcome. Wheris, too, was a small woman, thin-faced but wearing a warm countenance that to Kirah seemed continually on the edge of laughter.

Realising that Weyllan was not going to fulfil his duty as a host, Kirah turned to Wheris with a smile and asked her if they would like something to eat.

"Yes, thank you!" was the immediate reply. "We have been walking for some time since our last stop. If you allow it, I would be happy to help to prepare it."

A small beaker of the last of their beer was found, then some cold meat from the previous night, with some freshly baked wheat bread to accompany it. The men were becoming more animated as they found out about each other and ate automatically as they talked, so Kirah took the opportunity to begin a conversation with Wheris.

Nyren, she was told, came originally from the mainland, living near the coast far to the south of the point at which Kirah and her men had crossed the water. He had arrived as a young lad nearly twenty summers before, travelling with his uncle and mentor, heading for the Plain, but had instead made themselves a home on the southern chalk-lands. Wheris was a local girl and had singled out Nyren within a year as her partner in life, although he hadn't found this out for another year or so. They had had three children, but sadly only the boy Nykhin had survived. Both parents doted on the boy, who it seemed still managed to keep his independence and had inherited and begun to demonstrate his father's abilities as a stone-changer, if not yet as a seer.

After the meal, Weyllan announced, "You are welcome to stay with us for a short while. Indeed, if you wish to stay longer, we will welcome your company, but we will need to put up another hut for you. What we should do now, however, is go and pay our respects to Atharon, our chief, and let him know you are here."

In the end, Nyren stayed through the rest of the moon-cycle. Kirah helped the men set up a light shelter of bent saplings and hides, then when Kefhan came home a few days later, they began to repair the little furnace to make more metal knives. By adding a handful of blue ore to the pieces of Weyllan's worn blade and another of Nyren's with a broken point, they produced enough copper to make four blades; two to replace their own knives and two for trading on the journey.

For it soon became clear to Kirah that Weyllan intended to go with Nyren when he headed off on his prospecting quest, taking the opportunity to travel further on to the hills whence came the blue-grey stones with which the first Spirit House had been ringed. She had talked with him several times about these ancient stones; she knew that he was convinced they held the key to breaking the grip of Urda and her part in blocking the power of the Temple. She knew now he would not rest until he had traced the source of the stones and found a way to regain control of the ancestral spirits linked to them.

Over the next few days, as they harvested their little field of grains, Kirah often found herself worrying for Weyllan's safety, but was well aware that it was not her place to stop him going. But when Kefhan voiced his intention to join the others in this new adventure, she put her foot down firmly and immovably.

"Kefhan, my love, I know you wish to go with your brother, and to play a role in this adventure, but you are a father now; your family need you here to provide for us. We need you to hunt and to watch over our animals up on the Plain. I love you both, but only one of you can leave this time.

You are my rock, and Weyllan is our dreams; he should go on this dreamer's quest while you must stay behind."

Kefhan looked crestfallen, but Weyllan just shrugged. "I fear there is no argument you can raise against that, brother. I promise to come back whole to tell you both about it all before winter sets in again."

And that, it seemed, was that. Weyllan took a spare cloak, packed some food and made several new arrows to fill out his quiver, and within three more days, he and their visitors were gone.

CHAPTER FOURTEEN

Late in the day, we crossed the watershed, descending towards the great wetlands below. You could see a good distance from up here, across the marshes to the low ridges that flowed into the hill country to the north, off to our right. Below us, the landscape was a mosaic of vast reed-beds and open water that caught the early autumn sunshine, glimmering like a thousand crystals amongst the brown of the reeds. This web of waterways, lakes and marshes stretched as far as you could see towards the sunset, broken only by occasional low ridges covered in ash and willow, from some of which the smoke of farmsteads rose vertically in the still air.

From the middle of the marsh there rose the Isle of the Dragon, with its tall oval ridge like an upturned boat; the back, so they said, of the sleeping beast, with its tail running out behind towards the sun. I had heard from time to time tales of these strange, magical creatures, but had never seen any evidence of one. Except for the spirit beneath the Sacred Hill at home, and I wondered, not for the first time, if that denizen of the underworld was the reality behind these dragons; not a living creature at all but a demon come out from the spirit realms. To the local folk, it was a place of mist and dark spirits to be avoided if possible. My first sight of it did nothing to gainsay that opinion.

We spent the night at a small clutch of farmsteads on the shore with farmers who supplemented their larders with some of the abundant fish and fowl that lived on the wetlands. Fish were almost never eaten elsewhere on this island, so it took us a while to get used to the muddy flavour again after so long.

The next morning, we set out to cross the marshes in a log boat paddled by our host's brother and sons, while he worked the steering paddle at the stern. Nyren, Nykhin and I all took our turns at the paddles, although I think those stocky folk could have carried on happily all day without our aid. I have rarely seen so many different boats as we did that day. It seemed that every household owned several for different uses: canoes of elder and birch bark, log boats of every size, one or two flat-bottomed plank boats, and a score of the small round skin coracles they called koryak in their dialect. These were everywhere, skipping across the water with one or two paddlers, often with a dog or even a couple of pigs tethered in the boat with them. The men fished from these boats or sometimes hunted the waterfowl along the edges of the reeds. Canoes and log boats were better to take into the reed-beds after moorhens and small birds, or simply to get from one place to another quickly, as we were doing.

The depth of the water varied considerably, sometimes so shallow you could wade through it and keep your breech-clout dry, at others deep enough to cover a man over his head. Deep enough for the water spirits to pull your feet down and bed them in the mud, to cloud your sight, confounding you in the swirling murk until you knew not which way was up, drowning in the darkness even as they mocked you. I shivered at these dark thoughts, drawing my cloak more tightly around me. We entered another bed of reeds, the brown stems crowding around us. They rustled threateningly, increasing my apprehension with every length we paddled. The boat grounded, floated free, then hit the bottom again.

"We need to walk the boat through here," said our host. "Keep your shoes on, or you will get your feet cut on the reeds." He was right, for although the water was very shallow, my ankles and legs were soon covered in scratches.

"At least the water is too shallow for the spirits to take us by our legs and drag us away," laughed Nyren nervously.

I was glad to hear that I wasn't the only one finding the place eerie; I acknowledged him with a grunt and a smile."Perhaps they *are* trying to take us," I joked. "Their claws are tearing me to pieces!"

The others joined in the laughter, but our host assured us we would get used to it. And so, we did, for we had to walk the boat through three or four shallow stretches that day, becoming quite familiar with the procedure by evening.

There was a wild beauty to this landscape that warmed my soul in spite of the evening chill on the water, but my nascent love for the marshes died when the sun went down and the air filled with humming, biting, night-flies. The only option to being bitten by each of them in turn was to squat in the smoke of the fire until your eyes watered and your throat was too parched to talk. That one night was enough to quash any positive feelings for the wetlands forever.

We camped under a tree for the night, waking in the morning to the smell of fish cooking on a spit over the fire, overseen by the two young lads. The night-flies were still about, but by this time seemed dazed and disinterested. Or perhaps they were overfull, sated from a night of feasting on our blood. Either way, they let us alone, so after a quick meal of the fish and some bread washed down with watery beer, we were on our way again, reaching the coast shortly after noon.

The tide was low; the wetlands were separated from the sea by a wide bar of muddy sand, more than an arrowshot across but never much over my height above the water on our side. We stayed in the boat, rowing north along the inner shore until late in the day we came to a small hamlet, a cluster of ten or so huts and lean-tos where the bar rose above the tide line high enough for some grass and a few trees to take root. On our side, several log boats were drawn up with two koryaks on the grass, whilst on the channel shore, two masted boats lay tilting towards one another amidst a web of nets spread out on the grass to dry.

At least the salt air kept most of the night-flies away, and we spent a much more pleasant evening than the previous one there with the coastal fishermen. Over the course of the meal, we negotiated a passage across the sound and along the coast a way towards our destination in exchange for a handful of my barbed arrowheads and a tiny nugget of gold. We also learned that the people of the far bank of the channel spoke a rather different dialect to ourselves; we were told that we would have to learn scores of new words if we were to converse with them. Our current hosts then started bombarding us with the words we would need to greet folk, to ask our way, and to thank them for whatever hospitality they offered. Before we went to bed, I sat up for a while, reaching out to the water spirits to ask for fair weather and a safe journey. I did not fully cross to the other side, but somehow felt I had been heard by someone.

· · ·

The crossing proved uneventful; with the tide behind us, we shot across the water at an exhilarating speed. Then we made our way along a coast of low cliffs and muddy inlets to a rocky headland, where several caves were visible above the tide as we sailed by. Once again, the sailors plied us with words to learn, for rivers and hills, for headlands and animals, but there were so many I remembered only a few from that telling. We lost the wind as we turned into the wide bay beyond and had to paddle towards the shore until we picked up a light breeze filtering down the broad estuary behind us. Then we were able to raise the big deerskin sail again to push us gently along close to the shoreline. Broad mud flats backed by steep hills were replaced by more cliffs and rocky points. A short way past a small outcrop, the boatmen spotted a safe place to land and brought us ashore beside the mouth of a stream that flowed through several channels across the beach down into the bay.

That valley ran off in the wrong direction, so the four of us shouldered our bags and set off along the shore in search of a stream that led inland the way we needed to travel. We did not have to go far. We were soon following another little valley in past a confluence, then up a path that climbed the side of the combe to the hills beyond. We followed one of the ridges towards the afternoon sun, then dipped down into a pretty valley with a small homestead at either end. In the centre stood a single house with daubed slate walls and a stone roof, the like of which I had never seen before.

Beside it as we approached, we could see a small pool fed by a bubbling spring, overhung by a great and ancient willow. An old man came out of the house to greet us with a raised arm and a friendly "hallo", beckoning us to join him.

I still remember him as if he was standing before me now, for his appearance was as extraordinary as his house. He had a long grey beard and shaggy locks tied roughly into seven braids; his clothing was of ill-matched animal hides roughly sewn together, decorated with animal bones and teeth tied on with leather thongs. But his voice was warm and friendly, and he spoke our language quite well, his accent close enough to the folk of the marshes on the other side of the channel to be readily understandable to us now.

"I am Teyrin, Keeper of the Spring. Welcome to the Vale of Daela, whose pool this is, and by whose bounty we all enjoy such good health and long life."

I could not argue with that; he looked to have seen at least fourscore summers himself. I decided that the spirit of the spring was a force worth keeping on our side. I bowed my head to show respect.

"Greetings. we are strangers here; is there a proper way to ask the blessing of this spirit on ourselves and our journey?"

He smiled, nodding, and led us to the edge of the spring."You are a seer," he said, as if it was obvious. "Open your mind with a greeting; experience Her for yourself. Your companions can offer their thanks and take the water in their hands as is the usual practice hereabouts."

So, I did as he suggested, kneeling beside the spring with one palm flat upon the surface, closing my eyes to seek the way through to the lady of the spring. I was not kept waiting long, as almost immediately a vision appeared before me, not of the young and beautiful nymph I had half expected, but of a short, mature woman with a lined face that nevertheless radiated warmth and a powerful life-force. Her mouth moved soundlessly as the words once more appeared in my mind without passing my ears.

"Welcome, Stone-changer, welcome to you and your friends. I am Daela, guardian of these waters and the valley from which they flow. You seek the source of the ancient stones you have in your Spirit House; you also, I see, hope for news of your kinsman. The first we can help you with, but you are the first of your kind to pass through my land; I know nothing of your …aah, your grandfather?

"For the source you seek, look on the far side of the mountains for both the rocks and those who once used them. A seer there will tell you what you need to know; she may even have news of your other quest. I see also that your companion seeks a source for the stone upon which you both work your magic. Tell him that from the hill she must travel two or three days towards the midsummer sunrise, where he will find what he seeks. Drink of my water, leave a gift for my friend here and you will all have a safe journey. Long life I cannot offer you; it is mine to give only to those who stay in my valley and the hills around it."

Without waiting for a reply, Daela faded back into the waters and returned me to my own world. Only a ripple on the pond showed that anything had happened. I cupped my hand into the spring, taking a few draughts of the water as directed. The others had waited for me, so we crossed together into the little house, where Teyrin produced bread and some cold stew for us to share with him. I liked the old man, and in view of his friendship with Daela, I gave him two fine gifts; a small copper blade and a tiny amulet of bone covered with gold foil I had made at the smelt with Nyren a few days earlier.

We left shortly afterwards, following his directions, following a narrow track around the hillside, down into a straight valley, carved by a gentle brook which flowed towards the setting sun. Then our path led us upstream, beside a larger river that ran south to the sea in the bay we had left that morning. We saw several small farmsteads, sometimes alone, or in small clusters of two or three families, but nothing you could call a village. We spoke to a number of the folk in them, but despite our lesson with our sailing friends, we could as yet understand only a little of what they said to us.

Continuing far upstream, we walked until just after sunset, stopping for the night in a copse of trees on a more open terrace where our river was joined from the far side by another. I remember how peaceful it was in that valley, with the rippling sound of the water flowing by thirty paces away, and the evening birdsong as the light faded, the sky turning from pink through orange to purple. Tomorrow would take us to the mountains, and we would see if we could find the way across that Teyrin had described to us.

As it transpired, we did not cross the hills until the day after. The morning was spent ambling up the meandering valley, crossing the river several times at convenient fords, taking time out to shoot a pair of young ducks for our meal and roasting them on a greenstick spit at midday. By mid-afternoon we came to another confluence where the valley widened out, where we stopped at a farmstead for directions. The occupants advised us to leave the crossing until morning, and we spent the night in a guest hut they kept for their children's families when they visited, which from their account, they often did.

The weather changed in the night; we awoke to a world full of dull grey light and a persistent drizzle that continued throughout the day. We crossed the river for the last time and climbed the first range of hills, following deer paths through the gorse, the woods of the valley beginning to give way here to upland bogs.

We made offerings at a wayside cairn and stopped a while to look at a circle of small stones, quite newly built by their appearance. They were the same bluish-grey as our own ancient stones, and some had similar small white patches as well. I felt a shiver pass through me as I looked on them and knew I was close to the source of their power. There was nobody about to ask, so we said a greeting to the spirits there then carried on our way towards the rocky tors on the ridge beyond.

Next, we skirted a particularly boggy stream and climbed up its valley to a saddle between two peaks, at last seeing down the northern side of the hills past numerous stony outcrops on the slopes before us, down towards the distant Sunset Sea. The view was astounding, even in the rain, so we sat down to admire it for some time, taking a well-earned rest at the same time. Then the clouds closed in and the world was shut off from us. We started down the hills towards some smoke we had seen in the distance.

After that, we walked between two stony tors, skirting a long tongue of stunted woodland that licked at one of the outcrops, then went down across the bracken and mossy bog-land to a broad river valley, where after some searching, we finally found the source of the smoke we had seen from the hilltop. The shepherd's wife who greeted us pulled aside the hide door cover and let us in to dry by the fire while she warmed a little beer for us. She told us that if we wanted information, we should continue across the river to the home of their seer and mother, Tulria by name, who she thought could tell us whatever we needed to know better than anyone else in the valley. So, when the drizzle eased off, we set out on the last leg of our journey beneath a watery sun that sank slowly towards the sea.

Tulria was a formidable woman, who wore her untold summers with an ease which could only be admired, with a big frame, meaty arms, and a hearty laugh to match her physique. Her husband was tall but wiry, a quiet man by comparison, and a foil to her in almost every way. Yet it was soon apparent they thought as one being, so that whatever one decided the other was already acting upon. It was a display well worth the observation, and I often found myself admiring their closeness.

At first, our conversation was limited by our poor grasp of each other's language, but as the days passed, Nyren and I gradually learned enough to say more than please and thank you, and how long it would take to walk from here to there. Wheris and Nikhin, on the other hand, seemed to have the gift of tongues; within a few days, the boy was prattling away like a native speaker. We used him as our translator until his mother, and eventually we men, caught up.

Tulria was a rich source of information about the stones that had come from this area, about their magical properties and the legend of their disappearance. She told us how, many generations ago, a man they knew as Mynradys had been ousted as head seer for his people, and rather than stay to work with his successor, he travelled far towards the sunrise to find a new destiny. Some years later he had returned with a flotilla of boats carrying a great band of warriors, demanding he be given the ancestor stones of the great circle. He had travelled, he explained, to the very centre of the cosmos, and there had seen a sacred place of great power. If he was to set up the circle anew at this focus, the power of their ancestors would be so mighty as to dominate all the peoples of the world, and perhaps all the spirits of all the seven realms as well.

In the end, they had held a great council at which many people agreed to the venture, and many families even packed up to go with them to live at the heart of the universe. Over the next year or so the stones from two ancestral circles had been uprooted and carried down to the sea, where Mynradys had them loaded two to a boat to be ferried over the water to his new home. They had also taken with them the bones of several prominent people from each of the circles, to act as messengers to the other worlds.

Tulria laughed at this point. "Whatever power they managed to harness where they re-erected the stones, none of it ever seemed to make its way over the sea to us again! Certainly, no spirit I have dealt with in my life has ever heard a whisper of any influence from our stones, or the ancestors for whom they work now. Nowadays there is no one living here of Mynradys' line, and very few who claim kinship with those who went off with him. Those of us who chose to remain have never rebuilt the circles in our lands; the power is gone from those places. Instead, we scatter the ashes of our revered ones up on the mountain among certain of the tors there, and we use the power of Wobai direct for our prayers."

I immediately thought of the stone circle I had seen on our way up the mountain. Evidently, some local people still made use of stone spirit houses. But I said nothing to spoil the story we had just heard. Another time, perhaps.

The weather in those first days was not good; between the rain and the low white wall of cloud, there were whole days when we could not see the hills a short walk away from us. When the weather finally improved, we were taken up the mountain again to see the stony outcrops and learn more about them. Each tor seemed to have its own personality, to gather around it rocks of particular shapes or qualities and each one, or more accurately the spirit in each one, seemed in competition with the rest to pile their boulders together in ever more impressive arrangements. One outcrop was composed of fist-shaped angular blocks piled up on a base of a dozen or so much bigger versions of themselves, whilst another added a large number of longer blocks arranged like bundles of sticks in spiky crests against the skyline.

These last I could quite see being used as standing stones and ancestor stones in a circle, each one imbued with apart of the spirit of the tor from which it came, adding that power to the strength of the ancestors buried beside them. For there was considerable power here; you did not need to be a seer to feel the presence of the spirits around you. I found the whole ridge so overwhelming that I returned to Tulria's homestead that evening with a dreadful headache and retired to bed immediately we had eaten.

CHAPTER FIFTEEN

Two days later, Nykhin and I walked a short distance down-river along the wooded valley to a small saddle where we were told one of the removed stone circles had stood. The site had evidently been untended for generations; the woods had encroached upon the place to such an extent it was hard to make out the circuit of the bank that had been built to enclose the decommissioned spirit house. We mounted the low hump that remained and walked the circuit before descending into the centre. A few of the trees had patches stripped of bark and painted with dark ochre, showing where some at least of the local families still paid their respects to their ancestors, or perhaps used the site for buri-als. There was a small shrine in the middle where the sad remains of moons-old floral offerings still lay rotting, but I felt no power there, nor any force pulling me towards the spirit world. We stayed only a short time, then crossed the river at a ford to visit another source of spirit stones, about which Tulria had told us.

Lying stretched out in a river bend was a low ridge of rock no higher than the taller trees, with well-grazed meadows on three sides between it and the river, so that the outcrop seemed to extend from the woods like a finger pointing at the sunrise. In stark contrast to the circle site, this place buzzed with energy, and when I touched the stone cliff, I was instantly enveloped in the aura of the spirit. This showed no human-shaped avatar to communicate with me, nor was I aware of any understandable message coming through from it. Instead, I felt submerged in a depth of time passing beyond comprehension, of a consciousness of immense age that acknowledged me and empowered me without the need for language or signs. I had no vision, but I felt that I could easily have lifted one of the great slabs that lay around the outcrop with one hand, could I just find its point of balance.

As I was experiencing the spirit of the tor, Nykhin was looking around, tugging on my cloak, as he pointed towards a small house at the boundary between the meadows and the forest. A man stood outside, looking at us with interest. We waved a greeting, then strolled over to meet and pass some time with him. He turned out to be a youngish fellow of an age with myself. Greeting us with a cheery grin, he invited us into his home with a wave of his hand. His father, he told us, was expecting us, and wanted to talk to me.

In the gloomy interior, it was difficult at first to make out any detail, but we could see on the far side of the little summer fire a hunched form from which a pair of fiery eyes watched our entry. The old man told us his name was Rathon, and that he had been waiting for my visit for some time.

"You see, young man, as soon as you arrived here and I heard your story, I knew our paths would cross. I knew your grandfather, albeit for a short while, so that I do not remember more than a sense of his touch and the smell of his body when he held me in his arms. He was my father, which as I suppose, makes me your uncle!"

At this point, I felt suddenly a real need for the pot of barley beer that our younger host pressed into my hands. I tried to pull myself together enough to take a large swig of the musty liquid. I had told Tulria about my other quest, but she had claimed no knowledge of my ancestor Kefhan's visit; I was beginning to believe he had perished on his way here all those years ago. Now here was someone who not only remembered my grandfather, but claimed kinship with me through him. I sat down abruptly on a log-end, staring at the old man whose features I was just able to make out as my eyes adjusted to the flickering shadows in the hut.

"I must have been just a year or two old when he went away. He told my mother he had been away much longer than he had intended, and needed to go back to tell his people what he had discovered about the stones in their spirit house – the ones that came from this outcrop and the others around here. He never returned. I suppose he must have died long ago now, but my mother never stopped hoping to see him walking across the ford and up the clearing to the house. Not this house, of course. Their home was over there, about twenty paces or so; if you look hard, you can still see the flat patch where it stood."

He smiled vaguely to himself, remembering, I suppose, the house in which he grew up. "She would have been so happy to have met you. She loved your grandfather very much, you know, and there is such a family resemblance in your face, that it would have brought him clearly to mind, I'm sure."

"So, he must have been here two summers or more?" I queried. "Do you know what it was he discovered that made him feel the need to return?"

Rathon looked somewhat puzzled at this new enquiry,

but rallied his thoughts and came back with an answer after only the briefest of pauses. "I was very young, you know; it was probably several summers later that I discussed Father's departure with my mother, and *that* all happened a great many more summers before now. But I remember being told that he thought it was important that the stones did not each have their own spirit, but that each was simply a part of the spirit of the tor; I think you may have experienced for yourself the different way that power expresses itself. He thought *that*, too, was worth telling his friends at home. There was also something about the legend of Mynradys and the people that went with him that worried him in some way, but I cannot remember the details, I am sorry. He apparently told Mother that some people would not be happy at all with what he had to say!"

We were interrupted at this moment by the entry of a young woman, who had the strangest effect on me. I felt straight away a connection with her, and that she would somehow be significant in my life, but when I discovered she was Rathon's daughter and therefore my cousin, I put my feelings down to sensing that link. She was introduced as Fenratha. I saw her as a slender, wiry young woman, with freckled cheeks and straight brown hair who smiled shyly at us when her name was spoken, before busying herself about the room getting some fruit and cold lamb for us to eat, and refreshing our pot of beer. Despite her shyness, she was a good host, and managed to create such a relaxed atmosphere around her that we ended up staying in the house talking well into the afternoon. When finally we left, she insisted on walking with us as far as the river, to send us off with a warm invitation to return as soon as we liked.

I did not know why, but I felt drawn back there. I began to visit Rathon and his family quite regularly, walking the woods or hunting with Fenratha and her brother Rathonan. I found I enjoyed both their company and the novelty of my newly discovered family; we spent much of our time talking about our family and our pasts. They were naturally fascinated by my story, especially the differences in the lifestyle I had left behind.

One day we walked towards the mountains, up through one of the forests of twisted oaks and birches that covered the lower slopes, their trunks and the rocks and rotting branches beneath them covered with moss, between which grew sedge grasses and the forest mushrooms that the pigs loved. These were domestic swine and not for hunting, but we flushed out one or two hares with a few fowl which we took a shot at. Fenratha, I discovered, was an excellent shot with her bow; we spent some time discussing our techniques and found they were very similar. She, too, could see the arrow path between the bow and her target, and like me, she felt the pain of her kill as it happened. There was more to this young woman than her shy exterior gave away.

We came out of the woods at an ancient burial cairn, closed up and being taken over by brambles and bracken. I offered a greeting to the spirits there, but received no reply. They can be a surly lot, our ancestors, when they are not cared for and regularly made to feel important. Does that shock you? I'm old enough now to be entitled to speak my mind sometimes. The spirits know what to expect of me; they would be disappointed by anything less. But I digress.

On that day we walked on from the tomb and up onto a ridge, a foothill of the main range, where we came across several standing stones of a type very like those at our Spirit House on the Plain. Rathonan told me this was thought by many to be all that remained of one of the temples dismantled and taken to the Plain, but he admitted that no one was really sure, as the missing circle had been the spirit house for Mynradys' lineage, which had died out many generations earlier. Nobody these days could confirm the story. Neither could he explain why, when Mynradys had done his great sacrilege, he had left behind these four stones. It was a puzzle indeed, but not one I felt worth investigating. Like the other site, there was little potency or presence remaining here, and presently we turned back towards their home for a pot of beer and some stew.

The moon waxed and waned, then began to swell once again while we tarried at Tulria's homestead with the People of Morahan. I had found out what I could about the origins of the stones – I spent some time thinking about what I had learned and whether it could be used to make the potency flow once again at the Temple on the Plain. I had also discovered rather more than I had expected about my grandfather's sojourn here; I told myself my reason for staying was to find out all I could about my new family. I only realised later that it was one particular member of my family who was the focus of my attention, and that she was beginning to feel the same about me.

Matters came to a head one evening when Nyren drew me aside after we had eaten and asked me outright how long I planned to stay.

When I said I wasn't certain, he replied, "In that case, I must tell you I will be leaving in a day or two. I have been told of possible sources of the ores we seek in the mountains inland from here and need to investigate them before winter sets in."

"So soon? But in a few days, we will reach the time of balance, the midpoint when day and night are equal. I should stay to celebrate that at least with my family before I move on, and I *do* want to travel with you into the mountains."

Reluctantly Nyren agreed to delay a little longer,

putting off our departure until two days after the midpoint. I told Tulria of our plans and was surprised to see her frown at me, withdrawing into herself for the rest of the evening.

The autumnal festivities in this region were centred around a day-long feast, with dancing, drinking, and general merrymaking. The cooking fires were lit shortly after dawn, and by late morning, more than two hundred people had gathered together, and the little glade chosen for the feast hummed with activity. There was fresh bread, some of it flavoured with herbs, there was pork and mutton, and a selection of early autumn fruits, all washed down with different beers.

Then, shortly before sunset, the men gathered together as four large drinking pots were produced, filled with a heady mix of soured sheep's milk and blood, a ritual meal to sustain us through the rest of the evening. The women in their gathering drank beer and sour milk, and both meals were accompanied by a celebratory chant with prayers to the forest and river spirits. Both men and women applied spirit pigment liberally to themselves and each other, reds and yellows and whites, to indicate the living as separate from the spirits. Nyren and I took turns to paint each other's faces. I gave him a face that would unsettle any demon; who knows what he did to me?

When we were all ready, we formed up to process up through the woods to the mountain. The wind-twisted forest covered the lower half of the hillside, ending in a series of fingers extended towards the grassy hilltop and the stony outcrops that populated it. We halted beside the first of these, a crowned tor surrounded on three sides by woods. Tulria began to chant as we spread out on the slightly boggy meadow above the trees. Soon, two couples came forward with small bundles of ashes, the remains of three children who had succumbed to the fever that summer, and the burial rituals were carried out.

The whole process was repeated at the next stop, one of the largest tors on the crest of the ridge. Libations were made this time to the ancestral spirits and to Wobai, the ancient spirit of the mountain I had experienced on my first visit. Wobai was so old as to be considered neither male nor female, and I wondered whether it could be influenced at all by these brief ministrations and token offerings from the human world. Although once again I was affected by the mood and power of the place, I escaped this time without ill effects, so was able to join in the evening revels with the others, reserving my aching head for the next morning with everyone else.

I remember at some point Fenratha came to me, pulling me out to join the dance, and I recall enjoying myself far more than I had in several years. I laughed in her company, enjoying the closeness and warmth of the occasional embraces that were part of the dance. At the end, laughing like a fool, I drew her close and hugged her tightly, aware that she was not pushing me away, but returning the embrace with some enthusiasm. Then her father, smiling, came upto take her home with him, while Tulria and Nyren guided me to my bed in the guest house.

The next morning, I slept until long after sunrise, waking only when Nyren shook me to tell me Tulria wished to speak with us as soon as we had eaten. We quickly put on our leggings and smocks and, after swallowing a few mouthfuls of bread and dried meat, we made our way across the yard to Tulria's day house, where she was waiting patiently for us.

"I have been thinking about this for many days now, since before the new moon. Since you came here, I have known I would send back with you an offering for our spirit kin who now dwell in your Spirit House at the Heart of the World, but I could not decide what to send. I have been watching you, Stone-changer, and your growing friendship –or more, I think – with Fenratha; I have decided that she should go with you when you leave to return to the Plain, carrying with her a few of our ancestral bones bearing a message for the spirits there. I will teach her a suitable song of greeting and praise for our ancestors to sing at your Temple."

At first, I was shocked into wordlessness by this revelation, not least by the suggestion that there was something between Fenratha and myself. Then I was aware of a feeling of relief that I would not have to find the words to say farewell to her for some time yet. Nyren was grinning at me, highly amused at my discomfiture, and I forced myself to make a response to Tulria.

"I… I think you are reading too much into our friendship. Have you spoken to Fenratha? Are you sure she will want to come? And how will she get home afterwards? I mean …"

My attempted reply tailed off as I floundered in the sea of mixed feelings that burst from my head. Tulria joined in with Nyren's and Wheris' laughter as I frowned in embarrassment, then began to laugh with them as I realised that they were right; this was exactly what I wanted to happen.

"Thank you for your gift, Tulria, although I must still ask if you have spoken with Fenratha about this."

"Last night, young man, after you went off to your dreams, I caught up with her and her father on their way home. They both consented, and I am sure in the darkness that the girl was as relieved as you appear to be. When will you leave?"

CHAPTER SIXTEEN

We set off the following morning, walking towards the sunrise into the craggy hills of the interior. Nyren seemed in no hurry, and our progress was slow, for he kept turning aside all the time to examine an outcrop of rock halfway up the hillside, or to run a few handfuls of silt through his hands when we crossed a stream, or just to halt at every ridge-crest to admire the view. His expressive descriptions carried us all along with him, so I never felt frustrated, even though by the day's end we had covered less than two marches, half of what I would have expected. But the company was pleasant, so I settled down to this slow hike through the mountains, taking time to get to know Fenratha better, now that I had accepted her as more than just a cousin. We had at least a full moon-turn left before the first frosts of winter; the autumn weather was turning balmy and dry, so we were in no great hurry.

Shortly after dark, I found myself seated on the edge of our camp, looking at the heavens as the sea of cloud, which had hidden them through the day, finally faded away towards the south. I watched as the north star winked at me and I remember reflecting on this great spirit, the still-point of the heavens, the heart of the steady progression of the cosmos around us. Kylri, the spirit of the star, was the epitome of order, and the antithesis of Leus (or Loek, as we knew him back in my homeland), the lord of the wild wind and the personification of chaos. Order and Chaos, an opposition second only to Light and Dark. The two sets were linked at every level: day and night, the sun and moon opposing the disorder of darkness, the order of conscious thought and the chaos of dreams, even the star and the dark emptiness around it. We live in a world of opposites in conflict, always pulling our lives apart; the task of the seer is to find the balance point, to be for everyone the still-point of the community. No easy task, and I felt thankful that I was one seer among many on the Plain.

Then Fenratha came to sit beside me, and my thoughts turned to lighter, or at least lesser, things until we curled up in our furs and cloaks for the night.

Our intention was to follow the high ground between the river system to the north and the southward draining rivers on our right. But the watershed was broken and irregular, so it was not as straightforward as you might imagine. There was no braided track here in the fashion of our ridge path north of the Plain. We walked along a length of a trackway here, around an upland bog there, and followed sheep trails when there was nothing else. By mid-afternoon on our second day, we had turned away from the headwaters of the northern river, and were traversing a series of hills towards where the midwinter sun would rise. We had been told that this would take us to another valley which we could follow into the heart of the mountains, where Nyren had heard there were brightly coloured rocks and shiny flecks in the waters which might be the minerals we sought for our craft.

Gradually the woods closed in around us as we followed a path of sorts along the ridge, but we barely noticed, so engrossed were we all in a discussion about the recent celebrations we had attended.

Without warning, a boar broke cover in the trees to our left; it charged, squealing and snorting, through our little party. I went to pull Fenratha aside, but she was faster than me and leapt out of the boar's path, causing us both to land in a heap on the grass. Nyren was also down, I hoped unhurt, and the other two turned with us to watch the angry animal disappear into the woods. Then I wondered what had caused its sudden flight, and turned back to the other side of the path, to see a party of nine or ten men armed with spears and axes walk out of the woods, positioning themselves to surround us.

We hastily scrambled to our feet, grasping our weapons. Only Nyren had his bow strung, but his arrows were tucked in his quiver, and he knew he could never get one out and nocked before a spear was thrown at him. We were caught without a chance of flight or defence; the grins on the faces of the leading warriors showed that they, too, realised this fact.

"Do not attempt to fight it out, strangers, or we will kill you all!" pronounced the leader. "And though we may well kill you anyway, we would first like to know what you are doing creeping into our lands through these woods, instead of coming along the valley like a normal person would."

"Well," said a truculent Nyren, "you cannot expect us to know all your customs before ever we have met your people, and as for creeping in, we were making enough noise to wake the dead; hardly the approach of evildoers, you must agree!"

This provoked scowls and a growl of anger from our captors, but then Fenratha joined in, speaking fluently in the local dialect. "We came the direct way from the sacred mountains where dwells the spirit Wobai. We are seers and healers, travelling into the mountains in search of herbs and materials for our callings. We mean no harm. We will happily help you if any help is needed."

The naming of the mountain spirit obviously carried some weight, and they considered this explanation with slightly less aggression than before. I confirmed Fenratha's offer of help and added in stilted phrases that we had hoped for some hospitality rather than hostility as we passed through the valleys. Somewhat mollified, the hunters lowered their weapons and turned away along the path, indicating that we were to accompany them. Any feelings of relief were short-lived, as three of them fell in behind us, to ensure we couldn't escape back along the ridge.

At this point I was uncertain what they intended and as a result was a little concerned for our safety. But I had been in similar situations before in my travels, so perhaps it was my experience that allowed me to follow these warriors without too many immediate qualms. It could still go horribly wrong but - it hadn't done so yet, and there would be time enough to panic when blades were again drawn in earnest.

The path soon turned off the ridge and wound down through the woods to the river valley below. The trees stood tall and proud here, but the river when we reached it flowed fast along a bed fully eight paces across. Fortunately, we did not have to cross at this point; we walked along the bank into an area of settlement. It was not really a village, but the homesteads were much closer together than those of Tulria's people; frequent clearings containing a couple of huts, a fenced garden, and a small meadow for the livestock, each separated from its neighbours by a narrow strip of trees. Our escort drew up at one such house which the leader entered, only to reappear a few moments later with an old couple to whom the other warriors nodded their heads in deference. The couple approached us, and we repeated our story. They listened gravely, then shared a rapid whispered conversation between themselves before turning back to us, putting smiles on their faces and bidding us a belated welcome.

We soon learned that our welcome was at least partly down to Fenratha's claim that we were healers, for they told us of two youngsters nearby who lay in fever close to death after eating something poisonous they had picked in the woods. They had seers who had done their best to oust the malevolent spirits that had taken up residence in the children, but all to no avail. If we could save them, they said, the valley folk would be eternally in our debt.

"Not much chance of that," said Nyren in our own tongue. "We can't expect to have more success than their seers, and none of us is really a healer."

"But we must still give it our best try," I replied. "And Fenratha does claim some skill as a healer, so let us allow her to take the lead."

Fenratha herself, after some further questions, confirmed that she might be able to help. She asked for someone to fetch her some specific plants before we set off to the home of the poisoned children, a short distance along the valley in a clearing on an old terrace back from the river. She and I entered the hut, to be met by an overpowering stench of sickness, emanating from the two still bodies on the bed. Fenratha asked for them to be carried out into the light; the parents and our escort, now reduced to just two men, lifted the children on the hurdle bed and carried them outdoors.

With cool river water, she began to bathe her patients, while I tried to clear my mind to find a way through to the spirit causes of the illness. I had never tried this before and was therefore quite surprised when I was suddenly aware of grey shapes sitting at the head of each child. I challenged them with gestures and as had happened before, a reply formed in my head, although neither of them made an actual sound that I could hear.

"These children are ours now; you and your friend are too late. This one is already gone, and her brother will follow in the night. They are beyond your help."

"Who are you?" I thought back. "And why are you waiting for these children to die? Get away from them! Let us try to save them – you are not helping, even if you are not calling them to death."

One of them appeared to laugh, although the lipless grimace that passed as a facial expression would have better accompanied a howl."We are not here to help, nor will we hinder you. Our work is to receive their spirits when they emerge, and to guide them safely to their next existence in our world. The young one, as I said, is already past help. Her spirit will appear for us soon. The older child you are welcome to work with, but he is too far gone, I think, for your skills."

"Is there anything we can do to save him?" I asked.

"Your friend there will do what is needed. But do not expect too much of her; she has little experience in this illness."

I had spoken to spirits often enough by now not to be surprised at their knowledge of our minds and our abilities, so I said nothing, but nodded in farewell, letting myself drift back to the world of substance again. The plants Fenratha had called for had just been brought, and she was busy chopping up a tuberous root with her little flint knife, leaving the patients to their parents' care.

I repeated what I had learned, offered to help, and was passed some leaf to chop, while Nyren and Wheris made a fire on which to heat the mixture. It took but a short while to prepare a hot draught for the patients; the thick porridge in the bottom would be rubbed into their chests to cleanse the bodies of their fevers.

But as we turned back to the children, we could see that the condition of the young girl had altered for the worse; she was limp and had ceased to perspire. Her eyes were open, staring blindly; it took only a few moments to confirm the worst. Just as the spirits had predicted, she was beyond help and had passed over into death. The parents began to keen pitifully but obeyed Fenratha's motion to remove her body from the bed to allow us to work on the surviving brother. I was deeply impressed by my cousin's calm manner and confident authority; she was a born healer if ever I had seen one. I began to harbour some hope for the young boy in her care.

Little by little, I managed to get some of the liquid into the mouth of the young boy, while Wheris applied the poultice to his chest. When about half the soup had been swallowed, Fehratha indicated that we had done all we could; we sat back to wait and see whether the potion had done its work. The sun was by now resting on the ridge behind us. The long shadows were made more eerie by the continued keening of the women for the passing of the girl.

Night had fallen when someone brought us a little food: some barley porridge, a few chunks of dried lamb and a handful of crumbly ewe's cheese each. We washed it down with a little beer, after which I fell into a doze, waking well into the night to see Fenratha bathing the patient again. I rose to help her, and she handed over to me whilst she began to tip more of the soup into the boy's mouth.

"This will be his last burning," she said to me. "If he comes through this, he will recover. Can you still see the spirits with him?"

I tried to clear my thoughts and slip into the other reality, but it is never an easy thing to do when you are trying to, so for a long while nothing changed. Then, as I was about to give up, I saw out of the corner of my eye one of the grey shapes I had encountered in the afternoon, standing now a few steps back from the fevered child. It seemed unaware of my presence, staring intently at the boy. Then with a shake of its head and a gesture that might have been frustration, it turned away, fading rapidly into the gloom.

When I told her, Fenratha smiled for the first time since we had seen the children. She indicated that the boy's fever had broken at last. He lay there, still a little restless, but with a peaceful expression on his young face as his breathing eased and he slipped into a deeper sleep. Wheris had awoken as well and, putting a fur over Fenratha's shoulders, told her to get some rest while she watched the child until daybreak. I took my cousin by the arm to lead her a few steps away, where we curled up in each other's embrace and slept until sunrise.

By then it was clear that the crisis was over, and with some relief we began to discuss our next move. Fenratha wanted to stay for the girl's funeral. We readily agreed to this delay. It appeared that the two children were close kin to the old couple who we took to be the leaders of these people, and that as a victim of the summer fever, she was not to be laid out for cleansing in the usual way, but interred as she was in a stone-lined grave. The children's mother gratefully gave over nursing responsibilities to Wheris and Fenratha as she and her family prepared the girl's body for burial, busying themselves with other duties needed for the ceremony. Nyrhen and I were left at a loose end, so we took a most enjoyable walk along the river with Nykin, who spent the time pointing out various medicinal plants Fenratha had been teaching him as we'd travelled over the hills. I began to relax again for the first time since we had come into the valley.

As the shadows of evening crept into the valley, the ceremonies began. The washed and scented body of the young girl, dressed now in a clean doeskin tunic and bedecked with several strings of beads, was lifted into her father's arms to be carried to the graveside. We walked behind the family the short distance to the burial place. I was deeply affected by the loss of this child, who we had been unable to save; Fenratha was quietly weeping and I could feel the tears welling up in my own eyes until I blinked them away manfully. In the middle of the clearing a rectangular pit had been lined with thin slate slabs on the floor and sides. Another large slate lay against the pile of excavated soil beside the grave.

The women laid rushes in the chamber before the father lifted his daughter gently into the cist, placing her on her side as if asleep. The girl's uncle, a seer, chanted a farewell song as a wooden bowl of beer sweetened with mead was passed among the family as each, after drinking from the bowl, spoke a few words over the grave. The bowl was refilled to be placed in the cist along with a chunk of cheese for her journey to the spirit realm. The lid was fixed in place with a little clay, and we all helped to fill in the little grave with a few handfuls of earth before lighting torches to see our way back to the homestead for another drink and some honeyed porridge.

The next day we set out early, crossing the river at the ford and walking up a second valley directly towards the rising sun. Not that we could see the sunrise in the valley, deep beneath the canopy of trees, but we were aware of its arrival when the shadows strengthened and the morning air began to absorb a little warmth. We took our cloaks off, offering silent thanks to Lukan and to Gerash for the fine weather.

We made good time; soon after midday we reached the

headwaters of our stream and walked through a long pass across the watershed into the next valley system. We camped that night close to the river where it swung to the south around a range of very steep mountains that rose before us. We had been told that if we followed this river upstream for another day or two, we would reach the heart of the mountains, where several locals reckoned we might find whole nuggets of the sweat-of-the-sun, the sun-gold we sought.

Behind us, and to the north, we had been told of even more formidable ranges of peaks, but for us, they remained mythical and unseen, for throughout our journey we could never see beyond the nearest ridge or the next line of trees. The oak-woods were beautiful in their autumn colours, but the hills crowded in on me and had me constantly looking over my shoulder for the demons that I feared were sweeping towards us. I sat by the little fire we kept burning, thinking how used I had become to the open plain I now called home, and how I had changed since leaving the White Mountains and my home forest far away towards the sunrise.

All the next morning we followed the river around the side of the mountain range until the valley opened out and we found a ford where we could cross the water in safety. I was drawn along a clear path that led south up a hanging valley, so, with Nyren occasionally stopping to pan a little silt as we went, we made our way through the woods to a cold, silent lake in a great hollow amongst the trees. I knew at once this was a spirit lake of the kind I had seen in the White Mountains as a child. I felt very strongly the presence of the spirit who dwelt there, although transport into the spirit world eluded me that day. I offered a prayer at a small cairn that stood beside the path; then we sat down to rest while Nyren and Nykhin tested the waters for traces of the sun-gold.

The night was spent back near the ford; then, on our third day, we continued up the widening valley into a land once more dotted with cleared fields and pastures, each with a clutch of huts and shelters occupied by, as it transpired, most friendly and talkative farmers who slowed our progress to a crawl that day. But it gave Nyren plenty of opportunities to pan the river sands and that afternoon, he found our first flecks of sun-gold. There were just three of them, so after several more attempts, he shook his head, indicating that we should keep moving.

We showed the flecks to the family at the next homestead, but they seemed unimpressed or uninterested, I suppose because they knew not how to make anything useful from them. They soon changed when I showed them my little plait keepers that I wore when I dressed for ceremonies. Then they became quite animated, offering cheese and hides as exchange for one of them. I declined, knowing that I had not enough sun-gold left to replace them.

As we travelled further upstream, we began to find more grains of gold-dust, and as we traversed a particularly sluggish stretch where the river meandered back and forth between slight humps in the valley floor, we began to find enough to interest Nyren. We went to work in earnest, placing handfuls of the silt and sand from the bends in the shallow baskets he gave us, then sifting through the soil until just the heaviest particles remained. Picking the specks out was time-consuming, but by nightfall, we had forty or more grains, and Nyrhen was clearly pleased with our efforts.

We set up camp there the next day, building ourselves two enclosed shelters and an open-sided lean-to for food preparation. Nyrhen and Wheris took the one shelter with their son, while Fenratha and I set up home in the other. The rest of the day was devoted to panning the riverbanks on the slow-flowing outer edge of the bends, taking a few samples at each sandbank to find the best deposits. As the sun sank towards the cloud-capped horizon, Fenratha and I took our bows and went in search of our supper. We shot a hare and an old beaver, the pelt from which would far out-value the fishy flavoured meat. After our meal, we retired to our respective shelters. This was the first time since we had set out that we had had any privacy, and I was greatly pleased to discover that Fenratha had laid rushes down for just one bed, and when she lay down beside me and spread her cloak over us both, it seemed the most natural thing in the world.

Our group stayed in that place for over half a moon, near a sharp bend in the river, collecting almost a double handful of sun-gold from the silts, until we woke one morning to a sharp ground frost. Autumn was passing early into winter, and we should look to find better shelter. I talked with Nyrhen at some length about it but he still wanted to see if he could find the source of the sun-gold. He also wished to seek out a mountain where the tears of the moon had fallen; the moon-gold was to be found where the tears had stained the rocks blue.

In the end, we agreed that he and his family would stay in the valleys over the winter, while I would return to the Plain with Fenratha to take her ancestral bones to the Spirit House, there to deliver the message from Tulria. Before we departed, however, Nyrhen was insistent that we should build a fire to smelt the gold dust we had gathered so far and split it between us, so that I would have something to show for my journey through the mountains. Personally, I thought that Fenratha was enough in herself to bring back; a gift both for me and, as a healer, for the folk of the Plain.

It took several days to prepare for the smelt. We had to build the furnace and let it dry, roll some clay pipes around a small branch to help blow air into the furnace, and use some of our precious deerskins to make a pair of bellows that would breathe more air into the fire to melt the sun-gold. We collected wood and slow-burned it to get plenty of charcoal for sustained heat.

On one of these collecting trips, I was walking a short way behind Fenratha, carrying two long branches, when suddenly I saw her put a foot down right beside a coiled adder. I watched the serpent raise its head, beginning to strike even as I brought one of my sticks out in a wild jab, concentrating all my force into the blow. The adder's head recoiled as it was flung back into the bracken. Fenratha had jumped aside, and I crouched down to examine her leg, but she seemed unhurt.

Then I saw Nyrhen staring at us. "What just happened there?" he asked.

"An adder," I replied. "It was striking at her, so I knocked it flying with my firewood. A good hit, wasn't it?"

"I saw the snake, but that was not my question," said Nyrhen. "Look where you were standing – over two whole paces from the snake. You could never have reached it with that stick, even with the step forward you made. Which, it seemed to me, you did not finish until the serpent was already flying into the bracken. You never touched it. It recoiled and flew away all by itself."

He shook his head as I looked afresh at the scene and realised the truth of his words. I was stunned, then puzzled, until I remembered the occasion when I knocked the knife aside as Turac was about to be stabbed. I began to understand that this was a power within me that I could effect when there was a great need. As yet, I had no idea where the power originated, nor how to gain control over its use, but I vowed that I would learn both answers. For a moment I had a wild daydream that I would be able to move the stones of the Temple just by the power of my will, but then reality closed back over me, and I had to laugh at myself. I spent the rest of the afternoon trying to explain my feat – despite not understanding it myself – and my subsequent laughter to my friends.

At last, everything was prepared, although, just as for a moon-gold smelt, we had still to clear our path with the spirits. We fermented a little mead with honey from a hive we found nearby, made libations to the river and mountain spirits, then offered prayers and mead to Lukan for his gift of sweat for our decoration. When we were done, Nyrhen poured the molten metal into six small hollows in a piece of mudstone to make roughly egg-shaped nuggets of pure sungold.

I took with me a bag containing four of the nuggets, each the size of a lamb's knuckle-bone, enough to make several pieces of jewellery. Nyrhen kept just two, arguing that he and his family would find enough to make another smelt before they headed north in search of the other essence we sought, the moon-gold. I remember reflecting then, although not perhaps for the first time, how curious it was that we used male sun-gold for jewellery and female moon-gold for tools. Good things come when the oppositions are in balance; that is the way of the world.

During our stay there, we had visited with several of the local farmers, making friends while soaking up their knowledge of the mountains to help keep us safe and to find our way through them back to the coast again when the time came. So Fenratha and I knew we could shorten our journey home by heading over a low pass into the next valley before travelling up river and across the next range of mountains to a long river that we could follow all the way to the coast north of the marshy fens we had crossed on our way out from the Plain. Two days after the smelting, we packed our belongings and set out for my home.

With Fen at my side and the knowledge I had gained at the coast, I was filled with a new sense of power and assurance. I would return to the Plain and to fulfil my obligations and complete my quest. I had not felt such confidence since we had set out from the White Mountains two years earlier.

CHAPTER SEVENTEEN

Mikhan climbed the last part of the hill from the river, finding himself on the high point of a long ridge. His attention was drawn to something on the next ridge towards the sunset, a dark oval with a white ring around it. As he focussed on the distant structure, he was able to make out the huge stones and realised with a shiver of excitement that he was at last looking upon his destination, the famed Spirit House on the Plain. After a few moments, he began to wonder what all the fuss was about. Perhaps he should take a closer look.

He was unconcerned with the possibility that he might be recognised; almost two years had passed since anyone there had seen him, and then, there had been just five of the Plainsmen. What were the chances one of them would spot him, or remember where they'd last seen him?

It was a long time ago, yet to him, the memory was as strong as if it had been yesterday. He had been ill for months, first when recovering from his wounds, then a second time when he succumbed to some flux that had torn through Thorachis' people, killing several weaker souls as it passed.

What with one thing and another, it had been midsummer when he was finally ready and fit to undertake this mission, when he had at last packed his few belongings into a shoulder bag before setting off to the north where his vengeance awaited him.

He walked across the grassy down, enjoying the warmth of the autumn evening sun on his face, thinking disparaging thoughts about this place and the people who lived here. He was no seer, nor was he especially aware of the spirits or the Kas that made the world work, but when he came up the rise and stood before the Spirit House at last, he felt the presence of the sacred place soak through him and was moved more than he would ever admit. The spectacle of the enormous squared stone blocks with their amazing ring of stone lintels could not fail to impress, as did the view. Mikhan gazed at the grassy horizon, quite level all the way around, and was able to believe that he stood in the very centre of existence. He saw for the first time that there was something in the stories; that this Spirit House truly stood at the Heart of the World.

He dismissed the thought, putting his mind back to the real reason for his visit. The sun was low in the sky, and he would do well to find a place to stay while he plotted his revenge. He also needed to find out more about where the Stone-changer, and that lump of a warrior who'd accompanied him, lived.

Spotting a man walking with his dog away from the stones, Mikhan set off to catch up with him and draw him into conversation.

"You're not from around here," the Plainsman remarked. "Have you travelled far?"

"From the land near the great Spirit Path; two days' walk to the south. I thought to see for myself this wonder. But it is late in the day, and I think my visit must wait until tomorrow."

"Do you have somewhere to stay? The nights are growing chilly at this time of the year; you don't want to sleep out if you don't have to. I only ask, because I have an empty hut you are welcome to use for a few days if you wish to."

Mikhan smiled. Sometimes, it was just so easy! He could speak to the family, explore the lands around, and find out all that he needed to make his plans. His new friend seemed talkative, so he asked about the Temple as they walked, until he skilfully drew the conversation round to the presence of the Mainlanders.

"Yes, they are friends of the chief's son, Syllan. Weyllan is, it seems, a powerful seer. He was accepted into the fellowship of the Temple last year; they were all very impressed with him – and not a little jealous, I'd say. Then he brokered an end to a feud we'd had with our neighbours to the north. Quite a hero, he has become."

"He sounds intriguing. Perhaps I might meet him while I am here."

"You may have to wait a while, my friend. He took off several moons ago to the mountains by the Sunset Sea, to visit the place where our most ancient stones came from; he hasn't returned from there yet, nor will he manage to this winter if he's not already started out for home."

This was an annoyance. Mikhan had hoped for a short stay, and a quick resolution to his quest. Now it looked as if he might be here until the following spring. He would have to plan for an extended residence, but a longer stay also increased the risk that someone would find out who he was. That would complicate his mission considerably. But after two years, he was nothing if not patient.

·   ·   ·

By the last moon before the year's turning, the sleet and rain alternated with misty frosts to mark the arrival of winter on the Plain. Kirah had already packed away her potting tools and prepared two mounds of gritty clay to weather through the frozen moons, ready to use when the warm weather returned. She had also finished grinding up various roots for a store of medicines against the many ills of winter.

Today, she was hanging strips of venison and pork to smoke over the cooking fire. Kefhan had just returned from hunting with Syllan, bringing home his share of the meat they had shot. He was skinning and cleaning it ready for the pot, watched intently by his new companion, a brindle pup he had named Arrow, who was hoping that a few gristly bits might come his way. Young Ulrac was sleeping peacefully in their main house.

Hearing greetings called out from the next homestead along the ridge, she looked up to see their neighbours outside, gathered around two travellers who were being greeted with some enthusiasm. At first, she thought they were kinsmen of the family come to visit for the year's end, and she was just turning away when something made her look again. She recognised the stance and movements of the taller of the visitors and called for her husband.

"Kefhan! Kefhan, come here! Your brother has returned in time for the Soul Days. And he has someone with him – I do not think it is Nyren, or the young lad. Come and look!"

Kefhan recognised his brother at once and trotted off along the path to meet him, followed closely by Arrow, his canine curiosity aroused by the sudden flurry of activity. Kirah, feeling slightly light-headed, wanted desperately to follow him, but not wishing to either leave or wake her son, she opted to wait by the house for Weyllan's arrival.

She stood in the doorway as the three people walked up the path towards her, the two cousins laughing at some joke they were sharing. Kefhan had always been taller than his adopted brother and had grown up the more muscular and ruggedly handsome of the two.

Kirah smiled as she admitted to herself that this had been her main reason for choosing him over Weyllan, together with his straightforward openness and honesty. In his teens, Weyllan had had a dark side, a brooding nature that clouded his eyes even when he seemed outwardly jovial. That darkness had gone from him since they had come to this place, and he had come into his powers at last. Now, she would be hard put to say which of them she loved more, although her first loyalty would always be to Kefhan.

As the group came past the small barley field, Kirah realised the third person was a young woman or girl; certainly, several years younger than herself. She was tall and well-proportioned with strong, well-toned muscles on her arms and legs, and carried her pack lightly and her bow with confident familiarity. From her belt dangled a bag from which the tops of several plants protruded.

A healer like herself, then, and a huntress as well; a woman – girl – of strong character almost certainly, who walked into the homestead without a single qualm or misgiving. A warm look that passed between the girl and Weyllan gave Kirah the first indication that they might be more than just travelling companions. Then they were standing right there before her, and Weyllan stepped forward to sweep her into his arms with an affectionate hug and kisses on the cheek and forehead.

Kirah returned the embrace, then pushed him away to look into his face. "So, home at last, you feckless wanderer! We expected you back over a moon ago. But I see you had a reason to take your time and enjoy the journey." She grinned, working to keep the faint twinge of jealousy from her voice.

240 | T. S. ROBEY

"It is truly good to see you at last, looking so well. And who is your mysterious companion?"

"Kirah, sister, it gladdens my heart so much to see you, too. Our family grows ever larger, it seems. This is our cousin, Fenratha, the granddaughter of our grandfather Kefhan, from the mountains beside the Sunset Ocean whence came the first stones of our Spirit House."

As Fenratha smiled and stepped forward in her turn, Kirah noticed that Weyllan's words had the air of a prepared speech, designed to say just what he wanted them to hear and no more. Yet that one look she had seen was more intimate than befitted the friendship of cousins. Putting aside her inner confusion, she smiled warmly at her new cousin, and took her in her arms to ensure there was no doubt about her welcome. Then she led the way inside to show Fenratha where she would be staying.

"You are very fond of Weyllan, I can see," Fenratha began as soon as they were alone. "So am I. I hope our love will not cause any ill-feeling between you and me – I am quite excited at the prospect of having a sister for the first time."

Kirah was taken aback by this directness. "I honestly did not know the strength of my feelings for him until I felt jealousy at your closeness. But, no, I have no claim on him. I am content to love him as a sister and will try to love you too as my own sister. Then … are you sharing a bed?"

Her new sibling nodded solemnly at that. They then agreed that it might be best for everyone if a new house was built for her and Weyllan. Kirah collected a couple of logs for the fire and a beaker of beer, then took Fenrtha to rejoin the men outside. She was more eager than ever now to hear Weyllan's account of his travels to the western mountains and the Sunset Sea, and the story of how he had met Fenratha.

. . .

The following day, as the two couples sat in the courtyard eating their morning meal, Kirah was surprised to see a familiar figure approaching along the ridge. Tokhan greeted them all warmly, and looked at Fenratha with evident admiration. He would no doubt be even more impressed when he learned of her prowess as a hunter with the bow. Few women on the Plain hunted, whilst even fewer could call themselves good archers.

Once the introductions were over, Tokhan came to the purpose of his visit. "I heard from Syllan that you were back, Weyllan. He told me you had stopped in to see him and Atharon, and that you felt your trip had been a success. I am very pleased to see you back safely, but I fear I come as the bearer of ill news. I was returning from a visit to my cattle out on the summer pasture, to check that my nephew and his friend were looking after them properly. I came back through the downs on the far side of the Sacred Land, past a couple of homesteads there, when I saw a man who seemed oddly familiar to me. At first, I thought nothing of it; after all, I must have seen all the people who live locally at one time or another. But later, as I was nearing home, it struck me where I had seen him before. It was when we were down at the coast being held by Thorachis' people; he was the poison-arrow maker, the one we called Weasel-face."

Everyone was taken aback by this revelation except Fenratha, who waited patiently for an explanation. There was no doubt that if Weasel-face was in this part of the country, he was up to no good. Tokhan had gone straight back to the homestead the moment he remembered, but the man had vanished. The homesteaders could tell him only that the stranger had been passing through, and had stopped to share a meal with them. He had asked who the local leaders were, but on being told where they lived, he had not appeared overly curious. Both Tokhan and Syllan had kept a watch out, but had seen no sign of the man since.

Kirah broke the silence that followed this announcement."I am surprised he made no comment or further enquiry on hearing that he was in Atharon's territory. I think perhaps he already knew where he was. Of course, he might truly have been just passing through, and decided to keep a low profile as he was in enemy territory, so to speak. Or he might be hiding somewhere nearby, planning something unpleasant for us. We should all keep a good watch out for him, or for anything that seems not quite right. Fenratha and I can take a walk about the land and make enquiries while we look for any healing work that is needed. Talking to folk about their ailments is a good way to pick up gossip; if he is anywhere nearby, someone will know about it."

Her plan was, of course, a good one, so after a little more discussion, they agreed to follow it, whilst at the same time taking extra precautions against possible sources of poisoning. It had been many days since Tokhan's sighting; they could at least hope that Weasel-face had moved on or that Tokhan had been mistaken.

He departed, and the others finished their meal before setting out on their day's tasks. Kefhan and Weyllan headed for the Spirit House. They needed to formulate a plan for making the stones a better structure for focussing the spirit energy required to persuade the spirits to do their bidding. Kirah and Fenratha were not needed, so they set off to begin their enquiries.

Despite questioning the local people for several days, they had no results. Then, when they were travelling through an area of the Plain about half a march north of their home, they encountered an old woman who remembered something that seemed to confirm their worst fears.

"You are kin to Weyllan, the stone-changer, aren't you?"

she had asked Kirah. "I remember seeing a man such as you describe just before the last full moon, who asked after your family. He said he was a friend of your kinsman.Someone had told him the stone-changer was away,andhe wanted to know where hehad gone. I told him that Weyllan had, indeed, travelled towards the Sunset Sea and had been gone for quite a while, but was expected back by the winter. The stranger left without any thanks, muttering to himself as he went that he didn't know if he should follow or wait for him.The man said his name was Mikhan, I think."

Kirah reported the news back to the men, but apart from renewing their vigilance, there was little more they could do. If Mikhan had gone to the mountains after Weyllan, he would have to stay there over winter. If he had not – well, that was what they were looking out for. As Kefhan said to her later, it was frustrating, but they just had to live with it. But woe betide Weasel-face if any of them saw him on the Plain. This time, they would make sure he made no more poisoned arrows.

The next evening, all thoughts of Weasel-face were pushed to the back of Kirah's mind when Weyllan related the story of the meeting he and Kefhan had had with Atharon and his council. Syllan had attended too, but had not arrived until halfway through the discussion; Weyllan reported that it was partly due to his friend's support that the others had agreed to his plans.

Weyllan had explained to Atharon how he and Kefhan had devised a way to free the energy flow at the Temple by rearranging the smaller stones into a pattern that mimicked the shapes of the great stones with their lintels. He had argued that the stones from the Sunset Sea had been set up to make a double circle, but that this had been abandoned when it was decided to use the local stones instead. Now, there were two conflicting patterns, lacking harmony, that set the ancestors against one another and interfered with the ability of the seers to draw down enough power to influence the spirits.

Ursehan had been at the council. He, of course, had opposed the idea of moving the ancient stones, but had looked surprised when he was loudly supported by Atharon's son Athlan, who had recently been admitted to the fellowship of the Temple.

Ursehan had declared that the stones, as they stood, formed a barrier separating the circle from the inner cave with the great doorways of stone. They were to remind people of the sacredness of the space within. He had stated that he had never had a problem going into the spirit world inside the circle, and pointed out that Weyllan hadn't either, although he had had difficulty finding his way out again.

"That made me so angry," Kefhan said. "But Weyllan waved it aside, calling it a petty jibe at his ability such as we might expect from Urda's kin."

"Athlan went on to say that everyone was aware of the ills that befell them the last time they shuffled the old stones around," continued Weyllan. "He asked if anyone wanted to stir up those old enmities again, and said that we have the finest Spirit House in the world here, at the centre of everything, and should not risk everything for a slight improvement. He supported what Ursehan had said, that many of us were still able to travel to the other world from within the Temple. Only a few had been unable or found themselves restricted by the old design as it stands. He doubted our suggested improvement could make it any better.I addressed each of these points, emphasising that if the interference was cured, the improvement would be huge."

"What, exactly, did you say?" Fenratha asked.

"I tried to explain my belief, which is that, whereas the great stones from the downs to the north give homes to individual spirits, the ancient stones from the Sunset Sea each house a part of the great mountain spirit Wobai. When put together they form a single, powerful presence that could drown out the individual spirits of the new stones. The old stones and the new in their current positions work against each other to cancel any concentration of Kas. Repositioning them to mimic the larger stones will harmonise the power of the two sets of spirits; it should stop the interference and amplify the potency of the Kas for the seers to use."

This argument, Weyllan told them, had silenced his detractors. Kirah could not help but wonder if this was because they accepted his ideas, or because they had no idea what he was talking about. But she kept her thoughts to herself and listened as he continued his story.

"The nested circles will also provide a route for the circle dancers to draw down the Kas, projecting it into the centre for the seers to receive without a double barrier in the way. Harmony in the pattern will create a unity of purpose and encourage the spirits of the stones to work with *all* the various factions among the ancestors to send out a stronger signal to the Domashyi out in the world beyond the Temple."

As she watched Weyllan's animated oration in the flickering firelight, Kirah could easily see why his argument had finally won the council over. One after another, he said, the assembly had nodded their agreement and support for his idea. Syllan had spoken at length in support of the changes, until Athlan was at last convinced; even Ursehan had had to admit it was worth trying. There had been silence for a moment when Weyllan finished speaking.

"Then Atharon rose and swept an outstretched arm around to encompass us all.'I think that you have brought us all with you, Stone-changer!' he said. 'We will try your solution, and we will all work with one heart to accomplish it. We are too close to the year's end to finish the work before the Soul Days, so let us plan to begin when the moon turns and begins to grow again.' There was general agreement at this decision, for nobody wanted to start a project in the dying days, nor in the waning moon that will this year follow the midwinter festival. When the meeting broke up, we all filed out to make our way home in the mist and drizzle."

There was silence around the fire when Weyllan finished his tale. His retelling of the council meeting had been so real, Kirah could almost believe she had seen it for herself. She passed him the barley beer to wet his throat and looked at him in wonder; stone-changer, seer, diplomat and now, a storyteller. From an introverted, lovelorn youth, her kinsman had become a well-rounded man with the makings of a strong, charismatic leader; if he ever chose to take that step.

CHAPTER EIGHTEEN

I did not join the other seers of the fellowship in travelling to the other side. The memory of my last spirit-walking experience in the Temple was still vivid and, with my new plan made public, I thought it likely that I would be targeted again by Urda's kin. Instead, I joined the circle with the other dancers weaving in and out of the stones all night to the drumbeat. Occasionally one of us would pause to help channel the Kas into the seers who stalked around the centre of the circle, waiting for the power to take them through the gates to the other side. As they passed each stone, the dancers would strike it with a hazel stick to wake the spirit within, chanting as they did so:

> *"Souls wake, Stones hum, Spirits of our fathers come.*
> *Stone shake, Soul take, Mother of our fathers wake."*

As the seers began to walk with the spirits, the stone-beating stopped, and the chant changed to an extended ramble led by a caller standing at the entrance. Mostly out of breath by this stage, the dancers could manage little more than a whisper, repeating each phrase until they heard the next from the caller. The timing slipped, and the result was a hissing susurration that I found as mesmerising as the drum-beat that still padded along to keep our feet in time. Seers used the steady beat to maintain a link with this reality, helping them to make a smooth and speedy return when they were done in the spirit realm. Dancers would drop out of the circle for a drink and a rest, then rejoin in a convenient gap in the line when they were ready to.

I kept it up until well after midnight but dropped out before the first glimmer of dawn, after almost falling into trance myself several times. I sat on the bank for a while until Fenratha found me and sat down beside me. She took my hand, holding it while we watched the spectacle in the stones until the sky grew lighter. At last a faint glow in the clouds revealed that the sun had come back again.

The new year had begun.

As the day took hold and the last seers returned from their journeys, the dancers stopped circling. They separated into groups, discussing the night's action and exchanging experiences before they turned their steps towards their homes for breakfast and, for most of them, an unusual mid-morning sleep. We were joined by Kefhan and Kirah, walking as a family to where Turac waited near the southern causeway across the ditch.

He greeted us warmly. "Welcome, my friends, and a blessing on you all for this coming year!" He turned, indicating the ground to his right, just inside the bank and the circle of half-filled pits where the old stones had once stood. "The legend is that in this patch of ground were buried the remains of many of those who came from the Sunset Sea with the stones, and some of their children who settled here afterwards. Here, I think, is where you should place the message you have brought with you from their homeland, Fenratha."

She nodded agreement, and Turac handed her an ancient antler pick with which to dig a hole within the sacred circle. She bent to her task, turning up the turf and scooping out the soil beneath with her hands. Turac sang a calling-song to rouse the spirits; I clapped the time, joining in as the melody came back to me.

When she had made a hole as deep as her elbow, she straightened up, taking her bag of ancestral bones in her hands. Turac called on the spirits to witness the interment, while I blew a long call on his cow-horn. We asked them to receive their newly arrived kinfolk with friendship and goodwill. Then I knelt with my new wife, holding the bag open as she lifted out several small bones and laid them carefully in the pit. Last of all came a jawbone, the better to speak the message the remains carried. Then the bag, painted with seven magical patterns, was placed over the bones, and the two of us gently replaced the soil, tamping it down with our hands while Turac began to chant a short song of thanks to the ancestors for receiving the newcomers.

We were almost the last to leave the Temple. As we walked home across the down, Kirah took Fenratha in her arms, hugging her tightly to show her delight that our new kinswoman had fulfilled her duty so well. Then I took Fenratha by the hand, squeezing it gently before we all set off down the hill.

With my free hand, I turned her face towards me. "Your ancestors will be glad of the news from home, and to know that there is another kinsman among the living here again. It was a good idea of Tulria's; I hope you are happy with the little service Turac performed. And who knows, perhaps the departed you brought from your home will help to turn the spirits in favour of my plan to fix the Spirit House."

With the ropes ready at last and a few spares nearing completion, I, and the Children of Hatha gathered at the Spirit House on the day after the next new moon. It was a frosty morning, the light breeze chilling but steady. I, for one, was thankful for the calm weather; nobody wanted unexpected gusts of wind when the great blocks of stone were being manhandled from their holes. We were all aware that we would have to learn by experiment, for although the story-keepers knew tales that described the process, no one alive had ever actually seen a stone of this size moved.

After a lengthy debate, we began on one of the smaller stones at the end of the double arc between the outer arcade and the great gateways in the centre of the Temple. We learned quite quickly how to secure the ropes so that they didn't slip off the stumpy monolith. In some cases, we were able to use the larger stones to support the ropes as we pulled the smaller ones out of the ground.

Further trials clarified the role of the great timber frames over which the ropes could be passed, that we knew from the stories handed down since the building of the Spirit House. For each one, we excavated a deep trench into the chalk around the stone to loosen the hold of the earth on it. Even so, two ropes were broken and had to be replaced before we had the rhythm and the angles right, so that it was late in the afternoon before the first stone was lifted out and laid on a sled ready to be hauled out of the way by Syllan's team.

The second day began well, but when more ropes broke despite everyone's best efforts to pull smoothly and evenly, I picked up a broken end to take a closer look; most of the strands were frayed and uneven, but a couple seemed to have straight edges as if they had been cut part of the way through.

Shocked, I showed my discovery to the others. Syllan was not immediately convinced, but ordered a check on the spare ropes. They found that none of them had been cut or interfered with. He tried to reassure me that the breakages had been accidental, that no attempt had been made sabotage the work, but I kept thinking about the rope I had examined and remained suspicious.

I was not alone. Despite Syllan's efforts, many in both teams felt that someone or something was trying to hinder our work, and several questioned the wisdom of continuing. They settled down after a break to repair the damaged ropes, but mead had to be fetched for a libation, before they would return to work. This we made, while Turac and I chanted a purifying spell over the ropes and the site.

By the end of the day, another of the smaller uprights had been cleared and set aside. Syllan ordered three of the best warriors to guard the ropes that night to prevent any interference, then we made our way home together, chatting and quietly pleased with the progress.

Day three went well enough, and two stones were lifted, but the next day the teams of workers returned to the now unguarded Temple to find the ropes that had been placed ready to lift another stone had been untied and stolen, along with another coiled rope that had been left on site. We were now seriously short of suitable ropes and would need to preserve the remaining lengths if we were to finish the task. Syllan, Kefhan, and I went into a huddle to confer.

"When I find who is responsible for this, I will have them flayed and sacrificed to Lena!" Syllan was shaking with anger. "I'll have their heads on spikes by the guide stone ... I'll ..." He sat down abruptly as his anger affected his balance.

"We will have to find them first," Kefhan contributed.

"Now will you believe that someone is trying to stop this project?"

"No. This could be completely unrelated to the accident. And how would anyone think that stealing a couple of ropes would make us quit our work now? Someone has his eye on some good lengths of rope, that's all. I wouldn't be surprised if it was those Northerners across the river."

Kefhan shook his head at that. "Or it could be Urda's faction trying to make everyone think the ancestors are against us. Do you think if they thought the spirits were angry, that many of our teams would keep working? We need more guards to watch the Temple, as well as our rope store."

"If I allocate more workers for that duty, there will be fewer to pull on the ropes during the day," was Syllan's response.

That made me think for a moment. "We will never finish before the moon wanes if this continues. We need to get a second team working right away to double the pace. As for guards, if we store the ropes in the Temple, we will still only need one team of guards. But we don't need great warriors for such a job; some of the older men and other seers can keep watch just as well. We might even get the ancestors to lend a hand."

The others agreed, so while the rest of us set to work again, Syllan and Tokhan went off to gather more volunteers from their allies. By the sixth day, we had two full teams working by day and together we dealt with four stones, including one nearly two paces long. As the day shift packed up at dusk, five men of the Temple fellowship arrived to take on the night watch. I relaxed slightly, beginning to believe for the first time that this project might actually reach completion.

By the time of the next full moon, despite various

mishaps and suspected interference, our teams had managed to lift and store twenty-seven stones, leaving only the tallest ones in place, along with those that carried lintels flanking the entrance to the SpiritHouse. With the stones that had been removed to allow for the great gateways to be constructed, there would be over fifty stones available for repositioning.

I took a full day out to mark out the new single circle that was to replace the unfinished arc being dismantled. I remember that when Syllan joined me, he was surprised by the number of locations I had marked out.

"How many holes *are* there? And are you sure we have enough stones?"

"Last night I had a dream, a vision, call it what you will, but I was visited by a rook who told me to make the circle with fifty-six stones, the same number as those in the old circle. It will re-create the old in the new, and appease the spirits who have been troubled by the moving of their stones."

"But we do not have fifty-six of the old stones. Several were broken, and the remains are too small to use again. Do you propose we fetch more sandstone boulders to make up the numbers?" Syllan looked puzzled. "And I thought there was to be an inner circle too?"

"No, we cannot use the local stone. We will have to collect the stones from the lesser circle by the river, as Myrthis originally intended. It is never used now for ceremonies and has become just the place where people cast their kinsmen's ashes into the Ayn. Also, it is not to be a circle in the centre; I will mark out an oval, open on the one side, to reflect the arc of the five gateways."

Syllan did not look convinced, but could say nothing in the face of a solution from a vision. If this was what the spirits wanted, then this he would do. He directed his team to begin digging the pits I had marked out, and spent the rest of the morning selecting the stones that would be placed in the first sockets. I wanted the tallest stones reserved for the inner oval, whilst the rest would be arranged to have the tallest of them flanking the entrance. Even Syllan grudgingly admitted it was going to look very impressive, and a significant improvement on the tatty double line with several stones missing that they had just dismantled.

The following day, while Syllan set the first stones upright in the new circle, my team prepared to lift the first of the lintels from the arc near the main entrance to the Spirit House. We set up two frames, attaching a rope to either end of the stone, and with a co-ordinated effort lifted it clear of the tenons and lowered it to the ground without mishap. Our spirits riding high on this easy success, we set up three frames around one of the uprights that had supported the lintel, leaning them inwards until their apices touched directly above the stone.

We had used this system already a dozen times, and went about our tasks with familiar confidence. Two men dug around the base of the monolith to relieve the earth's hold on it, while others tied two ropes around it just below the old ground level. The ropes were run up the stone well past its mid-point where they were secured by the third rope, which would also provide stability when the stone came free. We had come close to killing several of our number on an earlier lift when the stone had suddenly decided to rotate wildly round in an arc, narrowly missing the heads of four of the men on the team. The third rope would keep the stone more-or-less vertical and make it easier to control. Just the same, I checked each cable for cut marks or weaknesses before the teams took up the strain.

Then the men hauled on their ropes while four of us

leaned on two wooden levers jammed in against the stone to try to jog it free. There was a long period of grunting and straining without effect; then someone noticed the stone shift slightly. Now we could all see it moving; a thumb's width, then another, the soil cracking around the base as the monolith began to pull free of the chalk. I called for more effort and, as every man and woman pulled on ropes or leaned on levers, the great stone finally broke free, rising majestically into the air to hang suspended an arm's-length above the turf.

The workers rested a moment, waiting for directions to move the stone. I cast my eyes over my teams. I was about to pass on to the third line, when a shock of recognition made me turn back to stare at one man on the second rope. Despite the growth of a light beard, I had no doubt at all that I was looking at Weasel-face and, in that instant, I realised that it must be he who was responsible for all the delays and sabotage we had experienced.

My shock must have been obvious, for the poison-arrow maker saw at once he had been identified. He let go of his rope and turned to run, barging his neighbours and cannoning wildly into another rope team as he did so. People were knocked over, falling against others who likewise lost their balance, disrupting everyone around them for one vital moment.

One rope pulled loose; another snapped taut as the monolith jerked and oscillated about its middle, the base swinging in a deadly arc towards me and my fellows. As we all tried to step aside, my foot caught on one of the falling levers so that I slipped sideways with one leg kicking upwards. The stone swung past, smashing into my raised knee as it did so, tearing a gaping hole in both my leggings and my leg.

A wave of pain and nausea shot through me as I toppled

down to hammer into the ground with a stunning jolt, cracking my legs together to release a second waveof agony that swept up my body and swamped my mind. There was a flash like fire, instantly extinguished as the darkness flowed in, and I knew no more for a long time.

PART III
BEYOND REASON

CHAPTER NINETEEN

I was aware of darkness. Deep, total, enveloping blackness in which I revolved slowly – or it turned around me, I cannot say which – sensing the void just as empty, just as absolute, in every direction. But I was aware. I did not see, I had no eyes; neither had I any sense of limbs or head or mouth, but I *had* substance. Substance without form, in darkness without end. I was aware for an age after how long of being unaware? A few moments? A day? All winter? Was it day, or was it night? I had no sense of time, no feeling of time passing, for in the darkness, there was nothing against which I could measure its passage. I was outside of time, or at the very centre of it, a still point around which the cosmos revolved somewhere out in the void. For a long time, it seemed, there was no time at all.

Then there was light. A single pinprick in the darkness, winking orange-red somewhere in front of me. Far away or at arm's length, I had no way of knowing, so I tried to be aware of being closer to the light. As I moved closer – or it came towards me – I could tell that it was more than a single point. It was a line – red, I knew now – that snaked away from me out into the infinite nothingness. I reached out with my no-arm and I grasped the end of it with my no-hand, and I drew myself towards it and drew it into me. The light spread through a hand, up an arm, and into my still shapeless substance, connecting my awareness to me, and me to the light. The Kas flowed from the life-line into my awareness and time began again.

Light flowed in, and images formed and flickered and went out like sparks from a fire. Some I could almost grasp, some so outlandish I still have no understanding of them, and many more that are gone forever from my memory. I saw my father, smiling and motioning towards himself. I watched an infant take a single, hesitant step forward, then another, then two more as it almost lost balance and tumbled into my father's arms. He lifted me – for I realise now the infant was me – and pulled me towards him, whispering to me as the image blurred …

I stood, an infant on new legs, and looked around me at the gently undulating grassland that stretched in every direction as far as the flat circle of the horizon that formed the edge between the earth and the sky. Around me and above me the air, clear and sweet, was passing through me and sustaining me, and above that, the realm of clouds, where the Turashyi, the sky-spirits, dwelt. Some days they laughed and cried and shouted and fought with each other, and sometimes they hid themselves away, revealing the uppermost realms of the heavens, wherein dwelt the great stars and Lukan and Lena, lords of the day and the night.

But my mother just smiled at me and said not to fret, not everyone was born to be a seer, and that I should be content with my skill with the fire-spirits and learn to draw the moon-gold from rocks. And my father said I should listen to my uncle and learn from him the art of making moulds and calling out the spirits of the stone and become a stone-changer. Then they walked away from me into night, and were gone.

Then it seemed I was flying, swooping close to the ground and up above the woods, my arms outstretched for balance and my head – I could feel my head now – raised to accept the wind streaming past. It was late in the day, and the sun was dipping towards the horizon little by little as I soared above the river with its golden splendour flashing off to my left. As it slipped over the rim of the world, I rolled over and began to rise through the air, my ascent just balancing the setting of the sun, so that it hung on the horizon for quite some time. I rolled again onto my back and let the sun slip away beneath me as the sky faded to purple, then to the deep dark blue of a stagnant pool, as above me the stars came out. I let myself rise towards them until I was sailing along the Aynturash, the river of heaven, once again at the top of the sky, with that ribbon of wonderful orbs that pulsed and glowed in the darkness whilst their spirits watched me with curiosity.

There was no balance to be achieved this time and anyway, I barely had command of the two arms I seemed to possess. The stars rose and fell at random, or suddenly shot across the heavens, narrowly missing each other as they passed by. One orb was much larger than the rest and I tried to float towards it, until I was close enough to see the shadows on its surface that resolved, as I watched, into a woman's face. A face neither young nor old, not beautiful but strong and captivating, serene and yet compelling. The visage of Lena, the moon, who seemed now to be aware of my presence, and made her words appear in my mind.

"Well, Stone-changer, look at you up here. Here, where you do not yet belong, where you should not be, and where you cannot stay, lest you lose the vision and tumble down to your end. But no, I see no death in you, not for many years,

Seer. I see your aura, and I see many years still to come if your destiny is to be realised. Perhaps one day you will join us here, but the road will be long and hard that leads you to a place among the Turashyi."

I felt her reach out and enter my cloud of being, placing within me a tiny, glowing, sphere which began to pulse gently with a rhythm I soon realised was my heartbeat.

"I gift this to you, Stone-changer. In time, it will open for you and you will receive the use of my gift. For now, it would do you harm more than good, so let it rest within you until the time is right. Now it is time you left and returned to the surface realm where you belong. Take care not to tumble as you go; I would hate my gift to be wasted so soon after the giving."

Without any effort or action on my part, I found myself sinking slowly down from the realm of the stars, through an endless bank of cloud that clung to me damply as it passed, then down towards a dark world dotted with the fires of a thousand homesteads, until I hovered a short distance above one in particular. I sank further, through the thatch and into the room below.

I was looking out from a bed of straw and hides, as if from my eyes, though I was aware at the same time that they remained firmly closed. I was a consciousness within, but not controlling, my body; an observer of my own situation. A woman came across to me and knelt by the bed with a bowl in her hand. She placed the bowl of thin soup in her lap and, using one hand to open my mouth, used a mussel shell to pour some of the broth into me. I felt myself swallowing, wondering how I was doing it whilst completely unconscious, but I think my awareness – my mind, if you could call it that – was not able to reason, only to watch.

Much of the coherence that comes into this tale now is the result of my turning each vision over and over in my head until the memories fall into a comprehensible sequence. How much the actual content has altered in that process I cannot say, but I think for the most part my telling is true to the meaning of my dreams and visions as I hung balanced between life and death.

I soon lost this vision, and I found myself once more outside, in the depths of winter, surrounded by scores of people in lines, straining at ropes. I guessed at once what I was seeing and turned to look behind them at the massive block of sandstone that slid up the slope behind them, the motion barely perceptible against the frosty grassland behind it. The stone lay on a sled with two pairs of diagonal runners, each one adzed smooth on the underside to create a level cross that slid along over two broad rails made from halved oaks with the upper part likewise adzed to a flat surface and greased with animal fat. In places, the rails lay directly on hurdles spread on the ground, but in the dips, they were supported by transverse poles of different thicknesses. A short distance behind the stone, workers were lifting the rails and rescuing whatever cross-poles they could, carrying them up over the hill and out of my sight. I was deeply impressed by the effectiveness of this system, it being such an improvement over the rollers we had been using to move the old stones around the Spirit House.

I moved on up the ridge and looked out from the crest. The rails extended perhaps forty paces down the slope to where teams of men were constructing the next section of the trackway. I guessed there would be a long period of rest at the top of the haul while the rails were laid all the way to the bottom of the slope. I looked away beyond the workers to the ridge beyond, where dozens of other men and women moved about busily around three more stones that lay a short distance from the guide stone. And just beyond that was the Spirit House, or at least part of it.

The five great gateways I could see, complete as I knew them from before – or rather, from afterwards, in my lifetime; for I had no doubt here that I was looking far into the past, seeing what had occurred nearly two long cycles ago. Around the gateways, the circle of stones was only half-finished and people were still working on some at one end of the arcade. I drifted closer, not flying as I had before, but simply changing my viewpoint by thinking myself to be somewhere else. It was one of the strangest sensations I had ever felt in a short life quite full of extraordinary experiences.

Around three stones at the end, they had built a platform of logs, something akin to a widely-spaced funeral pyre to look at, with a working area at the top of hide-covered hurdles. On this, half a dozen men worked in teams with heavy sandstone mauls, chipping away at the upper surface of the stones, levelling them to a charcoal mark along the side and leaving two conical studs standing proud. These would receive the lintels that were already in place on the platform, providing convenient benches for the masons to rest and admire or criticise each other's work.

There seemed a great many people involved in the work around the Temple, more than I would have thought were required. Many seemed to be just standing and watching, but it was not until one of them rose into the air and drifted on to the platform without the teams noticing, that I realised I was seeing the ancestor spirits gathered at the edge of reality to observe the construction of the new Spirit House.

Then a worker screamed, and I saw him cradle his hand as blood dribbled between his fingers. The spirit I had seen had been right beside him, but was now returning to the company of his fellows on the ground. I felt sure I had just missed an act of spirit sabotage, and moved in closer to see him better. It was no surprise to recognise him as one of

Urda's faction, one of those who had been with her when I was trapped in the Spirit House. And there was the seer herself, looking straight at me and whispering, with a wave of her hands that indicated a spell of some kind being directed my way.

Sure enough, the stones began to fade, and the spirits took on the translucence of the spirit realm as the grass and chalk faded to the fine grey sand I was coming to know so well.

Urda, her cronies forming up behind her, addressed me. "So, Weyllan, like me, you hover in this limbo between life and death. Like me, perhaps here is where you will remain forever. I curse the fate that trapped me here, but I rejoice that I may henceforth have you here to torment."

Two more spirits drifted into the scene. One jostled Urda, pushing her away."Let him be, you ill-begotten witch! Do you not think he has done your people honour? *And* he attempts to end this conflict and bring us all together again. Only your malice stands in the way, as it has with every change since you trapped yourself in limbo. For no matter how you rant, it was your own lack of caution that put you there, and ..."

"Get out of my way, Tyrac, or I will remove you myself. You know none of you can defeat me; I am here and yet not here, and your powers have no effect on me. Get you back to your underworld lair and leave us to our affairs!"

But the distraction had weakened her grip on me, and I was wafting away again, slipping through time even as my vision crossed the down towards the burial mound and Urda's Spirit Path. And there was the seer herself, walking along the freshly scoured path with her cronies – I suppose they were her advisors or friends in life – inspecting the various devices she'd had built along the path. There were lines of chalk boulders, a circle of freshly cut leafy boughs from the riverside, and single and double stakes hammered into the chalk banks at certain points, all to help her remember in her spirit-walk to perform special movements or say certain words of power.

I could imagine her walking and dancing along the path to who knows where in the spirit realm; then there she was, doing as I had imagined, dancing as a spirit along the way. At the same time, I could sense her body, in trance, somewhere dark – inside the ancestor mound at the end of the path. There were other spirits around Urda, watching her and listening to her words, following her towards – what? I looked along the spirit path to its far end on the ridge, and could faintly make out a huge shape in the gloom.

I willed myself closer, ahead of Urda, and moved wholly into this other spirit realm to look upon the most mighty tree I had ever seen, ten times the height of the tallest oak, with a trunk nearly twenty paces across, scaly and scarred. The leaves were also unlike any I had seen, similar to massive fronds of bracken or fern, the spread reaching almost the whole width of the spirit path, which was still just visible through the thin walls between realities. Running beside it was a gentle stream, perhaps the one that Turac had told me of, although I could see no spirit shelters for ancestors anywhere nearby.

I felt certain I was looking at the first tree, the mother of all others, still living in spirit on the other side. And Urda had found it, here at the Heart of the World, and built her spirit path to connect with it and – what? To rejuvenate the forest? To heal some disease? I wanted to know, but I was being drawn away, for something was wrong with Urda's sending.

Her spirit self had stopped, was standing confused, uncertain whether to continue or return. And the ancestors around her were losing interest and drifting away. I turned to look back at the burial mound to see what was happening, and saw Urda herself feebly struggling in the arms of an enormous bear, a primeval beast from the time of our ancient ancestors hibernating in the dark, trying now to tear her apart as they crashed around within the innermost chamber of the tomb. Aged timbers cracked and crumbled, and in the blink of an eye, the walls collapsed, half burying both woman and bear and sealing them alive deep inside the mound. Dust billowed out from the entrance as people fled in terror from the scene and Urda's spirit self flew back to the mound to reunite with her body. Yet something seemed to be blocking her and, as the dust settled, the wraith danced ineffectually around the entrance but could not find a way in.

As I watched, the spirit surrendered to fate and sat down wearily before the tomb with her head in her hands. For the first time since I had come to this land, I felt a pang of sorrow and sympathy for Urda. Hers was indeed a terrible fate, and one severe enough to turn any soul to malice. I wanted to go down to her and offer her some comfort, perhaps reach out to her as a friend, but once again my vision fever wanted me elsewhere, and the scene began to fade to darkness.

Sometime later, I found myself high in the air again, moving over a range of mountains, snow-capped peaks that grew more familiar as I passed along the range. These were the White Mountains of my home, towering spirits that had supported me in my childhood and been the source of my people's power to separate the blue stone from its moon-gold essence. Away to the north stretched the forests and clearings of my people, and there, as I searched, was the scatter of houses along the hillside that was my village. I turned my gaze a little upslope of the main settlement, to a clearing with huts that I recognised as the home of Orelac, my uncle. As before, I allowed myself to descend towards and then through the thatch, to stand in the room across the fire from my uncle. He was weeping, sitting on the hurdle bed with his head in his hands, very like the spirit Urda I had just left. Then he raised his head and stared across the room towards me, and I knew he could see or sense me with him.

"Weyllan, my adopted son, is that you? My eyes are weak now and do not see well in the other realms. Have you gone over then? Or is this a sending? Ahh, did I do the wrong thing to send you? Were you this unready that it has ended so soon?"

I moved around the fire to be closer to him and to make myself more visible, and I tried to answer him, my first attempt to communicate since I had come back from the darkness. But the words were fevered and made no sense even to me, so I shifted closer and knelt beside him to rest a hand upon his shoulder. A strong sense of something – pain, I suspect – shot through me from my leg and I hurriedly unbent it.

"So, not dead then, but without speech and probably near death and fevered along with it. Yet if you can control your sending this much when you are so ill, you have already come a long way, my son. And you still fight on; that cheers me immensely. You must keep fighting, my son. I have seen a vision of you as a seer of great fame, and the father of a dynasty of great chieftains. Of course, visions only tell us what *may* be, but I would like to hope you will achieve this destiny."

I tried to speak again without success, so instead I tried to converse as I had with Lena, from my mind to his without speech. "Father, I cannot see myself as a chief, although I am well-liked among my new people. Syllan's father is well established and has two strong sons to follow him, for they have begun to take as their chief the son of the old chieftain. I do not remember what happened to me, and I have not yet returned to myself to find out, but I feel what might be great pain in my leg."

I pondered what he might want to hear, and went on. "Your son Kefhan is well and is now a father himself, for Kirah gave him a son, Ulrac. I too have a wife; she is Fenratha, a cousin descended from your father Kefhan Wanderer. He went to the Plain where I now dwell, and from there went off to some mountains by the Sunset Sea, where he stayed long enough to father a second family. I have not yet found what became of him; that mystery remains."

"Then you must be sure to live," said Orelac, still vocalising his words. "A seer can, to some degree, choose when he is to die, and your quest is not yet finished. Search yourself and find the strength within you to heal your body. If you can do what you are doing now, you can most assuredly do that. As for the chieftainship, I have seen it and I believe it will happen. Perhaps not with you or your children, but with their sons and grandsons. You should return now and use your power to heal yourself."

That was easier said than done. I had no idea where I was, nor how to re-enter my body. At that time, I suppose I had no memory that I had done just that once already.

I had many more visions that flickered and faded in and out of my head, but the only one I remember now was the last, for it took me once more into the underworld of the ancestors. I slept sometimes, I know, because I had dreams as well as visions. I learned to tell the difference; both appeared dislocated, but the dreams drew on memories, experiences and aspirations from my life, whilst the visions streamed in images from the whole cosmos and from all of time.

That last vision, now. That took me down beyond the grey spirit realm of pale light and sand, and into the deeper world of caverns and halls where dwelt the lesser demons and stronger spirits of people long passed. As I stood there to take stock of my surroundings, I saw someone approaching me. He was, or had been, a man of perhaps forty summers, and even through the distortions of the spirit, I could see he had been well-built and good-looking, although even now there was a hardness of the eyes that spoke of determination and authority.

"Greetings, Weyllan stone-changer. Well met, I looked for you, and here you are!" I returned his greeting, and presently he spoke again. "I know you are interested in the seer Urda, and have had ... well, unfriendly encounters with her, am I right?"

I nodded, a little wary now. "And what is your interest in my affairs – or hers with me?"

"I am Kharis, and I lived on the Plain long before your Spirit House was built, before even Urda was born. When I came here with my people, our nearest neighbours lived down near the River and grew only enough barley for beer; most of their food came from wild plants and hunted game. We settled on the very edge of the Plain, a little sunset-wise from your temple, and ploughed our fields and planted our crops. The soil was thin, and within ten years, our fields were exhausted. We completed our Great House for our dead, at my insistence, but within a year the people turned against me and wanted to replace me as head seer and leader. I argued with them, and tried to forge links between our ancestors and the local spirits at the Heart of the World. But my rivals cut me down and slit my throat so that before I could get back to my people, I passed from that world into this one. The saddest thing is that as I lay awaiting my disposal, I came to see that they were right, and that we should move down-river and into the valleys where the soil was better. They buried me and left anyway, so that I sleep alone in my spirit mound, without companions of my generation, and without descendants to care for me or my home."

I started to reply, but as with my father, the words that emerged were meaningless.

Kharis laughed at my discomfort, but there was sympathy in his voice when he spoke again. "No need to say anything. It is because you are neither one of us, nor full of the Kas, that you have not the power of speech here. You do not belong here now, just as Urda is an outsider. She will calm down when her transition is complete, but that will not happen unless her body is found and her spirit fully released. But take great care, for she is not in her limbo alone, and her companion could be very dangerous if not treated properly."

Unable to speak my queries or, on this occasion, to *think* them to him, I tried to give Kharis a questioning look. He smiled again and went to answer me but as he began to speak, the vision faded.

For a while I slept, dreaming again of Fenratha and the love and care she was giving my body while my mind wandered all across the cosmos. Then I became aware of some altogether different sensations, none of them very pleasant. Foremost among them was pain. Not just an inkling of it as before, but a roaring, throbbing, biting pain that exploded from my leg and burned its way right through me and burst out of my head in a long moan of agony. I was conscious again; properly conscious this time, and all I could think of was that I wished with all my heart to return to my painless delirium or the darkness that had preceded it.

CHAPTER TWENTY

The first Fenratha knew of the accident was when she saw the hurdle being carried across the ridge opposite. A young lad, a nephew of Turac, came on ahead to tell her who was upon the hurdle and why. The bearers were not hurrying; Fenratha was terrified Weyllan must be dead. But she forced down her fear and examined him the instant the hurdle was set down, and found a pulse, although it was feeble and irregular. Despite the men's efforts to cover the wound and stem the flow, her husband had lost a lot of blood; she feared he hung just a hair's width away from death.

She sent the boy off to pass the word to Kirah, who was with a young mother at an outlying homestead, then set about gathering her healing materials. She mixed together a set of herbs, mashed them with a little precious honey into a poultice to spread across the wound, and brought out a bowl of moss to soak up the blood. Then she removed the blood-soaked dressing and cleaned the wound on Weyllan's leg with spring water, cutting away several loose flaps of dying skin with a flint blade as she did so.

The wound was a terrible one. The blow had shattered

the knee cap and driven splinters of bone into the surrounding flesh, ripping the tendons to shreds, and gouging a great hole in the front of his leg, twisting the lower leg to one side.

She spent some time sorting the ends of muscles and tendons, realigning them while laying spells on them to rejoin and heal quickly. Then she applied the herb poultice on a moss pad before splinting the leg and wrapping the wound with long strips of softened deerskin.

The external injury contained, she turned her attention to restoring Weyllan's life force. She rapidly prepared an infusion to kill the pain and stimulate the heart again, all the while calling the spirits to her aid. She built up the fire to cook a broth of liver mixed with ewe's blood and a little sour milk. While that was brewing, she fed him the infusion, trickling it slowly down his throat so as not to choke him. Then she did the same with the soup, all the time looking for any sign of returning consciousness.

There was none. Weyllan remained as still and unmoving as a corpse. Only the thready pulsing of his heart and the faintest signs of breathing indicated that life held on somewhere within him. When she could do no more, she had him carried inside, settling herself beside him as she continued her appeals to the spirits to preserve him and return the life force to him.

Kirah returned in the fading light of the day. Fenratha welcomed her sister and drew her into the hut, where they sat together, discussing the best ways to treat Weyllan before Fenratha began her vigil at his side.

For the next ten days, she spent most of her time with him, feeding him food and medicine whenever she could. Occasionally, she was forced away, to relieve herself or wash her face; at such times, Kirah or Kefhan watched over him. Kirah fetched whatever medicinal plants or powders were needed, joined Fenratha in her entreaties to the spirits, or brought her food for sustenance. Sometimes she fell asleep, and awakened to find that one or other of the family had covered her with a cloak and stayed while she rested. All the while, Weyllan lay as if dead, silent but for the slight rasp of his breath, just audible when she put her ear next to his mouth.

Then came the day when she noticed his eyelids flicker slightly, followed later by a twitching of the fingers on his left hand. But by mid-afternoon it had ceased, and he sank back into complete unconsciousness. This was highly distressing, and she walked distractedly around the house offering up prayers for his return.

The moon waned to nothing, then returned to a full-bellied circle again, until on the third night after the full moon, Weyllan's breathing and pulse strengthened. As dawn broke on the following morning, he opened his eyes for just a moment, filling her heart with hope.

Shortly after Weyllan's first signs of recovery, Tokhan paid Fenratha and Kirah a visit. He told them that he had been involved in the hunt for a man called Mikhan, who had escaped in the confusion after the stone broke loose. Exhausted from tending to Weyllan, Fenratha was eager to hear the story of the manhunt.

Once Weyllan had been treated and carried home, Tokhan told them, Syllan had tried to establish what had occurred, immediately recognising the description of the man who had caused the collapse that led to the seer's injury. He called for Tokhan and another warrior to find the man's tracks and follow them, then gathered together twenty more men to split into groups to scour the surrounding landscape in case the Weasel had gone to ground or had been seen by others as he fled.

By nightfall, they had a report of their quarry from herders away towards the sunset, so Tokhan and his partner caught up and were soon following a fresher trail. But it rained the next day, and most of the trail was washed out. The trackers followed slowly in the icy drizzle, knowing that Weasel-face would be drawing away from them if he continued to run. By the fourth day, they had to give up, as there was simply no trail to follow. The other teams had nothing more to report, and Syllan needed everyone back at the Temple to continue the work. But Tokhan's dislike of the poison-arrow maker was so strong that he had asked Syllan if he, at least, could keep looking, and the chief's son was glad to let him try.

Tokhan had roamed widely for many days across the lands to the south of the Spirit House, asking everyone if they had seen or knew of Mikhan, but no new leads were forthcoming. He felt deep in his belly that the Weasel would not have returned to Thorachis without definite evidence of Weyllan's death and must be hiding somewhere nearby waiting for news. Tokhan had decided to swing back towards the sunset further up on the Plain and try his luck there. Then, around the time of the moon-dark, his patience had been rewarded.

He met a man who had seen someone answering to Mikhan's description talking to an old woman outside her house a few days previously. Tokhan walked to the place the man described and, finding a small copse of trees over-looking the homestead, he had sat down to watch. The next day, he saw the woman emerge to sit in and enjoy a little of the weak winter sun. She had been there only a short while when a figure approached the house across the abandoned fields on the far side of the valley. As the man drew near,

Tokhan could see that it was Weasel-face. The woman went inside, returning with a small bowl of liquid, probably beer, and a couple of strips of dried meat for Mikhan. They talked for a while until the Weasel finished his drink, after which he took his leave and returned the way he had come.

Tokhan had risen and swung wide around the farm, expecting to catch up with his quarry on the far side. As he went, he spied two young lads herding some pigs, and sent one of them off to tell Syllan that their man was found, and to come quickly to help capture him.

By the time he crossed Mikhan's path again, the man was nowhere to be seen; nor was there any sign in the short grazed grassland. But a small stream flowed through the next valley and there was a straggling copse along its banks, good cover for a man to hide in. Tokhan had walked down to the water, then headed upstream, checking as he went for disturbances that might have been made by a person collecting water.

After only thirty paces, he found what he sought, a mudbank on which were numerous partial footprints pointing towards and away from the water. He followed them up the opposite bank and among the trees and shrubs that formed a thicket along that part of the stream. And there it was; a small trampled clearing with the remains of a fire and a patch of bracken nearby for bedding.

There was nobody there, and Tokhan feared he had been seen as he approached. He crouched quickly, and as he did so, an arrow whipped out of the bushes, snapping the hood from his head as it passed through the deerskin, and parting his hair. He reacted instinctively, throwing his spear back along the flight of the arrow and following immediately himself, crashing through the undergrowth to grapple with his attacker before whoever it was had time to nock another shaft.

Nothing. He found where his spear had pierced a bush to its very heart, but there was no sign of Mikhan. Then he heard a splash and the sound of someone running, back in the direction he had come from, but by the time he reached the crossing point, the Weasel had vanished. A full search resulted in sight of neither the man nor his tracks, which faded out a short distance from the trees. Tokhan had retraced his steps to talk to the woman, and to await Syllan's arrival.

And so, the search had resumed, but by the time the moon was full again, even Tokhan had to admit the trail had gone quite cold, and it seemed more than likely that Mikhan had fled the country, or returned to his home.

Tokhan warned Fenratha and Kirah to keep a wary eye open in case the man was still around, and left soon afterwards.

Over the next few days, Fenratha stayed constantly with Weyllan, tending to him night and day, bathing him to reduce his fever, feeding him febrifugal extracts and nourishing soups whenever he would take them. She watched over him as he slipped back and forth between consciousness and oblivion, then fell after a day or so back into the same state as before his awakening. Then once again he lay there, as still as death much of the time, with only the sweat of fever or the twitch of an eyelid to show that he was yet clinging on to life.

It was about this time that Fenratha's own sickness began, the revolt of her stomach against the blandest of foods, suffering weakness and dizziness well into the day. She began to worry, dreading the mornings, when the nausea was at its worst. She ate very little and grew weak with the effort of fighting both her symptoms and Weyllan's.

It was Kirah who diagnosed her illness one morning when she was keeping her company.

"You are with child! I remember the symptoms so well. Although I think perhaps you have it worse than I did. No matter, you can nurse Weyllan, and I shall nurse *you*. I was taught a few tricks when I was learning to heal, and Aslena taught me a few more. It is just the babe within you taking your energies and interfering with your body as it grows. We will counter that and have you feeling like nothing has changed, have no fear!"

To ease the burden, Kirah arranged for Aslena to come and help care for Weyllan, which she did only after considerable grumbling, with protestations of old age and worries about her animals (two goats and an owl with a broken wing that had elected to live with her after its wing mended). The goats were brought across the River to be kept with Kirah's own beasts, and the owl flew after her saviour as soon as it was dark, hooting softly outside the house for attention when it arrived.

One day, Kirah took Fenratha outside and got her sorting clay for the next season's pots. Fenratha was curious about the care taken over the material. "I have seen potters coiling clay back in the mountains, but there are always large grains within the coils. The potters say plenty of sand and stone in the mix makes the pots stronger in the fire, so that fewer of them break in either their making or in cooking with them."

"Yes," Kirah replied. "But large grains mean thick walls, and I wish my vessels to be lighter than their contents. So, I take out all the large, angular pieces and add carefully sorted fine sand to provide the strength. You have used my drinking cups, and I'm sure you can see the results are worth the effort."

Fenratha nodded and said no more, turning back to her

task with renewed attention. She was enjoying the distraction of having a different task to do.

The moon turned again and the first yellow rain-flowers came into bloom beside the paths across the Plain. The three women continued taking turns to care for Weyllan, and Fenratha suspected Aslena enjoyed the frequent company of friends as a refreshing change from her usual isolation.

Whenever Kirah was relieved of nursing Weyllan, she was occupied with her other patients, or sifting clay, or cooking for the expanded household. Her husband, Kefhan, was away much of the day, looking for Weasel-face or caring for their combined animal herd. When Fenratha and Kirah were too busy, he'd help at home by watching his young son, Ulrac. And so,the days of Weyllan's illness passed quickly, and Fenratha fell into the new routines as if they had been set thus forever.

A day came when Mikhan was seen down near the ford, heading up towards the settlement. Kefhan was with the chief and Athlan when they heard the news. so the two younger men scooped up their weapons and, with another warrior, ran to investigate. They spotted Weasel-face as he crossed a small winter brook in the same moment that he spied them and turned to flee. His foot turned on a wet rock, and for an exhilarating moment Kefhan thought they had him, but he leapt on to the bank and unslung his bow, drawing an arrow from his quiver as he did so. It was over in an instant. Mikhan turned and shot at the nearest target just as Kefhan did the same in the other direction, the arrows crossing in flight. Kefhan swore as his shot skimmed passed Mikhan's shoulder, but beside him Athlan staggered and fell to his knees, an arrow-shaft protruding from his shoulder. As Kefhan and the third warrior turned to tend to the chief's son, the Weasel disappeared into the trees on the other side of the stream. Kefhan knelt and plucked the shaft out while Athlan was still in shock, then washed out the wound with water from the brook to remove any poison that might be on the arrow. But it was all to no avail. He looked on in horror as Athlan's eyes rapidly turned milky and he began to sweat and twitch uncontrollably. The seizure lasted only a few moments before, with a final violent convulsion, the wounded man let out a last, rattling, breath and lay still on the grass. Kefhan looked wildly about him for a moment, realised Mikhan was gone, and left the warrior to look after the body while he ran towards his own home to warn the others of the Weasel's presence and to pass the word to Atharon of his son's death.

As he broke out from the trees, he could see another figure on the opposite slope climbing towards the homestead where Kirah and the other women remained with Weyllan. There was no hope of even coming within arrowshot of the man before he reached the huts, so Kefhan stopped and filled his lungs to release a mighty shout of warning that echoed around the valley.

Aslena and Fenratha were inside the house when they heard the shout, and although the words were indistinguishable, the cry itself was unusual enough to attract their attention. Fenratha got up and stepped to the doorway; the hurdle door was open to let in the light. She saw a man, perhaps a hundred paces distant, trotting up the path towards her, and at first thought it was he who had called. But then she saw the strung bow and the little figure of Kefhan on the far slope, waving madly to get her notice. An instant intuition sent an fearful shiver through her. She turned back inside to reach for her own bow, stepping into it and fitting the string in a single fluid movement. Snatching a couple of arrows from her quiver, she returned to the doorway.

The man was running now and had already covered half the distance to the house. Fenratha drew a slow breath to steady herself, then nocked an arrow and drew the bow. Mikhan stopped almost mid-stride at this unexpected action; a woman drawing a bow against him seemed quite beyond his comprehension. Then he reacted and lifted his own bow, picking out an arrow even as Fenratha loosed her shot. His own missile was on the bow when hers struck him just to the side of his breastbone. His fingers clawed ineffectually at the flights of his shaft for a moment as he tried to clip it onto his bowstring, then he let go both bow and arrow and staggered backwards as her second shot struck him two finger-widths above the first. He was dead even as he pitched backwards, tumbling several paces down the slope before coming to a halt against a patch of bracken beside the path.

She remained in the doorway, bow in hand, stunned at what she had just done. She watched absently as Kefhan ran up, breathless, and as Kirah emerged from her house, looked around her, and crossed the courtyard to put a comforting arm around Fenratha. She allowed Kirah to take the bow at last, then turned in her sister's hold and buried her face in the older woman's shoulder, sobbing with released tension and shock.

"I couldn't let him come closer, Kirah. He would have killed us all. I had no choice! Oh, Lena, I have killed someone! I ... I ..." Her voice trailed off, and the sobs took her over again. Kirah patted her on the back and kissed her hair gently.

"Now, girl, you have answered your own doubts. You had no choice. Sometimes the spirits demand a life to save a life, though this time I think you may have saved us all!"

Over her sister's shoulder, Fenratha observed Kefhan as

he checked the body to ensure that, at last, Weasel-face was finished. Both arrow shafts had snapped off, and the heads were buried deep in the body, so he left them there and walked up to join the others, enfolding both women in his arms and dropping his head on Kirah's other shoulder as even Fenratha felt the relief wash over him. She put her free arm around his shoulder and slumped weeping in their arms.

Kefhan went with Aslena to pass the news to Atharon. When they arrived at the chieftain's compound, they found Syllan there before them. He welcomed them in, his face wreathed in a huge grin.

Without waiting to hear their business, he burst out, "How right that you should be the first to know! The wife you and your brother found for me has just borne a son! They are both well, and he is as fine a young warrior as any father could wish for! I only wish Weyllan was here to share this joy with us."

But Atharon had seen the strain on Kefhan's face and was more aware of the events of the day.

"What has happened? What has become of the assassin, and why is my son not here with you?" he growled.

"I know not how else to say this, Atharon, but your son is slain. By a poisoned arrow." Kefhan spread his hands wide, palms up in a gesture of helplessness. "Fenratha slew the Weasel-face as he tried to approach Weyllan's home, and Kirah has gone to get some help to bring your son home."

Atharon's head fell forward and his shoulders slumped; Syllan's eyes grew wide with disbelief before he sagged down upon a log next to the fire.

"Was it quick? Did he suffer much?" he managed to mumble.

"It was over in a moment, Syllan. I barely had time to

remove the shaft and wash out the wound before he passed away. He was poisoned, so I must suppose he suffered some pain but, truly, only for the shortest time. Weasel-face was so quick to shoot; there was no time to take cover or dodge the arrow. I shot back, but my shaft slipped by him even as his hit Athlan. I am so very sorry that I was not able to prevent this, or at least take revenge on the instant, but that honour went to Fenratha. She shot twice, as true as any shot of my brother's; either shaft alone would have killed him."

There was silence in the house as the chieftain's family digested the news. Then Athlan's mother, who had been sitting in the shadow throughout the exchange, let out a wail of anguish and ran outside, breaking the spell that held them all. Syllan put his head in his hands, and his father slumped down beside him, staring at the fire. Aslena went out to comfort Sylwa. Kefhan stood awkwardly, unable to sit down or advance into the house without a word from his hosts. Gradually, Atharon pulled himself out of the pit and began to regain his awareness of leadership. He stood, a grim and worn expression on his face.

"Our thanks are due to you, Stone-changer, for bringing this news so promptly when I'm sure you had your own household to consider. I must ask you now to do one more thing for me, which is to go around the village and pass the word to the elders and seers, asking them to attend upon us here to witness the death of Athlan when your wife brings him home. Syllan, you must stand with me, for you are now my heir and must learn to lead our people when I go."

Kefhan, relieved to escape the confines of the house, bowed and trotted off to fulfil his duty.

CHAPTER TWENTY-ONE

I was underwater. Was I drowned? I could see, so probably not. I had been in the house, listening to Fenratha and Aslena moving about, preparing a meal perhaps, and then it had all faded out. Through the darkness of the tunnel, the sparkle of the fire on my closed eyelids became the sparkle of the sun on the surface of the water. Close to me, just a little way above me, it flickered and glinted off the wavelets that flowed across the surface, forming a lattice of lines glowing in rainbow colours across my whole vision. I could feel the swell now, lifting me and letting me down with each passing wave.

I was in the sea then. I tried to kick upwards, but I did not move, and it came to me that this was another vision, and I was simply an observer, there, but not there. I tried to look down and was surprised to see the bottom just an arm's length away, white with the crushed shells of tiny creatures who, I knew instinctively as I saw it, had died and left their bones and homes on the sea bed to be tumbled and weathered to a white powder. Here and there were patches of sand, the dust of mountains washed into the sea and thrown about by the tide until they caught in little potholes in the surface of the chalk bottom.

I remained above one such sandy hollow as I watched the sea drain away from around me until I was being swished around by the wash of the tide on the shoreline, and sand was settling out of the water around me to cover the chalk. And the wind blew gently, forming the sand into low dunes from which grew tall trees with stems like ferns and a crown of huge flat leaves splayed out from the top of the trunk. Their roots went into the sand and drew out the water from among the grains, leaving behind a gummy material which stuck to the grains and bound them together. Time was passing fast, I knew, flashing by me; I saw the changes as if just a morning passed. And the sand became stone, rocks that glittered just like the great stones from which our Spirit House and others were built.

Then the beach dissolved before me and became another – very different – shore, rocky and cold, with a lowering sky above and a hint of sleet in the air. And out in the bay, I saw a boat coming in under a half-open sail, saw them bring the boat about, furling the sail and swinging the boom across before carefully unfurling it half-way to catch the breeze on the other quarter. On this tack, the boat was able to run for the shore, a gravelly beach a few paces wide on the incoming tide.

It was a bigger vessel than I had at first thought, although still smaller than the one on which we had first crossed the sea to come to the Islands and the Plain. A man jumped into the shallows as the keel dug into the beach, followed quickly by two others. A large boulder was passed over the side to them, and they half carried, half rolled it up the shoreline and anchored the boat to it with a stout rope.

A young, travel-hardened woman joined the men in the surf, helping to push it a little further up the beach to keep it safe against the tide. One of them walked up to the rocky shelf that marked the edge of the beach and scanned the land beyond. As he turned towards me, I felt a jolt of recognition; it is the strangest thing to be staring at yourself through the mists of vision! But I looked more closely and realised it could not be me; there was a different shape to the hairline, and this man was longer in the leg than I. He also had two good legs, although when I had the vision, I was still largely unaware of the extent of my injury. So, a close kinsman, no doubt. My grandfather? Or some un-named descendant? I could not tell.

My vision wavered again, to clear into an image of the same people standing by a stone spirit house, a circle of angular blocks split directly from the nearby outcrops, their sharp corners pointing like spears at the overarching heavens. There was a ceremony occurring, the seers dancing to a complex drum-beat, some with arms raised behind them to receive the Kas, until one by one they reeled off in their spirit-walks to their personal visions. I remember thinking lucidly for a moment, wondering whether any of them was seeing me watching them, then discounting it as unlikely.

These visions must have brought me back to the brink of reason, for I tried to imagine myself back at the great Spirit House on the Plain. For a while, the visions tumbled past as I careered wildly about in time and direction. I was aware, in flashes, of activity among the stones; I saw people in outlandish colours, all the colours of a flowering meadow and more, people in woven fabrics with knives the length of their arms at their belts, walking among the stones of the Temple as the stood in various stages of disrepair.

I saw four men with hard jackets of plates that overlapped like the scales of Brwslyi, shining like moon-gold but the colour of clouds in the morning sun. One man faced the others and slipped a great wooden disc off his back and held it before him as another hurled a spear across the space between them. Then they charged him, and I saw him swing a hefty axe that all but took the arm off one of his attackers.

But the fight was too one-sided, for moments later one of the attackers slid a long blade around the axe-man's defences and stabbed him in his side. Even as his legs buckled, another drove his blade into the man's chest and he fell silently to the grass close to the centre of the Temple. The two killers paused to bind their fellow's deep wound before, half supporting and half dragging him, they made their escape, leaving the corpse on the ground, and the Temple forever defiled.

The wind rocked me, and I turned to my left as a new sun rose over the Plain. Stones had tumbled, stones lay broken, the circle was no longer complete. The great gateway that framed the setting sun was fallen, one limb lying broken on the ground, the other leaning drunkenly into the centre of the circle. The southern entrance was destroyed, with three lintels down and one upright fallen and another just a broken stump.

There were other visions then that I do not now remember, except for one or two. I saw what I think was the bog beside the River, but in my vision, it was a shallow lake, a big pond within which a clear spring bubbled up. The place was well wooded, just as it still is today, but the trees were in their full summer leaf. A great bear wandered into view, coming to drink at the waters, but there was something about it that was not as it appeared; a lightness of foot and an alertness that I had not seen before in a brown bear.

Then I saw, briefly, its reflection as it bent to drink, and what it showed was not a bear at all. This was a spirit beast, the guardian of the spring, and he looked familiar, although I suppose one bear must look much like any other. He waded in and paddled across to where the water bubbled gently, dipping his head into the water amid the bubbling spring, afterwards lifting it high to roar his approval of the day. For a moment, the beast seemed to become aware of something and swung aggressively towards me, seeming to glare at me through the mist of my vision. He growled at me as if in wary recognition, then swung away just as the vision began to fade.

I must have had my mind on injuries and healing, for I soon found myself watching a young woman hurrying along a path on the Plain, carrying an old leather bag full of freshly picked herbs. She reminded me of Fenratha, especially with the bag of herbs, but this girl was taller and had a set of the jaw that put me more in mind of my brother Kefhan. Then the scene shifted, and I watched her sitting inside a hut tending two patients on straw-covered hurdle beds. The one lay quiet, but the other was in the throes of a violent bout of the summer fever, tossing her head about and uttering strange moans and whimpers as if all the demons of the underworld were on her tail.

I sighed, thinking that this woman would almost certainly be dead before the day was out, and perhaps her companion with her. Many survived the sweating sickness that came every few summers, but hers seemed a particularly bad attack, and few were strong enough to make it through two such days. But the young healer seemed unconcerned, and doggedly continued to mix her febrifugal draughts and applications. She sang several little incantations as she did so, and spoke gently to each patient as she rubbed in the ointment. Then she opened their mouths, each in turn, to take a little of her herbal drink and in a while, the fevered woman settled into a peaceful sleep, while her companion's breathing became easier, and his expression less strained.

Later, it seemed I revisited this vision; I was surprised to see the two patients sitting outside the house in the late summer afternoon, hide cloaks wrapped about them as they talked together in low tones. To one side stood the young healer, talking softly to two older women. One of them suddenly smiled warmly and embraced the young girl affectionately, while the other just nodded approvingly. I had no doubt I had witnessed a healing of great power and that the young woman must be exceptionally gifted, and I wondered who she was – or would be, since my visions seemed still to be leaping back and forth through time as if it had no significance whatever.

There must have been periods when I simply slept, free of dreams and time-slips, and began the long process of recovery. Afterwards, I spent so much time analysing what I had seen, but I always came back to the idea that, whilst my body lay in the hut with Fenratha, my spirit was still anchored in the Spirit House where the accident occurred. It was for that reason that my visions took me back and forth through time with such bewildering frequency, for only there, in the very centre of the cosmos, could all time co-exist at once. There I was in a still point; while the storm of the ages tore on all around me, I was in calm air, in the very Eye of Time.

Gradually, the visions became shorter and less obviously significant, and always with me being a disembodied observer, with not even the amorphous body I had possessed in some of my early experiences. I still had no control over either what I saw or the outcome, and after the episode with the bear spirit, I had no interaction with the people and spirits I saw.

There was a time when I was watching someone at the fire, working the bladder to force air into the flames and raise the heat needed to release the essence of the stone. I saw him take the little pot of glowing liquid from amid the glowing embers and pour the sun-gold into three small moulds. Then I watched as he removed the cooled tablets from the moulds and selected one, beating it with an antler hammer into a thin, flat disc which he then trimmed to form a tidy oval. He took the off-cut and folded it before beating it into a long tang on one edge of his oval to create the blank for a tress-ring just like the ones I myself wore. His decoration, too, was almost identical in technique and content to the way I had learned from my uncle Orelac, and I gradually realised I was watching my grandfather Kefhan at work.

I saw him on a different occasion, and many a time since I have wished I had *not* had this vision or had not thereafter remembered it. When first my sight came into focus through the mist, I saw him climbing the wooded slopes at the edge of the Plain and coming out of the trees as he breasted the ridge and looked across the grasslands beyond towards the invisible Spirit House on the far side of the downs. He was seen by some herd boys who waved and called out as he strode along through the late summer haze, admiring the way the wind made the shadows dance with the light across the tall grass, and the rich tones of the sky around the great thunderheads building towards the sunset end of the Plain. One of the lads took off at a run ahead of him to tell them he was home and he watched with pleasure as the boy ran like a deer across the rolling hillside.

By the time the sun had slipped below the spreading bank of cloud, my grandfather was nearing home, walking below the rise that marked the ancient spirit rings of the ancestors, great oval circuits of segmented ditches, one inside the other. Out of the growing gloom, three men appeared, seemingly coming to meet him, as they altered their direction a little to intercept him as he passed the old place. They stopped a few paces in front of him and waited for him to walk up.

"Greetings, Useris, and you, Jysthan!" said my grandfather when he recognised two of the men. "What brings you out here to meet me, or is it pure chance that brings you this way?"

"No, not chance," replied Jysthan. "We heard of your return earlier and decided to save you the last march of the journey."

"Thank you, but since I doubt you are offering to carry me, I cannot see how you can shorten the journey. I would be happy if you would walk with me just the same and tell me all the news from the last year or so. That will make the journey seem shorter, at least."

Useris scowled then, and stepped forward belligerently. "We mean that you need not bother to walk the last march, Stone-changer. You are not welcome in our land anymore, and may as well turn about and take your footsteps and your false boasting somewhere else. Or go back to whatever burrow you have spent the last two summers in, and have them listen to you if they will."

"Ah, I am so glad to be back at last, to hear your charming voice and caring advice, Useris. I might have known you would not be here to wish me welcome home. But I have news to tell Yrthyn, and will wait to see if he is more welcoming, so I fear I will have to complete my journey after all."

With that, Kefhan shifted his pack to a more comfortable place on his back and walked past the three sour-faced plainsmen. He must have covered just ten or twelve paces, when, with a sharp exhalation of breath, Jysthan swung his bow from his shoulder, stepped through it and tensed the string, raising the weapon and smoothly fitting an arrow as he took a step forward.

Neither of his companions tried to stop him. In fact, Useris, with a wicked sneer on his face, imitated his kinsman and drew and armed his bow as well. Jysthyn shot first and missed, the shaft passing over Kefhan's shoulder a handspan from his head. I shouted a warning, but as before, none of them could hear me. Kefhan looked around in disbelief, then started to run, weaving as he went to disconcert their aim. Useris aimed, then loosed his arrow and buried it in Kefhan's pack, the shaft passing through the contents and into the man as he staggered before running on.

Jysthyn's second shot took him in the leg and brought him down, then both archers ran towards my grandfather, each one nocking another arrow as he went. They stopped four paces from my grandfather, who was trying to sit up and turn to get at the shaft in his leg. Both men shot from close to, hitting their victim in the neck and the side. He cried out once and fell face down in the field.

Jysthyn took a spear from the third man and walked around my grandfather until he stood close to the prone man's head. Then with a sudden lunge, he stabbed the spear into the base of Kefhan's neck and walked forward as he pushed it deep into the chest, looking for the heart. There was no escape from death after that blow, and as my vision faded and my head throbbed, I watched my grandfather bleed to death on the edge of the ancient spirit ring.

Did I see further visions after that? I cannot say, for nothing I saw could supplant that scene of horror in my addled mind, and the next thing I can recall with any clarity was the return of the pain, tearing into my head, filling my whole body until I cried out and was jerked unceremoniously back into the land of the living.

For a few days, I floated in and out of consciousness, adrift on a sea of pain and barely aware at the best of times of the people who came and went, or of the tender hands that washed my face and applied soothing poultices to my wound. Gradually, with the help of regular draughts from

Fenratha which took away the worst of the pain and left me in a light-headed, half-witted state of helplessness, I regained control of my head and the various parts of my body. Well, apart from my left leg, which would not be tensed, let alone moved, without a wave of pain that cut through all the opiates that my wife had given me, and made me cry out like a vixen on heat every time I shifted my weight.

After many days and nights, they judged the wound was stable enough to try and move me, and they bound my leg up tightly to a split pole that held it rigidly on both sides. Then Tokhan and Kefhan, with the aid of another man whose name I forget, lifted the hurdle that had been my bed for I know not how long, and carried me outside for my first view of the world since the ancient stone had shattered my leg and my life.

From the flowers I could see in the meadows, I judged that it was late in spring, four or even five moons after my accident. Kirah told me, as I swallowed my first unlaced barley beer in the cool evening air, that although the wound remained slightly inflamed, the skin had begun to grow back at the edges and that there was a good chance it would close up eventually. Then, she said brightly, I might learn to get about again with the aid of a crutch. The prospect did not exactly thrill me, but it seemed too late now to go back and let death take me. Besides, there was a new feeling coursing through me that I could sense when the pain subsided, one that promised a freedom of movement in my mind that I could never experience on my legs alone.

During those days, when the softness of spring slowly gave way to the heat and harshness of a hot, dry summer, I spent much of my time trying to recall the dreams and visions I had had in my delirium. For each one I remembered, I attempted to turn the jumbled images into a logical sequence of events, with people and places I could identify and who remained the same throughout the vision. Some were beyond recollection, and I had to let them go; others appeared so trivial and insubstantial I stored them away as simple dreams. Of the remainder, there were many I did not understand and some that indeed I have never understood to this day. Equally, there were others that fell into place as real events of the past or present, and some I guessed were fore-tellings of possible futures. I have recounted many of them to you in these ramblings, but believe me, there were many more.

Above all of them, I kept returning to that last horrific scene, the clearest and most lucid of them all. I had no doubt it was the truth, that this showed what had become of my grandfather. I could not see how Atharon could not have learned about it, from his father or from others, and wondering why he and his sons had chosen to lie to me so many times worried me. I knew I would have to pick my time carefully to broach the subject without alienating my hosts, but at that time I had no idea how long it was to be before I finally had all the answers to my mystery.

CHAPTER TWENTY-TWO

All that summer and through the following winter, I was confined to my bed, except when there was someone who could lift me and carry me outside. Kefhan and a neighbour rigged a hurdle seat for me that gave support to my legs, and they placed it close to the house wall so that I could lean back and look at the outside world for a while. Once when I insisted, they gave me a staff and helped me to my feet, but the pain when I tried to walk nearly made me faint, and the effort caused fresh oozing from the knee. So I bowed to the inevitable and kept my weight from my left leg.

I had no shortage of visitors. At first it was just my friends, Tokhan, Turac, Aslena, Syllan. Even Jahrain came from the Northerners' settlement across the Ayn once or twice to see how I was faring. And when there were no adults, I played with the children, for little Ulrac was growing fast and loved nothing better than to sit beside me and ask me about the 'ghosts' I had seen, and the dragon beneath the sacred hill. He would forget most of it within a few days, but some of it stayed with him and helped, I suppose, to train his mind to be the seer I was sure he would one day become.

The other child was rather younger, and our play was limited to her grasping my finger as tightly as she could and smiling a smile to melt any father's heart. For just a few days before midsummer, Fenratha went into labour and delivered to us a tiny bundle, a pretty little girl we named Meyrana, and I became a father. I am told a woman's first child is often reluctant to make its appearance and causes the mother long periods of pain (they assured me it was worse than anything I had experienced with my knee, but I was not entirely convinced) but Fenratha had a much easier birthing than Kirah had had. I think it was that easy birth that made Meyrana a happy, undemanding child and allowed us both to enjoy our first experience of parenthood.

Meyrana was not the only new addition to the family that year. At the height of the summer, in the midst of a thunderstorm and a torrential downpour, a small black dog limped into the house for shelter.

Kefhan made to push him out, but I stopped him, saying, "Look at him. He's as thin as a reed and twice as wet. And he has injured his leg. We cripples must stand together now and help one another. Let him sleep and warm himself, find him a few scraps, and when the weather changes, either he will go home or we will try to find his home for him."

That stray pup looked at me with such understanding and mute gratitude I knew even then that he would be staying on with us. By the following evening, I had named him Sorash – Shadow – for his dark colour and his emaciated state, so thin that he hardly seemed to be there at all. Apart from occasional forays out to catch a rat or to do whatever dogs do on their own, he remained by my bed day and night for the rest of the summer and through the turning of the season into winter. Once or twice he managed to get Arrow to join him for a romp around the homestead, with rough and tumbling melees whenever they caught up with each other. Most of the time, however, Arrow pretended to be too grown-up for such childish games, and lay tolerantly still as Shadow bounced around him until he ran out of energy and sprawled beside the older dog in the yard and regarded me with a cocked head as if he was wondering when I would get up and join in the game.

I was so involved with my new situation that it was only the approach of another midwinter that set me thinking about the work I had started at the Spirit House, and what, if anything, had been achieved by it. I found out from Kefhan that the work had been completed, but it was when I talked next to Syllan that he described in more detail what had been done.

"It took longer than we planned with all the distraction of hunting for Mikhan," he told me. "But in the end, we completed the outer circle and found enough ancient stones for a complete oval in the interior. They tried it out at the midsummer festival, and the seers said the two circles made a good path for the circle dance and the oval gave a good sense of separation for the centre space. Even Ursehan was quite enthusiastic!"

The name Ursehan took me back to my visions, and I wondered whether to say anything to Syllan about the murder of my grandfather. I decided to wait until I felt strong enough to confront his father, or even Ursehan himself, about it. But something else caused me concern.

"A complete oval? My idea was to repeat the cave formed by the gateways with an open arc of the ancient stones. If the entrance is blocked, the flow of power from the dance to those in the middle may still be blocked. I thought I made that clear."

"Obviously not!" Syllan bridled at my assertion. "You described an oval, and an oval was built."

"Then we will have to change it," I snapped back.

"Ho! Good fortune with that, my friend! My father was heartily sick of all the disruption and the wrangling that went on last winter. I doubt he will even consider further changes. And neither will many of the fellowship. If it works better than before, they will want to leave it as it is, and get used to it and enjoy the results without further changes. My advice, Weyllan, is to enjoy the praise and thanks that will come to you for your insight and sacrifice, and to say no more about more changes for a few years at least."

Being in no condition to go out and consult the brotherhood myself, or to face Atharon's bad mood, I let it go at that and said no more.

By the following summer, the hot, dry weather helped the healing of my skin and, thanks to the ministrations of my two personal healers, the wound on my knee finally closed over, and I was, for a while at least, free of padding and bandages. The internal liquids also dried up, and I found I was at last able to hobble for short distances with the aid of a stout staff. My leg dragged behind me and required effort to position before each step, but at least I could move between the houses of our little homestead, and walk out into the grass when I needed to relieve myself.

The reports I had from the Temple seemed favourable, and I took Syllan's advice and said no more about my ideas for further changes. Late in the autumn, I walked as far as the Chieftain's complex to see Atharon. He had been to visit only once, and that had been just a brief call to see how I was. I thought I should make the effort to pay my respects and discuss my future in the village. The trees in the valley were already half bare, but here and there was a colourful blob of orange or red to brighten the grey onset of winter in the woods.

Atharon seemed genuinely pleased to see me."I am very impressed, Stone-changer, by your progress. There are many who, faced with an injury such as you suffered, would have given up and died, or spent the rest of their days being carried to-and-fro. It is good to see you active again, although I also see that it has taken considerable effort on your part to get here. Sit yourself down, lad, and share a pot of beer with me. I heard you had some amazing dreams and visions when you were ill."

It was the most relaxed interview I ever had with the chief, and I felt unable to bring up the issue of my grandfather, but I told him (and his family and advisor who were present) some of the visions, and we wondered what they signified.

"It is not often one of our seers has a conversation with Lena herself," he said, much impressed by that vision in particular. "If she continues to favour you, perhaps we should arrange some ceremonies in her honour to return the favour she extends us. Talking of ceremonies, I hope you will be well enough to attend the solstice festivities this winter; we missed you last time."

And so, I agreed to resume at least some of my duties as a seer for my adopted people.

I began walking for a while every day, trying to extend the distance every few days as my strength returned. But by the time of the midwinter rites, I could barely make it to the old settlement and the wooden spirit house where our morning ceremonies would take place. Kefhan and Tokhan fashioned a wicker seat for me between two long poles, and they carried me across the ridge after the prayers at the wooden house, arriving in time to join the procession in the combe below the stones. I made my own way up the hill among the seers to attend the evening dances and rites.

I would not be able to dance, but Kirah supplied me with a long draught of her potion to open the senses, painted my face up, and I entered the new oval sanctum to try with the others for a vision. I felt I could probably achieve a vision state without any herbal assistance, but the mixture helped calm me and significantly lessened the pain that would have disturbed my mind after the strain of processing even the short distance up the hill. The dancing began, with the hypnotic rhythm of the drums and the eerie piping of flutes punctuated by long howls from medicine horns to rouse the spirits.

I sat on my throne near the edge of the inner space, my back to the great gate to the underworld, and swayed gently as I tried to call down the Kas into my shoulders. For a while, it seemed as if nothing would happen, but suddenly I lost sight of the Temple, and in a breath, was drawn backwards through the gate behind me and transferred completely into the sandy underworld of the spirits.

They were waiting for me when I arrived; Urda and her cronies, hovering before me in a malevolent arc of latent nastiness. I waited to see what they would say this time.

"So, Outlander, you are back again! I would have thought you had learned from your last experience here. And now you come back, having joined the ranks of the blasphemers and moved our ancestors' stones yet again! Yet even I have to admit you are a hard man to kill, Stone-changer, even with so strong a weapon as one of our stones."

"Did *you* have a hand in that, Urda? Or are you just claiming influence over someone even more twisted than you, so as to impress your cronies?" I placed the barbs deliberately to provoke a reaction; I wanted to know if she had indeed managed to influence Mikhan and the events of the winter before last.

"And as for the moving of the stones, I have tried to honour your ancestors with them again. Look; I have rebuilt the circle of fifty-six stones to bring the ancient circle within the new and unite them once more. Your ancestors' ashes and bones are still within the boundaries of the Spirit House and can integrate once again with the dancers in the Temple."

"And a random set of odd stones you have made of them, Outlander. Only the number matches – the stones themselves are all over the place!"

"I could not have replaced them in their original pits if I had been allowed to do so; how could I tell which stone stood where, to place it back in its socket? That past is gone forever, and we must work with what we have. The fifty-six stones and those in the inner ring between them must contain pieces of all the original stones, and I'm sure the spirits will be able to find their particular stone if they feel the need to. And *I* do not forget, even if you do, that all those stones carry part of a single mountain spirit, Wobai. Which one an ancestor addresses will matter far less than it would with the great stones. So, the circle is made again, of the same stones, and whether you like it or not, the spirits will be united!"

She was not used to being argued with, and swayed backwards, at a loss for words.

I pressed my advantage. "Urda, I am not your enemy. Neither are these people, whatever their clan or allegiance. I have seen the spirit path you made; I know what lies at the other end. I will take you there, so that you can find your way out of limbo, but I think you must bury your anger and your bitterness first, or you will never be free."

She laughed then. There was the bitterness I expected, to

be sure, but also more; a sense of helplessness and of fear that freedom was not a simple option.

"It's the bear, isn't it?" I guessed. "Something to do with the bear and the manner of your death?"

"Outlander, I would have travelled on many generations since, if I could. The beast holds me, in body and spirit, and without it, I have no access to the Kas I need to take me whole through to this world or the tree. I cannot break its hold, I cannot put the demon to flight, and no man alive can help me do so, or I would have had it done cycles ago."

"*I* can try. I think I have a way to solve this, but I need to have you and your kin on my side, not against me. I will do right by them, and by you, if you give me the chance."

"Even though my people killed your grandfather? I know that you know; I can read it in your thoughts. We believed he would make things worse and we killed him, as we tried to kill you through that useless assassin. How can you forgive that?"

"Urda, I know not how I will achieve that, nor when it will come upon me. But I will try. I am not one of these folk of the Plains, but I have come to love them as my own. This place is surely the very heart, the centre of all that exists, and they are its guardians, your kinsfolk along with the rest. It is time they, like their ancestors, were united, so that this house becomes what it deserves to be; the Heart of the World and the Eye of Time for all peoples, irrespective of their kinship. Help me, and let me help you!"

"We shall see," was her only reply before she turned from me and faded into the haze that hung over the sands like a mist of lost and formless souls. The place suddenly depressed me, and I turned to find a way out.

I was aware of a presence, and looked down to see Reya beside me. I felt much better, and smiled down at my spirit companion. Her words formed in my head as we moved along, she trotting and I hobbling awkwardly with my half useless leg that it seemed would stay with me even on the other side.

"So, Seer, you have outflanked your enemy and offered her friendship. An excellent move, if it succeeds. But you will need great power and great resilience to carry out your promise, you know."

"I know," I thought back."And I have no idea if I am strong enough. But I will do as I promised, and try."

"You should know that the gift Lena gave you was a power you can draw down when you need it most. You will have the power. Now the spirits are a jealous lot, the great as well as the small, and I have been told to tell you to turn your face to Lukan when he appears tomorrow, for, not to be outdone, he too would give you a gift. It is with their help you may win this battle, and you will owe them both everything for their gifts if you succeed."

With that, she turned aside and faded before I could reply. Then I felt myself fading too, and I slipped back through the gateway into the Spirit House as the dancers were giving up at last. The sky was grey across the River, although you could still see stars clearly in the purple sky on the other side of the Temple. Dawn was upon us, and the sun would rise to start the new year in just a short while. I had fallen unnoticed from my chair, but I could reach my staff, so with some effort I pulled myself to my feet and hobbled out of the stone house to find my family.

The night was almost over, but the spirits had not yet done with me. I sat myself down with Fenratha, little Meyrana, and Shadow, on the chalk bank a little way from the southern entrance, facing the point on the ridge where the sun was rising slowly from its journey beneath the world. Some say, I know, that when the sun sets, it passes through the underworld, but in all my times with the spirits on those pale sands, I have never seen the sun, nor any sign of a shadow anywhere. So, I believe there is a passage beneath the world where the sun goes each night.

I thought then, that if ever I flew in the heavens again, I would fly out past the horizon and see what I could see, whether there was an end to the underworld, or even, as one old sage once told me, a mirror image of our world beneath us, where Lukan shed his light when we were in darkness. I remember shaking my head at that thought, and hoped that if I lived to that age, my mind would last better than that sage's.

At last Lukan showed the top of his head above the ridge, filling the land before us with light and warmth. Almost immediately, I felt myself slipping away into my other state, crossing over into another place that looked just like the one I had left, except that my family and the others there became insubstantial, like pale shadows unaware of the other side I had moved into so quietly. And the sun-spirit spoke to me, in my head, with words that burned in my mind like a sun-gold furnace, and scored themselves into my memory.

"Greetings, Stone-changer and favoured of my cousin Lena! I see you have had my message from little Reya."

"Greetings, Great Lukan. She has indeed told me you wished to speak with me."

"That is so. Know that we watch you and speak to you, not out of curiosity, but because you have been chosen to steady the balance here at the Heart of the World, to make this spirit house a place of unequalled power, and to clear the way for that power to bring order to the cosmos for a hundred generations to come. Lena gave you access to great power to bend the world to your will, but your injuries have limited your strength to wield that power. So, I give you another gift; call on me when you need to, and I will give you, while you have need, the strength to absorb and use the power you have been given."

"Thanks be to you, Great Lukan. I will remember you and your gift, and will try to make sure others respect you as I do, in thanks for your kind offer."

"Kindness is not something we toy with, Seer. But we see the patterns in the web of fate, and try to guide certain mortals through them to strengthen the weave and maintain the balance that benefits us all, mortals and spirits."

Every gift from a spirit is a two-edged blade; the gift given is always to be balanced against the cost of using it. Wielding such power and using such strength would drain me and almost certainly aggravate my wound, and the burden of it, when to use it and when not to, would be a heavy strain upon my mind. More than one seer has been shattered by the pressures of wielding power, and been lost in the twilight, like Urda, for the rest of their life and beyond. So, it was hard to know what I felt about this new honour.

I knew both pride and trepidation, both excitement and uncertainty, but never resentment that I had been chosen to bear this burden, never a wish that I should not have these responsibilities and these extraordinary experiences. Those things I would not have missed for all the simple joy of an ordinary life, where the spirits were something you might be vaguely aware of a few times a year and where you had no control over your destiny. I would often feel bitterness and regret about my damaged leg or the loss of a dear friend, but never about my calling as a seer and the way it had grown beyond anything I had expected in my youth.

And the sun began its low arc across the winter sky, and the new year swam into focus around it.

CHAPTER TWENTY-THREE

Over the next year or so, I worked hard to build up the strength in my legs to walk longer and longer distances with the aid of my staff. Kefhan said that I should carve images on it like the ones that seers used back in our old home, but I shook my head and dismissed it all as showmanship. But when Kefhan took an idea into his head, it was hard to shake it from him, so when I was confined to my bed after a fall that set my leg oozing and throbbing for many days, he took my staff and carved its top into a good likeness of a smiling fox, in honour of my spirit guide Reya. I gave only the lightest of thanks to my brother, but secretly I was most pleased with his action and quite proud of my new symbol of power.

There was in my heart the knowledge that I had done nothing yet to fulfil my pledge to Urda, nor to confront our chief about my grandfather's murder. Another solstice came and went, but as I was confined to my bed with a fever from my leg, I did not attend. But as the fading white blossom of the thorn bushes warned of the end of spring and the start of another summer, I tried one day to walk to the Spirit House.

Stopping to rest at Urda's spirit path, I had a new vision of the ancient seer, this time without her usual gang of acolytes in attendance. She mocked me for my failure to carry out my promises and my poor health, raising my ire until I reached out to her and grasped her roughly by both arms, spinning her around to face along the path toward the late afternoon sun.

"You think because I am frail in my world that I have no power in yours?" I roared. "Look yonder; I reveal to you your destination!" I concentrated all my energy to pierce the gloom and to break through into the third place where stood the First Tree, towering above the little banks of the spirit path with its lowest branches halfway to the clouds.

"Now, doubt my abilities no longer, Urda. And do not doubt that I will take you there! But there are things that must be done first and permissions to be sought from the living; doing that is what my illness has prevented so far. I am stronger now, and I will do this before midsummer. That is my word!"

Why I made such a rash promise, I have never under-stood. I must have been so angry that I would promise anything, or perhaps, after all, I felt guilty at my failure. Whatever the reason, I now had a deadline; two moons at the most to persuade Atharon and Urda's kin of the rightness and necessity of what I wanted to do. I hobbled homeward, determined to seek an audience with the chief the next day.

So it was that on a warm but breezy morning, I took up my staff and walked slowly along the ridge to Atharon's compound. Syllan was on his way out as I approached, but turned back to join in the discussion. A young lad was sent off at a run to fetch Ursehan whilst I sat with the chief's family and exchanged commonplace news.

Presently Ursehan arrived, with Reirda in tow. Both gave me a strange look as they entered, one of mixed surprise and curiosity. I soon found out why, as Atharon brought the audience to order.

"We are here at the request of our seer Weyllan, who wishes to discuss a ... project – is that right? – with all of us. I have already been assured that it does not involve moving any stones in the Spirit House, so we may be easy on that front. What is on your mind, Stone-changer?"

I stood to address the others in the formal way, leaning on my newly carved staff for balance. "Thank you. You all know that I have had various dealings with the seer Urda, and that she has, for many generations, been opposed to the changes that have been made to the Spirit House, to the building and, more recently, with my alterations to the stone Temple. What you will *not* know is that I have spoken with her twice more, with a proposal that I hope will allow her to take her place with the ancestors and bring all the factions back together again."

"We wondered if this concerned Urda," Ursehan interrupted. "You should all know that both Reirda and I have this night past had visitations from our kinswoman's spirit, both with the same message; that you would come to us with a plan to bring peace to our ancestor and that we should agree to it, whatever it was. It seems you have not told Urda your full intentions, Stone-changer."

"No, because I felt that just making the promise to put things right was rash enough, without complicating it with detail that might be considered sacrilegious. Let me explain. Urda built her spirit path to connect your ancestral burial mound with the First Tree, which she found on another plane here at the heart of the world. She built the path as a gateway to reach the tree. But she was thwarted in her attempt by a demonic bear who grappled with her and brought down the mortuary chamber within the mound, burying the both of them deep inside. I told you how I saw this in my visions, and how I realised this was why Urda is trapped between the realities. I also spoke with another spirit, who seemed sure that I would be able to free Urda to travel on. After that, I spent many days considering how I might achieve it."

I made sure I had everyone's attention. "This is my solution. We must dig into the mound, levelling it if needs be, until we recover the bodies of Urda and the demon. Then we can take Urda, along with any others we recover, and build a pyre at the other end of the spirit path. I will go to the other side to open the gate so that those who wish to can go with Urda to the land of the First Tree."

"You wish to exile my ancestors along with Urda?" snapped Atharon, clearly angry at hearing another disruptive plan from me.

"No, they will be able to find their way back when they need to, with whatever gifts or learning they acquire during their stay. They will take their place as before, with your ancestors at the Spirit House, and I hope Urda will be with them, valued by all for the part she has played in this episode. For without her, it is unlikely I or anyone else would have seen the gate through to the Tree."

"What of the bear-demon? What is it, and what shall we do with it?" asked Reirda.

"The bear, too, must be caught in limbo. I had a vision of a bear-spirit that guarded the bog by the landing place, back when it was more of a pool. I think perhaps it took refuge in the mound, for winter or to rest from some injury. We should make a pyre for it somewhere else, and send the ashes down the Ayn away from the Plain."

"But that will pollute the sacred River, mixing with the spirits of the other departed." Reirda was outraged. "We should scatter the bones around and leave them for the birds!"

"For the sheep and cattle to chew on?" I asked, "So that we will all be infected by the bear's malice? No, I think that consigning them to the River is the best way. The waters will cleanse themselves, and like our other departed, the bear will complete the cycle and return once again to the earth from whence it came."

Ursehan frowned but nodded anyway. "It is a clever plan. I can see why you wanted our agreement, although I must say, I am not happy that we must desecrate our ancestors' tomb. But if, as you say, there is a demon trapped within, it may all be poisoned ground already. It would be better to dismantle it than to leave it damaged and still polluted. Urda said we should agree, and I do so."

Reirda looked at her kinsman, then with some reluctance, nodded her consent as well. Syllan signalled his agreement, and we all looked at Atharon.

"As with all your ideas, Weyllan, this one has the potential to go very badly awry. But on the whole, your schemes have worked so far; if Ursehan supports it and Syllan is in favour, I will give it my blessing too. The men that undertake this work need not be seers, but they will all need to undergo purification both before and after their work. Syllan, I give you charge of this project with Weyllan. It will be good practice for when you take my place as the leader of our people."

This was the first time I had heard Atharon publicly confirm Syllan as his heir, although we had all expected that he would be the chieftain's first choice with Athlan gone. I parted company with him, still full of the import of the things we had discussed, and I was almost home before I realised that I had still said nothing about my vision of my grandfather's murder. That would have to wait for another day.

. . .

Atharon wanted to delay the work until after the harvest, but Ursehan argued for an immediate start. Why, he asked, should we wish to delay the end of Urda's misery and pain? I supported his argument, rather to everyone's surprise, so the chief issued orders that every clan and line was to volunteer anyone they could spare to start straight after the next new moon.

Only about forty men and boys turned up for the first days, but we still managed to build five great sweat houses in three days. Turac came by to inspect the lodges, and together we made a spell of blessing for the place and the purification rite that would follow. More came to join us the next day, including a dozen or so women who took over one of the sweat houses for their own rites. After a day-long fast, the rest of us crammed into the other four lodges, perhaps fifteen or sixteen to each fire, and began the process of cleansing ourselves for the coming task. I led the chants and meditations in my lodge throughout the night, long after the sweat was done with and the fire damped down to prevent us overheating. We had to open the door-flap to let in enough air for everyone, and many fell to sleeping a long time before the dawn.

With the first rays of the sun, we stepped out into the morning chill and were handed our cloaks to wear by young attendants who had kept their vigil outside. I felt a surge of pride that we were doing this for someone so long dead, who had, to be honest, been a thorn in the side of most of the people present their whole lives. We had a ritual meal of porridge with watered mead and walked over to the ances- tral mound. Ursehan raised his arms and in a clear voice, called out to the ancestors to forgive us for the act of dese- cration, explaining what we would do for them to atone for any ill they felt. Then the first teams set to work, one working down from the top of the mound, the other digging into the broad end, where the entrance to the chamber should have been.

Soon they encountered pieces of decayed timber, some barely more than dark soil after such a long time, while others retained a recognisable form, although quite soft now to the touch. We worked in alternating shifts, and by sunset, we had exposed the main timbers of the chamber, without yet finding any bones. We stopped work and went to a camp prepared for us by another team where we would stay for the duration to maintain our purity of spirit. We ate our meat and fell quickly into sleep on whatever we could find to soften the chalky hill beneath us.

The next day and the day after that, we continued work, clearing the timbers and carefully searching the soil underneath for the bones of our ancestors. By the end of the third day, we had almost finished emptying the burial chamber and had a large stack of bones arranged around a makeshift shrine, but we had seen no signs of Urda or the bear.

All the bones we found had been moved many times, and stored with similar body parts rather than with the other bones of the individuals of whom they had once been part. These bones were ancestors now, a group of spirits with a corporate identity that had more significance than any individual. Seers could often still encounter them as single souls in our travels but for most, the ancestors became one great, inseparable, spirit. Syllan, Kefhan, Ursehan and several others gathered around a fire to discuss our progress and our options for the next few days.

Ursehan went straight to the point."All this has been a waste of time! We have desecrated the ancestors' house because this outlander said he dreamed we would find Urda here. And now it seems it was nothing but a sleeping fantasy.

How will we make it up to our spirits? This will require a blood sacrifice to put right, mark my word!"

"Weyllan has been right before, and his visions have always been accurate." Syllan was more conciliatory. "We have not found the very back of the chamber yet – there is no sign of the rear wall. We may yet find what we seek."

Kefhan weighed in as well, then others joined in, and the discussion went back and forth for a while. I found myself drifting off into a tired reverie, thinking of my bed with warm skins about me, and Fenratha beside me. Then I realised there was no campfire anymore, and the shadowy figure speaking to me was none other than Urda. What she told me brought me wide awake, back to reality.

"There is a second chamber!" I shouted to the group. "Behind the main burial room; a niche at the back that was enlarged by the bear for its winter nest. We have another two days' digging yet!"

"How do you know that?" asked Kefhan.

"Just this moment, I have had another vision. Urda came to me and told me to keep digging; that there was another chamber and that they are both there!"

The others were almost convinced, except for Urse-han."And why should we believe this? A vision, with no preparation? No inducement, and so conveniently timed? My spear, but you are a powerful magician indeed, Stone-changer! Or not, I think. My people and I will have no more of this. We are going home tomorrow, and you can finish your desecration alone. And if a blood sacrifice is needed, I know who I shall recommend for the honour!"

But Syllan supported me, and most of the others followed his lead. We would carry on in the morning, with or without Ursehan's kin.

Despite a constant drizzle that began at dawn and barely paused for breath the whole day, most of the men worked on until, shortly after noon, we found the collapsed roof of the low passage to the rear niche. There was nothing in it, so we dug on into the chamber beyond. That was a larger space, although the timbers of the roof only extended back a longish step; the rest I guessed had been hollowed out by the bear, with no roof supports at all. We ended the day in a much more optimistic mood; when the rain finally ceased, and a few stars showed themselves through the clouds, I felt quite confident at last.

Sure enough, we found the bodies early on the fifth day, although it took us most of the day to clear the soil and the remains of one massive timber from them, exposing them ready for lifting out. I will never forget the sight; Urda lay on her back with the great body of the bear across her chest, its skull badly cracked on one side where the timber had struck it a death-blow.

The strangest thing of all was the state of the bodies. After all this time, they should have been no more than bones, but by some magic, they still had most of their flesh, albeit withered and shrunken to a dark leathery brown. Most of the bear's fur had gone, but odd tufts remained, giving it an air of having severe mange, and its lips had peeled back to expose the teeth in a fearsome snarl that turned my blood to ice. Urda's last moments must have been terrifying, attacked by a monster in the dark and then buried alive, trapped beneath its bulk forever.

Or, as it turned out, until we came to her rescue.

The following day, we carried Urda's body and the bones from the tomb in procession along the spirit path to the far end, where two great pyres were built. I wondered which of the children of Hatha were among the bones here, and whether Hatha herself was about to go with her family to the land of the First Tree. A few bones were separately taken to the Spirit House to be laid to rest in the ditch, so that the spirits there could be informed of the latest developments and the resolution (I still hoped) of the Urda problem. When the pyres were lit, I took some of Kirah's special potion and settled down on one side to meet the spirits and guide them across the divide to the Tree. Atharon led the proceedings, with Turac as chief seer, and it all went as smoothly as anyone could expect.

As I opened the doors through to the Tree, the spirits of these ancient ancestors, led by Urda, filed past me, each nodding a 'thank you' as they went.

Urda stopped as she passed, reaching out a ghostly arm to touch me as her thoughts came to me. "Thank you, Stone-changer. You have earned your place here with these people. I am sorry I stood against you, and for my part in the fate of your kinsman and yourself. May you prosper and be honoured and remembered in your turn. May the Kas always come to you and serve you well!"

And she was gone.

Because of Ursehan's outburst and his withdrawal of help from the digging, Atharon ordered him to dispose of the bear's body. He was instructed to take it well downriver somewhere. There he was to burn the carcass and scatter the ashes to the winds, releasing the spirit from its limbo to go wherever bear spirits go. We watched them leave, a little procession of about eight of Ursehan's kin group, as they carried the carcass on a makeshift litter down the valley towards the Ayn, heading at first towards the pools and bogs along the riverbank before they turned aside to follow the stream a little towards the southern sea.

No one doubted that they would follow their instructions, and it was many years before we found out what they *actually* did that night. And by then, it was far too late.

CHAPTER TWENTY-FOUR

Nyren and Nykhin returned the moon after midsummer. They came not from the Sunset Sea, but from their home in the opposite direction, having returned there early the previous winter. Wheris stayed behind to nurse their new infant son, born earlier in the autumn. It was good to see my old friends again and to know they were well. Moreover, they came with a gift for me of a large bag of blue-tinged rock and a smaller bag of sun-gold nuggets and flakes. There was enough here to make nearly a dozen moon-gold blades and several pieces with the softer gold. Over a pot of beer with some venison provided by Kefhan, they shared many of their adventures with us, continuing the tales the next day and into the night following.

"The spring after you two left, we walked north for days and days through the mountains until we came at last to the sea again. We were told by local herders that there were places where we could find some moon-gold stone just inland, and we spent the entire summer prospecting for that, and panning the streams for the sun-gold. We were stalked by wolves, chased by wild boar, and even once seen off by a bear! But by the year's end, we had located a source of moon-gold rock, and at least three streams that gave traces of sun gold."

He took a sip of his beer. "We spent another year looking for the source of the river deposits without success, but we dug out several sacks full of blue ore and panned about as much again of the sun-gold as I have given you, my friend. We gave gifts to the local seers and still had as much as we could carry to bring home. We tried to involve a few of the locals in the smelting and mining, but they were very suspicious. Then there was a day when the earth shook, and the mountain fell, trapping Nykhin and a local lass. We got them out, but the chief threw us out anyway. We started home, but I took ill with a fever, and we had to stay most of the summer near one of the great rivers that run south to the sea from that land."

"Four years since we first met, and nigh on as long since we parted!" I said in mock admonishment. "We wondered what had become of you, Fenratha and I, or even if you had perished. It is good indeed to see you all back safe and well, Nyren."

"But you have not fared so well," he responded. "You have done yourself a foolish injury, by the look of it, and now I see you will not be returning to the mountains with me next year."

And so, I had to tell him the tale of my accident and all the other stories that followed from it, including some of the visions, the killing of Mikhan, the improvements to the Spirit House, and the finding of Urda.

Our guests stayed for many days, and we filled the time talking of our various lives until we ran out of things to say. Eventually, our conversation turned to the future.

We decided that before he returned to his home, Nyren would join Kefhan and I for a bonding smelt. We would again replace our knives from a mixed pool of moon-gold, and I made up my mind to make two pairs of sun-gold tress-locks like my own and my brother's, to give to our friends to show our kinship as stone-changers. But before we did, Idetermined to ask Atharon about the changes I wanted to make in the Spirit House.

As chance would have it, when I walked over to see Atharon, Syllan was there, with his young son Kyrthan in tow. I had not seen Syllan since the cremation of Urda's remains, and was distracted for a while catching up with my friend. But once the ceremonial beer had been brought and tasted – several times – I forced myself to come to the reason for my visit.

"It has been over three years now since we made the changes to the Spirit House," I began. "We have all seen and experienced the improvement that my changes have brought about." There was a nod of approval from Atharon, but Syllan, knowing what was coming now, looked concerned.

"But I was not able to supervise those changes, and there are others I would have liked to have had done which were not enacted because of my accident and illness."

Atharon's eyebrows were raised as he responded, "Your achievements are not forgotten, Weyllan. I have already heard that there is more you would like done. But the disruption was great indeed, and I would not wish more upon the brotherhood so soon after the last occasion. You have a lifetime ahead of you; time enough to make more changes when you are more attuned to the power of the Temple and are, perhaps, one of our elder seers."

"But, Father, this will not cause the same degree of disruption." I charged ahead, ignoring the subtle warning of the chief's words. "It will be an enormous improvement.

Right now, the inner circle is blocking the flow of power, and we need to …"

I got no further. Atharon's scowl was terrifying; the hand he swept up to silence me brooked no argument. He stood up for added emphasis as he shouted across the room, "*No!* I will not allow any further experiments or works to be undertaken! You have done what you were asked to do, and for that we are grateful. But it is *enough*, and the power flows quite well enough. No more changes, no more projects!"

"But Father, it is just a simple ch …"

"Weyllan Stone-changer, you have overstepped the mark! I am Chief here, and you are here as my guest, nothing more. You are *not* an elder of the fellowship, nor are you one of my advisors. I will not have you trying to tell me how to rule my people. Go now, or there may be consequences!"

I was angry now, as well, and when I heard that last remark, I was unable to stop myself from blurting out, "What will you do? Kill me, as my grandfather was killed? Was that on your father's orders, or was it just the action of Urda's kinsmen? Either way, your father knew of it and so did you. Yet you have consistently denied it and lied to me. What am I to make of *that?*"

There was a long silence. Atharon looked at his son, who shook his head in denial, looking understandably surprised by this turn of the conversation.

Then the chief turned to me, his anger as cold and sharp as a flint blade."How have you come by this information, to make such an unwarranted accusation in this manner?"

"I had a vision. I saw my grandfather shot and speared by two of Urda's clan, Useris and Jysthan by name. They murdered him on his return from the Sunset Sea. I know it was a true vision; I know the difference between dreams and visions."

"True or not, visions cannot be evidence in our justice,

and since both the men you mention are long dead, there is nothing to be done now."

"But you knew this. You have known it all along and have denied that knowledge to my face several times!"

"I had heard rumours, but there was never a body, nor any proof. My father decided it was better for all to let it go, and when you asked, I made the same decision. It was not why I asked you here. As my guest, I did not, and do not, want you starting feuds among the Children of Hatha. That is all I have to say on the matter. It is closed. Done with!"

"I cannot accept that, Atharon. Since I have come to live among your people, all I have done, I have done for their peace and wellbeing. I do not ask even now for revenge or retribution, but a little honesty would help *me* to close the door on the past. I ..."

"You have no further say in it!" Atharon interrupted me for the third time. "I will not be gainsaid and treated with such disrespect. You were asked here to show us the new magic of stone-changing and to see if you could improve the working of the Spirit House. The latter you have done, the other you have shown no inclination to share with my people. You have done what you came here for; you are free to go. You are no longer my guest, and may leave whenever you choose to! And should you need to speak to me before you go, you will ask for a time of my choosing, as other foreigners hereabouts must do. Go now. I do not wish to speak with you anymore!"

I stood in stunned silence for a while until he turned to his son and told him to escort me out. Syllan, equally shocked but also clearly angry with me, hastened to do his father's bidding. At least he gave me my staff before leading me outside and away from the compound.

"You fool, Weyllan," he said, when we were well away. "Why did you bring that up when he was already annoyed?

What did you expect? Now you have lost your special status here and your ear to my father, for he won't change his mind. He's as stubborn as an ox when he gets angry like that. Go home, and think about what you have done today."

Then he turned and left me to make my own way slowly back along the ridge to our homestead.

To be honest, Atharon's retraction of support made very little difference to our daily lives. We discussed it at length, talked to old Turac and to Aslena when she came by a few days later. I had not been exiled or ordered to leave, so we could still stay where we were. Our friends, other than the chieftain, were still our friends and I was still a member of the brotherhood of the Spirit House; I could still participate in the ceremonies there. Atharon had hardly ever been to visit, whilst although Syllan seemed to drop by even more rarely than before, he still went hunting with Kefhan and permitted Ulrac to play with his own young son. Kyrthan and Ulrac were becoming inseparable and, unknown to all of us, were busy forming a bond that would last them the rest of their lives.

I had not given up on making further changes to the arrangement of the old stones in the Temple but knew it would have to wait until Atharon had gone on and Syllan was chief. In the meanwhile, I met with and talked to as many of the other seers as I could to try to persuade them of the advantages of another change, so that when the subject was raised again, it would come from the brotherhood rather than from me. The response I had was very mixed, and many of the older seers wanted no further talk of changes. I began to wonder if I would ever see the project completed as I had originally envisioned it.

Just three days after my audience with the chief, Nyren,

Kefhan, and I repaired my furnace and built our sweat lodge to prepare for the double smelt we had planned. I would have liked Kirah to join us, but with three of us already there was no need for another pair of hands, and since Kefhan did not invite her, I felt it was not my place to do so. She was, anyway, quite busy decorating her next batch of pots – some of which, I should add, were bound for Atharon's household – and trying to keep young Meyrana's hands away from the fragile clay vessels.

We purified ourselves from dawn on the fourth morning, then applied a little paint as we did each time we smelted; although we did not set out into the spirit realm on these occasions, the act of painting helped remind us that this was still interaction with potentially dangerous spirits, and showed them we were fully prepared.

By midday, the fire was burning hot, and we placed into the first of the fire-pots the stone we would change. This was moon-gold ore along with the broken fragments of two old knives, so that the stone would understand better what was expected of it. Then we stoked the fire and worked the pair of little bellows Kefhan had made. It took a while to break down, but when it was ready, we removed the slag from the surface and poured the metal into three new knife-moulds. Then we made another three knives by placing a second fire-pot in the cavity left by the first one and repeating the process.

Nyren had an idea for a new use for some of the moon-gold. "We should draw it out into a thin string. Then we can cut it up to make needles or cloak pins, harder than any from bone and, like our knives, they can be re-made when blunted."

"Our father taught us that trick years ago," Kefhan replied, then nodded warily. "But we were never happy with the results, and the string was lumpy and uneven."

"Let me show you my way then." Nyren smiled at us."I have had good results and will happily teach you the trick of it."

So, we drew out several wires with the moon-gold. We were all impressed by Nyren's technique, far more efficient than the one Kefhan and I had learned back in the White Mountains. Then we all three sat for a while sharpening points and heating the other ends to make blob-heads to the pins.

The final smelt came late in the day when we placed in the furnace a fire-pot filled with crushed nuggets and ore bearing the brilliant sun-gold. There was enough there for a handful of liquid sun-gold – not that we were foolish enough to consider measuring it that way – and aside from the tress locks I had in mind, Nyren wanted some sun-gold pins and some sheet to cover small toggles or brooches. Kirah, too, had requested some sheet metal and we smelted enough to provide her with her needs as well. It was nearly dark by the time we finished, and having had nothing to eat since our ritual breakfast at dawn, we returned to the houses to devour a huge pot of stew, some bread and several beakers of barley beer before collapsing into our beds.

After Nyren left to return home, life returned almost to normal again. A few days later, I noticed that Brwslyi's scale had disappeared from its place among the relics on the shelf at the back of the hut. I panicked, thinking we had been robbed, until Kirah calmed my fears, producing the scale once more, although it was now edged with a narrow strip of sun-gold sheet, riveted into place with alternate studs of sun and moon-gold. She had decorated the strip with chevrons and dotted zigzags like those on her pots. I knew the symbols well and understood the magic that went into them.

This relic of my vision quest had been turned now into a talisman, a shield to defend me against who knew what evils. I was stunned by her gift, humbled by the skill with which she had worked the unfamiliar metal, and once again impressed to the depths of my being with the resource and abilities of this woman with whom I was fortunate to share kinship.

"This should be your insignia. Wear it when you perform as a seer, both to protect you and to remind the others of your powers. No one else has *ever* been honoured by Brwslyi in this way! Also, only you and Kefhan hereabouts can work the stone-changing magic that produced this border. I know you are not a boastful man but you have been slighted by Atharon, and others will look down on you now for that reason, so wear this with pride to remind them you still deserve their respect!"

I protested, but of course, she was right, and I have worn her talisman ever since, whenever I work or officiate anywhere as a seer. I believe also that it travels with me to the other side, where it is visible and impressive to those I meet there, so that it protects me even without the magic Kirah worked into the edging.

Winter came with all the coughs and ills that always accompany the cold weather. Each year some of the older folk would die, not of starvation or the cold, but from the attentions of the fever spirits who came among us to prey on the weak and unwary. They kept well clear of *our* homestead in those days, but they found a way into the home of our chief. Just over a moon after midwinter, the fever spirits took Atharon to join the ancestors. Fenratha had been to visit him when we heard he was ill, but there was little she could do. Moreover, the suspicious looks she received from both

Syllan and his mother persuaded her not to try any strong medicines, in case they should blame his death on her.

Turac took charge of the funeral arrangements, following instructions left by Atharon. The chief had been neither a seer nor a member of the brotherhood, so he could not be buried within the bounds of the Spirit House, but he had wanted more than just being consigned to the River after the next midwinter blessing. While the preparations were under way for the cremation, Turac organised a crew to dig a ring of pits, and throw up a bank to create a spirit wall around the grave. A circle of posts was erected within the boundary to form the spirit house for the cremated remains and any future members of Atharon's dynasty who wished to share it with him.

I was not asked to participate in the funeral proceedings, but we all went anyway to pay our last respects to the man who had brought us all here. Turac called the ancestors to witness, and Syllan lit his father's pyre to release the spirit within. No great signs or portents showed themselves among the flames or the smoke, and Atharon's spirit passed quietly from our world into the next. Kefhan and I went over to Syllan afterwards, and offered to join him in the vigil over the embers, but he spoke only to my brother, and seemed unaware of my presence. I soon left, dispirited and annoyed, to rejoin Kirah and Fenratha and the children. We returned home, leaving the family to grieve and watch over the ashes until they were cool enough to sort through for the remains of Atharon's bones. Kefhan joined us after dark for an evening meal, having been sent home by Syllan with his muted thanks for staying.

The next day, we all went back to watch the short procession from the pyre site to the chief's new spirit house. The cremation had been a sober occasion, but today there were drummers beating out complex rhythms, flutes whistling, horns hooting and howling, and pots of celebratory beer being passed around. Atharon was having a loud and enthusiastic send-off to leave the spirits in no doubt as to his status amongst the living. With the ashes interred, the digging crew were called upon to cover the grave with a low mound of chalk to mark it in white as sacred ground. Turac told me, as we talked afterwards, that some of the chalk had come from scouring parts of the ditch around the Temple, in accordance with a specific request from the chief. He was creating a new burial form to suit his belief that he was the founder of a dynasty who would rule Hatha's Children for many generations to come, and we all realised that this was, indeed, the beginning of a new era for the folk of the Plain.

That was how Atharon passed out of our lives and into the spirit world. Or, at least, I presumed he did, for from that day to this, I have never encountered his shade in my journeys on the other side.

CHAPTER TWENTY-FIVE

"Mother, how can I hunt with Kyrthan if I don't have a proper bow and arrows? Father says I can't have one for two more years!"

"And your father is right. You have not yet seen seven summers and could not pull a full bow if you had one. In another year or two, you will be ready. Then Kefhan will take you to cut your first full bow before they take you hunting. Until that day, you boys must make do with your light bows and stick to shooting tufts of grass or the odd squirrel."

"But Kyrthan's father said he would give him a bow this summer!"

"I doubt that. Kyrthan is younger than you and twice as dangerous anywhere near a weapon. Syllan has more sense than to do that, even if he lets his son think it will happen!" Kirah smiled at the disappointment on her child's face and shook her head at him. "Did you really think I would be so naive as to fall for that one? We used to try the same trick on our parents when we were children, Ulrac. It didn't work then, and it doesn't work now. But run along, and see if your friend has fared any better than you."

She watched him trot off along the ridge towards the chief's compound, where she knew he would meet with an equally disappointed Kyrthan. They would take their small bows and head off into the woods by the River and by noon would have forgotten all their tribulations in the excitement of stalking and generally terrifying all the small animals in the wood.

Syllan had been chief for a year now, and showed all the makings of a good leader who listened to his advisors and dispensed justice even-handedly and without bias. He remained friends with Kefhan, but his attitude towards Weyllan was unchanged. He barely acknowledged the seer when he came across in search of Kefhan. She had asked her husband to question the chief and try to persuade him to open up to Weyllan again, but Syllan simply changed the subject whenever the issue was raised.

As for Weyllan himself, Kirah thought he seemed restless, and often brought up the subject of his grandfather's murder. It played upon his mind, and he was unable to pass beyond the need for some form of closure, be it justice or simply an apology.

Spring slipped gently into summer until there was a day when she noticed a fierce light in her brother's eyes and watched as he gathered up his dragon-scale and staff to hobble off with Shadow along a path leading upriver towards the homesteads of Ursehan's kin. Kefhan, as usual, was nowhere to be found when she needed him. Fenratha was lying down, recovering from a bout of sickness caused by the new child within her, so Kirah set out herself to follow Weyllan and keep him from mischief if she could.

Hewas not difficult to follow. His crooked gait left a distinctive track in the knee-high grass along the edge of the path, and his progress was still relatively slow, although Kirah had to admit he was more agile than she expected.

The track dropped into the riverside woodland for a while, but she knew that it would soon emerge to climb the next hill. Beyond that ridge lay the scatter of homesteads that were the home of Ursehan, Reirda, and the descendants of Elluric, the half-brother of Urda, her closest living kin among the Children of Hatha.

Kirah stepped out of the woods, blinked for a moment in the sunlight, then staggered backwards to avoid the figure lunging at her from the shadows beside the path. Weyllan caught her as she fell, bracing his good leg and leaning away to keep her upright.

"Kirah? What are you doing? It's only me! I thought I heard someone following me – I'm sorry – what, what are you doing here?" His words tumbled out as she tried to recover both her composure and her balance. "I guessed where you were going, and *why*. I followed to try to keep you from doing anything foolish. You know this will only stir things up, and may turn Syllan even further from your old friendship."

"I have made my mind up," growled Weyllan. "I want to hear what Ursehan knows and how true my vision was. He owes me for saving Urda's spirit."

"Then I will come with you, and we can hear it together. You should not go alone."

"I am not alone, dearest sister. I have with me my spirit guides and a spine full of Kas. And my dog, if only he would stay with me!" He gestured towards the distant hound, happily and hopelessly chasing a hare across the meadow. "If they were to try anything, I am more than ready to defend myself. But I hope it will not come to that."

Kirah looked around her as she walked beside him, unable to sense any power or spirit presence, and wondered if her brother was bluffing, or had taken something unsuper-vised and was simply hallucinating. Without her potion, she could not see the spirits and demons that took possession of sick minds, but she had enough experience to sense their presence, and she felt nothing out of the ordinary in Weyl-lan's proximity. She knew he could store up enough Kas to move objects and perhaps even throw a person about; Fenratha had told her of the episode in the mountains, and she remembered the seer's description of the knife incident the year before that.

"You must be very careful," she admonished him. "Don't go using your power to punish them for the sins of their fathers; that leads to a dark path I would not see you take."

He smiled then, and put his hand out to cradle her cheek. "Do not fear. I am in control, and Reya is here to watch over me as much as to protect me."

They crossed the ridge side by side and took a path that led more directly to Ursehan's homestead. As they approached, a child who had been playing in the yard ducked inside, to re-emerge with two adults who stood to watch the seer's approach.

One of them, who Kirah recognised as Ursehan himself, called out, "Greetings, Stone-changer! What brings you visiting my house today? I am sure you didn't just come by to gossip and share a drink with us, although I will gladly provide a pot of beer to refresh you after your exertion."

Weyllan thanked him but said no more until he was seated on a log set outside the house for any guests. Ursehan was head of his kin line, so he had to be ready to advise and mediate between his people when they came to ask his help. His yard was set up for him to hold court, with log seats for a dozen people and a wicker-backed stool for his own use.

"When first I came to this land, I made enquiry after my

grandfather, whom I thought might have passed this way before me. You all denied knowledge of him. Then I found he had indeed been here, but left to journey to the Sunset Sea. Atharon swore that he never returned. Yet Urda told me he had, and that she had made sure he was dealt with when he did. And then I had a vision of his murder at the hands of your kinsmen; your father struck the fatal blows! Atharon's response was to disown me and send me away none the wiser, except that he ordered me to cease my search since all the actors were now dead. So many lies, so many denials, and so little truth. Now Atharon is dead. I have come here to listen to some truth at last, Ursehan. If the chieftain knew, then you must know as well, so tell me; what really happened to my grandfather?"

Ursehan coloured, then as Kirah watched, his expression changed to a dark scowl.

"You dare to come here to make demands of me, based on some delirious dream you had when your wife and family stuffed you so full of potions you would imagine whatever you wanted to? I would not bother to lie to you, Stone-changer, because I do not fear you. Neither your physical strength nor your spirit power can come near to harming me. You will get no answers from me today or any other day!"

Before Weyllan could recover and reply, there was a roar from within the house, followed by a voice, quivering with anger, calling Ursehan by name. A figure appeared in the doorway, a bent old man leaning heavily on a stout ash staff, blinking in the light yet still succeeding in glowering balefully at the unfortunate target of his anger.

"Father!" Ursehan cried. "You are not well enough! You should stay in bed. Leave this to me, please."

"I am well enough to hear still more lies and distortions spoken when you should be looking to heal the old wounds.

332 | T. S. ROBEY

Must I still do everything myself, until finally it consumes me?"

"He called you 'father'!" stammered Weyllan, exchanging glances with Kirah. "If that is true, then you must be Useris. Not dead at all, and the centre of still another deceit?"

The old man looked at Weyllan, and suddenly appeared both frail and weary. "Yes, I am Useris. Why they told you I was dead, I cannot understand, although I came close enough to it last winter. And you must be the seer Weyllan, who did what all of us before you not only failed to do but failed even to *realise* could be done. You understood what had become of our great mother Urda and how to free her, and despite all she had done against you, you released her into the place of her dreams. You deserve answers, Stone-changer, and you deserve truth. Let me sit with you for a while. I will answer your questions and try in my turn to set you free."

He paused before turning to his son, who stood in the yard with his mouth open and his arms frozen mid-gesture. "And you! You make yourself useful and fetch the beer you offered your guests, since there is no one here you can order to do it for you."

He lowered himself gingerly towards the log next to Weyllan. Kirah, still perplexed by the scene she had watched, stepped forward quickly and took the old man's arm, helping to support his weight as he sat down. She was rewarded with a beaming, gap-toothed smile and a surprisingly firm squeeze of her wrist from Useris. She smiled back, instinctively liking the old man, in spite of the evil she was sure he had done against her family.

"Just as when *you* first arrived," the old man began, "Kefhan's appearance here created serious rifts among the Children of Hatha. Urda thought he was a menace, and told us all to oppose him however we could. Unlike you, your grandfather was no mediator, and his confidence that he could fix the Spirit House infuriated many here. When he left, we were not the only ones to be glad of his going. The chief, Atharon's father, made his feelings very clear at the next meeting of the elders. Your grandfather was gone for so long – several years – that we were fairly certain he would not come back. Then one day, we heard he claimed to have solved the problem, and was on his way here to impress us once again with his brilliance.

"My cousin and I took medicine and travelled into the other world to speak with Urda. She told us to prevent any interference with the Temple by whatever means we could. So, we went out to meet with your grandfather Kefhan when he came in across the Plain, and tried to persuade him to stay away. He was so dismissive that he angered us, so we struck him down and slew him. It was a terrible thing to do, and we were tormented by our actions, which we instantly regretted. We brought the body back here and burned it – with the proper ceremony, I promise you – before giving the ashes to the River. Then we held a council and decided to tell our chief what had become of your kinsman. I fear we coloured the narrative in our own favour though, so that Yrthyn would not see any need to punish us."

Kirah saw Weyllan struggling with this information. She was worried that at any moment he would explode and strike the old man, but he just managed to control his emotions.

When at last he spoke, his eyes were wet with tears of sadness, and he shook his head as if to clear it of the conflicting voices within."So, I was right, and Atharon's family knew all along the fate of my grandfather. *And* who was responsible. Yet still they let it go unpunished. I cannot decide what to say, I ..."

His voice trailed away as Kirah put her arm around his shoulders and pulled him close. Shadow trotted up, tail wagging furiously, to lick his master's face, and Kirah's arm, indiscriminately.

"I said I regretted our actions then," Useris spoke into the silence. "And I have done ever since. When you arrived here, I travelled to speak with Urda again and told her we would not help this time. That perhaps it was time for something to change, and that she should let the living move on. Even then, nobody saw how to resolve the situation until you showed us the way. You are a better man than any of us, Weyllan, and I suspect a more powerful seer as well. I humbly ask your forgiveness for our foul behaviours, as you found it in you to forgive Urda, and free her spirit at last."

Weyllan nodded and touched Useris on the shoulder. "After all this time, there seems little advantage in harbouring hatred for you or seeking revenge for the murder of my kins- man. I regret that it has taken you and your chieftain so long to tell me the truth. Forgiveness, yes, I can give that. But do not expect trust or friendship, or any further acts of kindness on my part. Our business is done from this time forward!"

Kirah took Weyllan by the hand as they turned away, leaving the homestead without another word or a backward glance. Nothing was said until they were almost back in the woods.

"What will you do now?" Kirah was still a little fearful of his answer, but he soon reassured her.

"I must rest first. Then I must speak with Syllan. I have blamed him along with his father for saying nothing, but after all, he was only doing what he was told to. I think I must try to heal this wound before we consider our next move. Thank you, sister, for being there with me – and for me!"

The next day, Kirah learned that the first case of the summer fever had been reported, and for the next moon, she and Fenratha were busy along with every other healer treating the victims of this feared illness that always took several people off with it. Fenratha continued her work despite the serious concerns of both Kirah and Weyllan for of the child she carried within her.

Turac was, among his other attributes, a respected healer, and remained busy despite his advancing years. He and Fenratha were among the most successful in treating the scourge. No one knew how to cure it or prevent it, but the better seers and healers were able to keep their patients comfortable and give them the strength to fight back. In the end, Turac's own guardians failed to shield him from the malevolence of the spirits that spread the disease, and he fell ill himself. Despite the personal ministrations of both Kirah and Fenratha, the spirits burned up his soul, and he died as the moon waned to darkness again.

Kirah listened with the rest of the family when Weyllan told them of the meeting the fellowship had called to discuss the funerary arrangements for the old seer, a distinguished member of the group. Several of the seers had advocated that Turac's remains be buried in the Temple enclosure, where in times past the ancestors were laid to rest. This was a rare honour, one that had not been gifted in anyone's memory, but most of them felt that Turac richly deserved the distinction. He was the right person to renew the link between the living and the ancestors now that Urda was at rest, and the spirits were more amenable.

The old seer had died about ten days short of midsummer and was cremated in time for the celebrations. So, on a warm, mostly sunny day, Turac's closest friends and relatives gathered at the wooden spirit house next to the sealed-off village to walk with the old man's ashes as he took his last journey down the Ayn, then up the path that led over the ridge to the Spirit House on the Plain. Weyllan limped along with them, with Kefhan and Kirah to support him should his strength fail him. The pace was slow, not only because of Weyllan's limp, but because several of Turac's nearest and dearest were almost as old as he had been, and they were no better at walking the distance.

By the time the group arrived at the Spirit House, it was mid-afternoon, and already Kirah could see a large crowd gathered outside the ditched enclosure. Many were there to join in the general festivities and to watch the sunset ceremony with the dance that followed. They would light their family fires after darkness, and dance their own dances; there would be gifts exchanged between the kin groups, and feuds ended or called to truce for a while. Many healers not involved within the Temple would also take this chance to see their patients or take on new cases, especially where the need was beyond just herbal treatment, and required spirit healing as well.

Kirah had to wait outside the stone circle but watched closely as they placed Turac's remains on the flat stone before the Sun Gate along with other pots holding the ashes of others who were passing over today. The dead would keep a vigil with the living through the night, to be warmed one last time by the midsummer sun as it shone over the horizon and into the heart of the Spirit House. Then, Kirah knew, they would be collected by their relatives before being consigned to the waters or to some special place for whichever line the person had belonged to.

Only Turac was to take his place among the ancestors inside the Temple boundary. Kirah was very proud of her close association with such an illustrious person, joining the others in a prayer to the spirits to honour him as he became one of them.

As before, Weyllan did not dance, but took charge of a

drum to beat the rhythm out faithfully for the others. It seemed, though, that he was not to be permitted to pass a ceremony in the Spirit House without visiting the other world in person, and Kirah was not surprised when his drumming faltered. She watched as he fell back against a stone, eyes flickering and his hand jerking in the air to the rhythm without ever touching the drum-skin. Kefhan was dancing and saw nothing so, with the early ceremonials over, she decided she could safely enter the Temple and stay with Weyllan's body as he journeyed to who knew where in his mind.

When he returned to his body, he was sweating profusely and Kirah touched his chest to feel his heart was thumping away in his chest. His experiences on the other side must have seemed so real to him. In the absence of Fenratha, she bathed his face as he lay back against the stone to recover, and watched over him as the night came gently to an end and the sun broke through to bless the dead upon the altar.

When he recovered, he related his vision to her. "I was aware of a change in the beat of the drums and was surprised to see the Spirit House filled with strangers, dancing the same dance but in a light drizzle that soon soaked through everyone's clothes. Nobody seemed to notice me tapping my drum out of time with everyone else, and I gradually realised that this was another vision. I began to look around with greater interest. The first thing I noticed was that the inner-most circle of the Old Stones was no longer complete, and that the remaining ones were all the tallest survivors of the collection. I could see that several of them had been exchanged for ones I remembered from the outer circuit and with a rush of warmth I knew that my plan for the final changes to the Temple would one day come to fruition.

"The rain increased in tempo, but the dancing continued, and many of the seers were being cared for by supporters while they travelled somewhere in other realities. In the very centre of the space was a shallow pit in which lay two broken spears and four or five bent or snapped moon-gold knives, longer than any I had ever seen or could imagine making. Now and then, one of the dancers would run into the centre and spit derisively on the heap of dead weapons, to the accompaniment of a ragged cheer from the others. I thought that this must be booty from a raid or a feud. I felt strongly that such behaviour was for dancing near a homestead and had no place here on this of all nights, when the healing of conflicts should be everyone's main concern."

Weyllan stared off into the distance, as if trying to recall every detail of the vision."As I sat there, I began to feel through the stone at my back a rumbling of power, of resentment, as if the ancestors and the stones themselves agreed with me. The rumble grew in intensity as the rain fell harder and harder, until it was a loud hum that I felt everybody must be able to hear. Indeed, several of the seers came back from their spirit journeys and looked around in some confusion, obviously puzzled by the air of menace that had descended upon the Temple in their absence. Then came a loud groan from the air itself, and the dancers faltered in their steps and the drummers, one by one, ceased to beat the rhythm. Several changed to a rapid beat to call back the seers who remained out on their travels.

"Another great creak, and a sound of stone rending against stone, and suddenly we all saw one of the uprights of the Sun Gate begin to move and tip towards the centre of the space. With a fearsome crash, the stone tore loose from the earth and hurled itself to the ground. pulling down its massive crosspiece with it. Both stones fell across the altar, cracking it through, and as the lintel rolled onto its side, I had to draw in my legs and pull myself upright with speed to avoid having my feet crushed. People were running in all directions away from the Temple. As I wondered what I should do, I felt the vision fading, and I passed through the darkness and back into my own time, where the dance continued smoothly as if nothing had happened."

Turac's remains were buried a little after sunrise, but Kirah could tell that for Weyllan, it had been a more than usually sombre occasion. With the shadow of the future still sharp in his mind, he told her, he felt with foreboding that Turac could be the last of his people to join the throng of the ancestors in this way.

CHAPTER TWENTY-SIX

"I know not what you hope to gain from this meeting," began Syllan, when he finally consented to see me nearly a half-moon after midsummer. "I hold by my father's words. There will be no more changes or disruptions in the Spirit House; that matter is closed."

"I have not come here about that, my frien ... my chieftain." I was trying to strike a conciliatory note. "Many days ago now, I spoke with an old man, Useris, who was one of the men who murdered my grandfather. I cannot entirely forgive him, even though I see now how he was driven by the misbegotten malice of Urda, but I did not and do not seek revenge or recompense for his actions."

"Then what do you want, Stone-changer?"

"Syllan, there was a time not long ago when you would have called me by my name, or acknowledged our friendship. Are those days gone now that you have become a chief? It was at your direct request that I came here, it was as a result of the task you and your father set me that I am injured so that I cannot, even if I wished to, make the journey home to the White Mountains. Will you not warm your heart towards me again and let us talk this through as friends?"

"Weyllan, you have done much that is good since you came here. I freely acknowledge, both as an individual and as leader of my people, the debt we owe you. But you have also caused division and exposed ills that should have been left buried, so for my people's sake, I cannot treat this matter as a friend. Those times are behind us for now, and I am your chief as long as you abide in our lands. You must do as I say or face the consequences!"

I was quite taken aback at this high-handed rebuttal. I had hoped to rekindle something of our old friendship and deal with this matter in that way, but now it looked as if any attempt to take it further would be met with open hostility. Just the same, I had to try to make my feelings understood.

"I know that vengeance will not put this right, nor bring back my grandfather. It would be my right to ask you to get me some recompense, but I realise that would cause a split with your people. All I hope to find out is why you and your father felt it necessary to lie to me time after time, to deny what you knew to be true. You could have told your father about me, that I would not want to interfere with the balance here, that all I needed was the truth. And that is all I ask now."

It was foolish, I know. I should have kept my silence.

Syllan had grown visibly angrier through the exchange, and now his voice rose further as he spoke. "I did not know you well enough to vouch for you in this matter, and I am not sure I know you well enough *now*. I did not know at first about your grandfather, and when I did find out, my father told me not to interfere with his decision to tell you nothing. At the time, I behaved out of loyalty to my father and my chief. Now I understand his reasons, and I would have done the same. How dare you call us liars, and presume upon my goodwill this way! You have already had the protection of the chieftain withdrawn; now I withdraw my friendship! Another word and I will have you exiled. Leave now, while you can."

He turned his back to busy himself with something in the family shrine, so that there was nothing I could do but bow and take my leave. My farewell was ignored, and I hobbled homeward in a despondent, miserable mood.

The harvest season was warm and dry, the small crops of grain for bread and beer were collected and stored before the rain returned amid gales that blew whole branches from the trees. The world prepared itself for the onset of winter.

One cool but sunny autumn evening, two men strode up the path to our homestead, carrying the heavy back-baskets and bags of long-distance travellers. I was sitting with Kefhan and our wives around a small fire, enjoying the evening sky as a stew of hare added to the left-over remains of a piglet bubbled on the fire. We all rose to greet the newcomers, who introduced themselves.

"I am Tamkris, of the People of Tamwyr, from the shores of Lake Ulu, and this is my travelling companion, Sterhun. We come following a vision we shared at midsummer, that on the Plain at the Heart of the World was a seer who would bring balance to the land. I have spoken to my kinsman Jahrain, and we think the man we seek is you, Weyllan Stone-changer."

Well, I was both flattered and flabbergasted by this pronouncement. I attempted to explain that far from bringing balance and harmony, I had barely escaped being cast out from the Plain, and it was unlikely that I would have any influence over events in the near future at least.

Tamkris frowned, then shrugged, answering in his

musical northern accent, "Sometimes the balance can only be seen once it is in place. And usually you have to rock the cradle before the baby sleeps. That it has not yet come to pass does not mean that it never will do so. We are no more certain of our role in this than you are of yours, but my instinct tells me we have come to the right place. Will you tell us your tale?"

I nodded and, when Fenratha brought us a pot of barley beer, the talk turned to my adventures since leaving home. The two sisters had heard it all before and sat back from the fire, talking quietly together. I listened with half an ear while still retelling my familiar tale.

"I am glad this bout of fever is over at last," said Fenratha to Kirah in a low voice. "I am not certain, but I feel the absence of my guardian spirits and worry that I have lost them. Whilst they are gone, I fear I cannot carry out any healing in safety."

"You are wise to avoid risks in that case, especially as you are near to your time now," replied Kirah. "But do not worry too much. They do sometimes go away without warning. Their loyalties and priorities are not the same as ours, and I believe that they must sometimes go off to refresh their power, just as we have to."

"I agree. Within another moon, I will give Weyllan a son and all will be well. I do hope they decide to return before then."

"Just as I said, my sister, do not fear. The fever is passed by, and nothing likely to threaten us will happen in the next few days. Your guardians will return, and all will indeed be well when they do!"

I was inclined to agree with Kirah, but you can never be too careful; I decided to make a spirit journey when our guests had gone to see if I could locate my wife's spirit guardians and persuade them to keep a better eye on her as she came nearer to her time.

When we woke the next morning, our two visitors asked to be shown the Spirit House. I happily agreed but suggested we go first to see our chief, as I was sure Syllan would like to greet two visiting seers. Tamkris shook his head, saying that there would be plenty of time for that afterwards, and that they were eager to see our Temple as soon as possible. I saw no real harm in this, so after a light breakfast, we set off across the Plain to the Spirit House.

I showed them Urda's spirit path and told them of my resolution of the problem of that seer's negative, baneful, influence. Then we walked up the hill to the entrance of the Spirit House to the guide-stone and the two guardians. As they stared across the bank at the Temple beyond, I watched with amusement as their jaws quite literally sagged open, and they stood open-mouthed in wonder.

Sterhun was the first to recover his wits. He turned to me, his first words breaking the spell over his companion as well."By the rocks and raging rivers, I have seen some wonderful things in my journey here, but this is beyond them all! There are bigger ditches, there may even be bigger stones, but I have never seen any shaped and balanced together quite like this."

Tamkris just nodded agreement, so I led them forward, pausing at the guardians to tell the spirits who I was bringing within. As we went, I began to explain how the stones were not simply balanced upon one another but were held together with joints styled on those used in timber houses. I felt some pride that I was now a part of this wonder, this house of stone, at the Heart of the World. I turned to look outwards and showed them how the skyline had levelled up as we came into the enclosure, so that it seemed our Spirit House sat at the very centre of existence. The effect was slightly marred by the grey clouds that had rolled in while we crossed the ridge and climbed up to the Temple, but they were experienced seers, and could sense the truth of my words despite the fine drizzle falling on us.

Both men offered prayers of greeting to the ancestral spirits and the others who dwelt in the Temple, giving their blessing and asking for the same in return from the resident powers. Then, as the rain grew harder, we left by the south entrance and stood a moment looking out at the view before it became blurred by the downpour.

"We should get back across the River to Jahrain's home while we can still cross over," said Tamkris. "I hope that this is not a sending from the spirits showing their disapproval."

I tried to assure them that I thought that unlikely, but in the end, they both insisted on leaving directly for their kinsmen's homesteads, and I walked home alone. They promised to return in a day or two to meet our chief but said that, for now, they just wanted to be safe away from any ill omens. I decided I would walk over to see Syllan the next day to explain their behaviour to him, and perhaps it might be a neutral topic on which we could talk while we began to mend the bad feeling between us.

Dawn brought a sky that was a uniform grey from horizon to horizon, and for the first time in many moons, we sat indoors to eat our first meal away from the damp chill of the outside world. Even the dogs stayed in, curling up beside the fire for as long as they were allowed. We were just beginning to discuss our plans for the day when we were interrupted by the noise of several people arriving in the yard, and Tokhan appeared in the doorway as he gave a loud and unnecessary knock on the wall to announce himself. He looked abnormally flustered; I looked past him to see several warriors gathered in the yard outside, and I remember wondering what had happened to set off this early alarm.

Kefhan grinned "Hello, Tokhan, what is it? Are we needed? Give us a moment, and I will get my bow and be with you!" Suddenly the day, at least for him, looked to be much more interesting than it had a few moments before.

"That would not be wise, my friend, for the purpose of our gathering is *here*." Tokhan shuffled his feet nervously, avoiding our eyes. "I don't know any easy way to say this, but … Syllan has issued an order of banishment for Weyllan. He is to leave the territory before sunset, or face execution. And since he would probably expect me to carry out the sentence, I am here to make sure you go, and try to sort it all out from a safe distance. I am really very sorry to bring you this news." He spread his hands to emphasise his feelings.

My first reaction was disbelief. I had been threatened before, but hardly expected my old friend to carry out the threat. I was not sure he even had the authority to do it without consulting the elders and the fellowship of seers, but Tokhan assured me he could do as he pleased in this respect. He reckoned that most of the people would back their chief's decision unless it was completely crazy. That seemed to me an apt assessment of the order, but I said nothing. We began discussing what to do.

Fenratha was driven to distraction and in floods of tears but was adamant that she would come with me. Kirah was unwilling to leave before firing her current batch of pots, as she rightly feared they would not survive a trip on a sled in their present state. Kefhan was uncertain, wanting to speak to Syllan and to try to change his mind before we packed up everything; he was in no doubt that if I had to leave, he and Kirah would follow as soon as they could.

"You are welcome to try, Kefhan my friend," said Tokhan, without enthusiasm. "But not today. I have already tried, and was shouted out of the house for my pains. He is adamant. This has been brewing for some time, I reckon."

"But what set it off now?" The answer was already forming in my mind as I spoke the words.

"It was your visitors. That you entertained two ambassadors from another people and did not take them immediately to meet your chief. Not a wise move; he felt it was a deliberate slight and an assumption of power he does not believe you should wield. I must say I can see his point, although I am sure you did not really think that at all. But I am surprised you did not present them to him. Where are they now?"

It was my turn to shake my head. "I tried, Tokhan, but they wanted to rest first, then they wanted to see the Spirit House, then they decided to go back to their kinsman across the River when the rain came. Tell him I am truly sorry, but I intended no slight or challenge to his authority. Although, if I know Syllan, it will make little difference now he has made up his mind."

Tokhan nodded but said nothing. So, we returned to our discussion and decided that we would all go, and carry our essential belongings that very day. My brother and his wife would then return for a few days to finish their tasks before moving the rest of our homestead, including our winter store of grain and roots. Once across the Ayn, Fenratha and I would try to find a site to set up home near the Northerners' settlement.

Kefhan pulled our little sled around into the courtyard, and we began to bring out our belongings. We loaded Fenratha's medicinal supplies and enough food to last us several days while we built a new home across the River. Fenratha was still so upset, she had made herself unwell, but she tried to take charge of the packing, deciding what to take now and what to leave until the final move was made.

Before we left, I asked Tokhan if I could pay one last visit to the Spirit House to say farewell. He was, as always, sympathetic and amenable. He even arranged for two of his companions to carry me in the litter Kefhan had made, which had not quite fallen apart where it lay to one side of my house. As we travelled across the ridge and down towards the spirit path, he came alongside the litter and talked to me.

"This may not be forever, Stone-changer," he began. "Syllan is upset, and like his father, is prone to make hard judgements when he is in such a mood. Pride will keep him distant for a while, but it would not surprise me if in another couple of summers, I was sent to help you move back again."

I reached out a hand to grip his arm, partly to thank him for his kind thought, and partly to reassure him I was alright. "I think I may have pressed him too hard and too often to gain easy forgiveness. This has been forming in his head for several seasons, since before his father died, and his heart has been hardened to me for a long time now. I do not feel that I will return here in body, at least, but my spirit is not done with this place, for I have seen my kin here in visions of times yet to come. Fate has set my path for me, and I must walk where I am bidden, in this world and the others."

Tokhan was silent for a while, until we approached the massive way-marker at the entrance to the Spirit House. Then he spoke, wagging a warning finger at me only half in jest. "Now, old friend, we are here for farewells only! No great spells or curses, please. No anger in this sacred place; though I hardly need to say that to *you* of all people. And nothing that will bring me dishonour for letting you come here. Take your time, it is only a little after midday, and there is ample time before the sun sets for you to be across the River. We will wait for you here unless you want a companion to safeguard your body if you travel to the other side?"

I shook my head and stepped out of the litter, taking my staff from Tokhan for support. Then as I passed between the guardian stones, the outside world became blurred and distant. I walked across the short grass, kept cropped by the Temple goats, who scattered at my intrusion. I was thankful to have the place to myself that day, so that no one would see the tears that formed in my eyes, trickling down my cheeks as I bade farewell to the stones and the spirits that dwelt inside the great house.

I hobbled around the circuit between the great stones of the outer ring and the ancient stones of the inner, greeting some of the stones I knew by name, touching them one last time to reconnect with their individual Kas and waken them to my presence. Then I entered the inner oval of stones and stood at the very centre of the Temple, turning to each of the great Spirit Gates to call my greetings. By now I could feel around me the presence of the spirits, the sense of movement and of power just an arm's length away on the other side, and I knew I was surrounded in several realities by spirits wondering why I called to them alone at midday on an ordinary day.

I reached out my arms to either side, stood as straight as I was able, and bent my head forward to admit the power I called down upon me as I began to chant. I had no drummer, but in my head, the beats were loud and the rhythm rapid. I even heard the horns several times as I tried to place my spirit where I could see into each of the five levels at once while I kept a conscious presence in the now of the Spirit House.

I had never attempted this before, and only believed it possible because Turac had told me it could be done, though he had not managed it himself. I felt the power surging through me, glowing hot as I channelled it in five directions at once, and I looked around in the hazy light to see the translucent shapes of scores of spirits around me. I opened my mind and gave them, as best I could, what I understood of the situation. I wished them well, and Tokhan would have been happy to know I specifically asked them not to blame anyone, least of all Syllan, for the fate that had befallen me. I said other things, and asked a few favours as well, before I closed my eyes, raised my head and released my hold on the spirit realms.

I was exhausted and had to sit down on the chalky ground for some time to gather my strength again as the stones stood dark and brooding, watching over me as I recovered. At last I stood up and walked to each gate in turn to bid them goodbye. As I put my hands to each stone, I could feel the response of the spirit within, some giving just warmth, some channelling Kas into my outstretched arms as if I were a dancer in the solstice circle dance.

At the Sun Gate, I remembered my recent vision of its collapse and searched within the stone for any signs of weakness. At first there was nothing, but then I sensed the faintest of tremors in the future, the very beginnings of movement in the rock far below me in the chalk that would one day lead to it toppling down upon the stones in the middle of the Temple. I knew then that my vision had been true, and that this would one day break the power of the Spirit House beyond repair, leading in the end to its abandonment. I also knew with certainty that this fate was far in the future and that the Spirit House would remain the Heart of the World for dozens of generations to come.

I returned to the centre, sang a short song of farewell,

then walked out to rejoin Tokhan and his companions. They regarded me in some awe as they helped me onto the litter and carried me towards the ford to meet my family. Tokhan said nothing, but later told Kefhan they had all heard the drums and horns within and seen the glow of fire from the centre of the Spirit House. He said they were very concerned for my safety, but nothing would have induced any of them to enter the Temple while all that was going on around me.

We cut across the ridge to meet my family near the ford. They were already there, resting. One of Tokhan's men had given Kefhan a hand to pull the sled, and they had made the short journey at a normal walking pace; they had been waiting for some time. It was already mid-afternoon, so with the days getting noticeably shorter now, we knew we should lose no more time in crossing. The Ayn was high from the recent rain; at the centre of the ford, the water was easily waist deep and flowing strongly. Kefhan and I set about gathering brushwood to tie in bundles beneath the sled to give it added buoyancy, then manoeuvred it to the edge of the River. Tokhan told two of his warriors to help us guide it across, and I turned to him with some concern.

"My friend, are you sure you should be helping us like this? Not that we do not value the assistance or the friendship behind it, but we do not want you to make trouble for yourselves on top of ours."

"My orders were to see that you left the territory before sunset," he grinned at me. "No one said I should not help to ensure that it all went smoothly. I will deal with my chief if he has any objections, have no fear."

"And we would be glad to help even had Tokhan not asked us too, Stone-changer. He is not the only one who is sad to see you and your family leave us. Say no more about it," was the unexpected comment from one of the men directed to help.

So, the four of us pushed the sled-raft out into the current at the upstream edge of the ford and hauled it across the stream, coming to shore within two paces of the downstream drop into deeper water. After a short rest, we crossed back over to collect our personal packs, the women, and my little daughter Meyrana. I tried to lift her onto my shoulders, but Tokhan gently took her from me and put her on his own back, saying that I should take care of Fenratha as we crossed. We filed into the water, and I felt the deep chill again, despite having already been in twice before. As we slipped and shuffled our way across, I held on to Fenratha's arm, although I'm not sure who was supporting whom.

Then, just a few paces short of the far bank, Fenratha slipped badly and plunged backwards into the stream, dragging me with her so that we were both underwater in an instant. We tumbled over in the flow, banging knees, elbows and heads as we did so, until I managed to jam my good foot against a stone, hauling us both back to the surface, gasping and spluttering. I tried to steady myself, but her body swung against mine, our legs became entangled, and down we went again.

Kefhan reached us then, hauling Fenratha to the surface. Without the encumbrance, I was able to regain my footing and stagger upright by myself; between us, we dragged the limp form of my partner to the bank where Kirah joined us to help pull her up onto a low terrace. We rubbed her arms with our hands, with grass and with moss to dry them and invigorate her, but there was no response.

It was Kirah who noticed the blood forming a pool by Fenratha's knees, and it was she who realised what it meant. "She's miscarrying!" she cried. "We have to stem that flow or she will die!"

So, saying, she began to pull aside Fenratha's sodden tunic to add wads of grass between her legs where we could now all see the steady trickle of blood. Kirah sent Kefhan to fetch more from the supplies in the sled, and Tokhan went into the trees around us to find anything absorbent. Kirah took the medicine pouch and mixed up a poultice of woundwort and alkanet and other herbs, chewing the mix to a wet pulp before pushing it inside her patient to the entrance to her womb. Then she added fresh moss and other leaves, among which I recognised dock.

"It's not really the right thing for this job," she said, "but I think the leaves may help to stem the blood flow. I fear she has lost the babe already, and who knows how we will get it delivered from her."

As the sun set, Fenratha opened her eyes for the first time since the fall, turning her head slowly towards me. "I am sorry, my love, to add this to all your other troubles. I shall try to get up in a while. I just feel a bit dizzy still, and numb…. I cannot feel my legs. Weyllan, are my legs alright? My baby – is my baby well?" She had started to raise herself on to her elbows as she spoke, but now she closed her eyes again and lay back, exhausted but muttering incoherently to herself.

She lost consciousness again as the darkness grew around us and by midnight, she had gone. We sat in shock for a long time, until the first pale glimmerings of dawn appeared over the hill before us. Tokhan stayed with us, sending his men back to report to Syllan. As the daylight took hold, he helped us to load the body onto the sled and, taking a rope with Kefhan to pull it, led us at last away from the River and up to the hillside where Jahrain's people lived.

Kirah took my arm to support me as I staggered after them, lost in a world of grief and recriminations. I simply could not accept that my world had fallen apart to such a degree in the space of a single day. I had lost my love, I had lost my hope, and it seemed as if I had lost all purpose to carry on. I was not at all sure I could carry on, nor whether I even wanted to; despair wrapped me in its cloak and drew me away down the darkest path I had ever followed.

PART IV
DARKNESS AND LIGHT

CHAPTER TWENTY-SEVEN

Fenratha was cremated a few days later, with Kefhan and Kirah taking charge of most of the arrangements, while I sat on a log outside Maklyr's guest hut, unable to deal with any part of reality, unwilling to release her from my mind, sinking into darkness and unable to kick out to rise again into the light. I blamed myself for not trying to recall Fenratha's guardian spirits, I blamed Syllan for our exile, and I blamed Tamkris and Sterhun for arousing Syllan's wrath. It was only with difficulty I managed to rouse myself to attend to my duties at the funeral, to take the lead and light the pyre and make a short and probably garbled eulogy.

I understood that her ashes were to be honoured with a special treatment reserved for healers, as she had made herself well-loved and respected all over the Plain in this way. I did not consider myself much of a healer, although when I said this to her later, Kirah laughed derisively.

"Really, brother? You, who have healed the rift between feuding tribes, who have re-forged the link between old ancestors and their distant kin, who have made whole the Spirit House and soothed the wound left by your own grandfather's murder? Oh, Weyllan, you are a powerful healer; just because you do not involve yourself in the healing of individual ills does not mean that you would be ineffective if you did. You are a healer on a grander scale than most of us, so do not belittle your powers, lest they desert you in chagrin."

Still, I was surprised to learn from Kirah that there was a fellowship of healers alongside that of the seers of the Spirit House. Many of our seers, such as Aslena and Diera, were also effective healers with a place in both groups. The Healers traditionally scattered the ashes of their dead in a small spring at the head of a stream that fed into the River just north of the sacred hill, and Fenratha was given this honour as well. I learned that when Kirah had been here a year or so, she was invited to join, undergoing an initiation that included drinking from the spring, thus absorbing some of the strength and secrets of her predecessors. Quite unknown to me, because I was near death at the time, Fenratha had been similarly initiated into the group to boost her powers to heal me. She repaid that investment ten times over with all the lives she saved or helped in her short stay with us on the Plain.

My leg never fully healed; all Fenratha's and Kirah's combined skills could not keep the wound from reopening several times each year, if I accidentally knocked my knee, or lost my balance because of the twist in my leg. Each time, the pain returned to haunt me for days, often for a whole moon cycle or more, before the oozing stopped and the blade-thin flesh sealed over it. I knew that the poison was always there, deep inside; I could quite literally feel it in my bones. But the ministrations of those two superb healers had kept it in check, stopping it from eating away at more of my leg, so that I still had both of them to balance on, even if my left leg would bear only a small part of my weight and always dragged when I tried to hurry anywhere. I was lucky to be alive; I freely acknowledged the debt I owed to both of them.

Once we had settled in our new home, I did not often venture very far from it. I had dreamed of travelling with some of the Northerners when they went home (they often discussed this but never seemed to get further than I towards setting off). I was not permitted to cross the Ayn to visit the Spirit House or friends on the Plain, although my exile didn't prevent them from coming to me, and many did, to the continued annoyance of Syllan. The other members of my family were not affected by the order, so Kefhan would sometimes hunt with Tokhan, but he and Syllan avoided one another on such occasions.

Kirah would sometimes cross onto the Plain to visit sickly friends or patients, or to trade her drinking pots. These lovely vessels were thin-walled for lightness, a definite improvement over the local styles, but that same asset made them more prone to breaking. Added to that, the content of the beakers was usually beer or mead, the effects of which meant it was to be expected that they had a short life-span and needed regular replacement.

Kirah always coiled her pots in the middle of spring, working hard for four or five days to finish two drinking cups or a single big cooking pot, then catching up with her healing or household duties for the next few days before allowing herself another long clay-coiling or decorating session. In this manner, she would have enough pottery for a firing by early summer, and would sometimes get another in before midsummer. With three or four firings a year, she was able to meet the demand for her wares, even having vessels left to barter with new customers. In return, we received meat and bread or beer, or the grain to make our own. I could no longer till the field, so that most years we were unable to do more than tend a few herbs and pick wild fruits from the trees and bushes nearby.

In the third year after my exile, the summer fever returned, and took Kefhan from us. There was little enough warning; one day he came in complaining of a headache and slight dizziness, making us think at first that he had a cold. Then the sweating began, until by morning he was in a high fever. Kirah did what she could, aided by the seven-year-old Meyrana and my sad efforts, but he just slipped deeper into the abyss. By nightfall of that same day, he was dead.

We sat in the darkness, the three of us, with our arms around each other and tears rolling down our cheeks as we contemplated the gaping hole that had appeared in our lives. When Ulrac came home from a day's adventures with his best friend Kyrthan to find us like that, he went over to his father's bed and sank silently beside the body, regarding it in disbelief.

As dawn crept over the hills, Kirah and I managed to rouse ourselves to get some breakfast together for ourselves and the children, and face the bitter reality of life without Kefhan. Ulrac had covered his father with his cloak; after a while, he shook himself and began to help do what needed to be done.

We carried Kefhan's body to Kirah's work hut so that we could cleanse their house. I lit bundles of herbs to chase the demons away, and placed scented water in a pot to boil on the fire. Then Kirah and I began to sing Kefhan's death song, recounting his many acts of goodness, generosity and bravery, calling on the spirits to care for him as he crossed over into their country. A distraught Ulrac went off to tell our neighbours and the community leaders – for we had no chief in this mixed band of northerners and exiles.

Although he had experienced a few visions, Kefhan had never practised as a seer, preferring as I had once done to concentrate on the magic of fire that transformed rock to metal, or to be my support and my anchor when I ventured off into the beyond. As a result, he had never joined the fellowship of the Spirit House or any similar group, and had no official status higher than the ordinary farmers or tribesmen. Yet to us, he had been the heart of our little household; we mourned him like a chieftain.

Maklyr and some others came by later that day, to help build a pyre. We cremated our Kefhan the next day, setting his soul free with more prayers to our ancestors and the ancestor spirits of the Plain. When the fire had died, Ulrac and I gathered the ashes and placed them on a little raft of leafy boughs to float down the sacred River towards the sea. Over the next day or so the water would gradually take the ashes, returning them to the earth through the river bed, before the raft broke up and released the remaining ashes into the stream to disperse. By that time his spirit would be well on its way to the other world, depending on whether he decided to stay near us on the Plain, or to make his way home, to the White Mountains. We would know soon enough, for I would be looking for him the next time I travelled into the spirit world, and would soon know whether he was nearby or not.

Young Ulrac came to me a day or two later with a worried look on his face that went beyond the grief and loss he was feeling.

He stood before me with his head hanging, staring at the ground in front of me."My father is dead. I am too young to be the head of the family. I don't know how to do that. What am I to do?"

What could I do when he came out with that? I took him in my arms and held him tight for a moment. It couldn't last; our heights were all wrong. I was sitting on a log-end stool; he at eight already stood a hand-span over my head in that position. But he seemed reassured by the gesture.

I smiled as I told him, "I am head of the family now. I will look after you and if I need to, your mother. Mind you, she may spend more time looking after *me* than I do her. So, just as my uncle took me in when my father died, so I will do for his grandson; you will be my son in all matters. Does that quiet your heart?"

"When we were in the house in the night, and I sat beside him, I thought I saw him," said the boy. "In my head, so clearly! He stood there and talked to me for some time. I'm sure I was awake, though. Or was it just a dream? Did you see if I was sleeping?"

"I did not hear or see you sleep that night. Tell me more about what you saw. How did it start, and how did it finish?"

"It's hard to say. I was looking at his face, the firelight flickering on his cheeks and eyelids so that they almost seemed to move. The rest of the room seemed to fade into darkness, but there was his face, lit up at the end of a dark tunnel. Then his eyes opened and he spoke my name. I got up, walked through the tunnel to where he was waiting on the other side. He held me for a while; he said how sorry he was to be leaving, how I should take care of Mother, and how I must be the man of the family. I was terrified, but I tried not to let him see. So, I just nodded. When I asked if we could still go hunting together, he answered that he would always be there at my side; that if I needed him, I should just ask and he would help me. There was some other stuff too – I can't quite remember – then it all went swirly, and I sort of fell back through the tunnel again, back into the hut."

"You have had your first vision, my son. You have the gift

– or the curse – as do all our family, and it has begun to show itself. I will have to talk to your mother about what you have told me."

My new son looked me in the eye. "Will you take my mother as your wife now, as she's your brother's widow, like they do on the Plain?"

I was taken by surprise at his frankness, and I stumbled over my reply."Well, there is no ruling that says I must do that in this land, although it was our practice in my home-land, but I think your mother will have strong views about whose decision that would be. We have not discussed it, but I suppose we will need to do so at some stage."

"Don't you like my mother then?"

"Ulrac, Kirah is as close to me as was your father. I love her very much, and we have always been a single household, but you are talking about a change in our relationship that we have never even considered, and that would need careful discussion. Leave it at that for now, young son!"

Then I struggled to my feet, bustling away indoors to hide the storm of emotions that were flooding in, now that the gates had been prematurely thrown open. For all my experi-ences in the other realities, the adventures I had had and the dangers I had survived, I had no idea how to broach this particular topic with Kirah. I knew within a few breaths that I wanted to take her as my wife, that the love I felt for her was so much more than I had admitted to, but I was utterly ignorant of her feelings for me. What if she had none, or at least none beyond the accepted familial bonds? What would I do if she laughed at me for even considering the idea of marriage? I strode around the hearth two or three times before I realised that I would find no answers there, that I would have to wait for the right moment – one when Kirah was at least present – to decide the question.

My thoughts shifted to another path, and I stopped

pacing as I put my mind to the boy's future. He needed something to give him purpose and to occupy his mind; I thought it time to tell him of my plans. I went outside again.

"Ulrac, I have been thinking about your vision. It is not unexpected, given our family history, and now that it has manifested itself, we cannot let you face it without proper training. Also, I will need someone to assist me with any smelting I do in future, so I think it time you became my pupil and learned to be a seer and a stone-changer. What do you think of that?"

He was silent for a while. Then gradually, his face cleared. He said breathlessly, "Do you really mean that? Really? Of course! But what about Mother? Will she be happy for me to do this?"

"We will have to talk to her, of course, but I think it is inevitable, and she will have realised that long ago. I don't think there will be much of an objection."

Thus, Ulrac began his formal training as a seer. He was not alone for long; before the end of that summer, he had persuaded me to let Kyrthan train with him. Since the two had become inseparable and shared everything anyway, and because I would rather Kyrthan learned through my words rather than the interpretation of them by an eight-year-old, I agreed without much resistance. Kyrthan had a condition, however (you could tell he was a chief's son already, putting conditions on my gift to him), which was that his father was never to find out in case he ordered a stop to the training. He insisted that we keep the whole affair a secret from anyone connected with the Plain or Syllan's circle.

Nykhin returned that summer. It seemed he had met a young potter when visiting among the Northerners on his previous visit, and had been unable to forget the effect she had on him.

So, he came back to make Yarta his wife if he could, and found she was only too happy to oblige, having suffered in the same way as him for the whole year.

Yarta was dark and pretty, and talented enough in her craft to have been shown by Kirah how to make the new drinking cups in the Mainland style. The Northerners believed that a young man should live for a while with his wife's family, thus easing her transition from daughter to wife for all parties, so the new couple set up home along the ridge from us.

Nyren, Wheris, and some of her family came by as summer turned to autumn, so we held a great feast to celebrate Nykhin's marriage. We all donated a pig or some venison for the meal, while Kirah and others brewed whole urns full of barley beer subtly flavoured with herbs for the guests and visitors. Most of the Northerner community joined us; even a few of the Plains folk stopped by, including Tokhan and a small clutch of seers from the Spirit House led by Dobris, whom I had not seen for several years. He came to sit with me during the evening, when the talk soon turned to the Spirit House and goings-on among the fellowship.

"The last few celebrations we have had, both at midsummer and the year's end, have been trouble-free for the most part. Since Urda's passing to the spirit world proper, she has left us alone, whilst the others have all come together to support our living community. We have had good harvests and relatively healthy herds; indeed, we have enjoyed good health ourselves. This has been the first summer in three years that the fever has come upon us. The ancestors have done their work well; the spirits have given us prosperity. But among the seers it is a different matter; we seriously miss the strength and guidance of men like yourself and Turac.

"Because Syllan is not a seer, men like Ursehan try to use

the fellowship as a way to get more power. His faction sow dissent and counter any moves to support the chief or his wishes. It will not be long before he feels strong enough to issue a challenge for the leadership of the Children of Hatha. Without your support, I fear we will not be able to prevent Ursehan from winning the contest."

I have to admit that part of me was thinking that if Syllan was without us as allies, it was his own fault for deserting us to support his father's duplicitous behaviour. On the other hand, I would not feel safe living so close to Ursehan if he became leader of the Plains folk. There seemed little I could do about it either way, but it left an uneasy feeling in my mind and a gnawing discomfort in my belly.

I composed my response carefully. "You will have to unite the opposition within the fellowship to make sure Ursehan doesn't gain control. Speak to the other seers. Tell them of his underhand tactics and his threats to my family. Get them to stand together to vote down any changes which will increase the power of Ursehan or Reirda and the rest of that pack of wolves. And if you haven't already done so, invite Nykhin to join the brotherhood. You will need allies, and he can also keep me informed. You may find that this increases your own influence and status, Dobris; who knows? You might even find yourself in the place of Turac or Tufakin one day soon."

He laughed at the thought of that, but I had spoken with at least a little foresight. I felt he would make a good leader for the seers; certainly, I would give him my support. We talked about less weighty matters after that, and I felt myself warming to the humour and humility of this young seer as I had the day of my initiation. When the feasters began to thin out, and his friends came by to take him home, I was moved to tell him to come again to visit whenever he wanted to, whether he needed advice or just company.

He seemed genuinely pleased by my offer, grasping my arm firmly before he turned to leave. I looked back towards the fire to see Kirah smiling at me, indicating that she was going to bed and that I should do the same. I thought back to my conversation with Ulrac; would I be taking Kirah as my wife? It felt like we'd been married for years already. I did as I was told and hobbled off to my hut to sleep off the excess of beer and meat I had eaten at the feast.

CHAPTER TWENTY-EIGHT

Kirah paused for a moment on the path as a waft of blossom-scent swirled around her on the breeze. Everywhere she looked, she could see flowers, on the trees, on bushes, and among the grass of the meadows. She loved the spring more than any other time of the year; the beauty that swamped her senses helped keep her mind in the present. It stopped her thoughts drifting to memories of a past that was gone forever, that came back to haunt her and taunt her, churning up the guilt, the pain she felt over the loss of Kefhan and Fenratha. Guilt which was further complicated by her subsequent feelings for Weyllan, the pivot around whom all their lives had revolved.

If she was honest with herself, she had always loved him; well, certainly since they had come to these islands and he had grown into his destiny. But did she love him more than she had Kefhan, while he was still alive? That was the question that kept coming back to her, one which she tried to avoid thinking about too much. Weyllan himself had said it was irrelevant since they had all loved one another enough for none of them to feel jealousy or inadequacy in their little family. Now, he said, there was just the two of them, he and she were more aware of the direction of their affections, and they felt them all the more strongly because of it.

Such pragmatism was small help to her when the guilt jabbed its blade into her head, but the overwhelming scents and sights of the countryside in spring were among the few things that could wash all those thoughts from her mind. She sighed, then pressed on towards the homestead at the head of the combe, where her patient was waiting to have her poultice renewed.

The old woman who she was tending to on this day lived in a cluster of four or five homesteads two ridges north of Ursehan's house; she was, indeed, one of his clan, a relative of Urda's. There were no friends or enemies in Kirah's calling, just people well and not well. Her business was with the latter. Unlike Weyllan, she was still free to cross the lands of the Children of Hatha to work among Syllan's people, although as time went on, younger men and women chose nearby healers to tend them. After four years, Kirah's patients closer to home were mostly older women. It didn't matter; there were enough people who were glad of her skills among the Northerners and the mainland settlers to keep her busy.

She put her mind to some of her newer patients to keep her feelings for Weyllan from resurfacing to fill her head. Since their little group had crossed the Ayn, three more little families had come to live with this displaced community on the edge of the Plain. One was a headed by a seer from the mainland with some ability, and another had a daughter, Yarta, Nykhin's new wife, who was trained as a potter like herself.

Kirah and Yarta had begun to work together, so that no antagonism would grow out of competing for customers, an arrangement that so far was working well. In reality, Yarta was doing most of the work, while Kirah travelled around practising her healing art. Meyrana seemed to enjoy working with either of them, although Kirah suspected that when she was older, it would be healing rather than potting that would rule her life. Already, Meyrana knew all the lists of plants, their uses and effectiveness, could dress wounds to stop bleeding or putrefaction, and could read the minds of patients almost as quickly as could her late mother or Kirah. Soon Kirah would introduce her to the secrets of travels in the spirit realms, until one day she would be a famous healer with little time for making drinking vessels.

Kirah had now almost reached the homestead she was heading for, so she brought her thoughts back to the present and the problems in hand.

The matter of her relationship with Weyllan came to a head a few days later when she and Meyrana were walking along the riverbank collecting supplies from among the varied plant-life that grew there. The child was always relaxed with her aunt, so they talked as they worked.

"Kirah, this morning I saw Father looking at you with such a dreamy smile on his face. I think he admires you very much!"

Kirah was by now used to Meyrana's directness, but was still a little surprised by the sudden change of subject. "The feeling is mutual, girl. We have respected each other's skills for many years; it is nothing new."

"No!" insisted the youngster. "This is different. I mean admires like – like young people in love admire each other. And – and I know he has visited you in your hut sometimes these past few moons."

Kirah blushed deeply. She and Weyllan had thought themselves very discrete in their occasional rendezvous. It was embarrassing to think that they had not fooled a girl of nine summers for even one turn of the moon.

Seeing this, Meyrana quickly carried on, "It's alright, really it is! You have both lost someone dear, and you have both always loved one another – anybody can see that. And my friend told me that among the Lake people it is usual for a man to take in his brother's wife, even if he has one of his own. It keeps the family together, she said. So, I was thinking, are you and my father going to do that? Are you going to marry him and become my mother?"

Kirah sat down heavily on a fallen tree-trunk, staring at her small companion. "We talked about it just yesterday, you know. It is a tradition among our people around the White Mountains, too. So, we have been considering announcing our marriage. But we felt we should discuss it with you and Ulrac before we told the world. We didn't know you knew – we had no way to know that you would understand. And ... I am babbling a little, aren't I?"

An immediate nod came from the grinning child, who then raised her eyebrows, taking Kirah by the hand. "So, I'm tired of calling you my aunt. Can I call you Mother now?"

"Ulrac will be home tonight from the Plain. We will talk after supper and decide how to announce it to our friends. Let's finish the work in hand and get ourselves home early, shall we?"

They had decided to tell Aslena first about their marriage, and, if she consented, planned to organise a small wedding feast at her home, it being closer for the Plainsfolk to attend. So, the following day, with Ulrac in the lead, the whole family set off for Aslena's little farm across the valley on the sacred hill. As Kirah had discovered, Ulrac's support had been guaranteed since his talk moons earlier with Weyllan but, typically, neither of them had ever felt the time was right to tell her. She was greatly relieved to find that everyone was united in their opinion, and all that remained was to announce her marriage to Weyllan.

When they arrived, they found the old seer sitting in the sun outside her house, staring dreamily into space while the last liquid boiled away in a pot on the fire. The little stew she had been preparing was beyond saving, so Kirah and Meyrana immediately set to putting a new meal together. Aslena had forgotten all about it; indeed, she seemed unsure, when asked, whether she had been cooking at all. Indoors, the hut had not been swept for days, nor had she cleaned her knives and pots properly – almost all of them were dirty. Aslena swore that everything had been cleaned the previous day; she was offended that they thought she had left food-covered things on the shelf.

As they all sat down to eat the food Kirah had cooked, Weyllan said quietly to her, "This is not the first time we have found this; I think our dear friend needs some help. I have an idea. What if we stay here while we prepare for the feast, and gradually move our possessions here? There is plenty of space to build a new hut."

At first, Kirah hated the idea. She did not want the disruption of moving again, and she expected that Aslena would have strong objections. In the event, the old woman seemed glad to think that she would have neighbours and people to talk to each day, so she embraced the suggestion gladly.

Weyllan evidently realised more persuasion was needed to convince Kirah. "We have already said that this is more neutral territory for the Plains people. They would be able to visit without making an obvious journey to our present home with the Northerners. It is both closer and more discrete. Also, it is not so far for you to travel to see your patients in either direction. It will work, you know it will!"

She had to agree it did. Within days of moving, even as they finished plastering their main house, she felt a great contentment wash over her. When she noticed it, she was pleasantly surprised; she felt as if she had, at last, come home.

Aslena just smiled when she told her, and waved an arm to encompass the Sacred Hill. "You and young Weyllan belong here, as do I. Wherever we come from, this is where we put down our roots."

The wedding feast, far from being a small affair, was attended by so many people from both communities that Kirah lost count of the guests. Tokhan came from the Plain, and Dobris, as well as young Kyrthan who brought along both his mother and grandmother Sekerta, who was on a visit from their home north of the Plain.

Syllan did not attend, but Kerta took the couple aside to give them private greetings from their erstwhile friend."Despite his apparent antipathy, he misses you, Stone-changer, and wishes you both a long and happy life together. But do not expect him to change his mind. His pride will not allow him to go that far."

"I wish he would," replied Weyllan, sadly. "I was justified to question his family's behaviour, but I caused him no real offence, I thought, and I do not understand why he continues to bear me a grudge like this. I will gladly apologise for any slight I caused, real or imagined, if we could once again be friends. Tell him this, please, and send him our love whatever he does. I have no ill-will left in me over this affair. Indeed, sometimes I heartily wish I had never found out the truth if it might have avoided this outcome."

Kerta promised to take Weyllan's appeal back to her husband but again shook her head, telling them not to expect a reply.

After she had gone, Dobris sidled up to them, one hand cradling a large piece of pork while the other gripped a small pigskin full of barley beer. "It allows me freedom to circulate," he said, by way of explanation. "Waiting for the pot to be passed around ties me to a group of revellers for too long to my mind, so I always carry my own supply. I wanted to speak with you."

"That is fairly obvious," Kirah remarked, making Dobris look around to check if his presence had been noticed by anyone.

Reassured, he turned back to his hosts.

"Ursehan is at it again. He is using his wealth – and I suspect that of his clan – to make gifts to seers in the brotherhood so as to ensure their support. I'm certain he is going to make a bid to be acknowledged as leader of the seers soon. I have tried to warn people against him, but they think it is just jealousy, and nobody seems to take me seriously. There are a few who, like us, cannot abide the man, but many more are with him than are against him."

"Well, you will just have to keep trying." Weyllan leaned towards him conspiratorially. "Sooner or later, he will show his true character, and you need to be in a position to ensure everyone understands the implications of supporting him. It will work out, but there may be pits in your path before you win through."

Dobris then went on his way, chatting to people he knew and total strangers with equal ease.

Kirah smiled at her new husband. "I don't know if he has the force of character to be a strong leader, but as an advisor or a negotiator, he is perfect. It would be good for the Plainsfolk if he stood beside Syllan as leader of the seers."

"My thoughts exactly!" chuckled Weyllan.

CHAPTER TWENTY-NINE

We soon settled into the new place, feeling as if we had in some way always been there. There was one disadvantage from my side, that I had to walk further to see anyone or to ask for help. But I soon found that people would come to me with even the slightest excuse, and we had a steady stream of visitors to the homestead, coming either for my advice or Kirah's healing. Some also came to barter for pots or my arrowheads, although there was less demand now that local potters and knappers were working out our techniques, making their own versions of our goods. We didn't mind; we had plenty of food and work to occupy us. The children grew and listened and learned, playing about the farmstead, enjoying the long warm summer, then the golden shades and leafy paths of autumn. We were happy.

Winter came in hard, fully a moon before the solstice. We had early snow with day after day of freezing weather. We were all amazed at the angry turn of the seasons and all caught colds. Aslena struggled to keep going, then took to her bed with a fever. She was old and very frail now, with perhaps seventy summers behind her, and sadly she had not the strength to fight her demons. She passed away just ten days before midwinter. We held her funeral and cremated her remains as quickly as we could to allow her to be taken to the Spirit House for a final blessing before passing over to the other side.

This was the moment when I resented my exile the most. For my friendship with Aslena and her close connection to my grandfather made her almost kin; not to be able to enter the Spirit House with her ashes and participate in the passing rituals was hard to bear. In the end, we asked Dobris to carry the urn in for us. We decided that I would secretly attend with my family, joining them as soon as I could after dark.

On the ridge between the Spirit House and the River was an old pit enclosure, built during the dark years after the construction of the Great Circle at the source of the Aynash River, when it seemed the spirits had abandoned the southern Plain for the downs to the north. I sat myself down there as the sun began to sink in the heavens, and watched the procession wind up from the River, crossing the ridge north of me, then assembling in the combe for the formal approach and entry to the Spirit House.

As the sun dipped close to the horizon, I could see the shadows spreading in the valleys, until a deep booming blast from a wild cow's horn was joined by a dozen higher notes as the procession of seers and urn-bearers began to climb the hill to the guard stone before the Temple enclosure. With the light fading fast, a few torches were lit among the climbers, but I could see little beyond the torch-light, and could not make out Dobris in the crowd.

We were to be denied a sunset on this occasion, as Lukan sank slyly into a low bank of cloud, hiding himself from view, but he still lit the clouds with swirls of pink and red highlights that almost had me slipping into a spirit-walk away from anyone else. I fought the sensation. I stood up to walk down to the Temple and join my family, as the horns sounded again while wild drumming broke out from within and without the ring of stones.

It was fully dark by the time I had crossed the valley and climbed the ridge to the Spirit House. Already numerous fires had been lit outside the enclosure; the sound of drumming was to be heard from some of them, where family dances were to be held, and seers not engaged in the Temple could cross over for individuals or kinsfolk, to contact departed loved ones or to find new spirit guardians for souls who had lost theirs or had none. There were hundreds of people here, perhaps a thousand or more, milling around between the fires in ones and threes so that the whole place seemed full of activity. I had arranged to meet Kirah and the children near the guard stone, finding them without trouble where they stood talking to Jahrain and some of the Northerners.

The entrance was as good a place as any to watch from; we settled down at the Northerners' fire close to the ditches, and unpacked the two pots of beer we had brought and a little of the food for our supper. Inside, the fires were lit and the seers were chanting to call in the ancestor spirits, with drums and rattles adding to the noise designed to wake them from their slumbers. Then a single voice rose above the others to greet Lena and whatever other spirits graced us with their presence tonight. The call was muffled through the stones so that I could make out none of the words, but I knew the form well enough by now to follow the rites through. I also recognised the voice. It seemed Ursehan had arranged to have himself lead the prayers, if not the whole ceremony. Dobris had not exaggerated, and that irksome schemer was advancing himself faster than I had expected.

We had drummers at our fire, too, so during the night Jahrain and another seer journeyed to the other realm, bringing back news for some of their companions. I took a drum, helping keep the rhythm steady for them, but I was not in the mood to go myself and managed to stay within the bounds of our reality, even when I fell asleep for a while before the dawn.

The cloud had rolled in overnight, and the sun did not appear all that day, but we knew Lukan was back in the sky doing his work to warm the world and give us all our share of the Kas he had gathered in the underworld where he had spent the night. Although the wind stayed away, it was still cold, with occasional snowflakes drifting down out of the snow-grey sky. We were eating the last of our food in the dull morning light when I saw Tokhan and Kyrthan walking by ten paces or so from us.

They both saw me; the warrior checked his stride a moment before looking away and striding on. I was surprised at his reaction, and not a little hurt, until Kyrthan suddenly appeared at my side.

He made no formal greeting as befitted a student for his teacher, instead simply saying with a smile, "Tokhan tells me he has not seen you here today, which is a good thing, for if he had, he would have been duty-bound to report your crime to my father. I was puzzled by what he said, because for the same reason I had not seen you either, nor have I come to speak with anyone at this fire. Tokhan hopes that wherever you are, you stay safe and get home before there is any trouble, for you never know who might seek to misbehave after a night of dancing and drinking."

His grin by this time stretched from one ear to the other, and with a cheeky wink he turned away, then twisted back to tell me as he fled, "I'll be over the day after tomorrow for my lessons – tomorrow I am off hunting with my father!"

We all laughed, but we took the hint. We packed our pots and skins away, scooped the dead embers up to take home for good luck and doused the fire before we all left for home. Jahrain waited a little longer with Kirah to collect Aslena's remains to take with us; she herself had asked to have her ashes scattered upon the top of the sacred hill where she would help to shelter Brwslyi, as he had sheltered her for so many years.

The embers must have brought us luck, for apart from a few days of snow and freezing weather to follow, we had a mild, if wet, winter that blossomed into another beautiful spring. All in all, it was a very mellow year; the harvest was good and the beer we brewed tasted exceptionally fine; we received such good trade and gifts of food that we ate well all summer. We were given a handsome brindle pup which we gave to Ulrac for his own and, of course, there was the birth of little Aslena to bring us all together just in time for the autumnal mid-point celebrations.

If only every year could have been as happy and peaceful as that one. There were less pleasant things going on, but they affected us only indirectly. That was the year reports began to circulate of people going missing as they travelled across the River in one direction or another. There were five such reports that summer, although two of the missing people subsequently turned up, having been to visit distant relatives and stayed longer than planned, perhaps because we were not the only ones to make fine beer from the harvest!

The others were searched for by their kinsfolk without success, but people go missing every year, and usually they have simply gone away without sharing their reasons or destination. When, however, two more disappeared in the same area the following winter, there was talk of something wicked living on the Ayn. Some said there must be outlaws who had wandered upstream into our territory, whilst others muttered darkly about evil spirits and fearsome demons.

Tokhain and Jahrain talked about it, agreeing to send patrols along the Ayn, each on our respective sides of the water, and to mount guard on the crossings. They saw nothing. As winter turned to spring, they halted the patrols, assuming that the danger had passed. Then another young lad disappeared, and the rumours flew back and forth once again.

Fool that I am, I allowed much of this to pass me by without using my skills to go looking for a cause. Had I done so I might have saved a few lives, but I was enjoying a very full life that left me little time for outside concerns. I had as a wife the woman I had loved for a dozen years at least, I had two beautiful, intelligent daughters, one of whom was fast becoming a superb healer and the other – just as impressively – was already learning to walk and talk. I also had two excellent young students who were not only showing great potential but enjoyed their learning so much I felt quite young in their presence. I had not myself been an attentive student in my youth, but now I was only too happy to pass on the knowledge I had gained, the secrets and the understanding of the many worlds a seer travels in.

CHAPTER THIRTY

Ulrac enjoyed life with his new father but was at his happiest when Weyllan was teaching him, often with Kyrthan, the arts and secrets of stone-changing or spirit healing. Kyrthan, as the chief's son, had numerous duties set by his father. He could not always escape across the River for lessons but came whenever he could. Ulrac's father, for his part, seemed happy to reprise his words of wisdom and warning in the certainty that his pupils would benefit from the repetition. Some of what the boys learned was basic stuff about the structure of the worlds they and the spirits lived in, whilst some of it was darker and more magical, the words that helped to bind spirits and stone to your will, words that drew in or released the Kas, or others that called forth the essence of the rocks to flow as moon-gold or sun-gold. And woven in with them, over the years of training, came the story of Weyllan's life: his journey, his adventures in this world and others, his delirium and his wanderings through time then and on many occasions afterwards.

Ulrac and Kyrthan learned to understand the three-fold

division of the cosmos in which living creatures and spirits dwelt.

"Three is a number always associated with things of the spirits and things of the mind," Weyllan told the boys. "There are three spirit realms: the heavens, realm of light; the realm beneath, a place of sand and darkness; and the realm between, this landscape that we share with the spirits. In each, there are resident spirits, creatures of the cosmos, immortal or nearly so, who live within and are of the materials and forces of each world. Our ancestors can move between them, though many remain in the sandy wastes below us, some not by choice, being bound by curses or darker magic like that which held Urda in limbo. The two realms of the spirit, of light and darkness, are each divided into three, an upper and a lower level, with a surface between the two that is a place in itself but is neither one nor the other. Likewise, our land is but a skin drawn between light and darkness, where both exist but neither rules supreme. So that seven, too, is a number of the spirits and of great power, encapsulating all of existence. The seer must learn to find his way through all these, to know how to get in and, most importantly, how to leave, or he may be trapped in spirit form until his mortal body wastes to nothing. It has happened before; it almost happened to me, and it will happen again. Listen well, lest it one day happen to you!"

Ulrac held his father in the same awe as Kyrthan, the other Plainsfolk, and most of the Northerners, for Weyllan had become widely acknowledged as the most powerful seer of his generation, surpassing even Turac in his abilities. People would come from far away to consult him on a variety of matters and, although he did not consider himself a healer, he would sometimes undertake spirit journeys on behalf of a supplicant, looking for a suitable spirit guardian or providing spirit-strength to fight an illness. He would also gather the Kas to himself and pass it into his patient to help them heal themselves, but he would never work with herbs or potions. *That*, he told anyone who asked, was Ulrac's mother's business, and his knowledge of the subject was more likely to kill than cure.

Mostly, Weyllan would give advice, or travel to one of the spirit realms to seek it for his visitor, to help solve problems other than those relating to health or injuries. Unlike most of his fellows, he could slip almost effortlessly into a trance, travelling directly to where he needed to be and returning, usually with valuable insights, within a very short time indeed.

But then, as he told his students, time was a thing of the mind and not of substance. There was time that was past, time that was now, and time that was yet to come. A seer could pass from one state of time to another and back again, so all had to exist at the same moment. Time, Weyllan explained, was man's way of organising his experience of events so that they made a story, in the same way people say there are four winds or four directions, to make sense of something when they all know that really, there are *scores* of directions and winds. Ulrac dutifully learned that, but if he was honest, he didn't really understand it. At least, not until many years later, when he was powerful enough to find out just what Weyllan had meant.

For Ulrac and Kyrthan, time passed slowly, as the years spread out before and behind them seeming very much in a fixed order. Ulrac had not been included in his new 's exile, and would sometimes travel with his brindle hound, Badger, to see Kyrthan at Syllan's homestead. There they would hunt or work together. They spent time with Kyrthan's siblings, his sister Hathis and younger brother Athlan, although the boy was just six and too young for most of their activities. Hathis was a good shot with a bow, so she sometimes went hunting with the boys. She would also go with her brother when she could to visit Kirah and Meyrana, where she learned at least the basics of healing from them. Ulrac thus saw her often, finding he admired her more and more as time went by.

From Aslena's homestead, now his family home, Ulrac had a clear view towards the sunset, down the valley to the River and across the plain towards the Spirit House. To the right, the houses of the Children of Hatha where Kyrthan and his family dwelt were hidden behind the ridge, whilst on the other side, the houses of the northern Lake People were mostly masked by the high plateau which protected them from the cold North winds. There, too, lived the various newcomers from across on the mainland, like Nykhin and his family, along with four or five other families who had arrived in the last few years.

The fame of the Spirit House at the heart of the world was attracting many visitors, and quite a few chose to settle in this relatively open land. Syllan, after exiling Weyllan, had made it clear he wanted no more continental metal users within his lands, so they settled as near as they could to the boundaries of the Plain, which meant in reality amongst the Northerners, who welcomed the newcomers with beer and laughter.

So it was that on a day when Weyllan had his young apprentices working his furnace to test their learning, Ulrac looked up to see a man running and stumbling up the valley from the River. The runner did not follow the usual path that swung south to the settlements, but kept coming straight towards the stone-changer's smoke at the head of the combe. He called a warning to Weyllan, who stood up to take a better look, leaning on his staff as he stared down towards the distant figure.

The man staggered several times and seemed near exhaustion, while his route became more erratic as he climbed. When his father called to Ulrac to leave the fire and go to the runner's assistance, he needed no urging, and leapt from his seat, running excitedly down through the grass to meet the newcomer. The man was sweating and shaking from exertion and shock, so Ulrac took his arm to help him up to the enclosure and the seat nearest Weyllan. He settled down next to the men, in case further assistance was needed, as Kyrthan hurried over to join them.

Weyllan greeted the man. "You are Emaris, one of our newer neighbours from the mainland, are you not? What has happened that you rush so to bring the news to *me* and not to the settlements?"

"I was walking home from the flint workers' mine and thought to cross the Ayn by the bog there. I wouldn't normally go near the place, but it was daylight, and I was in a hurry."

"I understand. Many folk find the place unsettling. It is a point where the separation between our world and that of the spirits grows thin, and even those without any power can feel the nearness of the spirit realm around them. It is a place that seers once used to cross between the realms, but there is little residual power there these days."

"That may have been true before, but..." Emaris' voice tailed off.

"Please go on. I did not mean to belittle you."

"I was close to the River, walking quite quickly, when I heard a scream from the bog. I thought someone must have become mired, or fallen into deeper water, so I changed direction and went to help. What I saw was far more horrible than I could have imagined."

He paused to catch his breath before continuing. "There were more screams, but then it went quiet. I came into a clearing by the edge of one of the pools, and there it was! It was eating someone, taking great chunks from his belly, both of them covered in blood...."

"*What* did you see?" interrupted Ulrac, receiving a glare from for doing so.

"It was a bear." Emaris lowered his head and shook it despairingly. "Not just any bear. It was enormous and .... it looked more dead than alive. The fur, what there was of it, was tufted and grey, and the skin between looked like rawhide, all dried and twisted and pale. The eyes were hollows. It heard me come out of the woods; it turned towards me and I just ... it was like looking through two holes into the night. Nothing. No colour, no light. Dead. A demon."

Weyllan leaned forwards. "And then what happened? Did it attack you?"

"I don't know. I mean, I didn't wait for that. I fled back to the River. I half ran, half swam across just where I reached the water. I thought at first to run for the settlement, but then I thought you would need to know. And if anyone could protect us, it would be *you.*"

Ulrac watched as his father absorbed the information Emaris had just given him. It was clear he had some inkling of what it was all about, or at least what it might all mean.

Weyllan turned his attention to the boys. "Our practice here is done for today, I'm afraid. Ulrac, get your bow and make your way across to Jahrain to tell him all that has happened. Get him to find out if anyone is missing, and put out a warning not to go near the old bog, then return here. Kyrthan, damp down the fire and tidy up here. When you go home, make sure you go across at the northern ford; keep away from the River where you cannot see what is in the reeds or on the far side. Tell your father what you have heard; make something up and don't tell him the word came from *me*, but make sure he spreads the warning abroad. And if he doubts your tale, tell him people are saying it is Bellik returned to plague us again."

The words sent a shiver up Ulrac's spine. Could his father really think that Urda's nemesis had returned from the dead? The beast had been cremated and its ashes scattered on the Ayn. Nothing had ever returned to corporeal form after a send-off like that. But Weyllan looked grim, and made a motion with his hands as if to push Ulrac into action. He needed no further encouragement, and charged up to the house to retrieve his bow and spear.

Jahrain and Maklyr came over the early the following morning, while the family were still finishing their morning meal, wanting to know what action Weyllan recommended. They brought with them an unexpected visitor. A man called Sterhun had the day before returned from the north with news that Tamkris had died, and felt he should come to the homestead with the news of his kinsman's passing.

Listening to the conversation, Ulrac learned that nobody seemed to be missing who had been due home the night before, but that did not preclude the bear's victim being a local man. Jahrain had spoken to Emaris when he finally made it home, establishing that the Mainlander had been unable to recognise the victim, either by his face, which was bloodied and partially turned away, or by his clothes.

Much to Ulrac's surprise, his father seemed unsure as to the best way to proceed. But then he explained that he needed to know if indeed this *was* Bellik in some demonic reawakening, or something mortal that could be destroyed by normal means.

The men were still discussing that when three more people entered the courtyard. The man in the lead was Tokhan, but to everyone's astonishment, the next man in line was Syllan himself, followed by the seer Dobris.

As soon as he entered the hut, Syllan opened the conversation without preamble or greetings. "My son tells me he came to visit young Ulrac yesterday, where he heard some news of a most serious nature. Let me be clear, I have no objections to my son's friendship with your boy, Weyllan, or I would have said something years ago. I am here not to talk about that at all, but to assess the value of the news he brought home. He said you think Bellik is in the bog and has killed someone. How reliable is that story?"

"First, Syllan, welcome to my home. And you Tokhan and you, Dobris. I am always pleased to see any or all of you here." Weyllan's tone of voice alone suggested some level of rebuke to his old friend for the lack of courtesy he was showing. "As for Bellik, we are at a loss to imagine how the creature has come back, if indeed it is that demon our witness saw. I must try to find out from the other side what is happening down there. I tried last night, but what I heard was inconclusive. It may, of course, be another bear-demon come to terrorize our communities, but such creatures are hardly commonplace."

Syllan stood silent for a moment, then his shoulders drooped as he looked down at the fire. "I am sorry. I apologise for my lack of manners. There is enough between us without my making it worse, and I did not intend to do that. My greetings to you all, Stone-changer, and dear Kirah, and your fine offspring. Ulrac and Meyrana I know, but I have not yet had the pleasure to meet your youngest. She is named for Aslena, is she not? A very bright and pretty thing she is too. Please forgive me, all of you."

He seemed genuinely upset, and Ulrac sensed that everyone was moved.

His mother replied in a conciliatory tone, "Welcome after so long, Syllan. Your transgression here is forgiven. Sit down – have some broth and bread with us, please."

"Thank you, I have eaten already. Some water would be welcome, though!" The chief looked at Meyrana, who immediately ran outside to the rain pot to fetch a cup of water. "I can see you need still to make sure of your identification. How soon can you find out? And in the meanwhile, what can we do to help?"

"I have spoken once before with Dobris here about a man who is using unpleasant methods to advance himself. That same man was responsible for the disposal of Bellik's body. I cannot believe that if they followed my instructions and cremated the beast properly, that it could reappear here after such a long time. So, you need to question Ursehan and his team to make sure they did as they were meant to. I will try to find out through a spirit journey; perhaps, Dobris, you, too, can try your luck that way. I will get word to you if I learn anything. I hope you will keep me informed in the same way."

The Plainsmen nodded their agreement. Syllan added, "We will send word with my son, and you could do the same. That way, we can make them earn their leisure as befits their approaching adulthood. My Kyrthan spends little enough time preparing himself for his future role as leader of our people!"

"*Your* people, Syllan. By your actions, they can no longer be mine. And perhaps you are looking for his future in the wrong direction."

Ulrac could tell his father instantly regretted his words. The chief had been making a gesture of friendship, and he had pushed it aside.

"I did not come here to change my decision, Weyllan, much as I regret the unintended suffering it caused you and your family. It was your inability to measure your words and actions that led you here, and I see that failing is with you still. We will co-operate to fight this menace, whatever it turns out to be, but do not expect to use it to slide back across the Ayn. *I* am chieftain there. Until you accept that my word is law and submit to it, you will never be allowed back into our community!"

With that, he stood up abruptly. Without waiting to see if the other men followed, he strode out of the house and down the path towards the River. Dobris and Tokhan shrugged apologetically and followed, and Tokhan turned to wave back at the homestead as he went off down the hill. Ulrac waved in response, but when he turned back to the hut, he knew Weyllan hadn't seen the gesture. His father had his head in his hands and was staring into the fire, his face a mask of frustration and despair.

CHAPTER THIRTY-ONE

The visit from Syllan brought the memories of that terrible time flooding back, making me ill and out-of-sorts for several days afterwards. As soon as I was able, I took some of Kirah's special draught and tried to cross over to find out what it was that had taken residence in the pools of the bog. Ulrac, for the first time, came with me to the spirit realm while my wife stood by to aid us in this world. We had little luck, although Ulrac was very proud to have been able to stay with me when we crossed over and to have travelled there with me a while. I must admit, I was impressed with his performance myself; I began to believe for the first time that he might grow to be a better seer than me.

But for a long time, it seemed that none of the spirits we saw would talk with us, or they drifted away as if we were not there. At last, however, I saw two familiar faces; we directed ourselves over to join Turac and Aslena.

We asked what they knew about Bellik, to which Aslena replied, "There is a darkness about that place; we cannot see more than glimpses of events. But we have seen some of those who have passed over as a result of the evil that lives there. By the descriptions, it has to be Bellik. She has killed a dozen or so who have entered her little woodland territory. They describe a great she-bear with rotten flesh and poisonous claws. She should have been destroyed, but the demon she became with Urda in that tomb must have found a way to carry on. Her strength is growing, too. She works some dark magic in that bog of hers; we have felt the ill and pestilence she is creating. We suspect that she has found a way to inflict her ills upon passers-by she cannot reach in her body, for at least two have died of fevers who passed too close to her lair."

"You will have to find a way to destroy the demon," Turac put in. "We cannot get near her, and now she is awake again, she will certainly fight. But you, without meaning to, were the one who gave her the chance to live again. It will be for you to finish her, I suspect."

All of which took us no further, but made me feel worse than ever. I came back to my body depressed and angry, ready to pick a fight with anyone. My family wisely kept out of my way for the rest of the day, until a pot of beer and an exceptional sunset lifted my spirits and brought back my good temper. But I still had no idea where to go next, even though I lay awake much of the night trying to come up with a plan of action.

A day or two later, Kyrthan brought me news from Syllan and Dobris. The seer had had little more luck than Ulrac and I with the spirits, but he had spoken to Ursehan who had loudly denied any wrongdoing. Dobris was not convinced, and with Syllan, interviewed two of the men who had been with Ursehan's party taking Bellik to the River for cremation. Their story made everything clear at last.

They both admitted to their chieftain that there had been

no cremation or disposal of the remains into the Ayn. They had decided to take a short cut through the bog to get to the landing-place where they would build their pyre, but had found the path overgrown, and the corpse they carried was several times caught fast in the undergrowth. When they came to cross one of the shallow pools, Ursehan had slipped, dropping the bear's body into the mud. He finally exploded. He had cursed me and everyone involved, then had kicked the corpse further into the pool and ordered them all to turn for home, leaving the remains to rot away in the bog.

Ursehan was meant to be called before the chief to answer for his dereliction of duty, but he had disappeared. His family, including old Useris, claimed not to know his whereabouts. Syllan was apparently furious both with Ursehan's whole clan and with me, whom he blamed for precipitating the whole disaster. Once again, I fell into despondency. My health declined so much that I caught a dismal cold and was laid low for many days. By the time I recovered, Ursehan had been found and taken before Syllan.

I heard that Dobris had laid before the chief and elders his list of Ursehan's machinations, the aim of which, he said, was to regain leadership of both the brotherhood and the tribe for Urda's kinsfolk. Syllan and the others agreed that whilst Ursehan's ambition might be legal, the abandonment of his duty had shown him to be unreliable as a leader, and had put his people in danger. When Syllan announced his decision after discussion with the elders, nobody stood to voice support for the disgraced seer. He was given the same order of exile as me; he was escorted from the council, and by sunset that same day, had been forced to leave the lands of the Children of Hatha.

I thought that that would be the end of the Ursehan problem, so I turned my mind to the remaining issue, which was to somehow vanquish the resurrected Bellik from this world and make the bog a safe short-cut once more. I decided to seek help from beyond by undertaking a full vision quest, in the hope that the full purification and preparation would bring me to the answers I so desperately needed. We set to at once, building a sweat lodge and gathering the materials for the ceremonies. Ulrac and Kirah kept me company during the ritual – I thankedthem both for their support and for the excellent drumming they provided. Then I set off alone to the top of the hill, to the same spot I had gone to at my initiation, and settled down to await my vision.

In fact, I had two. The first was of little help, so I soon interrupted my journey and came back. The second came upon me early yesterday, as Lukan broke the skyline to warm my back. Reya came to me as a kite once more, circling around me two or three times before settling on a stunted bush just to my right. I greeted her warmly as both a good omen and an old friend.

"And again, greetings to you, Weyllan Stone-changer! It seems you have landed yourself in the stew-pot once more. It is a life's work to keep you alive and on top of your destiny."

"Then you know what faces me, and why I need a solution," I replied. Then, seeing her ruffle her feathers and open her wings in exasperation, I added, "I mean, I know I have to destroy the beast. That much is obvious. But *how* to do it is my problem. I do not know any magic that will kill her, nor have I the strength or weapons to harm a demon. My bow will not do the job, I fear."

"I cannot answer those questions, nor am I here to do so. But there is one nearby who can, and he lies under our very feet. It is time to meet Brwslyi again, Stone-changer."

As I watched, I saw Reya's shape blur, changing into her vixen form again. She turned to me. "Are we ready?"

She set off through the bracken at an easy lope, although I had to shamble as fast as I could to keep up. Once again, I noticed the encroaching darkness, then as the vixen disappeared in front of me, I remembered to shut my eyes and use my inner vision to see the tunnel. It was there, a slightly grey patch in the darkness, with the tip of Reya's tale just disappearing into it. I followed rather more confidently than on the previous occasion and was ready when we came out onto the boulder-strewn plain on the far side.

This place, I felt, was somewhere beneath the sandy wasteland where I usually went to meet the spirits, but I was not at all certain if it was the realm of the first tree and the clear streams either. It was a place apart, a space between the walls of other realities. I felt terribly isolated in it. There were no tracks, and I had to follow my spirit guide again as we wove our way between the shadowy boulders all about us.

Once more, we came to the black wall and the stairway between the two stone gates, and passed through them. As before, Reya stopped, motioning me to go forward by myself.

"Tell me, Reya, why you will not go into the presence of our scaly friend in the next chamber?" I asked, only half-expecting an answer.

"Brwslyi's power is very ancient; it draws readily upon spirit power such as my own. He would take what I had and leave me unable to return with you. I also hear that he has a particular dislike of all dogs, including foxes, and I am not able to transform here without drawing his attention. I will wait here. You will be fine. He likes you."

So, I walked in the direction she indicated around the wall and into the vast white-walled hall amid the piles of Brwslyi's treasure, until I came once more into the presence of the dragon. He opened one enormous eye, tilting his massive triangular head to regard me more directly; then the hissing and growling began as his words formed in my mind.

"Well met, Weyllan of the White Mountains." He clearly enjoyed the wordplay. "And to what do I owe this honour?"

"The honour is mine, truly," I proceeded to relate the story of Urda and Bellik, leading to the position I now found myself in. Brwslyi listened, blinking acknowledgement occasionally until I had finished.

"And what do you think I can do about it?" he said.

"I came here for advice. You are perhaps the oldest spirit I have encountered after Lena, who spoke to me in my delirium some years gone by. I hoped you could give me some direction to help me find a way to overcome this demon."

"And have you brought me a gift to exchange for my insight?" asked the dragon-spirit.

I cursed myself for having forgotten the gift, then had an idea. I took out my little moon-gold knife and cut off my braids, complete with the sun-gold tress-rings that held them in place.

"I give you these, the finest I have made. Is that a suitable trade?"

Brwslyi said nothing to that, but began to answer my main query. "I was aware of this Bellik, Stone-changer, for I keep a close interest in the ... ebb and flow of power in the lands and realms around me, and the folk of the Plain have always held me in some regard. Respect deserves the same in return, so I do what I can to help them from time to time. But you? You have come far, as I predicted, but somehow, they have seen fit to throw you aside. You owe them nothing, yet you are preparing to take a huge risk on their behalf. Take my word; there is great danger in what you intend to do. Why would you do that?"

That made me pause, for I wasn't all that sure why I was taking this burden upon myself.

"I feel some guilt that I did not make certain that Bellik was destroyed before. More than that though, I fear she threatens the balance of the lands on both sides of the Ayn. She draws in the darkness and feeds off the Kas of my friends. I have a feeling that I am the only one who can make her stop. I must try to restore the balance, or I will have failed in what I came to this land to achieve."

"Well, well, Weyllan." The throaty chuckle rumbled across the vast hall again. "I am glad that at last you understand what you have been doing for all these summers. And you are right. Destiny has brought you to this point; it is you and you alone who can restore the balance. Bellik is a powerful foe, but you have in your possession several weapons that can tip the balance in your favour. You have your own strength and the Kas you draw down; you also have the gifts of Lena and Lukan which give you more power alone than most of your fellow seers. You have the gifts I gave you on your last visit. My skin is very strong, and the talisman will keep you safe from fatal harm. But you will need your own unique weapons to kill the beast; those of lesser men will never do what you require of them. You could succeed, but I cannot see the outcome of this endeavour, for my vision is clouded, and that worries me somewhat."

He looked down at my gift of gold and snorted quietly. "You should keep your gift, fine as it is, for I fear my answer was not worthy of a gift after all. Take care, Seer, and use your power wisely!"

The eye closed, and the big blue head settled to rest on the uppermost coil of his body. The interview was ended. I had little option but to leave, so I picked up my sawn-off locks and made my way back out of the hall to where Reya waited for me. We set off together to return to my reality on the hill above my home.

It was mid-afternoon when I started down the hill; I realised I had been gone for most of the day, although it had seemed much less to me. As the sun sank gently towards the skyline in the late summer afternoon, I was mesmerised by the beauty Lukan spread across the Plain before me, with golden highlights and deepening blue-grey shadows in the combes. I ambled slowly down towards the homestead, oblivious to my immediate surroundings and almost entranced once again as I went.

So, I was surprised, as I rounded a large clump of bushes and bracken, to be confronted by a familiar figure, striding towards me with anger in every movement of his body.

"You!" he called out. "Cursed Stone-changer! This is all your doing. All your fault."

"Ursehan, do not blame me for your own misdeeds and irresponsible carelessness in dealing with the spirit world," I replied as he drew to a halt a few feet in front of me, ruddy-faced with anger and exertion, his leggings and smock freshly streaked with dirt and dark, damp patches of sweat.

"So, you know! That is an admission of your guilt. You still manage to control that fool Syllan as well as your pet seer. They both turned on me, sneered at me just as you are doing now. And now I have no home, and it is your fault."

"I have no influence over Syllan, but it was inevitable that he would eventually realise that you meant to usurp the chieftainship. Just as it was fated that someone would find out it was *your* orders that allowed the demon Bellik to survive and regain her strength to the point where she, too, threatens the balance in our little existence here. They did not need my intervention to act against you – in the light of the charges, I think you are lucky to still be alive!"

I have never learned when to keep my opinions to myself. That remark was all he needed to lose his temper completely.

"Curse you! It's you will die today. I will finish your meddling as my father finished your grandfather's!" With that, he pulled a polished flint axe from his belt, stepping towards me as he raised it above his head. I was still full of Kas from my vision and the experience of my walk home, so that as I backed away, I swept up my arm in a backhanded swing that missed Ursehan by a long arm's-length but still pushed him back on his heels.

I moved forward and swung again, this time knocking the axe from his hand, propelling him backwards to the ground with his legs doubled up beneath him. I knelt on his arms as I drew my own little dagger, jerking his buckskin shirt up to reveal his bare chest and lifting my arm behind me to strike him between the ribs.

Then a curious thing happened. I heard clearly in my head the hissing growl as Brwslyi spoke to me. "He is finished. Do not spend your power on him. Save it for tomorrow and let him run away up the hill. Leave him to me."

"But he will never find his way to your world. He is useless, corrupted!"

"You forget; he has been here before. I will open the door to him, and he will stumble in. We shall see how he behaves when he finds his way to me. Let him go now."

Against my better judgement, I did as I was told, standing up off my foe. He looked at me briefly with a mixture of fear and loathing, then staggered to his feet.

"Go now, and never return. For if Syllan does not kill you, I shall. Go *now!*" I almost spat the words out. He needed no further urging. Leaving his axe on the grass, he sped away in a stumbling run that took him on a spiral path towards the hilltop. I watched him until he was a small speck on the hillside, then I turned for home again.

He is gone now, and I hope Brwslyi is right, and he is gone for good this time.

CHAPTER THIRTY-TWO

By the time Weyllan had related his adventures on the hill to his family, it was growing dark. Ulrac had finished the delicious stew his mother had prepared for them on his father's return, and proceeded to wipe the bowl clean with a chunk of bread. The dogs had curled up near the fire to sleep, and his mother was putting young Aslena to bed.

Ulrac belched quietly and looked across the low flame at Weyllan."What next, Father? How do you interpret the dragon's advice? Do you have a plan? Will we go the bog to fight the monster?"

"I am not sure what he meant by 'my unique weapons', unless he was speaking of the moon-gold blades I make and my arrowheads. But I cannot believe that such a small knife could seriously injure such an enormous beast as Bellik. One thing I *am* certain of, though, is that I will be doing this alone. Neither your mother nor our collected ancestors would forgive me if I were to allow you to be maimed or worse by taking you with me. You will stay behind so that, if I fail to come home, you will be head of the family and have to assume the mantle of manhood a little early."

For Ulrac, the crushing disappointment he felt at this pronouncement was alleviated by a rebellious relief that fluttered through his chest and flared, unwanted, into his head. Did his father think he was unready to stand beside him and face a foe so fearsome? Did he think that he ...? Even as Ulrac told himself to heed the logic of his father's argument, his heart shouted defiance, and his belly was full of tiny birds flying about in panic. He tried to object, but Weyllan was adamant, although he *did* promise to ask for volunteers among the northern warriors to give him assistance when he went after Bellik. The talk continued for a short while until Weyllan, yawning expansively, led the others to bed for the night.

It was to be a short rest, as well before sunrise, with just the glimmer of dawn in the sky behind the hill, Maklyr and another man came knocking at the house to wake them all. As he struggled to rouse himself, Ulrac heard the newcomers say that another person had disappeared. This time it was a young lad of seven summers, Verhain by name, who had been searching along the River for some missing pigs and had not returned in the night.

Ulrac watched his father's face harden as he gathered his weapons about him. He picked out a stout spear and thrust it into the embers to soften the resin around the point. While that was happening, he took up Brwslyi's scale, hanging it around his neck, and lifted his bow before deciding against it as a weapon. When the spear was drawn from the fire, he wrenched out the flint point and inserted the blade of a moon-gold dagger for which he had never got around to making a handle.

As he bound it tight, he turned to Ulrac. "Now, remember what I said. Stay here, and keep the dogs with you. The beast would tear them to pieces. No arguments, now. I have to do this without you, and trust to Brwslyi's vision. He said that with this talisman, I cannot be seriously harmed. If I can survive *this*," he pointed at his knee, "then I can survive any injury the beast may deliver."

"Father, you are rushing into this without enough of a plan. You have taught me always to plan carefully in dangerous situations and not to face them alone, yet here you are, about to break your own rules. Delay a while; the boy may yet turn up. And when you go, take me and some others along. You promised to take some warriors with you!"

"Yes, the lad *could* be safe. But he could also be alive somewhere, with that bear-demon about to make a meal of him. There is no time to go around asking for volunteers. I must go *now*. And I do not want to have to be looking over my shoulder to worry about you and the dogs. Please, Ulrac, do as I ask this time! I am going now."

He turned then to Ulrac's mother and took her in his arms, then did the same to his daughters. He embraced Ulrac, then took up his carved staff and left the house, shouting to Shadow to stay put. The family watched together as Weyllan hobbled off towards the River with the two Northerners.

As soon as he was gone, Ulrac turned to his mother. "Mother, I cannot stay here. I must follow him and try to keep him safe if I can. You *know* I cannot wait here!"

She looked deeply into his face and shook her head sadly. "Even if I ordered you to stay, you would go. I can see that. Take the dogs and keep out of the fight, I beg you. I feel you may be able to help in some way, although I cannot see it at all clearly. Go, but your safety comes first! Before your father's, and before the dogs or anyone else's. That you must promise me."

He nodded consent and went immediately to gather his bow and weapons. Calling the dogs to him and commanding them to silence, he set off after his father, already little more than a dot in the valley below.

Ulrac had to keep well back to avoid detection and, by the time he entered the wood across the River, Weyllan was lost to his vision. Shadow quickly found his trail, entering the thicket with confidence, so that Ulrac and Badger had simply to follow his lead. He wound through the underbrush until he heard his father bellow out a challenge, so changed direction and ran directly towards the sound, coming out from the thicket quite suddenly at the water's edge.

On the far side of the pool stood his father, facing a ramshackle heap of branches and logs from which appeared at that moment the largest bear Ulrac had ever seen. Bellik stood upon her hind legs, towering head and shoulders above Weyllan, her hide a patchwork of bare skin, scars, and remnant tufts of dead fur. As she emerged, Ulrac could see tucked under her arm the limp form of the missing child, but on seeing Weyllan, she tossed the infant aside as she roared out an answer to the seer's challenge.

What followed, Ulrac always found difficult to interpret when he retold the story afterwards. The two antagonists stood less than two paces apart, staring at each other, quite motionless, for what seemed an age. Whether they were mind-talking or just trying to intimidate one another, he was never sure, but he took advantage of their concentration to slip quietly around the edge of the pool to a place where he could see the child sprawled on the ground.

Bellik let out bellow of rageand charged at Weyllan, who stepped asideto land a hefty blow to the side of the demon's head with his staff. It had little effect, as the bear spun around to take a deadly swing at him. Weyllan dodged again, nearly falling when he took too much weight on his bad leg.

Once more, they stood apart, each perhaps trying to gain some mental advantage over the other.

Bellik was now fully five paces away from the child, with her back to Ulrac. Seeing his chance, he signalled the dogs to stay put and ran forward to inspect the body. Little Verhain was still breathing weakly, despite having bled profusely from numerous rips and bites. As yet, the demon had not begun to feed on the boy, who was still more or less whole, but Ulrac held out little hope of his surviving the rest of the day. He lifted the child in his arms and trotted back to where he had left the dogs. As he stood for a moment considering his next move, he saw the demon launch another attack.

Despite the bear's apparent decrepitude, she was extremely swift and sure-footed on the loose stones and silt of the shoreline. She closed with Weyllan, throwing a pair of vicious blows at him. He avoided one, but the second hit him full in the chest; he was only saved by the dragon scale he wore which deflected the worst of the blow. One claw hooked the cord of the talisman in passing, tearing it from his neck, leaving a bloody red weal in its wake. He staggered back, trying to fend Bellik off with his staff. Another wild swipe from the beast knocked it from his hand, and he fell back against a branch overhanging the water. Immediately, the bear stepped forward, catching Weyllan in both arms to squeeze the breath from his lungs.

Again, Brwslyi's scale saved him, for when the beast clasped Weyllan with his makeshift breastplate to her chest, she screamed in pain and staggered back, clutching at the place where the sun-gold rim had burned her. With one great paw, she tore the scale from her and sent it spinning into the shallows, then aimed yet another blow at Weyllan.

Ulrac gasped as, instead of retreating, his father stepped inside the swinging arm to close with Bellik again. As the beast tried once more to close her arms around him, he seemed to grow in stature, thrusting his makeshift moon-gold spear point under the bear's ribs and into her chest.

Bellik screamed again but tightened her grip as both combatants staggered further into the pool. At that moment, Shadow could take it no more and charged barking into the fight, closely followed by Badger. The bear turned her head, in so doing losing her balance altogether and toppling forward across her opponent. Weyllan was trapped beneath her as they fell, submerging them both even as his spear sank deeper into her chest. Her head came up briefly, the eyes rolling as she tried to focus on the approaching dogs, then it fell forward, and both she and Weyllan lay still.

For a moment, Ulrac stood in shock, not believing what he had just witnessed. Then he realised that his father's head was completely underwater and he ran forward to do what he could. Kneeling beside the trapped body, he tried not to retch at the stench of burned flesh and rotting demon. He lifted Weyllan's head into his lap, cradling it in one arm, tilting it to the side and shaking it as much as he could to dislodge the water in his mouth.

He tried to think straight, then remembered something Fenratha had taught him. Leaning over the limp body,he placed his mouth over his father's and blew hard down his throat. The water bubbled up and some dribbled out as the air flowed back, so he tried again. This time,Weyllan responded with a convulsive cough; water poured from his mouth as he choked and spat.

His eyes focused on Ulrac and he smiled weakly."You could not ... stay put, then. I asked too much ...aah, but I'm glad to see you. Is she dead at last?"

"She is dead, Father. Can you not feel the weight on your chest? Here, let me try to pull her off you." He looked around for something to support his father's head, and founda large-tussock of coarse grass which he was able to pull free and use to keep Weyllan'sface above the water. Then he took hold of the wrecked body of the demon, pulling with all his strength to move the creature, but without success.

"You will not move her alone," said his father. "And really, I cannot feel the weight. I cannot feel much at all. So, kneel beside me and ... listen, for I think I will ... soon be away from here."

"You must live!" cried Ulrac. "I promised. And you have not finished teaching me – or Kyrthan. Stay with us, please! Father!"

"I cannot stay this time, son. You have heard all I have to tell you, you and Kyrthan both... The rest you will learn ... by experience, the same way that I did. Listen, you will make your family ... proud of you – I have seen it. Both you and Meyrana will be ... known ... across the Plain ... and beyond."

The pauses had become longer and the voice more a whisper as Weyllan said these things. He gazed at Ulrac a moment more, then he closed his eyes for the last time, and passed over into that other place he already knew so well.

CHAPTER THIRTY-THREE

I lowered my father's head back on to the turf and tried again to move the carcass on top him, but it would not budge. I sat for some time with him, lost, lost in every sense of the word. Then I felt Badger nuzzle me, pushing beneath my arm to get my attention, and slowly I came back to the moment. I remembered the boy lying in the bushes, and roused myself to see to him. He was very weak, hardly breathing at all, with such dreadful wounds and bites that I was amazed that he was still alive. Since I would have to fetch help to move my father, I determined to leave with Verhain at least, although I doubted that he would live long enough to thank me.

I hefted the boy across my shoulder and made my way to the southern ford with Badger at my heels. I was vaguely aware that Shadow had stayed behind, so I tried to keep in my head that we must come back for both him and my father. I hurried as fast as I could, calling upon the spirits to help Verhain, but they were not listening or had already decided otherwise for, by the time I reached the first home-stead, where I could send someone to fetch Jahrain with more help, he was dead. I sat in despair with my head in my hands for an age until Jahrain and several others arrived to shake me gently from my reverie.

We went back down to the bog, through the thickets to the pool where my father lay, and between us, we pulled Bellik off his body. The demon was already falling apart, so rotten had her carcass been; a putrid black sludge oozed from her body into the water around us. The others began to look around the rickety tangle of wood and skins that formed the demon's lair, collecting together the bones of her victims from where they lay scattered on the ground. Jahrain himself carried my father when we left, as I strode alongside with his staff and the cracked dragon scale, followed in silence by both our dogs. We took him straight home to my mother, who received her second dead partner with a tear-stained face and a bleak look in her eyes that I knew would take me months to ease away. She held his torn body as we discussed for the first time what we should do.

My mother wanted to ask Syllan to have Weyllan buried in the Spirit House, but the others doubted he or the fellowship would permit that. The Northerners wanted to cremate his remains and scatter them on the hill with Aslena's, but Mother had other ideas. She decided to go with our own ancestors' tradition, to have him interred, raising a mound over him for our offspring to remember for generations to come. Then we set the funeral for three days' time and sent out word to let folk know, should they wish to attend.

It was agreed that Verhain would be buried soon after my father and that the remains of Bellik's other victims would be buried with the child. Several men went back to the bog the following day to collect more of the bones scattered about Bellik's lair, and to finally cremate the carcass of the bear. To their amazement, they found the carcass already decomposing; they struggled to find pieces big enough to burn. The waters, they told us later, had turned a murky brown, while many pebbles around the shoreline now seemed to glow with the colours of the moon-gold when it flows out of the rock.

The day of the funeral dawned dark and sombre. I would have wished for warm sunshine to provide an air of peace to send him off with, but he probably made a special request for just the opposite. As I was learning, being a seer was as much about effect as ability.

Jahrain had prepared the ground at a spot overlooking the site of Weyllan's victory and thence on to the Spirit House, which stood just out of sight below the ridge across the River. I hoped my father would be able to see the Temple from the top of the mound when it was finally raised.

I had spent time planning the event with my mother. As Weyllan's nephew and adopted son, I would celebrate his life; broadcast his achievements to both the mourners and the waiting ancestors, just to be sure they knew what a significant personage was crossing over. Atharon's ceremony was our starting point, blended with what Mother could remember about the ceremonials from her homeland.

Our little procession set out from our homestead on the Sacred Hill led by Dobris as officiating Seer. Jahrain, with three of his fellows, carried the hurdle on which my father's body lay, followed by my mother and me, with the girls in tow, then a dozen or so others for whom this was the closest point at which to join the proceedings. Along the way, as we skirted the homesteads of the Northerners and recently arrived Mainlanders, more folk joined the line. I saw Nykhin and Yarta with a small group come out to meet us, and was overjoyed to see that his parents had made the journey across to be with us.

Mother greeted Nyren and Wheris warmly, then, to my

surprise, gave a cry as she embraced the man who accompanied them.

She turned to me. "Ulrac, this is Cuhal, a seer we all stayed with when we travelled across from our homeland to get here. Cuhal, this is my son by Kefhan, who I am sure you remember. But tell me, how did you come here so speedily?"

Cuhal smiled at her, "The ways of the spirit world are strange to us here. I did not know, but I was led to understand I needed to travel to the Island and seek out the seer Weyllan again. As it happened, I was staying with Nyren when Nykhin brought us the news, so we set off together."

"You are most welcome," I said, formally, in my role as the eldest male in the family now. They joined in behind us as we continued towards the burial site.

There must have been fifty people gathered there when we arrived, and we could see others coming up from the River. I took a moment to look around as the bearers laid my father on the ground beside the grave, a simple rectangular pit lined with plank walls. Off to one side lay several split logs waiting to be placed over the grave to roof the wooden cist. The chalk floor of the pit had been strewn with a thick bed of rushes and sweet grass, and as we watched, Dobris used his striker to light a small fire laid at the north end of the pit. At each side of the fire, he placed an incense burner filled with lumps of resin which he would heat from the embers as soon as there were any.

I turned to look at the crowd that now gathered around us, pleased to recognise so many familiar faces. There was my friend Kyrthan, and Sterhun with the flint miners Pithan and Suaric. Mother went to speak to them when they waved for her attention, so I joined them to greet my friend. Then another man came forward and, greeting us formally, introduced himself as Rathonan, Fenratha's brother and therefore my cousin. We embraced him, inviting him to join the family group.

"Our Mother Tulria called to me eight days ago," he explained in response to Nyren's enquiry. "She ordered me to come as fast as I could, saying she felt a great darkness over my family and that I would be needed. I assumed my sister would be here, but I stayed last night with Tokhan and he told me the news. I have come too late, it seems."

"You are still most welcome, cousin." I took his arm as I spoke, "And there was nothing really you could have done, even had you come four days ago. We were all just observers in the final days."

Dobris seemed to be taking his time to begin, so I walked over to him to ask him if there was anything wrong.

"No, young Stone-changer," he said; the first time anyone had ever addressed me thus. "But I am waiting for someone who promised to be here. I think I saw his party cross the River a short while ago; they should be with us soon."

My curiosity was short-lived, if not my surprise. For moments later, a small party came into view up the hill, and I saw at once why the seer had waited. Tokhan led the group, with Syllan and Kerta behind him, with another I recognised as Afron, Kerta's father. They approached us directly, greeting my mother and me, first formally, then with sympathetic embraces.

"I think the time is overdue for us to heal the rift between us," Syllan announced. "I wish I had done so when last I met Weyllan, but we were both so stubborn and too proud to bend. Of course, Kirah, you and your family were never exiled, so you are free to cross the Plain whenever you wish, but let me make it clear that you are also welcome to attend the Spirit House. And," he added, addressing me, "young Ulrac, you are free to join the fellowship when they deem you ready, as I am sure you soon will be. We are here to say our farewells to an old friend, one with whom I should never have quarrelled, fool that I am, and to heal the wounds between us all before they fester into feuds."

He turned to Jahrain and the little group of bearers then. "And this same peace offering I extend to all of you on this side of the Ayn, those from the Lakes, and those from the Sunset Sea, and now also to those who have come among us from the lands towards the sunrise. I claim no chieftainship over you unless you one day choose to ask for it, but you are free to come and go as if we were all one people. For in truth, that is what we are; the people of the Plain at the very heart of the cosmos. Jahrain, you and your fellow seers may use the Spirit House again, and are welcome to join the fellowship if they will accept you." He stepped across to the Northerner, clasping his wrist in greeting, his broad smile shining with his relief and joy.

After that, the ceremony began, although it seemed almost an anticlimax in the wake of Syllan's announcements. The man had certainly learned how to make an impressive entrance! My father's body was laid on its side in the cist, his knees drawn up and his arms crossed. He wore his favourite bracer on his left arm, with his best moon-gold dagger in a sheath on the upper arm. Two of Yarta's freshly made pots were placed before him, filled with a porridge of cheese and bread and meat for him to feast on as he travelled through the desert world. Mother placed another beaker filled with barley beer behind his head.

Dobris signalled the drummers to beat a rhythm out as he chanted a call to the spirits to attend and to listen to the eulogies and vows made at the graveside. The horns blew, and women shook rattles, until the cacophony was quite horrendous. At length, even Dobris felt we had the attention of the spirits, everyone within two days' march at least, so he raised his arms for silence.

I stepped forward."We stand here to bid farewell to a man who has changed our lives, all of our lives, in some significant way. My adopted father Weyllan was always driven by the need for truth and balance, sometimes to his own detriment, but often to the good fortune of others around him. He was a great seer who stepped into the whirlpool of time and saw on the way many things from the past, and many which are yet to happen. He was one who could move among enemies to make them friends again, who could heal wounds and balance the lives of others, even when he could not manage to do the same for himself. Now, he has given his life to reset that balance in our world, to make our land safer for us all. Let us remember him, and bring him to mind when we wish for his skills to help us in the days to come."

Then my mother took her turn, facing each person in the congregation as she spoke of the deeds Weyllan had done that involved them, until it seemed that she addressed almost everyone there. At the end, she held up Father's two long braids, still with the sun-gold tress-ringsaround them, and another of his moon-gold knives, reminding them all that it was Weyllan who had brought them these wonders, and who had taught the first of their people the magic to do it for themselves.

At this point she looked straight at Kyrthan, causing his father to turn to him in surprise, which quickly changed to comprehension as it dawned on him the reason behind his son's frequent absences over the last few years. I was pleased to see that they exchanged a look before Syllan put an arm around his son and turned back to smile at Mother, shaking his head ruefully at his own foolishness. I was also amused to notice that Kerta displayed no surprise at all. She must have known for some time, perhaps for years, what her son was doing on his visits to us.

My mother placed the objects on a folded doeskin cloak,

then placed her gifts in the grave alongside her husband. This was the signal for others to make their offerings and give thanks. I placed Father's favourite anvil stone at his back, then a bag of flints beside his head, mostly blanks and works-in-progress for him to deal with as he needed them in his next life. Pithan placed next to the cheese porridge pots a similar bag of useful tools for his journey. Nyhen gave a moon-gold knife, while from Wheris came a belt of woven wool with a fine stone ring, and Rathonan donated a stunning red stone bracer to the riches within the grave.

The women began distributing beer around the gathering, while Yarta and some others pronounced a stew of pork and venison ready, calling for people to bring their bowls and collect some. One beaker containing stew, and another of beer, were brought to the grave and placed carefully next to Father's body.

Then Dobris produced Weyllan's quiver with a dozen of his arrows in it. Mother removed them all, selecting one of his own shafts, and one made by Fenratha. Kneeling beside the grave, she leaned these gently against his hip. I took one at random and placed it next to hers along with another to represent my father Kefhan's gift. Jahrain, Nyren and others followed, a few of them using their own arrows with heads made in the new barbed style introduced by my father. Dobris placed a last one at Father's feet and stood to offer another prayer, after which several other mourners came forward with odd bone or stone gifts for the soul of the man who had given his life for their safety. I was moved to tears. As the ceremony drew to a close and the lid was placed on the cist, my mother and I held each other, weeping for the soul we had lost.

He was our anchor and our teacher, our fulcrum and our horizons, and everything anyone needed between. He had been the focus of our lives for so many years that we really were uncertain how we would go on from this point.

As Jahrain's team placed the roof over the cist and filled the grave, I released my mother to the arms of Yarta and Wheris to accompany her home. I stayedbehind, to help dig the boundary ditch.

With the spoil from that ditch, we raised the waist-high mound of earth and chalk that would mark for all eternity the resting place of Weyllan, the first metalsmith at the Heart of the World, and the greatest seer in the Eye of Time.

EPILOGUE

Now here I stand to watch the mourners depart, turning away family by family, friends with friends, slowly walking back down the hill towards their homes. They will go back to their lives, their briefly interrupted lives which, thanks to the man who was my uncle, my father, and my friend, will never be the same again.

I climb the little mound and settle down at the top to be with him for a little longer. When my time comes, I will be with him again. I smile to myself; perhaps I can even join him in this mound if I become worthy. Weyllan had no grand ambition to be buried as a man of power, in a mound and circle of his own; I feel the same. So, it would be enough of an honour for me to join my mentor and kinsman in this grave, as in the afterlife. Time will make its own decisions.

At last the sun reappears from behind a broad belt of cloud now edged with gold and red, burning up the evening sky, sinking sedately towards the far downs at the edge of the Plain. Its great disc touches the hills, setting them ablaze one last time for my father's spirit, to light his way to the Spirit House where it will dwell until the next Long Night feast. He will stay among his spirit friends and allies until perhaps Lena opens the way to the star realm where he will shine over us all for the rest of time. I stand, bringing the Spirit House just into view above the far ridge.

Now I see my father's spirit as a wisp of mist speeding towards the stones. I watch as it is joined by other spirit mists rising from the grassy slopes. More join him, until they merge together to build a wall of mist that rolls and flows across the Plain towards the Spirit House and the setting sun. At last, in glorious company, Weyllan is going home.

I can feel building within me the pain, the loss and grief gnawing at my gut, sniffing at my soul. I feel it building, blocking my throat, closing the airway and forcing my breaths back down inside me. It tries to cloud and control my thoughts, to make me follow him to the Temple and on to the stars beyond. But I will go in my own good time. Hot brands burn at the corners of my eyes while bees sting me high within my nose, bringing a tear to each eye, blurring my vision within and without.

I pinch my nose hard between my thumb and finger to kill the sting there and close my eyes on any further tears. I flex my chest, opening my lungs for air, raising my arms in salute to the dying sun as I call down a prayer to Lukan. I draw a deep breath to still my racing thoughts, forcing back the pain, then let it out with all my force, pushing the grief beast out and away from me as I do so. I use my hands to waft away the bad spirits, to cleanse myself. The sun warms my face as I feel the pulse of life beat through my body once more, slow and potent, powering up my mind and my soul to take on the mantle my father left behind. I am alive, I am whole. I am one with the land and my father, my uncle, my teacher. The cosmos is complete around me; I am one with the whole of existence, filled with its power and its knowledge.

As the dusk settles and the world darkens, I see across to my right a new light, a bright fire lit on the slopes of the sacred mountain, Brwslyi's Hill, yonder across the valley. My mother has lit the fire before Aslena's house, our house now, and is calling me home to end my vigil. I shall go presently. One day soon I shall return across the Ayn to claim my Hathis, and in time we will be united before the house of Syllan, now and always our chieftain and father. Together we will make and raise a son who will rule these people after his grandfather's death. A leader for both the native people and the new folk who are coming to us over the sea. A new age, a new beginning. I have seen it in my vision; it will come to pass.

TO THE READER

Thank you, reader, for reading my saga. I hope you enjoyed it, and found it both entertaining and perhaps educational, too. The best way to thank me for writing it is to leave an honest review on Amazon, and I would be grateful if you did that.

This is the story of a real person, known to us today as the Amesbury Archer. All we know about him comes from his burial; his bones and the artefacts with which he was interred. Whilst those remains reveal glimpses into what must have been an extraordinary life, there is still so much missing. I have tried to put the flesh back on to the bones of the story, and in so doing to paint a picture of his world. This is Britain at the end of the Neolithic, centred on the mystical landscape of the Salisbury Plain, the home of the island's most famous megalithic monument: Stonehenge.

Throughout the book, I have tried to present as accurate a picture of life and religion in the Neolithic world as I can. Since the period is a popular one for research these days, I am certain that some of my descriptions will make archaeologists in a few years wince and chuckle at the naivety of it all. But when written, my descriptions of the landscapes and economic life on the Plain, around Avebury, on the Somerset Levels, and in Wales, were in line with current thinking.

My interpretation of the religion of the time begins with the work of David Lewis- Williams who followed the trail from San ethnography in southern Africa, through the symbolism embodied in cave art across the world, to the carved stones of the Neolithic in the Near East and Britain: he suggested a widespread belief system interpreted to lesser mortals by a part-time priesthood we today refer to as Shamans. Since Shaman is a term strictly appropriate to Siberian and Arctic peoples, I have used the more neutral term "Seer", accepting the risk that they may be taken for seer-wizards popular in fantasy fiction. I hope neither side is offended by this, as I suspect that wizards have their origin at just the time of my novel, perhaps even with the seers and stone-changers of whom I write.

A word or two about houses. When excavations at Durrington Walls (the sealed-off village in the story) revealed the floors of Neolithic houses, they were among the first known in England. The absence of remains has long concerned archaeologists, as house remains are well documented from northern Europe and even from the stony edges of the British Isles. I have taken this absence as a sign of generally dispersed populations - where small homesteads are common and many houses are semi-portable, so that they leave hardly any trace behind. I expect that this interpretation in particular, will be challenged and perhaps discredited in the near future. I remind you (and myself) that this is just a novel: please enjoy it as such.

If you want to find out more about Stonehenge and the Neolithic world or its religion, go to:

The Eye of Tim:
   https://eyeoftim.blogspot.com/

T.S. Robey Author facebook:
   https://www.facebook.com/tims.robey.1

Printed in Great Britain
by Amazon